UNSUITED

. . . .

ERICA TIPPETT

TEMJA

Temja Publishing

MELBOURNE, AUSTRALIA

Temja Publishing
Melbourne, Australia
Web: www.ericatippett.com
Email: admin@ericatippett.com

Cover design by Martin Strong
Book Layout ©2017 BookDesignTemplates.com; Icon by Freepik

A catalogue record for this book is available from the National Library of Australia

Unsuited/Erica Tippett—2nd edition.
ISBN 978 0 6453215 6 2

ACKNOWLEDGEMENT OF COUNTRY

I wrote this book in various locations on the lands of the peoples of the Kulin Nation and published it from the lands of the Boonwurrung/Bunurong people. I pay my respect to the people of the Kulin Nation and their Elders, past, present and emerging. I extend my respect to all Aboriginal, Torres Strait Islander and First Nations people.

FOR DAD

I dedicate this book to my dear dad, John. He was the opposite of the father portrayed in this story: always kind, polite, loving, adventurous, and the most placid person you could meet (in the very best way). Dad was a rock for my family, a firm foundation from which we could grow and thrive. He instilled in me a love of footy, growing veggies, and the fundamentals of managing money. But most of all, a love of story. He would read me stories at bedtime and many nights we stayed up past my bedtime so we could finish a chapter. When he passed away in 2015, I made a vow to my husband that I would write a novel. It came after many years of thinking about it and saying to myself, "One day, I'm going to write a novel". The writing journey I embarked on merged years of tinkering with writing and produced a handful of short stories and a nonfiction book chapter. But my ultimate goal was the novel.

Here it is.

I hope you enjoy it, and it inspires you to act now on whatever it is you've been thinking about or meaning to do for years.

Time is finite for us all.

There will always be many more similarities between people than differences. But while the similarities are often invisible, the differences tend to stand out and demand attention.

—ERICA TIPPETT, 2021

CHAPTER ONE

Evalie walked into the Xoha pop-up application centre on a Tuesday lunch break. She bit the side of her lip and clenched her free hand into a fist. Thoughts raced through her head. The pain of sharp fingernails digging into her palm brought her back into the sparse room. She took a deep breath and joined the orderly queue of people (mainly women) that snaked out in front of a thin metal desk. Behind the desk was a heavy metal door engraved with a triquetra in the middle. *Unity of three*, Evalie thought.

The quiet cool was a relief from the heat and bustle of the overcrowded Melbourne street she had left behind. One day soon, she hoped, she would leave these streets behind forever.

"How long will this take?" a red-headed lady ahead in the queue said to the person beside her.

"They're supposed to be really quick, once your application is all in order," the person replied.

"I've been waiting for twelve minutes," the man behind them quipped.

The person rolled their eyes at the redhead and they both giggled. "Well, you'll just have to wait longer because we're in front of you," the redhead said mockingly. She turned and raised her eyebrows at the man. The man blushed a little and looked at his feet. The line inched forward.

Evalie noticed the growing queue behind her. She watched a woman in a white flowing dress dotted with delicate purple flowers arrive through the double glass doors. The woman stopped at what looked like a water dispenser and pressed her hand on the top, spreading her fingers. A blue light shone, then an arm came up, and she lifted her sunglasses for a retina scan. Evalie looked at the six people who had joined the queue behind her. She bit the side of her lip again. After watching another newcomer repeat the process at the small machine, Evalie began to sweat despite the building's efficient air conditioning. The line moved forward again, pushing in tighter towards the desk.

"Did you sign in?" Evalie asked the girl behind her, who frankly did not look old enough to be there.

"Yeah, of course I did," the girl responded.

"Oh, right," Evalie said. "Um, I didn't. Would you mind holding my spot? I'm on my lunch break and have little time."

"Are you serious? That is one thing they are crystal clear on in the application information. No changing procedure. No cutting lines or subverting the process. I'm not risking my spot for you. You should have read the instructions. It's all there, the sign in, the queuing, everything."

Evalie's cheeks burned.

"Maybe you should come back later," the girl finished, crossing her arms in front of her.

"I, well. Yes, I read ... but ... you're probably right." Evalie left the line and went over to the strange machine. *How could you have missed this on your way in? Stupid girl,* she thought. She looked at her watch and shuffled her feet. Then she headed for the door. Leaving the cool haven behind her, Evalie walked out into the bright summer's day.

* * *

The next day, Evalie left her desk a few minutes early and hurried down the stairs to the street. She half-walked, half-ran, and was at the application centre in record time. She checked in with her handprint and retina scan and joined the small queue. A big smile planted itself on her sun-kissed cheeks. Evalie hummed to herself, a tune she had heard on the way to work that morning. She didn't know what it was called, but it was very catchy. She made a mental note to find out later.

When she reached the front of the queue and was staring at the large metal door behind the desk, Evalie realised just how large and foreboding it was. It appeared at odds with everything Xoha was supposed to be.

"Good afternoon, Evalie," the person behind the desk said.

"Oh, hi. Hello," Evalie replied, stepping up to the desk.

"I'm sorry we won't be able to help you with your application today. You need to grant us access to your birth details." The person spoke in a soft voice and Evalie leaned closer to hear.

"But I did—"

"Correction. We need permission from your father for us to access his DNA contribution details."

"Oh, right. I'm really sorry. I thought he had given permission. He said that … he was supposed to …"

The person shook their head slowly and shrugged their shoulders. Evalie blushed and looked down at her feet.

"See you tomorrow perhaps?" they said.

"Um, yeah, hopefully," Evalie said. She turned and walked away.

"Don't forget, all applications for this round close Friday," the staff member called after Evalie. She turned back, studying the person's face. It was round, unlined, unfreckled. Evalie blinked twice, then nodded. She turned away and left.

Once outside, Evalie took her phone out of her small pink handbag. She flicked to recent calls and pressed the top number. She listened to the ring tone. One, two, three, four, five, six rings.

"Hello?" a gruff voice answered.

"Hi, dad, it's me," Evalie said.

"Ugh," came the response. "Watta *you* want?"

"I uh ..." Evalie mumbled. She chewed the thumbnail of her right hand. "I just needed to remind you about providing permission for the background check."

"Oh, that. I think I lost the details."

"I sent them ..." Evalie checked her tone. "Never mind. I'll send them again after we finish this call." There was no response. "Dad?"

"Hmmm. What's it for again?"

"It's really important," Evalie replied. "For a work thing. Can you do it soon? I can't, uh, progress without it."

Neville grunted in reply and disconnected the call. Evalie held tight to her phone. She blinked back tears, scrolling to find the message. She pressed 'Send' trying to ignore the three identical messages she had already sent to that insufferable man.

Her pulse beat fast in her ears as she rushed back to work. At the door to the lobby, she saw Naomi walking in ahead. They met in the lift.

"Hey Evalie, how's things?" she asked, pressing the "Up" button.

"Oh, fine," Evalie lied, feigning a smile. The pair entered the lift and pressed the numbers for their respective floors.

"Hey, you heard about that promotion yet?" Naomi asked.

"No, not yet," Evalie said, avoiding eye contact.

"Well, I think it must be yours this time. You worked so hard on the Jones project. It's got to pay off soon."

"I hope so," Evalie shrugged and left the lift. She checked the time and hastened her steps. When she got to her desk, she collapsed into her chair. She pressed the back of her hand to her forehead; it was burning hot. She saw a message from the boss's executive assistant and opened it hastily.

Evalie,

Mr Francis needs to see you at 1:15 p.m.

Regards, Arielle

She glanced at the clock on her computer.

1:19 p.m.

"Crap!" Evalie said. She hurried off to the big corner office.

"Hello, Evalie," Arielle said as Evalie bustled in through the glass door. "He's been waiting for you. Go straight in."

Evalie's pink cheeks turned crimson. She reached for the long, slender door handle and paused, inhaling deeply. Evalie planted a big smile on her face. Then she opened the door.

"So glad you could make it, Evalie," Mr Francis said. He looked up from his desk and followed Evalie with his eyes until she sat, awkwardly, in the empty seat in front of him. Evalie's co-workers, Tommy and Leo, occupied the other two seats. "I was just telling your colleagues here that I have reviewed your promotion applications and your recent project work. Tommy and Leo have already given me their thirty-second pitch for the Mako file. Now it's your turn, Evalie.

Remember, this file is a significant step up and comes with fifteen percent salary increase and that office over there." Mr Francis pointed his thick stubby finger towards the office Evalie had passed a moment before.

She cleared her throat. "I've been working here for three years." She looked at her boss. He sat back in his seat with elbows resting on the sides of his overly large black leather office chair. "Over that time, I've seen many changes. Made many of them myself. Like amending the–"

"Yes, yes, we know all that," said Mr Francis. "You've written about your achievements in the application. I'd like to hear your plans for the Mako file. You've got ten seconds left."

Evalie raised her eyebrows and looked at Tommy, who sniggered. Leo looked down into his lap.

"I'm the best person for the Mako file, as I would manage it properly," Evalie blurted. "You know it's the truth. I'm the most experienced and I would ensure the money lost because of mismanagement would be recovered in three months and then triple the returns. I've–"

"Times up," Mr Francis said. "Very well. You've all said your piece. Now it's up to the Board to ratify the decision based on my recommendation. You will hear by Friday. You may all leave."

Arielle opened the door and hastened to the boss's desk. Tommy and Leo disappeared through the open door. They left Evalie sitting there, wringing her hands. She shot her boss an angry look that he either didn't catch or ignored. She swallowed loudly, rose from her seat, and walked out of the office.

Just as she sat down at her desk, Tommy appeared.

"That was intense, huh Evalie?"

"Yes, it was." Evalie raised her eyes to meet Tommy's. He was staring at her, almost through her. Evalie diverted her eyes back to her screen.

"Well," Tommy continued, still looking at Evalie, "May the best man win!" He threw his head back and laughed. Then he strode out of sight.

Evalie's nose twitched as she narrowed her gaze to her screen. She didn't even notice her vision blur. All she could focus on was a sudden ringing in her ears.

* * *

As soon as the clock ticked over to twelve, Evalie hurried out of the office. Once she reached the end of the block, she called her dad. The phone rang and rang and rang. The line rang out. She threw her phone back into her handbag and walked faster along the all-to-familiar route.

As she arrived at the application centre, sweat trickled down her forehead and into her eye. She wiped it swiftly with the back of her hand and marched through the door. She checked in at the machine and joined the medium-sized queue. The queue moved slowly. Evalie tapped her foot double-time on the floor. She checked her watch, then her phone, and sighed. Each time the queue moved forward; Evalie pressed closer to the person in front. When she reached the counter, she inhaled deeply.

"Hello, Evalie," the person behind the desk said with a smile.

"Hello. I just wanted to check if the background permission has come through from my father yet? I haven't been able to get hold of him."

"No, not yet, I'm afraid."

Evalie looked at her feet, noticing for the first time how shiny the floor was. "Is there any other way to complete my application?"

"Without the background check completed by both birth parents. Let me see." The staff member disappeared through the commanding metal door. As they went, Evalie tried to sneak a peek at what was on the other side, but they obscured her view. After a few minutes, they returned. "There is one way. Because the same company has employed you for over two years, you can get your boss to sign it off for you. Although there is a strong preference for DNA checks. I'll forward you the alternate employer check, so you have it there if your dad doesn't respond by tomorrow. Or you can wait until the next round."

"Right. Thanks so much. Can you remind me when is the next round again?"

"It's usually an annual process. However, because we've received so many applications this time, we may skip next year and open again the year after."

"In two years' time!" Evalie's face dropped. "I'll do my best to get it done by tomorrow."

Evalie walked out into the sunshine. She rummaged around in her bag and found an apple. As she bit into it, the sweet scent filled her nose and sticky juice dripped down her chin. Evalie wiped the juice with the back of her hand. She strolled back towards her office. Once she'd finished eating, she fetched her phone from her bag and pressed the voice command. "Call dad," she said.

The phone responded, "You have instructed me not to connect to that number. Please enable 'Calls to dad'. Would you like me to call your therapist instead?"

"No!" Evalie said as she hurriedly took control of the phone and navigated to recent calls.

Evalie bristled at the sound of her dad's voicemail. She spoke through gritted teeth. "Dad, it's me, Evalie. Please complete the background-check permission for me by tomorrow. I'll come over later and help you with it." She quickly hung up.

Evalie looked up to see a young woman in front of her. She was wearing a lovely mint-green dress with pink and white flowers on it. Three young men, teenagers really, approached along the footpath. They were having a lively conversation and jostling one another. Their eyes fixed on the woman as they looked her up and down. The woman clutched her handbag tight by her side.

"Well, hello sexy," the one in the middle called to the woman.

The woman flinched but didn't raise her eyes from the ground. The trio blocked the path and paused there.

"Wanna go on a date?" the same guy sniggered.

Evalie hastened her pace.

The woman was close to the group of men now. She looked up and smiled. "No thank you," she said politely, trying to edge past them.

The one at the end took a step forward. The woman quickly took a step back. Her heel caught in a grate, and she stumbled off balance. Evalie rushed up and caught the woman's left arm. The woman bristled, but relaxed when she saw Evalie.

"Excuse me, gentlemen," Evalie said loudly and pressed forward.

The man to their left stepped behind the other two and let the women pass. He muttered something to his friends, and the three laughed.

"Thanks," the woman said to Evalie as she let her arm go.

"Oh, no problem. It would be nice if you could walk down the street in the middle of the day without getting harassed."

"It happens all the time. I'm so sick of it. Anyway, thanks again."

The woman turned down the side street. Evalie stood at the corner and watched her go. Then she looked back at the way she had come. She saw the silhouette of the three walking along the path and shook her head.

* * *

When Evalie got out of the lift, the quietness in the office struck her. She hastened to her desk and looked at the time and her calendar. "Oh crap," she said under her breath. She stared at the all-staff meeting that someone had moved half an hour earlier. Evalie was ten minutes late. "My presentation." She sighed and closed her eyes.

The sound of her phone's ring tone made her jump.

Evalie grabbed her phone out of her bag and looked at the screen. "Oh, not now dad," she spat.

Evalie looked towards the large glass doors of the meeting room where her colleagues and boss were meeting without her. She bit her lip and pressed the answer button. She screwed up her face.

"Hello?"

"If you want me to do this thing. You need to come over and help me."

"Do you mean the background-check permission?"

"What else would I mean? Yes, that stupid nuisance."

"Okay, sure. I'm just at work, late for a meeting, actually."

"Well, come now or I won't do it. I'm going out in fifteen."

The ended call tone beeped in Evalie's ear. Evalie looked at her phone incredulously. She observed the meeting room and saw the legs under the glass shading. Evalie knew she would be missed.

"I guess this might just seal the deal on no promotion," she mumbled under her breath. Evalie tried to ignore the sinking sensation in her stomach. She picked up her handbag, turned, and snuck out of the office.

* * *

Evalie knocked on the old wooden door of her dad's house. She heard a muttering from within and tried the handle. Locked. After a few moments, she heard shuffling feet. The door opened slowly.

"Hi dad. Thanks for doing this."

Neville grunted. Then, shoving his phone in her face, he asked brusquely, "How do you make this work?"

Evalie took the phone and navigated to her message with the link to the permission. She pressed on it and up came two buttons—a green "Approve" and red "Deny".

"You just have to click Approve," she said.

"I know that. Blimey. Ya think I'm stupid, don't ya? Little smart ass. You've always thought ya smarter than me." He snatched the phone, accidentally pressing a button. "Now where's it's gone? Ah, this is hopeless."

"Maybe if we just go inside—"

"Forget it. I'm gonna be late for my appointment."

"Please dad, it will only take a second," Evalie insisted.

She reached for the phone and snatched it from him and went back to the approval buttons in an instant. This time she pressed on "Approve". A little trumpet sounded loudly.

"Done," she said, handing back the phone. "Thanks so much, dad." She smiled at him as he slammed the door in her face.

Evalie turned back to the street but lingered on the doorstep. She pressed her right hand to her chest. Her heart threatened to burst right through and jump out. An image popped into her head. She imagined her heart continuing to pulsate once free from her body and thumping all the way along the quiet side street before stopping, exhausted, and dropping into the corner drain. She shuddered. Evalie took a deep breath and closed her eyes for a few moments. Then she opened her eyes, straightened her posture, and walked away.

CHAPTER TWO

Evalie's gut churned as she waited for the lift. She stepped in and pressed the button for Level Eight.

"Shit, shit, shit, shit, shit," she said as the doors closed.

As she walked down the corridor, she saw heads turn to look at her. She hunched her shoulders and kept her head down. When she reached Arielle's desk, she felt the assistant's glare without looking up.

"Well, look who finally returned from lunch. You better have a good excuse. Mr Francis was fuming at the staff meeting. You really let him down, not being there for the presentation."

Evalie blushed a deep magenta. "Can I go in?" she asked meekly.

"Yes. But he's only got two minutes," Arielle snapped.

"That's more than enough," Evalie replied. She smiled.

The assistant rolled her eyes.

Evalie hesitated at the door, then knocked twice.

"Come in," came the call from within.

Evalie gritted her teeth and opened the door.

"Nice of you to join us," Mr Francis said.

"I'm really sorry," Evalie started, closing the door behind her and sitting down. "I had a family emergency. My dad is sick and he couldn't find his medication and well, I had to go over to his house and help him find it."

Her boss looked at her with raised eyebrows.

"Turns out he had put the box of pills in the linen cupboard between the sheets and the towels. The silly old fool," Evalie finished.

"And I suppose your phone wasn't working to call and tell us about this family ... emergency, then?"

"Well, um, I know I should have called, but you were all in the meeting and—"

"So, this happened after the meeting had already begun?"

"I, uh, I'm not sure. I'm sorry."

"Well, at least it makes my decision easier on the promotion. I certainly won't be recommending someone who has proven to be unreliable when it really counts."

Evalie dropped her head. Red blotches rose from her neck and patterned her face. She wrung her hands in her lap.

"If that's all, I've got work to do. And so do you," Mr Francis hissed.

"Ah, right. Yes. I do," Evalie responded. She looked at her feet, then back up at Mr Francis. "Please don't judge me just on this. I know I screwed up, and I let you down, but it was a one-off. Please take all my work into consideration, not just what happened today. I've always been so reliable. I just ... I had to help my dad." She pushed herself up to standing. Her legs were weak, threatening to collapse underneath her at any moment. She walked cautiously to the door and took one last look at her boss. His smug face wore a wry smirk. She closed the door softly and shuffled back to her desk. Evalie spent the remainder of the afternoon staring blankly at her screen.

* * *

Evalie flopped on her bed and kicked her heels onto the worn carpet. She lay face down, pressing herself into the covers until she couldn't breathe, then she turned her head to the side and gulped in a big breath of air. Her dishevelled hair covered her eyes, shielding them from the bright evening sun that poured through the window.

Evalie's thoughts wandered from the stifling little box of a bedroom where she lay, to the great spaces and standardised living quarters in the land of promise. The new system would take getting used to; she was realistic about that. But the promise of equality was enrapturing. She crossed her fingers, slid off the side of the bed, and sank down onto her knees on the floor. She moved her hands into a prayer, appealing to all gods of all faiths, young and old, to help her.

CHAPTER THREE

Evalie's alarm jolted her from sleep fifteen minutes earlier than usual. *Friday*, she thought as she jumped out of bed. She showered quickly and got ready for work. Evalie peered into the empty shelves of her pantry and sighed. She found some crusts in the freezer and popped them in the toaster. Scanning the dirty kitchen, Evalie scolded herself for letting the mess get out of control. While she stood, shifting her weight back and forth, she squeezed her left earlobe with her thumb and forefinger. Evalie rushed into her bedroom, found her mum's diamond teardrop earrings on the tatty bedside table, and returned them swiftly to her ears. Her pulse calmed. She walked back into the kitchen. Eyeing the blackened shards sticking out of the toaster, Evalie looked at her watch, grabbed her handbag, and slammed the apartment door behind her.

She waited for the old lift to arrive. "Come on, come on, come on," she said impatiently. The light didn't move off the ground floor. "Dang it!" she cried and flew down the three flights of stairs to the entrance. As she raced out of the foyer, she nearly flattened old Mrs Ferguson, who was trying, unsuccessfully, to get her little shopping trolley in the door. She saw Evalie and smiled.

"Be a darl won't you and help me with this, love?"

Evalie feigned a smile and held the door open wider.

Mrs Ferguson struggled forward.

Evalie tried to get a hold of the cart, but its maroon cover slipped beneath her fingers. "Here," she said finally, trying not to show her frustration. "Why don't you come in first and then I'll bring the cart."

Mrs Ferguson shuffled forward.

Evalie put her hand out and helped her through the door. The old lady's liver-spotted hand was deathly cold. Evalie shuddered and made a silent promise to herself not to end up like her, living out her final years here in this place. She yanked the cart through the door.

"Careful deary, that's got precious things in there, you know."

"Sorry, Mrs Ferguson. I'm just in a bit of a rush today."

The old lady took the handle of the cart and pushed it towards the lift. "Can't rely on young people these days," she murmured.

Evalie shook her head and bolted through the door. As she reached the bus stop, she saw a bus's red lights at the intersection up ahead. She looked at her watch again. *Just missed it,* she thought. *Why today? Why does this always happen to me?* Evalie slumped down on the bench to wait for her usual bus.

* * *

At her desk, Evalie got to work transferring files. A message popped up, interrupting her concentration. The subject line shouted at her.

ANNOUNCEMENT

It was from the boss. Evalie's stomach dropped. She hesitated, then opened the message.

Unsuited

Dear Staff,

I'm very pleased to announce that after a rigorous process, Tommy has been awarded the Mako file and, therefore, the promotion. I'm sure you'll all join me in congratulating Tommy on this fantastic achievement. It is truly well deserved. Tommy is proving to be a shooting star, having only joined the firm four months ago as a junior staff member. He has clearly benefited from my close mentoring. Please join us this afternoon at 4:30 p.m. for drinks and nibbles to celebrate Tommy and his great work.

Mr Francis

Evalie stared at her screen, blinking back tears. She checked the time.

9:02 a.m.

Evalie sighed and kicked the leg of her desk with her foot.

* * *

That afternoon, Evalie hid in the toilet. She could hear her colleagues talking and laughing in the conference room. Someone had put up streamers and balloons, most likely Arielle. It was as though Tommy's promotion was akin to a successful political campaign. Evalie felt sick to her stomach. That seemed like reason enough to stay in the stall until the fanfare was over. Then she could slink back to her desk, take her bag, and go home. Another day done. Another week of work survived.

Evalie cringed at the sound of the toilet door opening. Two sets of heels clicked on the tiled floor.

"Tommy is amazing, don't you think?" Evalie recognised Patricia's doting voice.

"He's okay, I guess," Naomi replied.

"I can't believe how quickly he's become an associate. It's a real inspiration."

Evalie heard the doors lock on the cubicles next to hers. She scooped her legs up onto the toilet seat and hugged them close. Her plain black slip-on shoes made a dull thud on the seat. She held her breath.

"Don't get your hopes up," Naomi said.

"What do you mean?" came the echoed response.

"Well, I mean, he only got this far, because he's a *he*. Evalie worked so hard for the promotion. She showed me her presentation and the results she achieved were impressive. You know, her work has more than tripled profits. There's no denying that she should have got it."

The toilets flushed and doors were unlocked.

"I heard she screwed up by not being there for that final presentation and she was also late for all those other important meetings," Patricia said. "I know she's your friend, but I don't think she really deserved it. If she did, I'm sure Mr Francis would have given it to her. He seems like a fair guy. Plus, she's not doing herself any favours by not showing up to the celebration today. A real sore loser, it seems."

The drier muffled the voices, and then they were gone. Evalie dropped her head onto her knees. She looked sideways at the toilet roll holder. She sighed, closed her eyes, and hugged her knees tighter.

* * *

Evalie heard the cheery tune of her phone ringing and raised her head from her mattress. "You've got to change that god-awful ringtone," she scolded herself. She reached for the phone and tilted it to see the screen.

Stella

She rolled over and answered the call. "Hello?"

"Hi Evalie, how are you? I've got big news. You're coming out tonight, so we can celebrate. Get dressed in that black number of yours. I'll be around in twenty minutes!"

"Um. Oh. Congratulations on whatever it is. But no, I can't tonight, sorry."

"Come on, it'll be my shout!"

"I'm really not up to it, S. Please don't make me."

"What's wrong with you, then?"

"I didn't get it," Evalie said. "I didn't get the promotion." Her voice trailed off.

"Oh. What? What do you mean you didn't get it? It was a done deal. You worked so hard for it! That's ludicrous. I'm coming over. Be there soon," Stella ended the call.

Evalie flopped back onto her stomach. She closed her eyes.

* * *

The door buzzer startled Evalie. She got up groggily from her bed and shuffled over to press the release. She glimpsed herself in the mirror. Her eyes widened. She grabbed a brush and hair tie. After tying her hair up, she tried to smile at her less scruffy reflection. All she could manage was a tight-lipped grimace. She lingered by her apartment door. At the sound of footsteps in the dingy corridor outside, she released the lock and opened her door a crack. Stella burst into the room. She put her bags on the floor and wrapped Evalie in a big hug.

"I'm so sorry," she said. "I know you deserved it. After all this time, hard work and bloody excellent results. It just doesn't make any sense. Obviously, your boss is an idiot."

Evalie broke away from her friend. "Thanks. He is. I know it's a bit ridiculous to be this upset about it. But it hurts so much after all those extra hours I put in. And truly, I can't see any reason for not getting it other than that I'm not Tommy, or Leo. It's bullshit." Evalie dropped onto the small sofa. "Do you know how long Tommy has been working there? Four months. Four piddly months." She slumped down on the couch.

Stella pursed her lips. She grabbed a bag from the floor and took it into the tiny kitchen. Stella rummaged through the faded kitchen cupboards and pulled out two unmatched wine glasses. She filled them nearly to the brim and brought one over to Evalie. "Here, to drown your pain." She smiled kindly.

Evalie took the glass and Stella retrieved the other from the bench. She sat down next to Evalie. Evalie peered into the bottom of the glass.

"So, apart from commiserating with you. I wanted to share my news," Stella said slowly.

"Oh yeah. I'm sorry. What's your news?"

"Tejas and I are engaged! Last night we went for our usual Thursday night date night. After dinner, we went on this romantic walk through the city and there was a guitarist. I found out later it was a set-up. You know, he'd paid the guitarist to play in the gardens, just for us. And there was a picnic blanket and champagne and chocolate-covered strawberries." Stella gushed.

She talked so fast, Evalie felt as though she were being pounded with word bullets.

"It was amazing. And after the picnic was done, he said all these really nice things about me. Who would have thought? About your old friend Stella! Then he said how much he loved me and, well, asked me to marry him!"

"Wow. Oh, that's marvelous. Congratulations!" Evalie looked down at her lap, then up at her friend.

Stella was staring at her. She burst out laughing.

Evalie paused, then laughed.

"You miserable bugger," Stella said. "You can't even pretend to be excited for me, can you?" She leaned across the couch and gave Evalie a big hug.

"I'm sorry," Evalie said. "I really am happy for you."

"No more moping then." Stella released her warm arms from around Evalie. "You're coming out with me for a drink, and that's that. You can *show* me you're happy for me. Or at least pretend for an hour or two. I mean, what are friends for?"

Evalie took a gulp of wine, then drained her glass. "You're right," she said, slapping the glass triumphantly on the ring-stained coffee table. She got up and headed into her bedroom. "Give me fifteen minutes and I'll be ready to go."

"Take as long as you need, dear Evalie. I'll be right here, drinking wine."

CHAPTER FOUR

The two ladies, dressed in their favourite heels and black dresses, walked with arms intertwined through the busy city streets.

"I can't believe it's this warm out still," Evalie said.

"It's like it's the middle of summer, or something," Stella teased.

Evalie prodded her side. "So where are we going, anyway?"

"To that place we ended up at last time, eighteen eighty-eight. It was better than the others, so I thought we might as well start there this time."

"Okay, sure."

"Thanks for coming out with me, Evalie. You won't regret it. We'll have fun, I'm sure."

"You are very persuasive when you want to be," Evalie laughed.

They turned down Fairchild Lane. Fairy lights hung across the balconies above the street. The door for Eighteen Eighty-eight was backlit with an orange glow.

"The city really is pretty at night," Evalie said.

"Good evening, ladies," the security guard greeted them. "IDs please," he held out his hand.

Stella and Evalie fumbled around in their bags and pulled out their IDs.

The guard took the IDs, glanced between them and the faces before him, passing the cards through the scanner. He returned them and nodded to the door. "Have a good night," he said.

Evalie managed a smile as they entered the bar. The dimly lit, softly furnished interior was reflected in the massive mirror that stretched the length of the substantial bar. She followed Stella to the bar and perched on a stool.

"What are you drinking?" Stella asked.

"Hmm, whatever you're having," Evalie said.

"Bubbles, of course!" Stella said, flashing her straight, white teeth towards the barman. He came over.

"What can I get you ladies?"

"Two glasses of the De Bortoli sparkling, please," Stella said.

"So, can you picture me having a big Indian wedding?" Stella asked. "You know, with all the bridesmaids and ceremony that lasts like a week?"

"Is that what Tejas wants?"

"Thank god, no! Could you imagine?"

"Will his parents put pressure on him?"

"Yes. For sure. Well, I think so. Although his mum was born here, and his dad has been here since he was at university. So maybe not. Maybe they'd be cool with a more Australian affair. Although he's considering not even telling them. Until later. Probably much later."

"Are you going to elope, then?"

"I think so. As much as we would love to have all our friends and *some* of our family at the wedding," Stella said, winking at Evalie, "we think simple is best."

Evalie nodded; her eyes fixated on the bubbles travelling up in lines from the bottom of the glass. They popped in quick succession on the surface, tickling her nose. The citrus scent was refreshing.

"So, will you be there? Will you be my witness?"

"Wow, Stelle. Uh, when are you planning it? Do you know where you'll go?"

Stella's smile dissolved.

"I mean, thank you," Evalie said quickly. "For the honour. Of course, I will … if I can."

"I know things are tight for you now. But don't worry about the money. We'll pay whatever it costs for whatever we decide. I just need you to show up. I *really* need you to be there." Stella touched Evalie's hand and looked into her friend's face.

Evalie met her eyes and smiled, nodding. "Of course, I'll be there. Wouldn't miss it for the world."

Stella laughed. "That's more like you. More like the Evalie I know and love. You've been absent of late. Now, finish your glass. I'm ordering another round." Stella threw her head back and cackled. "We've got to celebrate!"

* * *

"Wow, that place was really loud in the end. I didn't realise how much I'd been shouting in there," Stella croaked. "So, where would you like to go next?"

"Oh, aren't we going home? I mean, this has been great and all, but …"

"Evalie, it's nine thirty. We can't go home yet!"

"Right, well. Hmm. Why don't we just walk for a while? See where the road takes us?"

"You really are weird sometimes," Stella said, looking at Evalie.

Evalie smiled, raising her eyebrows.

They walked, arm in arm, back towards the central business district. As they passed a bar, people spilled out onto the street, and they stepped back. Evalie's foot slipped off the curb and onto the road. Her hands flailed behind her in a wild arc, and she took another step backwards to stop herself from falling. A bike bell sounded in Evalie's ear. She turned around to see a bike careening towards her, then it swerved and crashed into some garbage bins.

"Oh, shit!" Evalie said.

"What?" Stella asked, turning her head. She burst out laughing.

Evalie rushed over and put out her hand. "Oh, I'm so sorry," she said.

There was a muffled expletive as the person struggled out of the rubbish and took her hand. "Evalie? Is that you?"

Evalie studied the face under the helmet as she helped the man to his feet.

"Guy! Oh my god. You're back in Australia." Evalie stared in disbelief. "Are you alright?"

"Um, yeah, I think so," he said, brushing down his clothes. "Next time maybe look before you step onto the road, though. You could've hurt yourself!"

"I'm so sorry, I wasn't, uh, thinking. The people came out of that bar unexpectedly and I just sort of ended up on the road."

Stella came over. "You know this guy? Even better!"

"So glad to be of entertainment to you," he mock bowed to Stella.

"Stella, this is Guy. We went to uni together."

"Oh my god, that's Guy? The one who got the scholarship. Your Guy? I mean, the one you used to date?"

"Yes, that's him," Evalie said. She glared at Stella, willing her to stop talking. "Guy, this is my newly engaged friend, Stella."

Stella nudged Evalie in the guts. "I can't believe you ran into Guy or, well, he nearly ran into you!" Stella winked at Evalie.

Evalie shook her head, embarrassed.

"Hey Stella, congratulations," Guy said.

"Thanks!" Stella replied.

"Is that okay?" Evalie asked, pointing at the bike.

Frowning, Guy pulled it out from the bins. "It looks okay, except for that bend that isn't meant to be there."

"Maybe you better not ride it, just in case. Where were you headed anyway?"

"I was just going home. It's been a long day at the office."

"It's nearly ten. That is a long day. Let me help you walk it home, it's the least I can do. Again, I'm really sorry," Evalie looked at Stella.

"Well, I'm going to go," Stella said, taking the hint. "And see Tejas. He should have finished his errand by now. I'll see you on Tuesday, Ev." She gave Evalie a quick hug.

"Thanks, yeah okay, see you then. Congratulations again. Give my congrats to Tejas as well, won't you?"

"Will do," Stella said with a big smile. She looked from Evalie to Guy and back again. Then she walked off.

"Let me carry that," Evalie pointed to the helmet, still on Guy's head.

"Sure, thanks," he said, trying to undo the buckle with one hand.

"I'm really glad I ran into you. Well, glad I didn't *actually* run into you," he said goofily. He jerked at the buckle, and it gave way. "I'm glad to see you again." As he went to pass Evalie the helmet, she leaned forward suddenly, and it smacked into her head.

"Ouch," Evalie said.

"Oh shit, sorry!" Guy pulled the helmet back towards his chest. "I didn't … I'm so sorry. What were you looking at?"

"Your shoe. I thought it had a piece of rubbish stuck to it." Evalie rubbed her head.

"Right," Guy said.

"So, this means we're even then." Evalie reached for the helmet.

"Sure. Even." Guy looked at Evalie with concern.

Evalie laughed. "It's okay, don't look at me like that."

There was an awkward silence. Guy managed a half smile.

"Do you want me to take your bag as well?" Evalie asked.

"Nah, it's fine." Guy patted the satchel strap that crossed his chest with his left hand, then pulled his bike up onto the footpath. The front wheel squeaked as they walked along.

"I'll pay for the repairs," Evalie said.

"No, that's unnecessary, Evalie. Really, it's okay."

"But I feel just awful."

"Don't feel awful," Guy said. "I hit you in the head with my helmet." He looked at her and stopped.

Evalie stopped, too. She looked at him quizzically.

"You've got your mum's earrings in. You still wear them."

Evalie pressed her earlobe with her left hand. "Yes, of course. Every day."

Guy looked into Evalie's eyes. "So, how have you been, anyway? What have you been up to since you graduated?"

"I've been good," Evalie started. She looked at Guy's familiar face, long with a broad nose and pointed chin. His dark brown eyes shone in the streetlight. "Hey, I need to apologise for what happened with my dad. It was—"

"You don't need to apologise, Evalie. It was all him. You can't help who you are related to."

Evalie grimaced. "I suppose you're right."

They started walking slowly again.

"How was the National University of Singapore, and what was it like living in Singapore? Was it amazing?"

"It was. The course was phenomenal. You would have … well, there were lots of times I wished you were … it all seems like a bit of a dream now."

"How long have you been back?"

"It's been over a year."

"Right."

"How are you doing, anyway? What are you up to these days?"

"Yeah, fine. I'm working at Francis Consulting."

"Oh, wow. That's a good firm. Have you been there long?"

"I've been there since just after graduation. It's been three years now," Evalie chewed on her lip. "Actually, if I'm being honest, things have been a bit off for me lately." She stared straight ahead. "I keep getting looked over for promotions, Mr Francis is a wanker, my apartment is miserable and of late I've become more than a little concerned that I'm going to die there, sad and alone." Her playful tone had a hard edge to it.

Guy laughed nervously. "Oh, Evalie. I'm sure you're being dramatic. Maybe tonight is a sign that your luck is changing."

Evalie looked at him.

He winked at her, and she laughed.

"Maybe," she said. "Maybe."

They walked on, not speaking for a while.

"What have you been up to? What have you been doing since you got back?" Evalie asked.

"Well, remember how I did an internship with the Melbourne City Council during my undergrad?"

Evalie nodded.

"They got in contact just before I graduated from Singapore and offered me a job in their planning department. I've received two promotions already. They've been super impressed with all the ideas I've put forward," Guy paused. He cleared his throat. "You should have seen all the pomp of the graduation ceremony in Singapore, Evalie. It would have made you laugh."

Evalie smiled. "Yeah?"

"I was really disappointed I didn't see you at our graduation."

"Yeah. Well, I decided it would be best if I sat the graduation out, after all that happened. I needed to get a way for a while. From here. From dad. I kind of took a mini sabbatical."

"Right. I guess that was one way to deal with it. Anyway, it's good to see you now."

"You too. It's great to hear how well things have turned out for you. I'm really happy for you."

"Thanks," Guy said. "But even though things are going really well professionally, it's not all smooth sailing."

Evalie raised her eyebrows.

"It seems I've kind of bummed out on the relationship side."

"Oh, really?" Evalie cringed at the relief in her voice. "Me too I guess." She glanced sideways at Guy.

Guy took Evalie's hand. The bike wobbled in his right hand, but he maintained control. Guy's hand was warm and comforting. The two walked hand in hand all the way back to his block of units. The bike wheel squeaked now and then, marking their progress.

CHAPTER FIVE

Evalie sat on her couch, her knees pulled up to her chest. She sipped at a strong, nearly cold coffee. Her phone beeped from somewhere across the room. She looked towards the sound. A light flashed on the kitchen bench. She slowly rose and padded in bare feet to retrieve it. Her hand went to her left wrist, and she turned into the bedroom instead, found her watch on the bedside table and put it on. It lit up, and she glanced at the face.

10:15 a.m. | Saturday | 19 January

She picked up her diamond earrings from their little crystal box and put them on. After securing the second one, she walked to the kitchen and grabbed her phone off the bench. The text was from Guy.

Brunch?

Evalie smiled.

'Sure', she tapped back.

Delzano's, 30 mins?

'C u there!', she typed, then erased it. 'Lovely,' she wrote instead. She held her phone to her chest and breathed in deeply. Then she threw it gently on the couch and headed to the shower.

* * *

Evalie looked through the crowd of people at the tables outside the popular restaurant. The day was stunning—blue sky and not a breath of wind. Guy sat reading something on a tablet. He wore silver reflective sunnies that twinkled as Evalie approached. He looked up, closed the tablet cover, and placed it on the table. Then he stood to greet her.

"Good morning," he said, giving her a soft kiss on the cheek.

"It really is. What a magnificent day. And what a splendid view." Evalie sat down in the seat next to Guy so she could face the water.

The restaurant sat on the north bank of the Yarra River, a short walk from the centre of the city.

"It's even better now that you're here," Guy said.

Evalie screwed up her mouth. Then laughed.

Guy laughed too. "I knew that was going to come out wrong. Like some corny pickup line. Sorry. I mean, it's great to see you."

"Sure. Who can say no to brunch at Delzano's?"

"Oh, I get it," Guy teased, "You're only here for the food."

"You better believe it. Now what's on the specials today? I'm starving!"

"Big night last night or something?"

"Oh, not really. I was out drinking with a friend and when we were looking for our next haunt, I kind of caused a bike accident and had to cut the night short."

"A bike accident? That sounds terrible."

"No, it was okay. No one got hurt except a bit of pride and the bike wheel." Evalie smiled. "Seriously though, how is your bike?"

"It's fine now. I fixed it already."

"Oh, you've become handy, have you?"

"You could say that," Guy grinned.

34

A waiter came over to take their order. "What can I get for you today?"

"I'll have the Eggs Benedict and a short black," Guy said.

"And for you?"

"Um," Evalie said. "I think I'll go for the waffles. Oh, and an extra hot almond latte, please."

"Right. So that's an Eggs Benedict, waffles, short black and almond latte, hot. That's the lot?"

The duo nodded.

"Won't be long," the waiter said and moved to the table nearby.

"I've always wondered how they do that," Guy said.

"Do what?" Evalie asked.

"Go straight to take another order without putting the first one in with the kitchen. My memory is not that good. I could only take one order at a time."

"I think I'd be alright. It's all about having a system to remember things. You know, there's plenty–"

"Hey, did you see that?"

"What?" Evalie followed Guy's gaze out to the water. Two canoes were neck and neck, gliding along the murky brown river.

"That boat with the blue stripe was well in front and then the other one just came pressing forward and overtook it."

"Right," Evalie said. She looked down at her lap.

The world outside the restaurant engrossed Guy. His lips twitched, thoughts far away. After a few minutes, he turned back to Evalie. "So, what you got planned for the rest of the day?"

"Just the usual weekend stuff, really."

"Sounds boring. Want to hang out? We could go to the zoo. It's such a beautiful day."

"Oh, I–"

"Come on Evalie. Or did you just agree to brunch because you felt bad about my bike? Is this a guilt brunch, is that it?" Guy put his sunglasses on top of his head and raised his eyebrows.

"Well, I suppose my errands can wait. I haven't been to the zoo in ages. Unless you're just inviting me to the zoo out of pity for hitting me in the head with your helmet." Evalie smiled wryly.

"You got me. Brunch for my bike, zoo for your head. Even."

The waiter arrived with a tray of coffees.

"The short black," she said. She placed the tiny cup in front of Guy. "And the soy latte."

"Almond latte?" Evalie asked.

"Oh, um, sorry. That's right. I'll go get you another one."

"Don't worry," Evalie said. She extended her hand. "I'll have soy, I don't mind. Really."

The waiter looked at her. "If you're sure?"

"It's fine, really."

She left the drink and hurried off.

Evalie laughed. "Seems like they might have the wrong system."

"Huh? Oh, this coffee is good," Guy said.

Evalie sipped her coffee. Her face dropped.

"No good?"

"It's basically cold."

Guy sipped his coffee. "Mmm, mine's good. I'll order you a new one when the waiter comes back."

Evalie watched a runner on the path across the other side of the river. "Do you like running?" she asked.

"Nah, prefer riding," he said. "You?"

"Occasionally. Mostly on a treadmill at the gym. But if I ever need to really clear my head, I like to run by myself. I like the quiet." Evalie paused. "Where do you ride? Do you ever go on any of those charity bike rides or anything?"

"Mostly around the city."

The waiter returned with the food. "Eggs Florentine," she said, placing the plate down in front of Guy.

"Oh, I actually ordered the Eggs Benedict. Because I really like bacon," Guy said.

"Really?" the waiter asked. "I'm sure you said Florentine."

"No, he didn't," Evalie stated. "Maybe that was for a different table?"

"No, it was for this table," she said as she picked up the dish. "But I'll change it for you. It may take a while, though; the kitchen is flat out."

"It's okay," Guy said. "I'll give it a go. It looks awfully healthy with all that spinach."

The waiter put the plate back down. "Okay, good. And here are the waffles. Which you definitely ordered."

"Yes, thanks," Evalie said as the plate landed before her with a clank.

The waiter turned and left.

"Can I—" Evalie started. She looked over her shoulder. "I can't believe it! How could she stuff up your order, too? And before I can get a fresh coffee, she's gone."

Guy laughed. "I guess it's not our day." He looked down at his dish skeptically and started cutting a piece off. "Let me take you to dinner tonight, to make up for this brunch debacle. I know a really nice place down on Bridge Road. Do you like Mexican? Rosa's Cantina. It's great. What do you say?"

Evalie shrugged. "These waffles are great." She finished a mouthful. "Let's see how the trip to the zoo goes first, eh? We might be sick of each other by evening."

Guy smiled. "Oh, I get it, a test. I'll be on my best behaviour." He winked at Evalie.

A flutter travelled through her chest. *I forgot how charming he is*, she thought.

CHAPTER SIX

E valie looked at her watch.

2:03 p.m. | Saturday | 19 January

She leaned on the shady bench, her fingers tapping a beat on her leg. It was that song again, from the other day. Evalie shook her head. *I still haven't looked that up,* she thought. She got up and strolled back and forth outside the zoo gate. She watched the excited kids pulling on their parents' hands, urging them faster through the gates, anticipating the wonders beyond. Then there were the bedraggled ones coming out, hair all a mess, and food around their mouths. Some were asleep on shoulders and in prams.

Evalie retrieved her phone from her bag and wrote a message. "R u here?" She pressed "Send" and watched for a sign of forthcoming response, but there was none. She moved closer to the gate. Evalie turned and scanned the car park and the road in each direction, shrugged, and joined the short queue.

"Next," two cashiers said at the same time.

The couple and family ahead of her left the line. Evalie moved to the front of the queue. She adjusted her hat, so the wide blue brim wasn't covering her face. She dug into her favourite pink handbag. A nudge came from behind.

She turned, and the stranger said, "You're up."

"Next please," the cashier said.

"Oh, thanks," Evalie muttered. She moved forward to the window. She pulled her lip gloss out of her bag.

"Two adults?" The cashier asked.

"Just me," Evalie replied.

"Yes two," Guy said from behind her, reaching forward with his phone to pay.

"How did you?–"

"Sorry I'm late," Guy said with a grin.

"Know it was me?" Evalie finished.

"All done," the cashier said. "Scan here for the map if you don't have it already and enjoy your afternoon. The gates close at eight tonight."

"Thanks," Guy said. He scanned the map code. "Let's go!"

They walked through the main entrance.

"I knew it was you because you're unmistakable, Evalie," Guy said. He looked sideways at Evalie, then studied the map.

Evalie blushed.

"What do you want to see first? What's your favourite?" he asked.

"The monkeys."

"Righto, this way, please." Guy gestured to the left path.

The couple walked down the path out of the sun and into the dappled shade. As they walked further, the tree branches weaved together across the path, creating an emerald-green tunnel.

Evalie looked up at the tree canopy above. "It's so lovely in here. It's like another world."

The path led them to the first enclosure. They peered through the glass panel at the little creek, large log and dirt mounds covered in leaf litter that made up the otter's home. All was still. Some interested onlookers joined them. After less than a minute, they left. Evalie and Guy stood beside one another, nearly touching. Evalie glanced sideways, but Guy kept his attention fixed straight ahead.

"Hang on, I see movement," he whispered. "There!" He pointed to a dark shadow at the end of the log.

Two sleek bodies came into view. They slipped into the creek and began splashing around.

"They're so cute!" Evalie cried. The otters slipped out of sight.

"I think you frightened them," Guy chuckled.

"Oops, sorry." Evalie covered her mouth with a hand.

"Doesn't matter." Guy grabbed her other hand. "Let's go see the gorillas."

Evalie and Guy walked hand in hand to the gorillas, who were sitting with their backs to the viewing areas. They paused for a few moments, then continued up the wooden ramp to the primate enclosures. There were ten in total, displaying all kinds of monkeys. They gasped as a Black-and-white Colobus jumped from the ledge below the window to a tree over twenty metres away. Further along the compound, two Spider Monkeys were fighting over a piece of papaya. Guy and Evalie watched with interest to see which monkey would be victorious. The thick window muffled the screaming, but that didn't stop them from jumping when one monkey slammed into it.

Evalie looked at Guy and laughed. He pulled her in close and brushed her fringe out of her eye. Evalie's heartbeat quickened.

Guy leaned in and kissed her softly. He smelt like sandalwood and musk. Evalie kissed him back. She was overcome with giddiness and couldn't decide if it was the warmth of the day or this man before her. Evalie looked at his face. She noticed the once familiar mole at the top of his right cheekbone. He kissed her again. His tongue was soft and playful in her mouth. They sat down on a nearby bench, kissing passionately.

When Evalie looked up a few minutes later, a little child was staring at them. A bedraggled toy monkey hung limply from the boy's left hand, its long dusty tail dragging on the ground. He looked about two or three years old. He had scruffy brown-blonde hair, a stripy T-shirt, and blue shorts with patches of dust all over. Evalie blushed. Then smiled. The kid stared.

Evalie grabbed Guy's arm. "Time to go." She pulled Guy up off the seat. "It looks like we've become the exhibit. Plus, I want to see the seals."

"Okay, okay," Guy said. "I'm coming."

* * *

"We're just in time for the three-thirty show," Guy said. They entered under the sign that said *Wild Sea Habitat*.

"Great timing, huh," Evalie remarked.

They wandered along the nautical-themed path, with its heavy ropes tied to bollards; faded orange buoys; and an old wooden ship wheel leaning against a small, upside-down metal boat. The pelicans preened themselves as the couple walked past their enclosure. The couple turned the corner and before them was the grandstand. It was quickly filling up with spectators. Evalie found some seats towards the back, and they squeezed past those already in place on the concrete step benches, under a railing, and claimed their space. They sat with their knees touching. Butterflies fluttered in Evalie's stomach as she looked over at Guy from under her hat.

"You can take that off now, since we're well and truly under cover." Guy reached over and gently lifted Evalie's hat off and put it in his lap. "That's better. Now I can see your face. Beautiful."

Evalie smiled and looked down at her hands. When she looked up moments later, he was still looking at her. She leaned closer, and they kissed.

The entire world disappeared, and for those fleeting moments before the seal show started, it was just them, on a bench, kissing.

CHAPTER SEVEN

Evalie rolled over in unfamiliar sheets and opened her eyes.

"Good morning," Guy said smoothly.

"Good morning," Evalie replied in a muffled, sleepy voice.

"How did you sleep?"

"Good. How about you?"

"Very well. Better than I've slept for a long time." He grinned.

"Me too." Evalie shuffled closer.

Their bodies touched, and they kissed. Guy ran his fingers through Evalie's hair. They rolled over, so she was on top of him.

"An early riser, are you?" Evalie giggled.

"Not usually," Guy said. "But this seems like exceptional circumstances. Like it's going to be an exceptional day."

* * *

Guy stopped, puffing. "How much further did you say it was?"

"We're nearly there."

"That's what you said fifteen minutes ago."

"Trust me, the view is worth every bead of sweat."

"I was happy with the view down there. In fact, you can't get much better than the view I have right now," Guy said. He looked up at her backside.

"Ha, well, you'll just have to keep walking after this view, or it will soon be out of sight!" Evalie skipped ahead along the rocky path. The sea breeze whipped at her hair, and she brushed her fringe to the side. She reached into her pocket for a hairpin. She found one, along with something else. Evalie quickly secured her hair with the pin. She pulled the folded paper out of her pocket as she walked up the final three stairs to the viewing platform.

"Wow," she said to herself, taking in the view along the coast. "Gets me every time." Evalie watched the waves roll towards the beach in the curved bay. In the distance, on the rocky cliff, stood a lighthouse. Shipwreck Bay wasn't called that for nothing. Guy joined her on the platform.

"Made it," he said, puffing. Guy leaned against the wooden rail. He whistled. "I hate to admit it, but you're right. It is better up here, and worth the pain."

"It wasn't that bad, was it? Truly?"

"Um. Yep. It was." Guy took in the view, then turned back to Evalie. "What's that?" He asked, gesturing to Evalie's hand.

Evalie unfurled the paper. She saw the code for her Xoha application submission and quickly folded it back up. "Nothing important. Just a shopping list." Evalie shoved the folded paper into her pocket.

"That's archaic, isn't it? A paper shopping list. Don't you shop online?" Guy asked.

"Oh, yeah, of course I do. But sometimes I write myself notes so I don't forget something. I seem to remember things better if I write them by hand, you know?"

"Fascinating," Guy said. He moved closer and clasped Evalie's hand in his. They smiled at one another.

Evalie pulled Guy in and kissed him. After a few minutes, they separated slightly to take in the view once more.

The pair stayed there, in a half embrace, until the sun set. The yellows, oranges, pinks and purples painted the dusk into their memory and the red ball of a sun slipped silently over the horizon.

* * *

Evalie walked into the office at 8:59 a.m. She stood at her desk and checked her messages. She hummed a tune while she typed a response to Tommy's request for more background information. Evalie realised it was *that* same song. It had turned into an earworm. Evalie tried to think of another song to replace it, but couldn't. She lowered her adjustable desk and sat down. She thought about her magical weekend. The day slipped past, and she left work at 4:59 p.m., with a spring in her step.

That night as Evalie lay alone in her bed, she thought of Guy and smiled. She unfastened her diamond earrings and placed them gently in the delicate crystal box that sat on her worn bedside table. A message popped up on her phone. She leaned across so she could read the screen.

Goodnight XX

Evalie grabbed the phone and typed out a response.

Sweet dreams XX

She put the phone back on the table, rolled over, and closed her eyes. She was pretty sure her own dreams would not be sour.

CHAPTER EIGHT

E valie sat at her desk, daydreaming. Her phone's message tone brought her back to reality.

Lunch?

'Yes!' Evalie responded.

See you outside your building at 12:30 p.m.?

'Perfect,' Evalie typed back. It was 10:03 a.m.

"Only two hours and twenty-seven minutes to go," she murmured. "Suppose I should try to finish that report."

Evalie flicked between screens, typing, cutting and pasting text, editing using voice commands. After a while, she sensed someone looking at her, but kept working.

"Ah, hum."

Evalie looked up. It was Tommy.

"What are you working on there, Evalie?"

"The Zalinski report," Evalie said.

"You were meant to finish that yesterday."

"It's nearly done. Just have to finish the final edit."

Evalie completed a quick spell check, running through the prompts at lightning speed.

"But you–"

"There, all done." Evalie smiled. "I've just sent it to you."

"Oh. Next time, get it in on time."

As he walked away, Evalie pulled a face at his back.

Naomi was walking towards Evalie's desk. She laughed.

Tommy turned.

Naomi smiled at him. "Morning Tommy," she said.

"Yeah, whatever."

* * *

Evalie grabbed her bag and slipped away from the office. Outside, the air was warm on her face. She saw Guy straight away.

He was leaning against the bike stand. He smiled as she approached. "Hello," he said.

"Hello," Evalie said. She kissed him gently on the lips.

"Hungry?"

"Definitely."

"What do you feel like?"

"Sushi?"

"Sounds good. Where do you usually go for sushi?"

"Just round the corner," Evalie signalled with her hand and they began walking, "at Kimiko's."

"I haven't been there."

"It's fantastic."

"So, how's your day going, anyway?"

"Not bad," Evalie said. She furrowed her brow.

"That good?" Guy asked.

"Much better for seeing you," she smiled, and took his hand. "Come on slow coach, I'm hungry!" She pulled him along.

He laughed and let her drag him a few steps before matching her pace.

As they waited in line for their sushi, Evalie shifted her weight from one foot to another. "Do you ever get the sense that people are trying to quash your ideas at work?"

"No. Why do you?"

Evalie furrowed her brow. "All the time. It was bad enough before. I could never get any airtime. But now, after the promotion, Tommy is acting like he's some kind of god. It's really gone to his head. And his ego was big enough before. Now it's colossal."

"Maybe it's just the way you're approaching it."

"Sorry?"

"Could it be that you're jealous because he got the promotion and not you?"

Evalie glanced at her shoes.

Guy kept talking. "Perhaps take a step back. Or just follow along for now. There might be space for your ideas later once Tommy's had his time in the sun."

"Umm. Well. Maybe." Fire burned in Evalie's cheeks.

"Order fifty-three," the man behind the counter called out.

"That's us," Guy said. He stepped forward to grab the tray of sushi rolls.

Evalie watched Guy as he picked up the tray. A sense of discomfort settled in her stomach. She brushed it off as hunger.

The couple sat down at a spare table under the shade of an umbrella and ate their lunch in silence.

* * *

Evalie saw Stella's hot pink top from across the street. She checked for cars, then jogged over to the park bench. Stella stared at her phone, oblivious to the world around her.

"Hey," Evalie called out.

There was no response.

"Hello? Stella?"

Stella looked up and flashed Evalie a broad smile. "Oh, hey there," she said. "Shall we go?" Stella stood, putting her phone in her pocket.

"Sure. We've got plenty of time. We can meander, I guess," Evalie said.

"Consider it a gentle warmup." Stella grabbed her yoga mat from beside the bench and slung it over her shoulder.

The pair walked along the crushed rock path that wound through the park. Their shoes made crunching sounds with each step. The tall palm trees hushed them as the gentle breeze caught their tall fronds.

"How weird was it running into Guy on Friday?" Stella prompted.

"This again? I thought we got all this out in our text message marathon on Sunday!"

"Oh, no, that was just the beginning. This is too good. I can't believe it still. After that messy break up and you wondering if you'd done the wrong thing. Making yourself sick thinking you'd walked away from the love of your life. But knowing what happened with your dad, well, where do you go from there? Then, suddenly, there he is. Rising out of that garbage like your love phoenix rising from the ashes."

"Are you just hanging onto this because you're engaged now? Planning a double wedding in your mind or something?" Evalie said wryly.

"A double wedding! Your idea, not mine. Wow, things must be moving fast."

Evalie gave Stella a gentle side bump with her left hip.

Stella laughed. "Okay, easy now. I get the message." She looked curiously at Evalie. "But what are you going to do? I assume nothing has changed; with your dad, I mean."

They stopped at the pedestrian crossing and Evalie smacked the button, avoiding Stella's gaze. Evalie sensed Stella's intense gaze. It seared the side of her cheek as they crossed from the shady park over to the plaza that led down to the beach. The evening sun still had an intensity that burned at her skin. A faint seaweed smell danced on the warm summer breeze.

"It's hot out here, isn't it?" Evalie said.

"So, we're changing the subject then, I suppose," Stella replied.

Evalie grunted. "I sure hope I don't get lost halfway through, like last week. What do you think of the new yoga teacher, anyway? I think she's good, but I miss Bain. He was some fine eye-candy, don't you think? I wonder how he's going up in Queensland."

"Alright, I'll play along," Stella said. She shifted her gaze to the blue-green water that shimmered with sun diamonds. "I think Natasha's much better than Bain. Last week I really got into the flow of it. I like the sun; I need to up my tan, so I don't look so ridiculously ghostly next to Tejas, anyway. You should see his ass in the new boardies I got him." She whistled softly. "I've got my own eye-candy these days, I guess." Stella looked smugly at Evalie. "Perhaps you've found your own now, too."

Evalie snorted and skipped ahead of Stella, joining the small collection of yoga mats and acquaintances down on the sand.

CHAPTER NINE

Popcorn began overflowing from the machine. Golden yellow, it inched ever higher up the glass. Evalie breathed in the buttery scent and sighed.

"What movie did you buy tickets for again?" she asked.

"Enforcement X," Guy said in a robotic voice. "How can you forget? I only just told you yesterday after I bought the tickets.

"Yeah, right. Sorry."

"Are you okay? You seem a bit distracted."

"Yeah, I'm fine. Did you order ice cream as well, or just popcorn?"

"Ice cream, of course. I'll get your favourite."

"You're the best," Evalie said. She cuddled into Guy's side, and he put his arm around her. "You know my favourite flavour is boysenberry, right?"

"Next," the cashier called.

Guy broke away from Evalie and stepped forward, scanning his phone on the reader.

Evalie walked over to the corner of the busy counter to wait for Guy. She watched him converse with the lady behind the counter. She was young, with a flawless complexion and bushy eyelashes. His brown eyes shone under the bright lights, and his cheeks dimpled as he smiled in response to the woman's flirtations. *He is good looking*, Evalie thought. *Why wouldn't she flirt with him?*

After a few minutes, he walked back over, hands full of movie treats. "Let's go. Cinema three, isn't it?"

Evalie nodded.

As they rode the escalator, Guy held out the ice creams. "Here, take these. They're freezing."

Evalie laughed. "Okay, sure." She examined the packets, one chocolate, one strawberry. "Which one's for me?"

"What do you mean? The strawberry one, of course."

"Right. Of course."

The cinema was half full when they walked in. They found their seats and sat down.

Evalie put the ice creams down on the vacant seat beside her. "They *are* freezing." She rubbed her hands.

Guy passed her a popcorn bucket, and she passed him the chocolate ice cream. He smiled at her and leaned in. They kissed. The screen jumped to life and Guy drew away from Evalie. He settled back into his seat.

Evalie did the same. "You know how you said I seemed distracted before, well–"

"Shh. Tell me afterwards. It's starting."

"It's only the ads."

"I like the ads."

Evalie looked at Guy, her eyes glassy. He was looking straight ahead at the screen. She sighed and turned her attention to her ice cream.

* * *

"What did you think of the movie?" Guy asked.

"It was okay."

"I thought it was awesome."

The couple rose from their seats and headed out of the cinema.

Evalie rubbed her left arm with her right hand. "It was a little cold in there, wasn't it?"

"You should have told me you were cold; I would have given you my jacket."

"That's alright. Hey, do you want to go somewhere for coffee? I could use one to warm up."

"No, I can't tonight. I've got an early meeting tomorrow. I need to be on my game."

"Oh, okay."

"But I'll see you tomorrow, right? Your choice of activity. Any thoughts?"

They stepped onto the escalator.

"All planned," Evalie said. "Indoor rock climbing."

"Oh, nice one. Sounds fun."

Evalie smiled. "Do you think you can keep up?"

Guy laughed. "Pretty sure."

The couple dodged the groups of people huddled throughout the foyer and walked out of the main door.

"Well, see you tomorrow." Guy kissed Evalie and drew her in close. "Miss you already."

Evalie looked at Guy. She hoped he would read the concern on her face. They broke apart.

"Bye," Guy said. He gave her a little wave and walked off down the street.

"Bye," Evalie said. She watched him walk a few paces and then turned and headed in the opposite direction. Evalie walked slowly home, pondering how Guy could make her feel so good and so bad almost in the same instant. She wished he didn't make her feel so good. The sexual attraction was intoxicating. She closed her eyes and experienced a tingle in her crotch. She opened her eyes and walked faster. Why didn't he have time for her worries or concerns? Sometimes it was like he didn't even hear her.

Strawberry, what was that? she thought.

By the time she got home, she had warmed up and decided against the coffee she had craved on the long walk. Instead, she got ready for bed. After brushing her teeth, she noticed a message flash on her phone. It was from Guy. Her pulse quickened as she picked up her phone.

Goodnight XX

Evalie's face dropped. She wrote back.

Sweet dreams XX

CHAPTER TEN

The message pulse on Evalie's phone interrupted her concentration. She picked it up off her desk.

Lunch today?

Her heart pounded in her chest. Evalie crossed her legs tightly before the pounding travelled somewhere else. She swivelled in her work chair to peek out of the window. The sky was a patchwork of clouds.

'Yes! Maybe somewhere indoors?' Evalie wrote. She pressed send and watched her phone.

Meet you out front at 12:30 p.m.

'See you then!' Evalie typed back. She put her phone down on her desk and stared off into the distance.

"Evalie?"

Evalie blinked. "Huh? Oh, hi Arielle."

"So, can you make it to the one o'clock? You haven't answered my message."

"Today? What's that for again?"

"The meeting with Mr Francis and Tommy."

59

"Ah, no, sorry. I have a lunch appointment. Can you shift it to two?"

"Well, Mr Francis will not be happy. But I suppose so. Next time, answer my message." Arielle stormed off.

"Okey dokey." Evalie grinned at Arielle's back. She stared across the office long after Arielle had gone, thinking of Guy's muscly arms and his disarming smile.

* * *

Evalie walked out of her building at 12:29 p.m. She waited by the bike stand, wrapping her jacket tightly around herself in the cool air. "Summer in Melbourne," she muttered, shaking her head. She stood, hands in pockets, watching the passers-by with little interest. Six minutes later, she got out her phone and wrote a message. Then she stopped and deleted the characters. "Be patient, Evalie," she mumbled. "He's probably right around the corner."

Evalie noticed a bike rider coming down the street. "See?" She laughed to herself. The rider rode right past her. Her head drooped. Evalie busied herself with her phone. She flicked through various apps but looked up from her screen often.

Evalie lasted another five minutes. 'Everything okay?' she typed. Evalie sent the message and watched for a response. None came. She noticed Arielle walk out of the building onto the street and quickly turned so her back was facing the doors. She returned her attention to her screen. Evalie waited. And waited.

When someone touched her arm, Evalie nearly jumped out of her skin.

"Sorry to startle you," Guy said.

"Oh, hi."

"Shall we go?"

"Sure." Evalie looked at him. "What was the holdup? I was getting worried."

They walked down the street.

"Sorry, I was just completing some arrangements for lunch. It took longer than I expected."

"Oh, okay. What arrangements?"

"Come and see." Guy took her by the hand, and they walked towards the river. After a silent walk, they came to the dock at Banana Alley and there was a boat waiting. "Here we are," Guy said.

"Good afternoon, Miss Evalie," said a deep voice from onboard. There were three people lined up waiting for the couple. "Please, come aboard. Your lunch awaits."

Evalie looked at Guy. He nudged her forward, and she took the hand of the chef. She pulled Evalie on board and smiled.

"Welcome. This way, please." The chef led Evalie into the galley to a table set with a crisp white tablecloth, silver cutlery, flowers, and candles. Guy followed close behind.

"Wow," Evalie said. "This looks incredible."

Guy smiled. "You're incredible." He pulled out the chair for her and she sat down.

The boat pulled out of the dock and motored along the calm river. The chef brought entrees of freshly baked rolls and salad.

Evalie buttered a roll and munched hungrily on it. "This is wonderful, Guy." She looked at him, her eyes twinkling.

"I'm glad you like it. So, was it worth the wait, then?"

"Yes, for sure," Evalie said. "You could have just messaged me to let me know you were running late, though. It would have only taken a second."

Guy's face dropped. "Well, I–"

"Or you could have called and asked me to walk in this direction. You remember I only get an hour for lunch, right?"

"I just wanted to surprise you with something romantic. Isn't this better than work, anyway? You're always complaining about this or that, the minutia of your office's politics. Maybe you can skip the remainder of the day. It's not like you've got anything important going on at work. Call in sick perhaps?"

"Oh. Well, ..." Evalie looked at her salad and prodded a piece of beetroot with her fork. She looked up at Guy. "I suppose that's true. There isn't much going on at work," Evalie said in a glum voice. "I guess I could make up something. A sudden illness or family emergency." Evalie blushed as she thought back to the last time she had used the family emergency excuse.

Guy seemed not to notice. "That's more like it. How's your salad?"

"Delicious."

"Sparkling?" Guy asked. He pulled a bottle from the ice bucket next to the table.

"Sure, thanks," Evalie replied with a wry smile. "I mean, who could say no to that?"

They sat eating and drinking with only the hum of the boat filling the air between them. Evalie finished the last leaves on her plate and placed her knife and fork together in the middle.

"Done," she said.

"Ready for mains?" Guy asked.

"Oh, there's more? Right. Sure."

The chef poked her head through the door.

Guy signalled to her, and she disappeared again. "So, you know how I'm working on this big project at the moment," Guy said.

Evalie nodded.

"Rodger says I'm doing such a great job. Once I finish the report, he's going to put my name forward for a promotion."

"Really?" Evalie asked. "That's great, Guy, well done."

"Thanks." Guy looked across at Evalie. "I wasn't sure how you would take it."

"What do you mean?"

"You know, because you missed out on the promotion and all. Things haven't been very good for you at work lately."

"Come on, I'm not that shallow. Naturally, I'm thrilled for you. You deserve it. You're obviously doing a fantastic job. It's great to be recognised for it."

The chef came to the table with two bowls of gnocchi pesto, garnished with roasted cherry tomatoes.

Just as the chef placed them down on the table, Evalie winced at a sharp pain in her stomach. She pressed her left hand immediately to the sore spot. "Where's the toilet?" Evalie gasped.

"Are you okay?" Guy asked. "You've gone awfully pale."
Evalie shook her head.

"It's just through there." Guy pointed. "Here, I'll show you."
Guy led Evalie out of the galley and ushered her through the door. Evalie bristled as she entered the cubicle. She didn't know whether to sit on the toilet or bend over it. She sat and grabbed a sanitary napkin bag. Five minutes later, there was a knock on the door.

"Are you okay in there?"

"No," Evalie said, voice strained. Then she vomited.

"Is there anything I can do?"

"No." She vomited again.

A little while later she heard, "Evalie, honey, are you alright? The captain is turning the boat around. We'll be back at the wharf in ten minutes."

"Um," was all Evalie could manage.

"I'll just be waiting out here for you. If you need anything, yell out, okay?" Guy said.

Evalie hung her head in her hands.

* * *

After eleven minutes, they safely docked at the wharf. The boat rocked gently from the wash, bouncing back off the wooden structure. Guy helped Evalie off the boat. She walked gingerly along the gangplank and onto solid ground.

"Get well soon," the deckhand called after her.

Evalie raised her hand in acknowledgment.

"Let's get you home," Guy said.

Evalie nodded, her face pale and sullen.

"This is us," he said, leading Evalie to the waiting car.

Guy helped Evalie into the back seat. They rode in silence back to Evalie's apartment building. Once there, Guy helped Evalie upstairs and into her apartment. He helped her change into comfy clothes and got her a glass of water.

"Small sips," he said as he passed the glass to her.

"Thank you." Evalie grimaced instead of smiled.

"Do you want anything else? Can I get you a cool cloth for your head or something?"

Evalie shook her head. "I'm just going to curl up in bed."

"Sure," Guy said. "Feel better. I'll call you tomorrow." He kissed Evalie's forehead and left.

Evalie shuffled into her bedroom, put the glass onto the scratched top of her bedside table, and curled up in a ball under the covers.

* * *

Evalie raised her phone to check the time. The dull light of the screen hurt her eyes a little, and she had to blink many times before the blur came to be recognisable.

4:32 p.m.

Evalie couldn't believe she'd slept the whole afternoon and night. There were two messages from Guy. She opened them.

Hope you're feeling better. Call you tomorrow.

Goodnight XX

Evalie considered writing back, but it was too late, or too early now. Her stomach was empty, and her throat was dry. She put her phone down and raised herself up on her elbows. Evalie reached for the glass of water on her bedside table. She smiled at the thought of Guy giving it to her. Looking after her. Evalie took a few sips, then lay back down and shut her eyes. She saw the boat, and the table laid out for her. She heard Guy's voice. "I wasn't sure how you would take it. You missed out on that promotion and all." The nausea came rushing back and Evalie sat up, sweating. Then she hobbled quickly to the toilet. Her mouth screwed up in pain. Then she vomited. Again. And again. And again.

* * *

The morning clouds hung low and heavy on the city. The subdued light above her curtains was misleading. When she opened her eyes, Evalie sensed it was over. The twenty-four-hour bug that had ruined a special, romantic lunch, probably the most romantic moment someone had ever tried to create for her, was over. She groaned and stumbled to the kitchen. She needed food. Dry toast would do for now. No need to be brash and tempt the vomit gods. Just two pieces of dry toast and a glass of water.

Evalie sat down at her kitchen bench and chewed, washing each mouthful of dry bread down with a sip of water. It wasn't until she'd finished, put her dishes in the sink and flopped down on the couch that she considered the day or time.

"Shit," she said. She dialled the number for her boss.

"Francis Consulting, Mr Francis' phone, Arielle speaking."

"Oh, hi Arielle. It's Evalie—"

"It's nice that you finally called," Arielle said. "Where in the heck have you been? You better have a good excuse."

"I'm sorry. I've been sick. Really sick. Vomiting. Anyway, I won't be in today. Or tomorrow, probably."

"It's Friday, tomorrow is Saturday. I'll let Mr Francis know. He was fuming when you didn't show up for the meeting with Tommy on Wednesday afternoon and didn't call. I think he thought you were trying to get fired. He was certainly talking about firing you. And now you will miss the Dartmouth meeting. But I suppose we can't have you vomiting on the clients, can we? Make sure you get a doctor's certificate. Such a long absence needs an official letter."

"Uh. Okay. Thanks. I'll see you Monday, then."

Evalie ended the call and flopped onto her couch. She put her arms over her face and let out a long groan. Then she flipped onto her side and turned on the TV. The colours on the screen twirled in her vision. She closed her eyes tight and lay deathly still.

* * *

The following day, Evalie awoke on the couch. Her neck ached as she reached for her phone. She looked at the screen.

8:15 a.m.

She had three missed calls from Guy. At least her stomach felt better. And her head wasn't fuzzy anymore. She stretched and yawned. Her mouth was dry. She went to the bathroom and washed it out in the sink before lapping up some of the cool water. She was relieved that the seventy-two-hour sickness, or whatever it was, had passed. It was such a blessed relief.

She had just finished making a coffee when her phone rang. She quickly put the milk back in the fridge and retrieved the phone from the couch arm. When she saw the name on the screen, she sighed.

"Hi Stella."

"You're never gonna guess what happened!"

"What?"

"We booked a date. For our wedding. In Fiji. Next month. Twenty-third of March. Isn't it exciting!"

"Yes. That is exciting."

"What's wrong? You sound like I just told you your gran died or something."

"Sorry. I am excited. I've just been sick as. You know, vomiting. For like three days. I'm much better now, but still a bit washed out."

"Gross. Well, glad you're better. So, what have you been up to lately? Apart from vomiting, that is. I've hardly seen you, only at yoga and even then, you've been running late and seem to take off quickly afterwards before we can chat. Are you avoiding me?"

"No, actually, I've been hanging out with Guy. Like, most of the time."

"Evalie! You dog, why didn't you tell me?"

"I've just been really busy. We've been seeing each other nearly every day. For lunch dates mainly. We take it in turns to choose a place to eat. You know, on Wednesday he took me on a boat. It was all kitted out with a beautiful table set for two. There was just me and him. Oh, and the chef, deckhand, and captain. It was so romantic."

"Wow, Evalie. You haven't gushed this way about a guy since, well, I can't actually remember a time," Stella said.

"It was so perfect. Until I got food poisoning, or whatever, and started throwing up like it was an Olympic sport," Evalie continued.

"You were sick on the boat? How apt."

"It can't have been sea sickness. The water was smooth as glass!"

"It never seemed to matter to you. Remember that time we took the ferry to Williamstown?"

"Don't remind me," Evalie said with a groan. "My stomach can't handle that memory right now."

"We had been on the boat for a whole two minutes. I looked over at you and you were green."

Evalie groaned again.

"You spent the entire ride out on the side deck with the wind in your face. You didn't get any of the free food or drink. And that's not like you at all!"

"Speaking of free food and drink, a wedding, huh? Fancy you to be the first of us to get married?"

"Funny, isn't it? You aren't jealous, are you, Evalie?"

"Stop teasing me. I'm really not in a fit state."

"You were fine a moment a go when we were talking about Guy."

"Yeah, well."

"Why don't you come over? I can show you the wedding stuff. And I'll make you lunch."

"That sounds like a bride's request."

"You're damn straight. See you in an hour."

The buzzing of the ended call rang in Evalie's ears. "See you then," she said to nobody, as she picked up her coffee mug and took a sip. She screwed up her nose and pitched the brown liquid down the sink. Then she headed for the shower.

* * *

Evalie knocked again at the door. She shuffled her feet. Stella came to the door, peppermill tucked under her right arm and a pot in her left. The aroma of pepper danced in Evalie's nostrils. She twitched her nose and followed Stella's beckoning, shutting the door behind her and following the host into the kitchen.

"I'm so glad you're here, Evalie. This is my best ratatouille yet; I know it!"

"It smells fantastic," Evalie replied.

"I know! So, sit, sit." Stella gestured enthusiastically to a stool. "I can't wait to show you all the wedding stuff. Let me just put the rest of these herbs in." Stella tipped a small bowl of green flecks into the saucepan and gave it a gentle stir. "There. Okay, check this out."

Stella sat next to Evalie and shoved the tablet under her nose. The pictures of a wedding chapel on a cliff overlooking turquoise water scrolled before Evalie's eyes.

"Wow. This looks unreal."

"So, you'll come then, maid of honour?"

Evalie looked at Stella. "You bet!"

The friends swivelled on their stools and hugged one another.

"Now, don't worry about the flights and accommodation. We've got that covered. We got a ripper deal, too." Stella grinned.

"Oh, no, I can't let you pay for me. I'll pay my way. I know I have been struggling of late, but I think I can make it work."

"No Evalie, we insist. It was our decision to elope. We asked you to come with us. So, we will pay for the privilege. And we won't take no for an answer."

"Oh, well—"

"I mean it Evalie, we want to. I want to. You're my best friend. Sometimes I think you're my only friend, only real friend, anyway."

Stella got up and started clattering some plates. "You mean the world to me," she blurted. "Now, enough of that. Here, have some of this."

She took the saucepan and served some of the ratatouille onto the plates, then whisked them onto the table. The ice cubes in the water jug jingled against the glass. Evalie looked at all the goodies on the table. The plate of generously buttered breadstick slices and bowl overflowing with leafy green salad looked delicious.

"What a feast!" Evalie said, moving over to sit at the table. "How did you whip all this up in an hour?"

"Well, I must confess, I'd already started cooking when I rang. It looks alright, doesn't it? I think I've outdone myself this time."

"Isn't Tejas joining us?"

"No, he's gone to find a suit for the wedding." Stella sat next to Evalie. "You know the best thing about getting married in another country? They do pretty much everything for you. The hotel I mean. They have a package that comes with flowers, cake, and a photographer. All you need to do is find something to wear and show up."

"That sounds wonderful." Evalie's gaze wandered across the table and out the window. She had a piece of bread in her hand. Stella looked at her.

"You're thinking about Guy," she teased. "What it would be like to marry him."

Evalie blushed. "No, I'm not!"

Stella giggled. "You *lurve* him."

Evalie giggled. "Maybeee I just like him, a bit. Or a lot." She grinned broadly.

"Maybeee you should ask him to come to the wedding."

"What? Really? You wouldn't mind?" Evalie said, heart fluttering.

Stella just looked at her and grinned.

* * *

Hands in pockets, Evalie walked up to Guy's apartment building. She'd been mumbling to herself the whole way over, trying to get the words right. She hesitated at the door, then pressed the button for number 211.

"Hello?"

"Hi, it's me, Evalie," she sang.

"Hi. Come on up."

The door opened, and she walked into the lobby, choosing to take the stairs. She attempted to take her time so she wouldn't get out of breath. But as she climbed higher and thought about the prospect of Guy going to the wedding with her, she couldn't help but speed up. The door was open a crack. She knocked gently, and it swung open. Guy was putting a guitar back on its stand.

"Hi," Evalie said.

"Hello. To what do I owe this great pleasure? How are you? All okay now? That was a long time. You didn't call me back."

"Yes, I know. I'm sorry I didn't get your calls. I was sick in bed the whole time. But I'm all better, thanks. I just wanted to see you. And I wanted to apologise for–"

"No need to apologise." He walked over to her. They embraced. Then they kissed. "Come, sit." Guy gestured to the couch. "Do you want some water? You're all sweaty from your walk."

Evalie blushed. "Yes, water would be great, thanks."

Guy went into the kitchen.

Evalie looked around Guy's neat apartment. It was cosy, with a soft-looking brown U-shaped leather couch on a Persian rug of reds and dark blues, with just a hint of yellow. It was much nicer than her place, and much, much bigger. Two guitars sat in stands to the right of the big TV. The TV cabinet was full of DVD and CD cases, all neatly stacked. He must have been a collector. Nobody else Evalie knew kept those old relics anymore. She heard ice clinking and Guy returned with two glasses of water. Condensation had already trickled down the glass when he handed it to her.

"Thanks," Evalie said. She took three long sips.

Guy watched her and smiled. "So glad to see you looking well again," he said. "I was worried about you."

He sat next to her, close, so their knees were just touching.

"Really? No need to be. Just food poisoning or something. It was horrible, though."

"Yeah, food poisoning is never good."

"Hey, I have something to ask you."

"Sure, what is it?"

"Well, uh, you know how Stella is getting married?"

"Yeah, I remember you telling me that night we bumped into one another." Guy poked Evalie softly in the ribs.

"Well, they've set a date. Next month. In Fiji. And, well, I was wondering if you wanted to come. To the wedding. With me. If you'd like. But you don't have to. If you think it's too soon. I mean, I know we've only just started properly dating."

"I love you."

"Sorry, what? What did you say?"

"I'd love to, Evalie." He grabbed her hand. "I've never been to Fiji."

"Right, great!" Evalie said. "Me neither."

There was an awkward silence. Evalie was sure she'd heard him say it. But maybe it was just the sickness hangover making her mind play tricks on her. "It'll just be a quick trip, probably four days," she said. "The wedding is on the twenty-third of next month."

"The twenty-third?"

"Yeah, I know it's not a lot of time."

"No, it's not that. I have that work thing on then. I doubt I can get out of it."

"Oh, no," Evalie said. To her surprise, relief washed over her. "You can't get someone to cover for you?"

"I'll check with Rodger, but I highly doubt it. We've been planning this showcase event for months. I don't think he'd be okay with me not being there, since I'm managing it. I'll have to check, sorry."

"Oh, okay. Sure. Just let me know when you can, so I can tell Stella. She needs to know for the hotel booking and such. You didn't tell me about this big event."

Guy got a funny expression on his face. "Evalie, I told you about it the other day at lunch. Glad to see you were listening." He sighed.

"Right, no I remember," Evalie said, flailing. "The showcase event for the new green space plan, where there's been trouble with the catering and the schedule. I didn't realise it was a weekend thing, that's all."

Guy stood and took his half-empty glass to the kitchen, ignoring Evalie's empty one on the coffee table.

"Well, I've got some stuff to do." He stood in the doorway.

"I've upset you," Evalie said. She stood. "I'm sorry. My head's still not right after all that vomiting." She lifted a hand to her forehead. "I best be off then."

Guy walked her to the front door. "It's okay, Evalie. Don't worry about it. I'll call you tomorrow, after I've checked with the boss, okay?"

"Okay, sure," Evalie said.

They pecked each other on the lips, and she left. The happy butterflies that had been there on her walk over turned to a churning sensation that reminded her of her recent illness. She trudged glumly home.

CHAPTER ELEVEN

Evalie re-read the report. It was good. She fixed the odd typo and reformatted, so it looked slick. "Ready to send," she said to herself.

After she'd sent the report, Evalie lowered her desk and flopped into her chair, savouring the moment of completion. She wandered into the kitchen and made herself a celebratory hot chocolate. Evalie sat down at one of the long tables and sipped away, thinking of Guy. She couldn't decide whether she wanted him to be available for the trip to Fiji or not. At first, she was excited about the prospect but later relieved when the work commitment got in the way.

What did that mean? Maybe it's just nerves, completely understandable, Evalie thought.

She hadn't been away with a boyfriend before. It seemed serious, like they were taking things to another level. He was so attractive and there was no doubt about the fireworks between them. But had she heard him correctly? Did he say those three words?

Arielle came into the kitchen and made a cup of tea.

"Hi, Arielle," Evalie said.

"Oh, hello Evalie." She sat down at the other end of the table, scrolling through pages on the tablet positioned in front of her. "Can you believe this?" she said absentmindedly. "This Xoha controversy. When will it end? I can't believe they were recruiting in Melbourne recently. Who would ever consider joining a cult like that? It seems ludicrous!" She took a few gulps of her tea.

Evalie blushed. "You don't really think it's a *cult,* do you?"

"Nothing surer." Arielle drained her cup and stood, gazing at Evalie.

Evalie investigated the bottom of her cup as if searching for answers from tea leaves. The milky brown pattern gave her nothing. Realising Arielle was gone, she laughed at herself and rose from the seat. She put her cup in the dishwasher and walked back to her desk, shuffling her feet as she went.

* * *

"That's Evalie," Leo said. He pointed in her direction.

The courier had a massive bunch of flowers in his hand. He brought it over and put it on her desk. Evalie's eyes lit up. The heady floral scent filled the usually stale office air. Evalie breathed the fragrance in and signed.

"Sign here, please," the courier said.

Evalie took the electronic pencil and scribbled on the screen held before her.

"Thanks. You have a great day now, won't you?" The courier smiled.

"Yes, I will," Evalie said. She blushed a little. Evalie peeled the tiny envelope off the brown paper and opened it. She pulled out the cream-coloured card.

I hope these brighten your day.

I would love to come to Fiji with you.

Guy

Evalie smiled and held the card to her chest. Her heart beat wildly.

"Ooh, Evalie got some flowers," Tommy exclaimed loudly so the entire office could hear.

Evalie blushed.

"So, who's the lover boy, then?"

"Why do you assume they're from a man?" Arielle said indignantly as she walked past Evalie's desk.

"Yeah," Leo scoffed. "Though if they are from a man, and not your mum or something sad like that, I'd say he's got something big to apologise for."

Tommy laughed. "Apology flowers. He's probably been cheating on you." With that he strode off, like he was god's gift to man.

Evalie stood, hands on hips, mouth agape. All the comebacks swirled in her head, but none landed on her tongue. "He'll keep," she murmured to herself, without conviction.

CHAPTER TWELVE

Evalie rushed into her apartment, after practically running home from work. A silver envelope lay on the floor. Someone had pushed it through her door mail flap, which was odd because the couriers always used the mailboxes in the foyer. She wasn't even sure why the doors had mail slots, but guessed it was from years gone by. Nothing had changed in this apartment building for seventy years. Why should the apartment doors be any different? She left the envelope sitting there and threw her bag on the couch, kicked off her shoes, then headed for the shower. "No time to waste," Evalie muttered.

The warm water was delightful, and she remained in the shower longer than she had planned. Evalie sang a mash up of top hits while shampooing and conditioning her long hair. It was only once she'd hopped out, in a cloud of steam, she realised she didn't have a towel. She shook her head. *Silly girl*, she thought. Evalie shimmied the shower mat across the bathroom floor to the door, before dashing on tippy toes to the cupboard where she kept the towels.

She grabbed one and dashed back to the bathroom. Her foot touched the wet tile, and she slipped, clutching wildly for something to grab onto, to save herself. There was nothing. Evalie fell heavily on her left hip. She cried out in pain and lay half laughing at her stupidity, half crying in a tumbled mess on the bathroom floor. She gathered herself up, re-wrapped the towel around herself and hobbled the remaining few centimetres to the shower mat.

Evalie dried herself quickly; she was basically dry already by this point, anyway. She dabbed carefully at her hip, where a bruise was already brooding. After using the towel to wrap her hair on top of her head, Evalie put on her deodorant and creams. Then she padded out to the freezer and grabbed a half-bag of frozen peas from the back and a tea towel.

After throwing on undies and a bra, she flopped on the couch and held the ice pack gently against her hip. Evalie shifted across until the couch arm wedged the ice pack in, then released her hand. She studied her hands a moment, wishing she had time to paint her nails. Her eyes wandered across the small apartment and caught the envelope on the floor. Evalie shifted uncomfortably in her seat. The phone rang. Evalie launched off the couch, grabbing the frozen peas before they fell to the floor, and went in search of the phone. She stepped carefully into the bathroom and retrieved the phone from beside the sink.

"Hello?"

"Hi Evalie. Are you coming?"

"Guy. Yes. Sorry, I just need five minutes."

"Okay. I'm out the front of your building."

"Do you want to come up?"

"No, I've got a surprise for you down here."

"Right. Okay. That sounds exciting."

"Yes. See you in five."

"Okay, see you soon."

She ended the call and pitched the peas and tea towel onto the side of the sink. Evalie rushed into her bedroom and put on her little black dress. Delving through a draw, she found a purple silk scarf and tied it around her neck, then went in search of heels. After digging around in her cupboard and not finding her elusive purple stilettos, Evalie opted for red heels and sat on the side of her bed to fasten them. She swapped the scarf with her fake ruby necklace and grabbed her red clutch, shoving her phone in it. Evalie picked up her brush, then realised her hair was still soaking. She rushed back to the bathroom, avoiding the wet tiles, and did a quick blow dry, brushing out her long locks impatiently.

"That'll have to do," she said and left the mess behind for later. She clicked across the floor to the kitchen bench, snatched her keys, and walked out. Evalie thought about returning for a jacket, but was sure it had already been at least ten minutes since the phone call. She'd survive. Guy would keep her warm. Evalie smiled as she waited for the lift and smoothed her dress. She winced as her hand brushed over her tender hip. The lift came, and she pressed the button for the ground floor. She caught her reflection in the closed metal doors. The cheerful face with bright eyes grinned back at her.

Evalie gasped as she walked out of the building. Parked out front was a horse and carriage. Guy walked over with one hand out, the other behind his back.

"My lady," he said, helping her up the step. "You look stunning."

"Thanks! This is, well, magical." Evalie beamed as she sat on the luxurious velvet seat.

Guy sat down next to her. The driver clicked his tongue, and the horse walked. The carriage lurched forward, then rolled smoothly along the city street.

"Where are we off to?" Evalie asked.

"That's a surprise."

"You're full of surprises tonight."

"You have no idea."

Evalie looked at Guy and he grinned.

"Just sit back and relax," he said.

Evalie grabbed Guy's hand and shuffled in close to him. The cool night air ruffled her hair, and she breathed in Guy's sandalwood and musk scent. After clip-clopping through the city, they turned down St Kilda Road, then down Queens Road towards the lake. The carriage pulled onto Lake Street, and then she saw it. The lanterns hanging through the trees, the picnic rug, and the trio who started playing the moment they saw the carriage.

She gasped. "Guy, what's this all about? It looks so beautiful."

"This is a do-over of our boat date. Near the water, but safely on dry land."

Evalie laughed. "Good idea."

The carriage driver pulled the reins, and the horse stopped. It shook its head in its bridle and snorted softly. Guy helped her down from the carriage and thanked the driver.

"What a lovely idea. It's just my stomach." Evalie clutched her tummy with one hand.

"Oh, no. Really?"

"Just kidding." Evalie laughed. She threw her arms around Guy's neck. "I'm fine. Wonderful, in fact."

They kissed. A tingle ran up her spine and her tummy fluttered.

"Now, please, my lady," he said, taking her hand once more. "Come and sit here."

Guy led her through the trees. The lanterns swung gently in the breeze and Evalie shivered slightly.

"Are you cold?" Guy asked. "Don't worry, I'm prepared for that."

He led her to the cushions that were laid out on the small rise overlooking the lake. Neatly folded blankets were beside the cushions. Guy picked one up and unravelled it. He draped it around her shoulders. The sky was pink and purple, with stripes of cloud strewn across it.

"Thanks." Evalie snuggled into the blanket. "For all of this." She looked around at the romantic scene before her. "The sunset is lovely. You're lovely. I'm so glad we found each other again."

Guy beamed. "I'm glad you like it. But this is just the beginning."

Guy nodded to the guitarist, and she nodded back to him. The music changed pace to a light jazz number Evalie recognised but didn't know the name of.

"Sit down, please." Guy gestured to the cushions.

Evalie tried awkwardly to sit, but as she began to lower down, there was a shooting pain in her hip. She winced and let out a small groan.

"What's wrong?" Guy asked.

"Oh, it's nothing really," Evalie said.

Guy looked at her inquisitively.

"I slipped over in the bathroom earlier. It was really silly. I was rushing to get ready. Anyway, it's just a bruise. But I don't think I can sit there. Not in this dress, with these shoes."

"Maybe you'll have to take it off."

"Excuse me?"

"Your shoes, I mean," Guy said. "Maybe you should take off your shoes."

Evalie leaned on Guy and unbuckled her shoes. "That's better," she said. The grass was cool under her feet. She took a few steps, relishing the sensation. Then she arranged some cushions carefully and sat down. "All good," she said and smiled. "I made it."

Guy walked over to the icebox that was set up next to a small table. He had set up the table with a white cloth, a vase of flowers, two champagne flutes, and a cheeseboard with a knife. He busied himself preparing a cheese platter.

"How much time have you put into planning all this?"

"Ever since you were throwing up in the toilet. Well, at least, soon after."

"Well, that's very organised of you."

"Ah, well. Yes, I guess so. That was the last proper romantic thing I did, or tried to do at least, and it didn't work out as planned. I wanted to make up for it. I didn't want you to miss out. You were so sick."

"That's sweet of you," Evalie said.

Guy walked over with a bottle of bubbly and a champagne glass. He passed the glass to Evalie and opened the bottle with a little pop. She watched as he filled the glass with frothy golden liquid.

"Just sit back, relax, have a drink, and take it all in. And no more talking for now, eh?"

Evalie tilted her head, pondering Guy's intentions, and sipped her drink.

* * *

Only crumbs remained on the cheeseboard and the empty bottle lay close by on the grass. The remnants of chocolate sauce coated the bottom of a large bowl, which had strawberry tops in it. Evalie and Guy lay on the picnic rug, kissing. The band had long since departed and the lanterns were the only light in the dark, starless night. The cloud had thickened into a pillowy blanket after the sunset. Evalie's cheeks were flushed, and her pulse throbbed in her neck. They drew apart and Guy looked into her eyes.

"You know, these past six weeks have been the best of my life," he said.

They both raised themselves up onto an elbow. A lock of hair fell across Evalie's face. Guy brushed it back behind her ear.

"Evalie. You are the one for me. My one and only. I love you. Will you marry me?"

Evalie sat up, wincing at the sudden pain in her hip. "Oh Guy," she said. "I … I don't know what to say. This evening has been lovely, magical." She touched his hand.

"But," Guy prompted. The smile melted from his face.

"I just need some time to think this over. We've only been dating for a little while this time. I don't–"

"What does it matter the time?" Guy asked, sitting up. "When it's love, it's love. We were together before and when we broke up, it was just awful. Since we've been back together, it's been like a dream. I know you sense it too, Evalie. What are we waiting for? What are you waiting for? You do love me, don't you, or what has all this been about? Why did we get back together?"

"Well I, I really like you, Guy. You know I do. Please, just give me some time to consider. We're going to Fiji soon. It's our first trip away together. And my dad, well, it's just, I haven't told him about us yet." Evalie stared at her feet.

"Who cares about your dad or what he thinks of me? If he's still angry about me getting that scholarship instead of you, whatever. He needs to let it go. If you're so worried about your dad, we can elope. Like Stella and Tejas."

"I, well, I just need some time." Evalie looked up at Guy.

Guy's brown eyes flashed with anger, then pain. "I don't get you sometimes. You know I'm good for you. I'm the best thing you've got going on in your life. In fact, without me, your life would be a train wreck."

Evalie looked wounded. "I'm sorry," she said. "I didn't mean to hurt you. You know I don't want to make you sad. Or angry." She looked at his sullen face. "I just want some ... I *need* some time. You know I'm not good at this stuff ... I'm not good with c—"

"Commitment. That's a cop out, Evalie. I don't know why I thought you'd changed. But you seemed different. I thought you had, well, grown up. And I thought you loved me. I'm obviously some kind of idiot." Guy stood up angrily.

Evalie reached for her shoes and phone. "I'll call a ride. Do you want to come with me?"

"I've got to pack this up," Guy said. He gestured to the picnic. "And the carriage is coming back. I'll sort that out. You go."

Evalie looked at his face and cringed. Her stomach twisted into a knot. "Okay. I'll see you ... I'll call you?"

"Have you ever thought for maybe just one minute that the reason you didn't get that scholarship was because you're not good enough? I won it and I deserved to. It's been great for me and I will *not* apologise for that."

Evalie looked at Guy, eyes wide. "That's all I've ever thought," she hissed. "I don't need you to remind me." She turned away, tears streaming down her face. Then she turned back. She hesitated. Guy was hastily packing up the picnic, throwing plates and cutlery furiously into the icebox. Evalie set her mouth in a straight line and walked barefoot back down to the road, shoes in hand. As she stood beside the road, waiting for her ride, she wondered what the hell had just happened.

* * *

Evalie lay in bed, exhausted, yet so far from sleep. She leaned across and looked at her phone for what seemed like the fiftieth time since she'd climbed into bed. No message. Evalie looked up to the ceiling, barely distinguishable in the dull phone light, and gritted her teeth. She typed 'Sweet dreams XX' and hesitated, then pressed send. Evalie hoped Guy was okay. She hoped she was okay, that they would be okay somehow. Evalie tipped her phone gently back onto the bedside table, rolled over, and buried her head under her pillow.

CHAPTER THIRTEEN

Evalie lay in bed feeling sorry for herself. She turned over and sighed. The memory of the night before plagued her mind. Evalie got up. She put on her black leggings, rolling them carefully over the angry purple bruise on her hip. Digging through her bottom draw, she retrieved her sports bra and found her favourite running shirt. It had an image of a long road lined with palm trees on the front. After navigating her way out onto the street, she began jogging, then picked up the pace. She ran at full speed, focusing only on the path ahead. Evalie returned forty minutes later, sweaty, hungry, and thirsty, but with a clear head.

Evalie unlocked her apartment door with the key she'd stuck in the tiny pocket of her leggings. As she stepped through the door, something rustled underfoot. She picked up the silver envelope she had left lying there the previous day. Evalie peered at the label. It simply had her name, no address. She turned it over to find it fastened with an embossed triquetra sticker. She carefully opened the envelope, keeping the triquetra intact. Evalie pulled out the piece of paper inside and read:

Evalie,

Congratulations! You have been successful in your application to Xoha. Do not discuss this with anyone. NO ONE. If you wish to take the next step, you must attend the mandatory briefing at the time and place detailed below. Come alone. If you do not check in on time for your allotted briefing, you will lose your place.

12:00 p.m.

Monday 18 March 2041

646 Collins Street, Melbourne

Evalie stared at the neatly curved typeface. She turned the slip of paper over. It was blank. Evalie turned it back over and read it again. She sank down onto the couch. After reading it six more times, Evalie closed her eyes.

A knock on the door jolted Evalie back to reality. She shivered and stood to answer it.

"Evalie? You there?" Guy called.

She gazed at the letter on the couch and froze. Another knock.

"Evalie. It's me, Guy. I'd really like to talk. About last night."

Evalie's cheeks flushed. She stood silently, heart pounding in her chest. Her arm vibrated, and the merry tune of her phone rang loudly.

"Shit!" She grabbed the armband and ripped the Velcro apart. She pulled the phone out and pressed 'Answer'. "Hello?"

"Evalie, I'm sorry. I have come to apologise for what happened yesterday. I'm, um, standing outside your door."

"Oh, are you?" Evalie swallowed, trying to push the squeak down out of her throat. "I was just in the shower. I went for a run."

"Oh, okay. You must be hungry, or thirsty at least. Would you like to go somewhere and get brunch?"

"No, I can't today. I've got to meet Stella. Last-minute wedding stuff … you know." She cringed at the word 'wedding.' Her lip quavered. "Talk to you later." She ended the call and tiptoed into the bathroom.

* * *

"So, you really like this dress? You think it's the one?" Stella admired her reflection in the long mirror of the bridal salon.

"It's beautiful, Stelle, you look just beautiful. And it's very summery, I like the way the bottom floats out. Much more practical for a beach wedding than that other long slinky one."

"You're right. I love it! It's settled. This is the one."

Evalie smiled at her, but the smile faded as soon as Stella was back in the change room. She played with her phone absentmindedly and relaxed on the cushions of the opulent red velvet chair. The shop had an almost overpowering vanilla and patchouli scent. Evalie crinkled her nose and tried not to breathe too deeply. She put a hand up to her head. Her skin was clammy.

Stella made her purchase, and they left the shop. The doorbell rang cheerfully as they departed.

"So, where do you want to go for lunch?" Stella asked. She glanced sideways at Evalie.

"I don't mind. Your choice, bride-to-be."

They walked down the street in silence, Stella's big bag swinging between them. As they strolled along, the duo encountered a vibrant sidewalk café adorned with a generously sized awning with bold green and cream stripes. There were five tables meticulously set out beneath the eye-catching shelter. The tables that didn't fit underneath had their own matching striped umbrellas. All were overflowing with people, and a myriad of dogs were panting in various patches of shade. The delectable aroma of recently baked bread and rich coffee hung in the air.

"Oh, I love this place! Let's eat here," Stella cried with a huge grin.

"Best Burgers. No need to guess what their specialty is," Evalie said wryly. "Okay, sure."

"It's superb! Have you been here before?"

"No," Evalie said in a flat voice. Her heart wasn't in it, but she was doing her best to be cheerful for Stella's sake.

"You'll love it. I promise!"

They pushed open the door and stepped inside the busy café. They found a spot along the front window and sat down.

"I know what I'm having already. Let me know what you want, and I'll go order."

Evalie stared at the large, laminated menu. The font was too lively, and the words jumbled in her head. "What're you having?"

"The Wonder Woman, it comes with sweet potato herb fries and a green smoothie. See here?" Stella pointed to the menu.

"Right. Yeah, sounds good. Let me get them, though. It's more than my turn to shout."

"Evalie."

"I insist," Evalie said with a weak smile. She got up and joined the queue at the counter. She bit her lip as she waited. After she ordered, Evalie turned around and looked at her friend. Stella was beaming.

She sat half looking through the window and the door. As people entered, she nodded her head slightly to acknowledge them.

Evalie laughed. "You look like the happiest person on earth," she said when she returned to the table.

"Oh, I am. I hope someday you find your true love like I've found mine. Tej is just the best. I can't wait to marry him. I'm walking on air right now." She studied Evalie's face. "But you're not. What's wrong? Did something happen with Guy?"

Evalie bit her lip and looked down at the floor. "Well, yeah. He proposed to me last night."

Stella gasped. "What!" She looked like she might fall off her chair. She recovered herself and studied Evalie's face. "But that's not what you want?"

"It was just so sudden. I was at a loss for words. I mean, I really like him. But … I … well, sometimes I'm not sure that he gets me. Do you ever experience that with Tejas?"

Stella shook her head without hesitation.

"It's as if he sees through me or doesn't listen to me. And then other times it's not like that. I don't know. I'm just really confused."

"If it's meant to be, you'll know. What's the rush, anyway? You've only been going out for like two months."

"I know. That's literally what I said when he proposed, but it only seemed to make him angry."

Stella raised her eyebrows.

"It was soooo awkward, Stelle. It was just awful. He came around this morning to apologise. But I couldn't talk to him, I didn't know what to say. Seeing you today like this," Evalie gestured at Stella's face. "Well, I think I know the answer."

A waiter brought over two plates of burgers and placed them in front of Stella and Evalie. "Wow!" Evalie said. She picked up her huge burger and smiled. "Lucky I'm hungry."

CHAPTER FOURTEEN

Evalie entered 646 Collins Street seven minutes early. It was full of security personnel. They stood on either side of the door and spaced out through the lobby. She walked over to the desk. Two security guards looked up at Evalie. One stood.

"Can I help you?"

"I'm here for the Xoha session," Evalie squeaked.

"Photo identification, please," the guard said. He held out his hand.

Evalie rifled through her bag and took out her purse, thumbing her ID out from under its protective sleeve. She handed it across the counter.

"Thank you." He looked at her ID, then the screen in front of him. "Right, here's your pass. Just scan it at the lift and it will take you to the correct floor." He gestured to the lift, which had more security guards standing sentry on either side.

"Thank you," Evalie said.

She stuffed her ID and purse back into her bag and scurried across to the lifts. Evalie scanned the pass, and a lift arrived. The security guards blinked, but didn't make eye contact or acknowledge her.

Once inside, Evalie scanned the pass again. The panel flashed "Evalie". Evalie blinked. Maybe she was seeing things. The lift moved. She couldn't tell whether it was moving up or down. It smelt like candy floss. Evalie's stomach grumbled. *Should have had a snack before you left, you stupid girl,* she thought.

The lift stopped, and the doors opened to a dimly lit corridor. Evalie stepped out. It was empty. There was only one direction to go. She followed the hallway to a door. As she raised her hand to knock, the door swung slowly inwards.

The room was bright, with no windows. Posters of immense beauty covered the walls. Waterfalls, lakes, forests, snow-capped mountains and glaciers looked down on her. There was a small lectern at the back of the room and a semi-circle of chairs around it. A person stood leaning on the lectern, studying a screen. Evalie walked towards the chairs. The person looked up and smiled.

"Evalie. Welcome. We are so glad you are here. Come and take a seat."

Evalie smiled and sat down on the chair, just left of the middle.

"Thank you," she said. "Am I the only one here, ah, coming to this session?" She glanced at the other chairs.

The person looked at their screen. "Yes, it seems so. Well, at least it will be quick this way, and you can ask as many questions as you like."

The person left the lectern and came over with their tablet. They sat two chairs down from Evalie. "So, it says here that the instigation for your application was work-related?"

Evalie cringed. "Yes."

"And you believe you had the merit to advance, but you've missed out on many opportunities. Is that correct?"

"That's right."

"And you believe the reason is discrimination?"

"Yes."

"When you read the information on Xoha, could you believe it?"

"I knew it was for me, the first time I heard about Xoha. Even though it sounds too good to be true, in a way." Evalie looked down into her lap.

"Well, it is true," the person said. They paused.

Evalie looked up.

"Evalie. The reason it works is because of intelligent, remarkable people like you. And because of our strict application process, selection criteria and phenomenal technology. Would you like to see one of our suits?"

"Oh, yes, please!"

A person came through an unmarked side door carrying a grey metal suit.

"Here you go. Would you like me to demonstrate?"

Evalie nodded.

The person put on the suit. "The individual's chip and the location they are in activates it. Let me show you what happens when I put this chip in." The person opened a front pocket that was sort of like a pouch. They inserted a small chip into a slot inside. The suit turned a deep red. "See how it changed colour? And also, if I put the helmet on, that will change colour too." They put on the helmet. As soon as it was clipped into the suit, it turned from the dull grey to red, matching the suit perfectly.

"Remarkable," Evalie said. "I can't tell who is inside at all. I mean, I can't tell what you look like."

"That is right." The person's voice had changed. "You can only tell that the suit is red. Depending on where you were, at work, for instance, the red would mean something. Perhaps it would represent a particular team you were working in."

"Now that you have the helmet on, your voice sounds different, a bit robotic."

"Yes. That is obviously so you cannot make assumptions about my gender or get any idea of an accent from my voice."

"Are they uncomfortable to wear?"

"No, quite the opposite. They are fully temperature-controlled and regulate breathing. So, when you go between inside and outside it is always comfortable. It can withstand temperatures between minus twenty-nine and forty-nine degrees Celsius."

"That's phenomenal," Evalie said.

"Yes, it is, isn't it?"

The person unclipped the helmet and took it off. Then they unzipped the suit, stepped out of it and handed it back to their colleague, who was still standing there. The colleague disappeared back through the unmarked door.

"It sounds to me like you are ready for the next step, then." The person eyed Evalie. "But before we go any further, we would like to put you through the required medical assessment. It will only take a few minutes."

"Oh, right. Okay," Evalie said.

The person smiled. "Good. If you can just read this medical test agreement and sign your approval at the bottom, I will let the doctor know you will be through in a minute."

The person left Evalie holding the tablet and walked out through the side door. Evalie looked around the empty room, sighed, then read through the agreement as swiftly as possible. At the bottom, she ticked a box and scribbled her signature using her finger. She placed the tablet down on the chair next to her and rose to look at the scenic pictures on the walls. She was studying one of a lake surrounded by wildflowers when the person returned.

"Excellent, you have completed it then. Questions?"

"Um." Evalie tried to think of something intelligent. "Is there a medical review room, or do I have the test done here?"

"Oh, no, we have a dedicated room. Please follow me."

Evalie's stomach twisted. She wasn't hungry anymore. A fog of dread descended and her skin prickled with goose bumps. Perhaps this place *was* a cult, like Arielle had randomly said in the lunchroom at work that day. Evalie's legs suddenly seemed like rocks and her head light. The room blurred and the bright colours swirled before her eyes. Then everything went black.

* * *

When Evalie came to, she was lying on a bed in a small, white-walled room. She saw the usual medical equipment typical of a doctor's consulting room. There were wooden sticks for holding down tongues for throat examination, empty vials for blood samples, containers for other samples, and a metal kidney-shaped dish. They were all lined up on a set of metal shelves in the corner of the room. She lay there wondering whether to sit up. The door across the room opened, and a person walked in wearing a white coat. A stethoscope poked out of one of the front pockets.

"Hello Evalie, I'm Dr Frieder. I am here to do a medical for your application. How are you? The staff told me you fainted leaving the seminar room." The doctor's eyebrows furrowed.

Evalie tried to swivel her legs over the edge of the bed.

"No, don't move just yet. Tell me how you are feeling."

"Okay, well," Evalie began. She cleared her scratchy throat. "I'm much better now. I'm not sure what came over me. Maybe it's because I forgot to eat before I came here?"

"Hmm. Yes, low blood sugar can certainly cause people to faint. Let me take a look. Here, take my arm and raise yourself up slowly. See if your head is okay."

Evalie took the doctor's arm and crept her legs over the side of the bed. She pulled herself up to sitting, then raised a hand to her forehead.

"Are you okay?" the doctor asked.

"Yes, just a little woozy. Do you have any water?"

"Yes, of course." The doctor took a cup from a stack on the shelf and half-filled it at the small sink nearby. "Just sip it slowly, okay?"

Evalie nodded and took the cup, sipping some water. She thought of the last time she was told to sip water slowly. After vomiting. By Guy. Evalie was consumed by an instant, penetrating guilt. But the water was deliciously cool, and her head stopped swimming.

The doctor reached into the pocket of their white coat. "Here, have some jelly beans." The doctor handed Evalie a small packet of colourful lollies.

Evalie opened the packet and put two in her mouth, chewing slowly. She sipped some more water. "That's better," she said.

"Okay, then I think we should start. First, I will check your pulse and temperature, then I will listen to your lungs, take a blood sample and take your blood pressure, if that's okay with you?"

Evalie nodded.

"I will take your blood pressure last, to give your body a bit more time to settle back to normal."

"Thanks," Evalie said.

The doctor worked methodically and silently, checking Evalie's pulse, temperature, and listening to her lungs. They set up the vials for blood and then looked at Evalie with cool grey eyes. "Which arm do you prefer?"

"Um, my left, I guess."

The doctor nodded and tightened a strap around Evalie's left arm. A vein popped out proudly, and the doctor smiled a satisfied grin. Evalie shifted in her seat and turned her head. "Everything okay?" the doctor asked.

"Yes, I'm okay. I just prefer not to look."

"That's fine. You'll just feel a small prick."

Evalie shut her eyes and tried to picture the lake and wildflower scene from the poster. The needle stung her arm, but she didn't flinch.

"All done." The doctor put the last of the blood-filled vials in the dish and held a folded gauze to Evalie's arm. "Here, keep the pressure on this. I'll take your blood pressure on your right arm, then we're all done."

Evalie squeezed her left wrist to her shoulder to keep the gauze in place. The pressure cuff inflated uncomfortably around her right arm.

The doctor tapped on the screen in front of them. "Good." The cuff deflated. "Okay, you're right to go."

CHAPTER FIFTEEN

The person walked back and forth in front of Evalie in the large, bright window-less room. She sat in the same chair as before. The waterfall poster caught Evalie's eye. It seemed even more vibrant than it had earlier. "These suits have levelled the playing field like nothing that has come before," the person said. "If you are looking for career advancement because you deserve it, and for no other reason, then Xoha is the place for you."

"What happens if I ... if you don't succeed the way you plan to?"

"Evalie, you know you can always come back here, to Melbourne. Complete a full year, and if after that you want to return, you are free to go."

"How many people do that? How many people return to their old lives?"

"We have only had the one. But she was pregnant when she left. It was an early pregnancy that was missed. An exceptional case, I guess. Our medical tests are much more thorough now."

"How long have you lived in Xoha for?"

"I have been there since the beginning."

"Are you a Founder?"

"Yes. I have had the privilege of helping plan and create this new world for us all to share and enjoy equally. Evalie, it is the most wonderful place on Earth. I have reviewed your case and I think this is the right thing for you. There have been many others in your situation that have been suffering for years. Overlooked because of something that has nothing to do with being good at your job, or potential. Many are women. They are black. Or they have a disability. Many are LGBTIQ. Or short. Blonde. Red-headed. Not from an English-speaking background. They are ethnic. They are religious. Broke. Speak with a lisp. Or any combination of traits that mean absolutely nothing in Xoha. And when they get there, they thrive. Evalie, they reach their full potential. They find success, community, friendship, love, and it is all because of equality."

"It just sounds so great. Maybe too great, though."

"Do not listen to the doubters. There are so many that try to bring us undone. That call us a cult."

Evalie blushed. She pretended to fix her shoe.

"Or worse." The Founder continued. "They do not have any concept of what it is like. No one that has actually set foot in Xoha says any of these things. Jealousy can be a real problem. Many of the write-ups come from those who went through the application process and missed out. Disappointment can motivate extreme nastiness we have found."

Evalie nodded. "But the reason the application process is so stringent is to make sure only the people who will maintain equality get to Xoha, right?"

"That is correct, Evalie. You know all these things. You have committed to the process, and you have come out on top. Be immensely proud of yourself. And happy. This is going to be the best thing for you."

Evalie beamed. "I think it really is."

"So, are you ready, Evalie? Are you ready to leave your old life of discrimination behind and step into a brand-new world where you have no history, only a future? Where everyone starts with the same. A house that belongs to them. A job. Twenty thousand dollars and a suit that makes total anonymity a reality. What do you say, Evalie?"

"Yes. I'm ready!"

"Excellent. Then this is it. We will get your medical results shortly; finalise the arrangements and you will be on the next plane to Xoha."

"Wow, I can't believe this is happening. It feels surreal."

"The next few weeks will seem surreal. But you will adjust. We have an expert onboarding team filled with the best people to get everyone adjusted to Xoha. So, this is it, Evalie. Once you sign this agreement, you are with us. You will become a citizen of Xoha and renounce your Australian citizenship. Your journey starts now."

"Right now? Don't I come back after the results of the medical? Once I've got my old life sorted?"

"No. You wait with us for the medical results and then you go to our hotel while we make all the necessary arrangements. You will only be there for a short time, maybe a day or two, until the next chartered flight leaves. Let me see now." They looked at their screen. "The next flight leaves on ... Tuesday. That is tomorrow."

"Oh, right. Yes. The next flight leaves tomorrow. B... but what about saying goodbye to my friends? What about my apartment?"

"Leave all that worry and hassle to our expert team, Evalie. They have got it covered." The Founder stood next to Evalie.

Evalie looked at them, her smile beginning to melt.

The person put their hand lightly on Evalie's arm. "We have found that if people have the chance to say goodbye, it gets very messy. A clean break is much more effective, for everyone, in the long run."

"Oh," Evalie said. She gazed downward at her hands in her lap. Tears welled in her eyes.

The Founder sat down next to Evalie. "I know this is a lot to take in. It is natural to experience a sense of overwhelm. Just remember why you applied in the first place. If these matters are still an issue for you, if discrimination is still plaguing your life, give yourself this unique opportunity to live your best life. You will not regret it."

The two sat in the quiet hum of air conditioning for a few minutes.

Evalie finally spoke in a wavering voice. "What will you tell my friends and family, and my ah, boyfriend? How do you let them know I've gone but I'm okay? And sorry, that I'm sorry for leaving them." She looked at a picture on the wall of a sandy beach. "The wedding! My friend Stella's getting married next weekend. What will you tell her?"

"We have a tried and tested method. We send them a note and have them visit a trusted counsel. They discuss their anger, frustration, and pain with them. We find it to be effective for ninety-nine percent of cases."

"And what happens in the other one percent?"

"Well, the loved one does not accept it. Sometimes it results in attempted legal action against the Xoha Council. But there are no loopholes in Xoha. We have the best lawyers. We have the best everything. They were all exceptional people who did not make it to the top in the countries they have come from or were born in. People who didn't win the birth lottery but are winners at heart. Places where the majority lack agency to determine their life path. The only reason they did not make it was because of circumstance, not talent. We know how to manage these situations, Evalie, because we treat everyone as equal, and we have systems in place to ensure that nothing undermines our equality. People from across the old world, like Melbourne or London, Dubai or Singapore, Buenos Aires or Nadi, they cannot grasp this. They think the only way to fix inequality is by slow change, incremental progress. Or more likely, they do not want change at all. Because the inequality benefits those in power and that is how they like it."

Evalie wrung her hands in her lap.

"We have found that if you put everyone on an equal footing, if you share knowledge and resources broadly, and fairly, and if you give people the same chances, they thrive. It is remarkable. Something that is truly magnificent to be a part of."

There was a knock and Dr Frieder entered the room via another hidden door in the paneling.

"Evalie," Dr Frieder said. "I have your medical results. Good news all round. You are fit and well and ready to go to Xoha, if you accept your place. It looks like the fainting incident was low blood pressure, but you recovered nicely after the water and jellybeans. Do you have questions about the medical?"

"Um. No." Evalie studied her fingernails. "Yes, actually. What medical conditions disqualify you from proceeding?"

"There is no one thing that disqualifies you. We just need to make sure that we have everything we need ready and available to support our new arrivals," the doctor said.

"We recommend anyone who is pregnant, and did not know before they applied, to reconsider for the next round. But it is entirely up to them," the Founder added. "Okay, so that is everything sorted. We have checked off all we needed to discuss. Now it is decision time," the Founder said.

Evalie nodded slowly.

The Founder stood. "We will leave you here with this video playing and the Xoha guides and interactive materials. You can hop into our experience booth if you want to take a walk through one of our four bustling cities or a quiet leafy green suburb. Or experience our majestic scenery."

"Oh, I've been to New Zealand a couple of times. I know what it's like. It's just beautiful." A serene smile spread across Evalie's face.

"This is not New Zealand, it is Xoha. It is hardly comparable."

"Oh, sorry, I didn't mean to offend. I just meant the scenery. I'm familiar with the natural beauty of the land."

"Of course. No harm done. I recommend looking at the materials. But it is completely up to you. At the very least, take some time to think it all over and make your decision. Just press the button near that door over there when you are ready."

"Thanks, but I don't need any time. I'm in. Let's do this. I'm ready to sign."

"Are you sure, Evalie?"

"Yes! I've never been surer about anything in my life."

"Okay, fabulous. Sign here for me, please." They held out the tablet to Evalie.

She scanned the agreement text, ticked the four boxes and signed her name at the bottom.

"Excellent. I will arrange your chip now. It has only basic information on it. Think of it as a blank page for starting your new life in Xoha. You insert it into your suit on arrival. We add new information along the way, and it becomes a historical record of your progress. I will be right back with it."

Evalie watched the person leave through the hidden panel door. She rose from her seat and did a little victory dance. Then, suddenly self-conscious, she sat back down and ran her hands along her thighs, smoothing her pants and waiting for the Founder to return.

* * *

As she lay in her bed in the hotel that night, Evalie was too excited to sleep. There was a jittery tension in her legs. When she couldn't stand it any longer, she got up, rummaged through the clothes the Xoha team had brought from her apartment, and found some workout wear. She slipped out of her door, letting it close softly, and padded down the carpeted hall to the lifts. She pressed the button for the tenth floor and leaned back against the rail.

When she arrived at the twenty-four-hour gym, it was empty. Evalie buzzed through the door with her room key, grabbed a sweat towel from the neatly folded pile on the counter, and chose the middle treadmill. She walked for a few minutes, then turned the speed up higher and higher until her legs pounded the belt so furiously she thought she might fly off. Evalie pressed the down button and ran at a steady pace for thirty minutes. When she stopped puffing, hair a sweaty mess, she felt much better. She stepped off the treadmill and stood, bent over, hands on hips, gasping in air.

Evalie found some yoga mats in the small, mirrored room with a wooden floor and spent some time stretching. She began doing a few of her favourite poses from yoga class. As she moved from downward dog to warrior one, she thought of Stella. The thought sent a pang of regret through her gut. She collapsed onto the floor, lay back on her mat, closed her eyes and breathed. *In her heart of hearts, she'd understand. Hell, if anyone knows discrimination, it's Stella and Tejas,* she thought. Evalie's muscles relaxed a little. She lay on the floor for a few more cycles of breath. Then she stood up slowly and left the gym.

Back in her room, Evalie took a quick shower. She tasted the salt from her face, the residue of sweat from her workout. A job well done. She smiled with satisfaction. After drying herself and putting on some pyjamas, she wriggled back into the tightly made hotel bed. The sheets were crisp and cool on her warm limbs. She picked up the book she had popped on the bedside table. It had looked lonely on the shelf in the hotel room. Evalie rolled on her side a little and started reading. The introduction began with a brief history of inequality and the devastating effects of discrimination on individual lives and the progress of society. It was dense with references and quotes from Founders on how they had used negative experiences to drive the development of an innovative, equal society and established a new country, Xoha.

The feature box on the discovery of colerium, the metal used to make the suits, piqued Evalie's interest. It explained that colerium had many of the same properties as aluminium but was much stronger and more flexible. After reading a few more pages, Evalie fell asleep. The book slid quietly off the blanket and bumped onto the floor.

* * *

The next day, Evalie woke refreshed and ready to start her new life. She found a note under her door.

Evalie,

Your flight to Xoha leaves at 10:30 a.m.

Be in the lobby by 9:15 a.m. for the transfer to Essendon Airport.

Leave your packed suitcase in your room.

Xoha Transit Team

Evalie showered and washed her hair. She got dressed, packed her clothes and toiletries into her case. She grasped empty earlobes.

Evalie looked at the bedside table. No earrings. She glanced over at the other table. Nothing. Evalie wasn't used to having so much furniture in a bedroom. She looked in the drawers, then the bathroom. Evalie didn't remember taking the earrings off the night before. But she must have. She always took them off before bed. Evalie's heart rate rose and her cheeks burned. "Oh, where did you put them?" she said crossly. She searched the entire room again. No earrings.

"You've lost them. The only thing left of your mum's, and you've lost them. Stupid girl. I knew you couldn't be trusted with them." Her father's voice rang in her ears.

She burst into tears and sank onto the bed. She closed her eyes. *How can you just leave? This will destroy Stella*, she thought.

"You're so selfish, Evalie. How could you ruin my wedding? You're the only one I wanted there. My only true friend. That's why I asked you. You're more than family to me. Well, you were." Stella's voice was less cruel than her father's but sounded just as real.

Evalie's eyes sprung open, and she looked swiftly around the room. She was relieved to find she was still alone. *Guy deserves better than this*, she thought. She rested her head on her right hand, her eyes dropped to the floor.

"That's right. Walk out on me. You never were one to give things a real chance. Too scared of commitment. Glad to see nothing's changed." Guy's voice was bitter and left a horrible taste in Evalie's mouth.

She got up off the bed and went into the bathroom. She picked up a glass and half-filled it with water, then took a long drink. *What would mum think? What would mum do?* Evalie thought. She paused, waiting for her mum's voice. The silence surprised her. But then, she wasn't sure she could even remember what her mum sounded like.

The weight of yesterday's decision lay heavy in her heart, and her stomach churned uncomfortably. She sat on top of the closed toilet seat, knees bent, crying into a towel until she couldn't cry anymore.

* * *

Evalie looked in the big mirror at her puffy red eyes. *Pull yourself together, Evalie. This is the opportunity of a lifetime,* she thought. She splashed cold water on her face and used a face cloth to blot it dry. She looked in the mirror. Her eyes fixed on her plain earlobes. She raised her left hand to her left earlobe and squeezed the lobe between her thumb and pointer finger.

"The gym!" she shouted.

Evalie grabbed her room key and rushed out the door. As she waited by the lift, her stomach grumbled loudly. She looked at her watch. "You'll have to wait, I'm afraid," she said. Evalie patted her tummy gently.

When she reached the gym, she checked the clock behind the counter.

9:07 a.m.

The person behind the counter smiled. "Hello Evalie."

"Hi," Evalie said, once again taken aback by the hotel staff knowing her name. *Focus, Evalie*, she thought. "Um, I think I might have lost my earrings here last night. I really need to find them."

"Well–" the person said.

"Thing is, I've only got five minutes, as I need to be in the lobby by nine fifteen," Evalie blurted. "Have you seen them? Has anyone handed any earrings in?"

"No, no one has handed me anything this morning. We closed the gym at eight thirty though, because it is leaving day today. Would you like to have a look around? What equipment were you using?"

"Yes, please," Evalie said, rushing into the gym. "The treadmill," she called out.

She ran over to the treadmill and scoured the tray, which was empty, then the floor around. Nothing. She looked across the gym and through the windows of the small fitness room. She saw they had tidied it since last night.

"Was there a class here this morning?" Evalie called out.

The person walked out from behind the counter towards the fitness room. "Yes, there was a class at seven this morning," they said.

"Oh. I'll just have a quick look around. I used one of these mats and maybe my earrings fell out in here." Evalie walked over.

"If you do not find them, I am sure they will turn up. We can get them sent to you. What do they look like?"

"They are diamond teardrops," Evalie said. She entered the room and walked around slowly, studying the floor. "It's just they're kind of my good luck charm. And I'd like to have them with me when I travel," Evalie said gloomily. She bent down near the pile of yoga mats and started searching through them. "They're of sentimental value, really, that's all." Evalie dropped to her knees. Tears welled in her eyes.

The person came into the studio and started looking along the floor. "Maybe they have served their purpose now. You are fortunate they selected you for Xoha. Once you are there, you will not need to rely on luck anymore. You will get only what you deserve. You will start with the same as everyone else who is going today and everyone that has gone before. Like me."

Evalie looked up. "What's it like? Is it really as good as it sounds?"

"Oh Evalie, it is even better. Better than you could ever imagine."

"Thanks," Evalie said. She stopped searching and rose to her feet. "Those things you said ... maybe you're right. It doesn't matter about the earrings. I'm going to go to the lobby and start the trip to Xoha."

The person smiled at Evalie. "Good choice. Maybe I will see you there one day, although we will probably never know it. Have a glorious life, Evalie."

"You too," Evalie said. She walked out of the gym. As she waited briefly for the lift, she looked back and saw the person wave. A sense of relief washed over her. The nervous butterflies were gone and only the excited ones remained.

CHAPTER SIXTEEN

The lobby was emptier than expected when Evalie alighted the lift. She pressed her pink handbag to her side as she strode towards the counter. As she approached, the person behind signalled to the door. Evalie turned and saw a bus waiting at the curb. She looked at her watch.

9:16 a.m. | Tuesday | 19 March

Evalie had to stop herself from breaking into a run. She could see the bus was full as she climbed the four stairs. A person was standing at the front. They grinned as Evalie got on.

"And here is our last passenger. Take a seat. We are ready to go now."

Evalie walked down the aisle to the only remaining seat. She felt all eyes on her and sat down quickly, her face flushed.

"Don't worry," the person beside her said kindly, "We only just got on."

"Thanks." Evalie smiled. "Punctuality is my first goal for my new life."

The person laughed. "Mine is talking less and listening more."

Evalie looked at them sideways, not sure if they were being serious. They just smiled. "That's a good one," Evalie said finally.

They sat in silence for a while. Evalie saw the city buildings as they flashed past, wondering if this was for the last time.

"I can't wait to leave," the person next to her said.

"Yeah? You don't think you'll miss anything about Melbourne?" Evalie asked as they passed the big, waved roof of Southern Cross railway station and headed for the freeway.

"Not one thing. Oh, well maybe. But it's probably just a cliché. The coffee."

"I haven't heard anything about the coffee in Xoha, have you?" Evalie asked.

"No, I haven't. Only about the marvellous fresh organic food. I suppose I'll get over it soon enough. You can't stay in a place only for coffee now, can you?"

"No, I suppose you can't."

The bus cruised along, winding around and taking them high on the Bolte Bridge. It afforded views across the city on the right, the port of Melbourne on the left, and the residential areas beyond the factories of the western suburbs.

"What will you miss?" the person asked. They studied Evalie's face a while before turning back to the view out the window.

"Uh, mostly I'll miss my friend Stella. She's getting married next weekend, in Fiji. I was supposed to be her bridesmaid, her witness, maid of honour, I guess. She's eloping. I'm sure she's furious at me and will be glad I'm out of her life, for ... ever." Evalie couldn't stop the tears. They trickled down her cheeks and descended from her chin onto her blue silk blouse, where they pooled into a dark patch.

The person gently put their right hand on top of Evalie's left hand. "It's going to be okay. You've made a good choice. Stella will forgive you one day, I'm sure. And if she doesn't, it will become her issue, not yours. You shouldn't worry. You've decided to go to Xoha. This is the start of a new chapter. You'll meet a new Stella soon, maybe a bunch of them."

Evalie smiled. "You're very kind. The thing is, I'm sure I could only handle one Stella in my life."

The person chuckled softly. They removed their hand and placed it back in their lap.

Evalie studied the creases in the corners of their mouth and eyes and tried to guess their age. *This may be one of the last opportunities to do this. Judge someone purely by their looks,* she thought. She decided they must be in their mid-fifties.

"Is there anyone you'll miss?" Evalie asked.

"No, I ended all my relationships when I applied for Xoha. I cut myself off from the world in preparation."

"Was that hard? How did you know your application would be successful?"

"It was hard at first. And I didn't really know for sure. But then I realised how little I'd been getting from those relationships, anyway. And the more isolated I was, the happier I became. Plus, I always had a positive intuition about the application. The moment I applied for Xoha I thought I would be successful. The process went so smoothly."

Evalie snorted.

"Not for you?"

"Not so much," Evalie said.

Neither spoke for a few minutes. The low hum of polite conversation continued around them.

"I've always liked the trip to the airport, the sense of adventure of going on holiday. Especially overseas," Evalie offered.

"I've never been outside of Australia."

"Really?" Evalie asked.

"No. Never had the opportunity. I've always wanted to, though."

"Wow. But you've been on a plane before, right?"

"Yes, twice. I've been to Sydney, and one year I went to Tasmania. That was for a family thing."

"So, you've never flown for more than an hour before?" Evalie said incredulously.

"No. I grew up poor. My mum left dad when I was twelve. He was violent, you know. He was only violent with her at first, but when he turned on us, she got out. Had nothing but a few clothes, a couple of books and toys with us. She raised us kids, all five of us, as a single parent. Tough days, those were. I left school at sixteen and got a job at a warehouse. Being the eldest, I had to help support us all, you know. Had to do my bit."

"Wow. I, um, can't imagine what that was like."

"It was just the way it was. I didn't know any different. How about you? How's your family like?"

"Well. I'm an only child. I think I was a mistake. My mum never let on, though. She was the most lovely, amazing mum. She passed when I was thirteen. Car accident. And, well, my dad. He always blamed me for it somehow. He never got over it. Wanted nothing to do with me after mum was gone. He once said he wished he never had kids. Right to my face."

"That must have hurt."

"Yeah. He was the reason my application was so difficult. He didn't want to complete his part. And I, well, couldn't tell him the truth about what I was doing. I knew he would never understand, anyway. He doesn't have any idea what life's been like for me. And to be honest, he couldn't care less."

The bus merged onto the Tullamarine Freeway. They were getting close to Essendon.

"Did you have any problem with getting your dad's input?" Evalie asked.

"No, no, he's long since gone. Waste of oxygen, that one. The world is better for it. My mother's gone too, and most of my siblings."

"Oh, I'm sorry to hear that."

"No need to be. That's life, isn't it?"

"Hmm, I guess so," Evalie said quietly. "But you're the eldest." Evalie observed the person's twisted mouth and let it be.

The bus turned off the freeway, onto the highway that tracked the same bend to sweep north, only wider. They were close now. The conversation died down to an indistinct murmur. Evalie looked around her. The faces she could see looked slightly nervous. She was glad she wasn't the only one. The engine hummed down through the gears as they slowed for the intersection. The bus fell silent as they waited to turn right.

"When we get to the airport, we'll all head into Shed D." The staff member rose from their seat to address the bus. "That's where you will all get issued your suits. You must put them on before you get on the plane. They're all generic ones for transit to Xoha. Once you arrive, you'll receive your own personalised one. But the law says no one can enter Xoha without wearing a suit."

The bus turned, and they could see the airport buildings in front and a plane taking off.

"You'll find the suits extremely comfortable for travel. Plus, you can get to know how they work in an enclosed environment. Think of this as the first step in acclimatising to your new life."

Excited chatter broke out. The butterflies fluttered back to her stomach. Her neighbour noticed as she pressed a hand to her stomach.

"You alright, luv?" they said.

"Yeah. Thanks. Just excited and nervous, all at once."

"Me too." They smiled.

Evalie smiled back.

The bus turned left, then swung around into a car park, and stopped. The driver opened the door and cut the engine. They jumped out and waited for everyone to get off. When Evalie climbed down the steps, the smell of fuel hit her. She was queasy and a little lightheaded as they walked across the gravel to Shed D. They walked almost in pairs; few people talked. When they got inside, there was a small room sectioned off in the massive hangar. The floor was polished concrete, and the walls were crisp white, with enormous lights hanging from the overly high ceiling. Around the walls were wooden benches with a row of hooks above. Spaced out around the hooks were copies of the same soft metal suit that Evalie had seen during her briefing. The group spread out until everyone was standing in front of a suit. Two people wearing teal-coloured suits entered the room.

One suit talked. "Welcome, all." The voice was of medium timbre and the gender was indistinguishable. There was only a slight robotic sense to it, less than that of the suit shown to Evalie during her briefing. "It is time to get your suits on. You can wear whatever you like underneath—exactly what you have on now or you can take off some layers. As you might imagine, skirts and dresses are not particularly comfortable underneath. But what you wear is entirely up to you."

People began removing cardigans and long sleeves.

"You will not be hot or cold inside the suits. They adapt perfectly to your body and keep you at your optimum temperature. They are quick to adapt to each individual. Once you put them on, you will know everything is functioning correctly when this light here shines blue." They pointed to the light on the left shoulder of their colleague's suit. "If there's no blue light, or a flashing yellow one, something is wrong. If you ever have that happen, you must report to the closest suit master immediately. The suit master on this trip is me."

Evalie took her silk blouse off, silently scolding herself for the impractical decision to wear it that morning. She wondered if anyone had worn a skirt, but did not dare look around. She was glad she hadn't. Evalie guessed skirts and dresses were for wearing in private from now on.

"You will distinguish me by the colour of my suit," the suit master continued. "The metal changes colour depending on who is wearing it, what information is in the main chip, and where you are. My suit is a darker shade of teal than the other staff, to show that I am in charge."

Evalie left her camisole on and took her trousers off quickly at the last minute, trying hard to not look as self-conscious as she felt. She took down the suit from the hook before her and slipped it on. Evalie expected it to be heavier. She also expected it to feel more rigid, but it was smooth and malleable. What an intriguing material colerium was. She zipped it up and took one quick glance around the room before putting the helmet on. Almost everyone else was fully suited. They were holding up their hands in front of their helmets, like babies intrigued by the wonderful new experience of realising you have arms.

Evalie closed her eyes. "Goodbye former life," she whispered.

She gathered up her hair and pushed it to the back, pulling the helmet over the top. Evalie fastened the helmet to the neck piece. Her fingers felt as though there was nothing on them but the thinnest of gloves. There was no loss of dexterity. She breathed deeply and noticed the regulator kick in. She walked a few steps. The sensation was incredibly weightless. She held a hand up in front of her face, like she'd seen others do. It *was* fascinating. She barely felt like she was wearing anything. The temperature was perfect. Nice and warm.

"This is great," she said.

The voice that came back to her was different. She sounded like the suit master, only a little more robotic.

"Great, everyone looks ready. I see all the blue lights, which is wonderful." The suit master made an arc with their right arm, turning to look at each of the suits in front of them. "You will notice how your suits have changed to a pink hue. That is so we can tell you are new recruits. Pink is the common colour for anyone who is new, and for visitors. Before I forget, I am obliged by law to tell you that all suits in Xoha have an emergency button. You will find yours under your left armpit. It is inset, so you cannot accidentally push it. But do not try to find it," they added quickly.

Several pink-suited figures promptly put their hands down at their sides.

"Just know that it is there. It is connected to Xoha's law enforcement. If needed, you will feel for the indentation and press down on the button for two seconds. Law enforcement will then be able to track your location within a twenty-metre radius. Anyway, you will not need it on the flight. Hopefully, you will never need it. Alright, let us go. This way, please."

The passengers followed behind the suit master and the other teal suit. They headed out the door into the sunshine. There was a new buzz as people greeted each other and talked about their astonishing suits. As Evalie stepped outside, she noticed the visor in the helmet change to accommodate the bright light.

"At least I'll never get sunburnt in this thing," she said randomly.

"I was just thinking that same thing." The person next to her said.

They laughed. The strange sound of the laughter made Evalie laugh again. The group made a scraggly line of shiny pink that followed the leaders past some sheds and onto the tarmac.

Evalie climbed up the stairs into the small jet. It was welcoming, with large seats and a plush interior. Evalie smiled and thought about how it was just like the chartered jets she'd seen in the movies. She sat down in a spare seat and realised it swivelled. She felt like a rock star. Maybe a rock star robot. She sighed happily and sank back into her seat. The tension in her shoulders and neck evaporated. She put her seatbelt on and closed her eyes. The sound of her own breathing was rhythmic, and she soon drifted off to sleep.

CHAPTER SEVENTEEN

Guy saw the two officers as he cycled up to his building. They stood, pressing the door buzzer. Guy wondered which of his neighbours was in trouble this time. He rode up to the door and jumped off his bike. "Which number are you looking for?" he asked.

"Two eleven," the tallest officer said.

"Oh, that's me," Guy said. "Is there a problem? Let me just store this thing." He nodded towards his bike.

"Guy Brightwood, is it?" the other officer said.

"That's right. I'll just be a minute, okay?"

"Sure, take your time," the first officer said.

Guy opened the door to the foyer and let the officers in before him. He wheeled his bike through the back to the storage room and secured it on its stand. He glanced at the boxes piled high in his allotment. Some were full of antiques he'd inherited from his grandma and others held stuff he had shipped back from Singapore. None of it fitted into his apartment. He wiped his sweaty hands on his top and walked back out to the foyer, trying to look casual. "So, how can I help you?"

"I'm Officer Daniels and this is Officer Hassan. Can we go to your apartment, please? We need to speak to you in private."

"Okay, sure. Do you want to take the lift? I usually take the stairs," Guy said.

"Sure, the lift is fine," Officer Daniels replied.

Guy pressed the button, and the three waited in silence for the lift to arrive. "Busy day?" he asked as they alighted the lift.

"Not bad," Officer Hassan said. "How about you?"

"Quite busy," Guy said. He shot glances at the two officers. They both looked straight ahead. He sighed in relief as the lift arrived at level two and after the doors opened, he led the way to his apartment. He unlocked the door and opened it wide. "Please, come in. Can I get you a glass of water or something?"

"No thanks, we're fine. Let's sit down," Officer Hassan said.

"Right." Guy closed the door and joined the pair in the lounge room. He sat on the opposite side of the U-shaped couch, hands in his lap. He glanced around his neat apartment, then looked at the two officers expectantly.

"I'm afraid we have some bad news," Officer Daniels said. "It's about Evalie."

"Oh my god, what is it? Is she okay?"

"I'm afraid she was in a car accident this afternoon and she has passed away."

Guy sprang to his feet. "What do you mean? Evalie is dead? But she doesn't even have a car!"

"It was a hit and run. She was in an accident with a car," Officer Hassan said quickly. "She was walking down the street near her work when a car swerved onto the footpath. It was a high-speed incident. She died instantly."

"Oh, no. No, no, no, no." Guy slumped onto the couch, head in hands. Tears spilled down his cheeks. "I don't understand. How could this happen? She was fine … the other day … I … no, Evalie, no!"

"We're so sorry for your loss," Officer Daniels mumbled.

The officers sat there in silence, eyes on the floor.

After a few minutes, Guy stood. "I need some air. I can't breathe."

"Take it easy. Perhaps it would be better if you sat back down," Officer Hassan suggested.

Guy shook his head. "I can't believe it … I don't understand how this … can I see her?" He wiped his face with the back of his hand and wiped his hand on his shirt.

The officers stood.

"I'm sorry," Officer Hassan said. "It's not possible to see her. It was a terrible accident."

"The authorities have already packed up her things. There was a clause in her lease agreement. Anyway, we thought you might want these." Officer Daniels offered a small crystal box to Guy.

He took it in his shaking hand and opened the lid. "Her mum's earrings. Oh god." Guy closed the lid and slipped the box into his pocket.

"We'll get out of your way. Again, sorry for your loss," Officer Hassan said.

* * *

Guy leaned his bike against the old fence. He paced up and down, earring box in hand, rehearsing what he would say. Guy inhaled deeply, put the box back in his pocket and hurried down the path. He raised his hand to knock, then hesitated. He took a deep breath, then knocked. The door swung open, and the old man looked at Guy through narrow eyes.

"What the hell do you want?"

"I ... hello Neville, can I come in?"

Neville grunted. "I'm not one for entertain'in and it's late. What d'ya want?"

Guy's brow furrowed, and he looked at his feet. "It's about Evalie. Something's happened. I'd really prefer to tell you inside."

"Come in then," Neville said impatiently. He walked down the hall.

Guy entered the musky house and closed the door gently behind him. His bike shoes clicked down the hall in a manner Guy was sure Neville would find most irritating. He found Neville in the lounge, sitting on a faded leather armchair. The room was a mess. Dirty dishes and books covered what seemed to be a coffee table. There were piles of boxes in one corner of the room and the frilled lampshade cast shadows on the floor that accentuated the heavy stains on the carpet.

"So, out with it."

Guy stood awkwardly near the armchair. There was nowhere for him to sit. He considered pulling up a box but didn't think that would enamor him with the grumpy old man. "I had a visit from some police officers today. Did you?"

"No. Blimey boy, get on with it. I'm not interested in your trivia."

"Evalie's dead. They told me she died in a hit and run. They gave me these. I thought you should have them." Guy offered the crystal box to Neville.

"What?" Neville snatched the delicate box from Guy's hand. He looked inside. An ugly crimson mark rose up his neck and blotched across his cheeks. Neville raised his eyes slowly and looked at Guy. "What kind of officers did you say?"

"Police officers, they—"

"Did they show you any ID?"

"What? I don't remember seeing any. What does it matter? Evalie's dead."

"I knew I shoulda tried harder to stop her application. But it seemed inevitable. Shit. And there's no way in hell I'm keeping these. They're bad luck. The worst luck. You keep 'em." Neville shoved the box back at Guy.

Guy looked incredulously at Neville. He took the crystal box, enclosing it gently in his right hand. "What are you saying, what application, how was it inev–"

"Evalie's not dead."

"What do you mean?"

"Her mum's not dead, either."

"What?" Guy looked in horror at the old man. "I think you're in shock, it's understand–"

"I'm not in shock or off me rocker or anythin' else." Neville sprang from his chair. "Here, I've got somethin' to show you."

Guy followed Neville to a small bedroom. He slipped the earring box into his pocket and watched Neville rifle through the drawers of the wooden desk, which held a layer of thick dust on its top, like a soft blanket.

"Here," Neville said. He shoved a small piece of paper at Guy.

Guy took the paper and studied it.

Xoha Application

#4738902367

"I found it in the pocket of Lorraine's old jacket, right at the back of the closet. When I was ... when I was packing up her things. She musta thought she'd destroyed it. Unless she left it for me on purpose." Neville looked at Guy.

Guy watched the old man's face twist like a wet plank of pine. He looked back at the scrap of paper.

"They visited me after she left. Told me she had been in a terrible accident."

"But ... I don't ... Evalie didn't tell me."

"Her mum didn't tell me either."

"I've heard of Xoha, but I know nothing about it." Guy sank to his knees on the carpet.

"Here, I've got something that might be of use to ya. Hell knows I don't need it." Neville rummaged back through the same drawer. He pulled out a folder and pushed it across the floor in front of Guy. "I know it's not what you're used to, bein' paper, but I put it together when I was tryin' to understand why the hell she left me. Left us. I couldn't bear to tell Evalie the truth. I thought it was better left the way it was first told, ya know. No gain in tellin' the truth. And then Evalie was the spittin' image of her. So alike in all ways, it was scary. It was as if Lorraine was still here."

Guy pulled the folder closer and opened the cover. He was pale as a sheet and unable to stop his body from trembling. "I ... uh, thanks," he said.

"You can nick off now. Take that with ya." Neville gestured at the folder. "I'm tired and I want to get to bed." Neville shuffled out of the room.

Guy picked up the folder and stood. He pulled the folder to his chest and stared at the wall. Guy blinked himself back to reality and walked out into the hall, switching the light off and casting the little room back into velvety darkness. He couldn't hear Neville. Guy walked back down to the lounge room. It was empty. "Right. I guess I'll go then," he mumbled. He walked down the long hall and out of the dingy old house, hoping like hell he would never have reason to return.

CHAPTER EIGHTEEN

The bump of the landing jolted Evalie awake. She blinked her eyes a few times and remembered where she was; her dreams falling away but leaving a sense of unease. Xoha. So, this was it. She peered out the window across from her but couldn't see much. Trees. Tarmac. Grass. She glanced at the others in the cabin. Some sat up alert and looked ready for action. Others were relaxed, sitting right back in their seats, as Evalie had been. Evalie wondered if they were asleep. It was hard to tell. She could not see a thing through their helmets.

"Welcome to Xoha," the person in the dark teal suit said. Their voice had no inflection, but Evalie imagined the greeting to be warm. The suit master stood at the front of the plane, addressing the group. "We hope you had a pleasant flight. When we disembark, we will go into the airport terminal building. Each of you will be required to go into separate rooms to complete your registration and receive your official suit. When you come out, you will each meet a buddy who will take you to your new home."

The plane came to a gentle stop close to an airport building.

"Once you come out of the customs room, you will be known only by your Xohan identifier: the letter, number, symbol or nature word randomly chosen by our selector. Think of this room you are about to enter as your rebirth from your old life in Australia, or wherever you have joined us from, to your new life in Xoha."

The pink suits clapped. Evalie looked around at them. She clapped too, but suddenly felt silly. Like a lemming. Her cheeks flushed, and she realised with great delight that, for the first time in her life, no one could see her embarrassment.

The door of the plane opened, and the pink suits filed out onto the tarmac and up some stairs into the terminal building. It was evening in Xoha. The four-hour time difference from Melbourne and the four-hour flight time had eaten up much of the day. Evalie's tummy gurgled as they walked through a hall to a row of doors. She wondered what refreshments her peers had enjoyed on the plane. Something to eat. That would be her first order of business to address with her buddy. Evalie remembered her helmet and realised she would only drink in public from now on. Apparently, you could get almost any meal as a liquid in Xoha and drink it through the concealed metal straw-hole in the helmet. *I might just stick with smoothies or juices to begin with*, Evalie thought.

The pink suits fanned out, one at each door along the long corridor. Evalie walked along and stood in front of the first available door. She looked around to see if anyone was opening theirs. Everyone was just standing in front of a door. Evalie glanced at the door and realised there was no handle. She waited. The butterflies of the morning returned to flutter around her empty gut.

As the last few people found free doors, there was a stillness in the long hall. A beep sounded, and the doors swung open. Evalie took a quick look to her left and saw the others entering the rooms. Now she had the perception of being a cow in a long row of cattle. She had a sudden vision of cows being led to the slaughter. Evalie gulped. She drew in a deep breath and walked into the room.

The room was more spacious than expected. Wood panelling covered the walls, and down lights shone overhead. The floor was wooden, shiny. The boots of her suit tapped a staccato beat as she walked in. She suddenly realised she had no luggage to bring with her. As the door closed behind her, a person in a suit entered from the door on the other side.

"Hello, welcome to Xoha, we are so glad you have come. Take a seat and I will get you sorted."

Evalie's eyes flashed between the stool and the small couch. She chose the couch and sat down on its plush grey cushions. The person pulled out a small screen from the pocket above their left hip.

"Right, so I will log you into the system. Do you have your chip handy?"

Evalie's stomach dropped. "My chip. I put it in my handbag. To keep it safe. But I left it on the plane. I think we all did."

"You mean this bag?" The person gestured to the side of the room where Evalie's bag and suitcase lay.

"Oh, right. Yes. How did that get here?"

"We have a very efficient and silent luggage delivery system at the airport."

"Oh, that's great." Evalie smiled at the person.

They stared straight ahead. Or so she imagined. She could not tell where they were looking at all. It was a little unnerving. Evalie got up and brought her handbag back over to the couch. She searched through the pockets inside the bag. She was glad it was a small handbag.

"I know it's in here somewhere," Evalie said.

The person waiting didn't respond.

Evalie started removing the contents of her bag, making a pile on the couch. "I'm really sorry about this."

The person remained still and quiet.

"Ah, here ... oh no, that's not it." Evalie added her old mobile phone chip to the growing pile. It was surprising how much she had crammed in there. After retrieving the last item, Evalie sat staring into her empty handbag. "It's not here," she said finally.

"Oh. Really. Well, we've never had someone lose their chip before. Let me just–"

"It can't be lost," Evalie said. "I know I had it in my handbag when I got on the plane. How could it go missing?"

"I heard it was a bumpy flight. Perhaps it fell out on the plane," the person offered.

"Oh, was it? Maybe it did. How can I get back on the plane to check?"

"No one may re-board the plane after disembarking. I'll have to put a call through for the cabin crew to check the plane. This is most unorthodox. Wait here." They got up and walked to a panel located in the rear of the room, and a door swung open.

"I'm very sorry about the hassle," Evalie called out, but the person had already left.

Evalie waited for the person to return with her chip, or news of her chip. She sat on the couch, but soon became restless. She got up and walked over to the back wall of the room. There was no sign of a door or button. *How curious,* she thought. Not wanting to cause any more trouble, Evalie walked back to the seats. She tried sitting on the stool, but it was uncomfortable. She got up and paced the room.

After what seemed like an hour, but was only minutes, the person returned.

"Well, after a lot of effort, I've got your chip," they said.

"Oh, thank goodness. Thank you. Where was it?"

"It was in the compartment near your seat. It must have slipped out of your bag during the flight. At least we have it now."

"Oh, that's strange," Evalie said. "I ... well, yes, you're right, at least they found it." Thoughts flooded Evalie's head.

Maybe I shouldn't have fallen asleep.

What if someone was rummaging through my bag during the flight?

How else could it have fallen out?

I'm sure I zipped the chip safely inside the pocket where I usually put my keys.

Evalie tried to block out the unhelpful stream of consciousness. She slumped onto the couch and put her head into her hands. The unfamiliar touch of the helmet and suited hands connecting was not at all soothing. She sat upright once more.

"Let's proceed, shall we?" the person asked.

Evalie nodded.

The person plugged the chip into the back of their screen and waited. "Okay, all done."

"That was fast," Evalie said.

"Of course. Xoha's systems are undoubtedly better than those you are used to. I am sure you will adapt to the new pace," they said.

Evalie shot a questioning glance at the person. They didn't, or probably couldn't, notice.

"They will deliver your new suit shortly, via that same hatch where your bags came out. I'll leave you to get changed. Just leave the transit suit you are wearing on the hook above the hatch."

Evalie looked up at the wall behind and saw a hook she had not noticed earlier. It was the same colour as the wood.

"Your buddy will wait for you outside this door once you are all set. Remember to bring your luggage with you. Just walk towards the door and it will swing open. Oh, and before I forget, the random selector has chosen your new name, X."

"X?"

"Yes."

"Okay, I'm X."

"That is correct." The person walked to the back wall. "Good luck, X."

"Thank you," X said hesitantly. She remembered back to the words of the hotel staff member that morning. *But I'm not supposed to need luck here,* she thought. She hoped it was just a turn of phrase that the person hadn't been able to leave behind.

As the door closed behind the person, the room fell silent. X turned and saw the new suit, waiting on the floor near her suitcase.

"That was quick," she breathed. The robotic voice dulled her surprised tone.

X walked over and picked up the suit. She was still getting used to how things felt; the dexterity was astounding. She unclipped the chin piece, then pulled off the helmet and realised the room was quite warm. X took off the suit and hung it on the hook. She decided to change her camisole for a T-shirt and put shorts on. After rummaging through her bag, she found the pair of shorts she was looking for and changed her clothes. X saw the mess on the couch and swiftly returned all the belongings to her handbag. Then she stuffed the clothes she had taken off and her handbag into the suitcase. She had to sit on the suitcase so it would close again.

As X pulled on her new suit, she was amazed that it was even lighter and softer than the transit one. *I wonder if some people are naked in these things*, she thought. X smiled coyly. She finished putting on the suit, then put the helmet on and clicked it into place under her chin. Once she was done, she checked herself. X was glad to see the light on her shoulder was blue. "Ready," she said in an even tone.

X wheeled her suitcase towards the exit door. She looked for the sensor but couldn't see one and so shuffled closer until she was almost touching the back wall. X stopped. She shuffled to the right. Nothing happened. She took another few steps sideways. A door swung slowly open to reveal a long corridor, much the same as the one she'd entered through.

"Hello. Welcome to Xoha, X. I'm your buddy. My name is Sand."

The person was standing outside her door in a purple-tinged suit. The familiar voice was comforting, although X wondered if she would get bored with everyone sounding the same. She hoped that soon enough she would form a close friendship or intimate relationship and get to hear a person without their helmet and see them in the flesh. The idea of seeing someone without a suit on made her heartbeat quicken.

"Come on, there is so much to see. We should get started."

"Okay," X said. "I'm starving, though. Could you show me some food first?"

Sand laughed. "Of course. This way." They turned right and walked along the corridor. "The place up here sells the best smoothies. Would that do?"

"Sure. A smoothie is just what I'm after."

The corridor opened out into a small square of shops. X saw a couple of drink outlets and a gift shop. It reminded her a little of Canberra airport. X wondered if it was at all like Nadi airport. That's where she would have been arriving next week; in her old life. *I wonder how much Stella hates me right now?;* she thought. She dropped her gaze and looked at the smooth wooden floor.

"I know what you are thinking," Sand said. "This airport is so small. The size surprised me a little too, at first. We do not need a big airport here. Hardly anyone leaves, you see. We have some of the best tourism right here, within our borders. And they spread out arrivals of new citizens. As you know, it is quite the process to get here. Once they do, people are so happy here, they do not need to escape. After you have lived here awhile, it can also be unpleasant to travel somewhere where there are no suits and people are treated so unfairly all the time."

X was unsure how to respond. Sand stopped walking and X nearly bumped into them.

"Anyway, what flavour smoothie would you like? I can highly recommend the green kiwi."

"Sure, that sounds great. Will you get one too?"

"Oh, yes, good idea. Come up to the counter with me and I will show you how our payments work."

X wheeled her suitcase behind her and followed Sand to the counter.

"What can I get you today?" the person behind the counter said.

"Two green kiwis, please," Sand said. "Is that you, Moss?"

"Yes, it's me. Two green kiwis coming up. What name for the order, please?"

"Sand."

"Sand. Great to see you are volunteering again."

"Thanks. This is my buddy, X."

X waved, feeling a little foolish.

"Hi X, welcome to Xoha."

"Thanks," X said.

Moss got busy making the order.

"Is that weird?" X asked quietly. "Not knowing who you're seeing or speaking to unless you ask them?"

"Maybe at first. But you get used to it. Often, anonymity is a blessing."

X tilted her head to the side and gave Sand a look, masked by her helmet. *I guess this will just take some getting used to,* she thought.

CHAPTER NINETEEN

S and stopped at a path. There was a wooden marker with metal numbers screwed onto it, two and six.

"So, this is your house. Number twenty-six. You are going to love it," Sand said.

X looked at the pretty flower garden beside the path. The house was set back from the tree-lined street. Its combination of wood, metal and glass blended in with the natural streetscape.

Sand led X down the path to the front door, obscured from the street by a large flowering tree and the porch. X pulled her suitcase along, glad of its wheels. Sand stopped at the large metal door. It was the same style door she had seen in the pop-up application centre back home in Melbourne. It seemed like forever ago now. X pressed her hand against the cold metal, then traced the triquetra with her finger.

"Look familiar?" Sand asked.

"Yes," X said. "There was one of these at the application centre. I wondered why they had such a large, foreboding metal door."

"It signifies the privacy of home. This is your place. A sanctuary where there is no need for suits. But it should serve as a constant reminder about the difference between out here and in there. You will find the back garden private and expansive. Everything you need is in here. You will find detailed information about the house and the local shops. Also, about your finances, including bank account, investment portfolio and deed to this property. It is all in there, X. And here is your key." Sand pointed to X's forearm.

There was a slight rise in the suit X hadn't noticed before.

"You just press on the panel, and it releases," Sand said.

X pressed on the panel and up popped a flat piece of metal, a bit like the obsolete USB sticks she had found once in the back of a cupboard at work. She slid out the key.

"It goes here," Sand said, pointing to a slot to the right of the door. "It is like some hotel keys you might have known. You keep it in the panel inside and it turns on your power. It is unique to this house, and your suit. So, you cannot leave home without it. It goes back into the arm piece."

"That's nifty," X said.

"Yes, it is. There is more to your suit than meets the eye. Like the inbuilt guidance system, so you can never get lost. And the emergency button they would have told you about before you came here. Plus, you can choose your fragrance to circulate through your suit. You will find out about it all in the coming week. Enough for today, though. I will be back tomorrow at ten to show you around the neighbourhood and the city. You will have Thursday to settle in and Friday you have your work assessment. The Council will assign you a job next week and then you will be a fully functioning Xohan."

"Thanks for showing me all this, Sand," X said. "I really appreciate it."

"Sure, no problem. I will see you tomorrow." Sand gave a wave and headed back down the path to the street.

X put the house key in the lock. She waited for the door to swing open. Nothing happened. She waved her hand in front of the door. Still nothing. She took it out and turned it around. There was only one way that it would fit into the lock. Her stomach dropped, and her pulse thumped in her neck.

"Please open," she said. She touched her hand to the cold metal door. "Think, Ev–X," she cried, but there was no panic in the robotic voice that left her suit.

She spun on her heel and jogged down the path. She couldn't see anyone on the street. *Why didn't Sand stay until I was inside? What sort of buddy are they?* she thought.

X stood, hands on hips, looking up and down the street. It was a lovely, leafy street with a very wide footpath, no road. The marker at number twenty-four caught her eye. She walked closer, peering down the path, but couldn't see much of the house beyond. Like her place, the front door was obscured from view. She walked back to her door and gave it one last try. Nothing. She walked backwards and forwards at the door in case there was a sensor she had missed.

X moved her luggage to the side, ensuring passersby could not see it, and walked next door. The metal door at number twenty-four was exactly the same. She looked for the doorbell but couldn't find one. X knocked on the door. The soft thud didn't impress her, but she waited. She listened and heard only an unfamiliar bird call. It was so quiet. She knocked again, more loudly. A voice came from the panel above the lock.

"Hello. Can I help you?"

"Oh, hi. Can you hear me?"

"Yes."

"My name's X. I'm new here. My buddy left before I opened my front door. It doesn't appear to be working. I can't seem to get in." There was silence. "Sorry to bother you."

"Right. Well, I will get my suit on and be out in a minute. What number house are you from?"

"Number twenty-six. Thank you. I didn't know what else to do."

"You can wait back at your front door. I will be over soon."

"Oh, okay. Thanks." X wandered down the path, hesitating at the street. She turned right and walked back down her now familiar path to the front door she couldn't open. She stood, transferring her weight from one foot to another. *Did they say their name? What if they don't come?* X thought. She waited.

"How long does it take to get suited, anyway?" X breathed out slowly. She leaned on the top of the suitcase with the handle supporting her back. She heard soft footsteps approaching. As she tried hurriedly to stand, the suitcase rolled backwards, and she fell onto her bottom just as the person came into view down the path. She scrambled to her feet; her flushed cheeks hidden beneath her metal exterior.

"Hi. Thanks so much for coming," she said. X marvelled at the even tone of her voice through the helmet.

"This is highly irregular. But you are new, so I am making an exception."

"What's irregular about helping your neighbour?"

"X, is it?"

"Hmm?"

"Your name is X, right?"

"Oh, yes, that's right."

"X, we are not supposed to just go knocking on doors in the street. Maybe people do that wherever you have come from, but they frown upon that here. You should reach out to your network if you have any issues or contact the authorities directly. Neighbours are not really a thing here. It is all about privacy in your own home. Anyway, let me show you how the door works. Where is your key?"

"Oh, I'm sorry, I didn't know. Thank you. I'm really grateful you made the exception. It's here." X held up the key.

"Now show me what you did to open your door."

X put the key in the lock and stepped back, then forward. Nothing happened. X let out a sigh of relief, glad the door hadn't suddenly swung open and made a total fool of her.

"No, no, no. You are doing it all wrong. Turn it, like this." The neighbour turned the key 180 degrees and X heard a click and the door swung slowly open. "Then remove the key as you need it inside."

"Right. Oh, I feel so silly. I tried turning it but ... but not like that."

"Never mind. If you have any other problems, be sure to message your buddy."

"Thanks, I will. Sorry, what was your name?"

"My name is of no concern. Goodbye." The person turned and walked away.

X paused, mouth agape. She made a mental note never to knock at number twenty-four again. X turned back to the house, removed the key and stepped inside. She gasped. The room was beautiful. It had vaulted ceilings and wooden floors. Light flooded in through the gigantic windows at the far end and along the top of the left side of the angled ceiling. The furniture was sparse but looked high end, with tan-coloured couches, wooden tables and a large screen on the side wall. Her door thudded softly as it closed. She exhaled loudly. She found the slot on the inside wall to the right of the door and slipped the key in.

X walked around the lounge room and flopped onto a couch. It was so comfy—the exact opposite of her old tired one. She marvelled at the fact her entire apartment could fit into this giant room. She sat there looking around the room and smiling. After a few minutes, she realised something was missing. She had mistakenly left her bags outside on the porch.

X retrieved her bags and wheeled them through the house into the bedroom. The large wooden-framed bed stood like an oasis in the middle of the room. The carpet was soft underfoot. Her eyes shifted downwards towards her feet.

"Oh, you can take this thing off now, silly," she said.

She unclipped her helmet and took off her suit. She padded on bare feet through the large home to the laundry. Its tiled floor was warm. X put her suit into the refresh cabinet, hanging it up as per the diagram on the front. As she closed the door, the machine sprung to action, cleaning and sanitising the suit for the following day.

The cleansing room was as expansive as the rest of the place. After using the facilities, X flopped into bed, exhausted from the travel and excitement of her day. The sheets were gloriously soft. They smelt fresh with a hint of floral sweetness. X drifted off into a comfortable and dreamless sleep.

* * *

When she awoke, X was disoriented. She looked around the room and smiled. She padded through the house, lit by the rising sun, and stopped at the end windows. They looked out onto the loveliest garden X had ever seen. The lawn was lush and surrounded by trees and bushes of varied greens. There were pink, white, yellow, and purple flowers dotted around and a path that led through the trees and out of sight. X slid the lock on the door, and it opened silently.

The sound of birds flooded in and X, dressed only in her underwear, stepped onto the deck and then the grass beyond. She walked through the garden as if in a daze and returned to the kitchen, beaming. Her stomach grumbled like a bear waking after hibernation. She opened the fridge. It was full!

Stacked neatly were local products, all marked with the same 'made in Xoha' label. There were vegetables in the crisper and eggs in the door. She went to the pantry. It was full. Every cardboard packet had the same local label. She pulled out some cereal and opened the cupboard under the bench. It was full of earthenware, with a shiny glaze. She took out a turquoise bowl and filled it with cereal. She found the cutlery drawer and a spoon. After adding milk, she perched on a stool at the bench and wolfed it down. The cereal was delicious. After powering through the bowl, she sat satisfied, taking in the room.

She put the bowl into the sophisticated-looking dishwasher and as she put the spoon in, she realised it was engraved on the back of the handle. She read the engraving.

Made in Xoha for X

She did a double take. X pulled each piece of cutlery out of the drawer and found they all had the same engraved message.

"How curious," she said.

She returned the cutlery to the drawer, then padded off to the cleansing room to get ready for her day.

CHAPTER TWENTY

The door buzzer startled X from her daydream.

"Coming!" she called from the bedroom, doubting that anyone could hear her from the front door. She went to get her clean suit from the laundry. When she tried to open the refresher, it made a "do-doh" noise.

"What does that mean?" X asked the machine.

The door buzzer sounded again. X remembered her neighbour's intercom and rushed into the kitchen, looking for a button. She was wearing only a bra and underpants. She hadn't noticed an intercom button before, but she hadn't looked specifically. There was nothing on the wall that looked like an intercom.

A voice called out, "X, are you in there? Are you okay?"

She moved closer to the door. "I'm here! Can you hear me?"

"X."

"Where is the intercom?"

"I cannot hear you through this door. It has sort of one-way air flow, so you should be able to hear me."

"I can!" X yelled louder.

"If you can hear me, there is an intercom on the wall near the hall to the bedrooms. It is inconspicuous. It should look like a white metal panel near the light switch."

X raced down to the hall and found the white panel. "Now, how does this work?" she said to herself. She touched the cool metal and tried to pop it open. Nothing happened. She tried to slide it. "Maybe I should have read the information about this house," she muttered. X poked and prodded, her cheeks flushed pink.

"X."

She walked back up to the front door. Perhaps she should just open it a crack. Then they could talk unencumbered. She looked down. First, clothes. Just in case.

"You need to make sure you turn your key all the way to the right to operate everything correctly. Some things work with the key slid in, but others won't."

X looked at the panel. She had just slid the key in straight the night before.

"Why is this so complex?" she huffed.

X gripped the key and tried to turn it. It didn't move. She remembered the front door and pushed it to make sure it engaged all the way, then turned. It turned to the right and clicked. She went back to the panel near the hall and when she touched it, it lit up.

"Finally!"

"X."

"Hi Sand. I'm sorry about all this. I couldn't get the refresher open. Now I know why. I'll be there in a jiffy."

She ran back to the laundry and opened the door of the refresher and hurriedly put on her clean suit. She raced back to the front door. When she waved her hand past the panel, it swung slowly open.

"There you are. Ready to go?"

"Um, yeah, I guess so."

"X, your blue light is not on."

X looked at her shoulder. "Hmm, do you know why that could be?"

"Did you connect the chin piece properly? Here, let me look." Sand stepped towards X and leaned in, looking at her helmet.

X peered at the helmet in front of her, scanning for any sign of the human beneath. Even at this close range, she couldn't tell who Sand was. Male, female, skin colour, hair colour, eye colour. Of course, they could be speaking any language too. The auto-translation technology built into each helmet meant you heard everything in your preferred language. You could change the settings whenever you wanted to. X didn't imagine she would try that anytime soon.

"There," Sand said. "You've got to remember to press down after you engage the helmet. Listen for a click."

"That seems to be the telltale sign of most things around here."

"Yes, I guess it is. Shall we go now?"

"Are you sure I don't need to bring anything with me?"

"One hundred percent."

"Okay. Just let me get my key." X ducked inside and removed the key from the internal lock. She slid it carefully into her arm piece. "Safe and sound," she said.

"Here, you need to lock it. It's not automatic, so you cannot accidentally lock yourself outside. Just wave your arm in front and it should click."

X waved her forearm in front of the lock, and there was a click.

"Right, off we go then. Finally," Sand said.

X couldn't deduce what tone Sand intended with 'finally'. Were they upset?

"This place is going to take some getting used to," she said.

"Do not worry, you will get there. The transition is never easy."

X smiled. *They're not upset,* she thought. She sighed and followed Sand out to the street.

* * *

"So, where are you taking me first?" X asked.

They stood next to one another at the station, waiting for the train.

"I thought I would take you into the central business district to show you what it is like in our great city. Then I will take you to the gardens, the lake and on the way back we can visit the local shopping strip where you will find everything you need."

"Sounds great," X said.

The train came on schedule, and they alighted. There were only a handful of passengers in the carriage, so they found empty seats facing one another in the middle and sat down. It was the cleanest train X had ever seen.

"This train goes to the city. From there, you can take the train towards the natural wonders of Xoha, in case you ever want a change of scenery. We passed through one of the mountain ranges yesterday on the way from the airport."

"Oh, yes. I remember, it was stunning."

"There are also the lakes, ocean, and river. You can get to them from the stations between each city. There are four in all. They are exceptionally beautiful and worth a visit."

"Oh, of course, I read about them in the information." X paused, her mind brimming with questions. "There's so much to learn. How did you manage when you came here?"

"We are not really supposed to talk about our past to strangers, but the newbies always ask."

"Oh, sorry," X apologised.

"No problem. I think it is enough to say I had a really hard time settling in. I made all the faux pas and, well, do not worry, it gets better and easier. Once you have transitioned, it is amazing. It is well worth all the work. I guess that is why I volunteer. To make sure others settle in quickly and maybe stop them from making some of the mistakes I made. Not that mistakes are a problem. They encourage people to make mistakes here, as long as you learn from them. I just want people to experience what it is really like to be Xohan."

"That's nice. I mean, that's nice of you to be a buddy."

"Hey, look over there." Sand pointed out the window. "You will see the city in a minute."

X looked in the direction Sand had pointed. The city skyline was like no other X had ever seen. There was only one high rise building, the rest was a sea of green and brown.

"Is that it, where that tower is?"

"Yes, that is it. As we get closer, you will see the buildings emerge from their camouflage. I would ask you if you saw it from the plane, but I know you cannot, except for some of the solar panels perhaps, glinting in the sun."

"I didn't see anything from the plane."

"No?"

"I, uh, slept."

"Fair enough."

X looked down at her hands, folded in her lap. They looked strange to her, like they belonged to a grey robot.

"So, the train ride from the city to each of the three suburbs is twenty minutes." Sand continued talking as if on autopilot. "The suburbs are all residential with local shopping strips, like your Eastmiddle, and they fan out from the city. I am sure you would have seen the map in your house already, or perhaps you remember it from your briefing. Xoha is like a snowflake shape when you look at the layout on a map."

X shook her head slowly.

"Right, well, okay. I'll explain it more fully. Between each of the cities is a station halfway that leads to one of the four areas of natural highlight. It takes about thirty minutes to get to the mountains or the river from City East. As you know, there are no cars here and people mainly travel to the city for work, unless they get a job in a suburb. You cannot work in the suburb where you live. But you can work in a neighbouring one. I would encourage you to study the map. It might help."

"Okay," X said. "I'll do that." She made a mental note to study the map later.

"Travel in between cities is possible for work or leisure but restricted to the interconnecting railways."

X shifted in her seat. Perhaps Sand *was* a robot. The talking seemed endless.

"It is a unique set up and although sometimes I think I miss the feeling of driving down an open highway, the cities run so much more efficiently without cars. Once you experience it in action, I am sure you will not care about cars anymore."

X nodded her head as she peered at the remarkable city coming closer. They hadn't stopped at any stations since leaving Eastmiddle, which was a novel thing for her, as was living in the suburbs. There seemed to be a break in Sand's lecture.

"Why didn't the Founders go for electric vehicles? Couldn't people have still driven cars sustainably?" X asked.

"It is more about the road infrastructure. When they built this place from scratch, they had a blank canvas. When the Founders considered what the best layout would be, they quickly decided it was better without cars. You can always go to the Begapi raceway on the first weekend of the month when they have an amateur day, if you are desperate to drive a car. It is a lot of fun. They are the fastest electric cars ever made. They also have human-powered vehicles. Or you can get involved in professional racing if that is your thing. I should not assume you are an amateur. What I am saying is anyone can join in. So, you do not need to leave cars behind altogether."

The train slowed as they approached the city station.

"We are here," Sand said, rising from their seat as the train went into a tunnel.

X stood and followed Sand to the door. The high-speed train slowed on the approach and pulled up smoothly and gently into the underground station. City East signs lit the clean platform, and they followed some other passengers to the exit. The large lift moved noiselessly upwards and brought them into the street. Plants covered all the buildings, and each was three to five stories high. In between were garden beds of trees, shrubs, and ground covers.

"This way," Sand said, walking down a wide footpath that wound between buildings.

The crushed stone path had small grass plants lining either side.

"You do not mind walking, do you?"

"Not at all," X said. "It's lovely here. Although this is the least city-like city I've ever seen. Where's the concrete?"

"The city planners decided they would see how far they could get with minimal concrete. Turns out they got a long way. Because there are no cars, they do not have to worry about roads, only paths and tracks for the city rail. There is a light rail that winds through the city for those that need or prefer it. Walking is encouraged though."

"What sort of businesses are here in the city?"

"All kinds. From suit makers to food production, housing construction, financial services, and so on. It is all intermingled, accessible, and green."

"It's lovely." X admired the scene, taking a snapshot in her mind. It was very calming and completely at odds with the familiar Melbourne cityscape.

They walked on through meandering paths and came to a larger building made of sandstone with a small green creeper growing around the doorway.

"This is the main government building, where the Council meets—city hall, if you will."

"Wow, it's beautiful! Can we see inside any of these buildings?" X asked.

"Yes, you can. They are open once a month to visitors, unless you get a job there. Wood and stone and other natural materials dominate the inside of all the city buildings. You will see inside the testing centre when you go for your assessment. It is like all the others."

"Oh, right," X said. She looked down at her hands. "Is the test difficult? I mean, how do they make it fair for people that aren't good at tests?"

"It is amazing X, like no test you have ever had in your life. It is more like a series of games and puzzles you must figure out. And then there are conversations and writing and drawing and sometimes cooking. It is the most wide-ranging test ever invented to get a deep and true understanding of human capability. Do not fear it. Be excited. You are going to love it."

"Really?"

"Yes. Trust me, Xoha has it all. It is the most advanced country that has ever existed. And now you are a part of it."

"It sounds amazing."

"Come on, let us go up the tower. You can see Eastmiddle and the other suburbs from the top. It is breathtaking."

Sand led X into the foyer of the city tower. They paid the entry fee with their suits and walked through the gate. There was nobody in sight. They boarded the lift, and it sped to the top.

"Welcome to city tower," a suit said when they alighted. "Enjoy your viewing."

"Thanks," X said.

Sand laughed. "You know, that is just a robot."

X blushed. "Oh, it looked so lifelike. I mean, well, the same as us. How can you tell?"

"Um, I am not sure. I guess I know they have a welcome bot here. After a while though, you can just tell. I think it has got to do with their movements not being as fluid as a person's."

The view that surrounded X as she walked onto the glass-walled viewing platform took her breath away.

"Magnificent," she said in awe. The lack of tone from her helmet was underwhelming.

"It is," Sand agreed.

They stood, taking it all in. X could see the green brown of the city below them. To the left was an enormous expanse of gardens, wrapping around the city. To the right was a large lake, shimmering in the late morning sun. The city light rail wound in and around the buildings, and the fast rail lines carved three straight lines from the edges of the city. If you followed the lines into the distance, you could see where they stopped. The suburbs lay beyond. Even further into the distance, towards the south, X could see the mountains.

"Beyond those mountains are the suburbs of City South. They have the same pattern as our suburbs. Here, come around this side."

Sand led X to the other side of the large viewing platform. "Can you make out the ocean over there? It is a fair distance from here. Have a look through this." Sand passed X a binocular overlay for her helmet. A long, thin metal cord attached it to the outside glass wall of the tower.

X slipped it over her helmet. Everything went blurry. She slid her finger across the focus dial. "That's better," she said. X scanned the horizon, and the ocean sprung into view. "I see it. It's lovely." X looked at the dense scrub and sand dunes. After a few minutes, she took the binoculars off. "Do people visit the beach? I mean, do they go swimming, like in their suits?" X returned the binocular overlay back to its holder.

"Yes, well, you can get special swimsuits. They still protect your identity, but they are more streamlined and do not have any of the gadgets these have. You can purchase them from the authorities. You need to put in an application. But there are private pools where you can swim wearing whatever you like. The Council ensures careful management. You just have to make a booking. They have timed sessions."

"Oh okay. That makes sense. I guess. I can't believe I didn't think about swimming until now. There's so much about my old life that I think I might just have to let go."

"You know we have no cases of skin cancer in Xoha. Zero. There are benefits to this lifestyle. Of course, the Council encourages people to get some sun in their own backyards, but safely. The suits direct the Vitamin D directly to the skin while you are outside anyway, whilst filtering out the harmful UV."

"Wow, they really thought of everything in designing these things." X raised her arm, looking it up and down.

"They sure did."

"And you said you can't ever get lost here, right?"

"That is correct. Every suit links to the Xohan network, so your location can be tracked. If you press the emergency button, it connects directly to law enforcement, and they can see where you are."

"It sounds very safe."

"Xoha is the safest place on earth."

X and Sand strolled the remainder of the platform.

"I'm glad they made one exception to the no high-rise rule here," X said.

"Me too," Sand agreed.

* * *

That night X lay in bed, willing sleep to come. Images of the day flew through her head, intermeshed with scenes from her old life in Melbourne. She hoped that Stella and Guy were okay. She wanted so badly to send them a message, but she knew she couldn't. The communication system here was separate from the rest of the world. That was one thing she had read up on. Instead of the World Wide Web, they had the Xohan Web. The telecommunications network was closed and used sophisticated new technology that was lightning fast and impenetrable outside of Xohan borders. X sighed and flipped over once more. She began doing some yoga breathing and counting her breaths. She wondered if Stella was using yoga breathing to get through her betrayal. Despite these uncomfortable thoughts, a calm sleep soon descended.

* * *

X rolled over, dreams of Stella and Guy shattering and falling away as she took in her bedroom. Her bedroom. That she owned. In her new, beautiful house. She smiled and stretched out on her bed. The clock on her screen, which she'd left on her bedside table, was flashing red. "Oh, crap!" she said. "Seven fifty-five." X flew out of bed and into the cleansing room. She raced through her morning routine at a furious pace, celebrating like she'd won Olympic gold when she quickly located clean underwear in the gigantic pile of erupted suitcase that lay on her floor. "No time for breakfast, you stupid girl," she scolded.

After retrieving her clean suit and jumping into it, she stood, staring into a mirror. She was looking for a glint of who lay beneath the metal facade, but she was unrecognisable. X collected her screen and returned it to the front pocket. After retrieving the key from the internal lock, she shut the front door. She carefully placed the key in the forearm of her suit and swiftly locked the door. X rushed along her path to the street, willing her legs to move faster.

CHAPTER TWENTY-ONE

The person next to X leaned over. "Hi, I'm Elle," they said.

"Sorry?"

"Like the letter, L."

"Oh, right. That makes sense," X stammered.

The person looked at her. "And you are?"

"Sorry. I'm ah … um … I'm X. I'm just a bit nervous about this whole thing."

"Oh, you'll be fine X, don't worry."

"It's just I'm terrible at exams. And I know how important the results are. I really don't want to mess up my chance."

"You know this assessment is meant to differ from other exams, though. They talk about it being a holistic approach to testing intellect and capability."

"Yeah, I've heard. But the message doesn't seem to get through to my stomach."

L laughed. "Well, tell your stomach from me that this isn't your last chance. You will have other assessments along the way once you're in a job. To make sure you're on track and when they're looking to promote people."

"Did you hear that, stomach?" X said. Her empty stomach growled in response.

"Please make your way to your allotted room. The examinations commence in five minutes." The announcement came through speakers somewhere in the foyer, or maybe through her suit directly. She couldn't quite tell.

Either way, X heard it loud and clear. She got up from her seat and felt woozy. X put her hand out to hold the back of the seats but missed. Someone grabbed her arm.

"Easy there, are you okay?"

X tried to talk but words failed her.

"Why don't you sit back down for a minute?" They helped her into a seat. "Are you okay now?"

X nodded slightly. "Are you …" X searched for the words through the fuzz in her head. "Was I talking with you before? Are you L?"

"No. I was sitting back there." The person gestured behind them. "I saw you wavering as I was walking past and thought I should stop you from falling if I could."

"Oh, thank you. I didn't eat breakfast. I think it's just low blood sugar."

"Well, we'll have to fix that. We can't have you going into the assessment without eating anything."

"But there's no time," X argued.

"It'll be fine. You stay here. I'll be right back with a drink for you." The person turned and walked away.

"Are you sure?" X questioned.

They put their hand up in an unfamiliar gesture and disappeared through the crowd of moving suits. X fidgeted in her seat. She experienced a refreshing coolness. It was unusual. Normally, she would have been sweating profusely in a situation like this. The waiting was the worst part. Sand's reassurances muddled in her head with the lengthy instructions from the briefing she'd read yesterday. *What if that person doesn't come back?* The nasty thought made her clench her teeth. *There must be only a minute left. I should probably go to the room. What number was it again? Five.*

X chewed on the side of her lip. Her head was even more woozy. She was afraid to stand in case she fainted. This time, there was no one around to catch her. She wondered how long she could lie there before someone noticed. X smiled despite herself at the thought of her body sprawled on the floor like a robot run out of batteries. The smile quickly vanished. "Why couldn't you be more organised?" X scolded herself loudly.

"Here we are."

Someone was at X's left elbow. She nearly jumped out of her suit. They handed her a drink.

"Drink up. You've got about half a minute," they said.

"Thanks," X said, maneuvering the metal straw into her helmet. She took a big sip. The cool smoothie felt glorious in her throat. It washed the fuzziness from her head as it went down.

"Come on, we better get to our rooms. Where are you?"

"Five," X said. "I'm pretty sure."

"Me too. But I'm definitely sure." X pretended she heard a smile in their voice.

As they walked down the hallway, they saw the doors to the rooms swinging slowly closed.

"Come on," the person said.

They pulled her by the arm, and they ran to door five, catching it just in time. X slipped into the room last. There was a circle of chairs, full of identical, pink-suited people, except for one, whose suit was a deep magenta. X and her new friend took the remaining two seats.

"Nice of you two to join us. You just made it in time, I see." They looked at the time display on the forearm of their suit. "That's the first test for today, punctuality. Anyway, we were all just getting acquainted."

X shifted in her seat.

"As I was saying, we don't need to know names, although you can share your Xohan name if you would like. What we really want to know is something unique about you. It can be anything. And that's how your peers here will remember you. It could be something you've done or somewhere you've been, or a favourite hobby. I'll start. Obviously, you can always tell me apart, but that doesn't matter. I love to play the violin. So today I'll be Violin. How about you?" Violin said, gesturing to the person on their right.

"I love skiing," they said. "You can call me Ski."

X's stomach dropped as one by one the spotlight came closer. Her mind raced to think of something she liked that differed from what others had said.

The person who had helped her get the smoothie said, "I have always loved trees. From climbing them as a child to protecting them, or trying to, as an adult. You can call me Tree."

The circle fell silent. Violin nodded at her.

"Ah," X stammered. "Well, let's see. I learnt to juggle a while back."

"There you go," said Violin, "welcome, Juggler."

X cringed at the sound of 'Juggler' and her cheeks flashed scarlet. *At least no one can see my embarrassment,* she thought. *But really, X, Juggler?*

The last two people, Stargazer and Cartwheel, added their unique attributes to the circle.

"Thank you everyone. Now, let's go backwards and see if we can remember all these new names."

* * *

X looked up from her screen. She had nearly finished the personality test. The progress bar showed ninety-five percent complete. She saw Tree looking at her from across the table, well at least that's how it appeared to X. She looked behind and around her. Everyone seemed to be still completing their current task. She smiled, then realised it was impossible to see a smile through these helmets. X wondered how long it would take to adjust to the lack of facial cues. She raised her hand in a little wave. Tree waved back. She turned her focus back to her screen.

* * *

"Hi, Juggler, right?"

"Hi, oh, you can call me X. I'm a little embarrassed about the juggling thing now."

"You shouldn't be. It's cute. I'm known as Star in here." Star gestured around the room. "It's nice to meet a letter," Star said.

X laughed. "I met another letter in the foyer earlier," she said.

They sipped their lunchtime drinks.

"Are you interested in getting some fresh air? So to speak," Star said.

"Sure," X replied. "I'm nearly finished with this." She gulped down the rest of her drink and returned the metal cup and straw back to the table.

They walked towards the door.

"Hey, is that you, Juggler?"

"Yes, it's me. But call me X."

"Tree here. Are you going out?"

"Yes, to get some fresh air."

"I'll come too."

The trio walked out of the room and back along the wide wooden corridor to the foyer. It had a large wooden bench that ran all the way in front of the glass wall that looked out to the green and brown city beyond. The glass door opened automatically as they approached and the three pink suits walked out into a windy afternoon. Their suits turned grey as they left the building, unrecognisable from any other suit on the street.

"Let's go this way," Star said.

They walked down the hill and found themselves in the extensive gardens that wrapped the city.

"How are you both settling in?" Tree asked.

There was a pause.

"It's harder than I thought it would be," X confessed.

"In what way?" Star asked.

"Well. I, ah … I … guess the social side. Everyone looks the same out on the street. Which I know is the point, but it's hard to meet people."

"Have you looked up any interest groups?" Tree asked. "I went to a coastal ecology group on the weekend and met some fabulous people."

"Oh, I only arrived on the weekend," Star said. "I came to the city with my buddy on Monday. Apart from that, I've been hanging out in my house. It's amazing."

"I only arrived during the week." X said. "But that's a good idea. I'll look into the interest groups."

The three suits came to the lake that X had seen from the tower viewing platform. There were water birds of every creed and colour in and around the water.

"I've never seen so many kinds of birds," X said.

"That's the beauty of this natural city. The balance of human and animal life is incredible, the best in the world," Tree said.

"How long have you been here?" X asked.

"Oh, well. I'll tell you a little secret. It's a lot longer than the two of you. I've been here for six months."

"Oh, wow," X said.

Tree continued. "I'm redoing the assessment after taking some extended medical leave from work. My boss thought it would be a good idea that I get reassessed to see where I'm at."

"So, you've done all this before?" X pondered. "No wonder you seem so relaxed about it."

"It really does get easier," Tree said. "I love it here and can't remember what my old life was like. It's such a distant memory."

"We had best head back," Star said. "It's five to."

They turned back the way they'd come.

"Have you made any good friends?" X asked.

"A few. There's a group of four of us that meet at each other's house every other weekend."

"So, you've seen them unsuited? You know what they look like?" X asked.

"Yes. They're great people. I guess with time you don't think about the suit versus no suit as much. You get to know people by their mannerisms. You look for distinctions in the way people walk or talk. I mean, we all sound and look the same, but that's on the surface. Individuality still shines through. You'll see."

"I hope so," Star and X said simultaneously.

"Don't worry, everyone has the same experience in the beginning, in the transition phase," Tree attested.

"Can I ask, was your job very different back home compared to here?" Star asked.

"Yes. I had a low-level job back home. I had trouble getting promoted. My boss was a real, well, let's just say, my boss was a nasty piece of work. I moved up quickly after starting my first job here. It's a common experience."

The group entered the building. When they returned to room five, they saw everyone seated in the circle once again. They took the three remaining seats, X between Star and Tree. She was happy to have met some people and hoped she could stay in touch, particularly with Tree, who knew their way around. The facilitator rose from their chair and the group quietened down.

"I hope you enjoyed your lunch break. It's great to see people connecting and socialising. Now we move onto the group work portion of the day. We processed all your individual assessments to split you into groups. After that, we'll have a quick break and finish with a couple of outdoor activities."

There were murmurings amongst the group. X's stomach twisted a little.

"Why are you so nervous?" she murmured.

"Now, you'll see I have separated some tables. Each table has a screen with the members listed. Please find your table and sit down."

The large group rose from their chairs at the heart of the room and people found their tables and sat down. X wandered from table to table. When she saw Star and Tree on the same table list, her stomach twisted a little more. She looked at each table, but her name wasn't there. She approached Violin.

"Excuse me, but none of the tables have my name on it."

"Oh, really? And who are you again? To the group, that is?"

X stood there with a blank look on her face concealed by her helmet.

"What does the group know you as?"

"Oh. Um, Juggler."

"Right. Can everyone please check their table? Juggler can't find their spot," Violin said loudly.

X shrank back inside her suit. There were whispers from each table, then the group fell silent.

"How strange," Violin said, walking from table to table. "No, you're right, you're not listed at all." Violin walked back to where X stood. "I'll have to go sort this out. In the meantime, I'll get the others started."

"Can I just join any group for now? I could go with Tree and Star?"

"No. It doesn't work that way. The groups match the assessment results from the first half of the day. We can't interfere with the process. It's carefully designed."

"Oh," X said. She cast her gaze downwards.

"Okay everyone. You'll get specific instructions on your screen ... now. Each group has a box of materials in the middle. You have one hour to complete all the tasks, starting at one thirty on the dot. Please remember we are recording your group work. I just need to pop out to get something sorted for Juggler. Please read the instructions as a group and when you hear the siren, your box will unlock, and you can get started." Violin stepped out of the room.

The groups began reading their instructions. There was an excited energy in the room. X stood there, not knowing what to do while she waited. She longed to be with Tree and Star, although any group would be better than none right now. X shifted her weight from foot to foot. She watched the groups and saw that each had four members except the one closest to the door, which had three.

"Surely that's my group," X murmured. She moved closer to the group, debating whether to join them. She wished Violin would return. X strained her ears to hear the group's instructions. It seemed like they had to create a prototype for some kind of food that people can consume in public, whilst wearing a helmet. *Perhaps these are real Xohan problems the groups are trying to solve,* X thought. She smiled. Problems in Xoha. Did anyone actually believe that there could be a place where life was perfect, mapped out and calculated, fair, with no discrimination?

Perhaps she had been foolish in believing that her life was going to change, that she was worthy of promotion, headed for greatness. Maybe she was exactly where she deserved to be back home in Melbourne. At least she had Stella and Guy. How she missed them. A tear rolled down her cheek, and she raised her hand to wipe it away. She grunted. *The first flaw of the suit,* she thought. *You can't dry your eyes.* Just then, she felt something soft on her cheek, like cotton. It was a novel sensation, like a cloth inside her helmet. The tear was gone. *Wow, an automated eye-drying function,* she thought. *What will they think of next?*

X edged closer to the group. One member looked up.

"Are you interested in joining us?" they asked. "We could use the help."

"Oh, um. Well, Violin said to wait until they get back. They didn't allocate me to a group, for some reason."

"It can't hurt, can it?" the person on the opposite side of the table asked.

A siren sounded.

"The box is unlocked," the first person said.

X moved closer. She looked towards the door, then at the group of three right before her. They emptied the items from the box onto the table. The other tables were doing the same, and the atmosphere in the room was electric.

X sat down at the table. "Wow, what have we got here?"

"Looks like different food building blocks, and materials for new delivery methods or perhaps mouth screening," said the person who'd first invited X to join the team. They picked up a piece of cloth and studied it.

"You've probably already done introductions, or at least reminded each other of your names. Well, I'm—"

"Juggler, we know," the third person said.

"Yes, well X actually. You can call me X. I'm not so fond of Juggler."

The door opened, and Violin returned. They looked around the room.

"Oh," X said. She rose to her feet.

"Is that you, Juggler?" Violin asked.

"Yes, well, it's X, actually." X walked across to where Violin was standing.

"So, this is highly unusual, ah, X. They have assigned you to your own group. With just you in it. Come, sit over here."

"What? Oh, why? Can't I just join the group of three there? They asked for my help and—"

"Well no. Like I said before, you cannot just join a group randomly. This assessment upholds precise standards. It earns high regard because it follows precise standards, with painstakingly designed specifications, and delivers accurate findings. We can't have you changing that, just so you can even out the numbers. They do not strive for even numbers here."

"But I ... well ... okay. Do I at least get a box of materials?"

"Let me check. I have the details on this screen. Yes, there should be a box for you. Oh, it's a virtual box. Here, sit down at this table and I'll give you this. It has the instructions and the virtual box available right here."

Violin put the screen in front of X, and she looked at it carefully, her heart pounding in her chest and stomach churning yet again.

"Oh, yes. I see. I'll get to work then." X tried to focus her eyes on the text, but it danced before her eyes. She shut them and tried to calm her nerves by repeating to herself, *It's going to be okay; it's going to be okay; it's going to be okay*. She batted her eyelids open and was relieved that she could read the instructions. Her problem was about social inclusion and preventing loneliness in newcomers to Xoha. She was too stressed to see the irony.

X wondered how much time remained. She opened the virtual box and found some information on the interest groups Tree had told her about, airport buddies and workplace orientation. These were already things that existed. X knew she needed to come up with something novel to impress the, well, whoever assessed these tasks—perhaps a computer? She considered there must be a panel or a committee or something that analysed the results. X started writing words on a blank screen, her brow furrowed in concentration. "You've got this," she murmured.

* * *

"Time's up everyone. Thanks for participating in the whole group exercise so enthusiastically. I hope you've had some fun with the treasure hunt. They will contact you individually for an interview to receive your results. They hold interviews throughout the week. Those already working will know next week if they are ready for a promotion. Have a good weekend everybody. Best wishes for your successful careers. Remember, you or your employer can request reassessment from one month onwards. So, I might see you back here one day. Goodbye for now."

The group said goodbye to Violin and dispersed.

X turned to Tree, "that was actually quite fun in the end," she said.

"Yeah, you really seemed to get into that treasure hunt," Tree replied.

X laughed. "I guess I was just happy to be part of a group again. Are you going to the station?"

"Yes, I'll head home now. I'm itching to get out of this suit. It's been a long day."

They walked back through the city. The evening sun sank lower, and the trees glowed with golden tips to their leaves.

"This really is a beautiful place," X said.

"Yes, it is," Tree agreed.

They walked side by side along the path. They were so close they were nearly touching.

X bit the corner of her lip. "Hey, would you like to meet up some time for a drink? Then maybe you could come over to my place another time, for a meal or something?"

Tree turned towards her. "Don't take this the wrong way, but I only go to people's houses once I know them really well. You know, the five-time rule. I take that seriously. Sometimes it takes even longer than that to get to know what someone is like and have an inkling about compatibility. It's a big step to see someone unsuited. You're still new here and you're probably longing to see someone in the flesh again. I get that. But take your time, X. This is a tremendous opportunity to only make friendships and relationships with people you connect with on several levels. The physical bit comes last here. You will get used to it. But I know it's tough."

X blushed. She was glad she was wearing a helmet. They walked along in silence.

"I'm sorry if I've offended you. Who knows, our paths may cross again, and we may become good friends. I like to leave things to fate here. It seems to have the best outcome."

"No, you didn't offend me. I just feel a little foolish, that's all," X said. Again, she was glad that her suit concealed her appearance and tone.

"I don't think you're foolish, X." Tree touched her hand softly with the back of theirs. "Good luck with your assessment results and your first job. Well, here's the station. I had best be off now. Maybe I will see you around." Tree turned to take the stairs down to the platform.

X stopped and watched them go. They disappeared into a crowd of identical grey suits. People walked past her as though she didn't exist. Her stomach twisted, and she swallowed. X got the impression that even though she looked the same as everyone else on the outside, she would not find it easy to fit in here.

CHAPTER TWENTY-TWO

The morning was a haze of the previous night's drinking. Two empty bottles of local wine sat accusingly on the bench. As X cleaned up the kitchen after cooking and guzzling down a hearty breakfast, she had a nagging sensation that something wasn't right. X looked around the homely kitchen, into the cosy lounge and out the big glass doors to the garden.

She was worried about the job assessment result, that must be it. After walking around her garden and picking some ripe vegetables, she felt serene. She left her bounty on the doorstep and sat down on a deck chair. The sun was filtering through the leaves of the large Titoki tree. Its warmth on her skin made her sleepy, and she dozed off.

*

The office looked strange. It was almost like there was an indoor fog. Mr Francis walked into the room. "You didn't get the promotion, Evalie, because you're not good enough. I gave it to Tommy." He threw his head back and laughed. She spun around. Tommy and Leo were there, and Patricia and Naomi. They were all laughing. She had to get out.

She ran through the corridors, opening office doors, trying to find the lobby. In every room were more people laughing. Some were colleagues, some strangers. The three youths from the street were there. Laughing. The women from the pop-up application centre were behind another door. They laughed the hardest. She finally found the elevator and pressed the button. The button popped out onto the floor and then split apart into a hundred tiny black spiders. They ran across the floor.

She ran down the stairs. They smelt like rank water. She could hear a dripping sound coming from above. She couldn't bear to look up. When she got to the bottom and exited the door, she was in the park. It was pitch black and raining. She found a park bench and sat down, catching her breath. When she looked up, there was Stella standing on the path like a statue. Stella wore a dirty, ragged wedding dress and stared right through her. There was a flash of lightning and a massive crack of thunder.

*

X jolted awake. Beads of sweat ran down her nose as she jumped up from the chair. She looked through the window at the time display.

11:03 a.m. | 23 March

It was the wedding day.

X rushed inside, squashing a juicy red tomato on her way. She hobbled and half-hopped to the cleansing room. Her messy right foot marked the clean wooden floor as she went. X looked in the mirror and her wild eyes filled with tears. She just made it to the toilet in time to deposit her half-digested breakfast. After vomiting, she sank to the floor and her head lolled over her knees. Her stomach was empty, but a deep regret remained.

CHAPTER TWENTY-THREE

X got off the train with most of the people in the carriage. The grey suits filed out of the station in an orderly manner. She followed the crowd along the walking path, glad for both anonymity and company on her first adventure in the mountains. There were no dark glasses and layers of makeup needed to cover up this hangover. She had chosen 'mountain air' as the fragrance for her suit. It wasn't quite the same as being out in what she assumed was fresh mountain air, but it was benign. And even though she couldn't tell who any of these people were, it was comforting to be around them. She couldn't bear to stay home for a whole day on her own and didn't want to bother Sand on the weekend. Exercise and fresh air. That's what she needed. Although the latter didn't feature strongly when you were wearing a helmet.

The fork in the path came sooner than expected. X chose the trail that led to the river and waterfalls. If she still had energy after that, she vowed to try the summit track. The sky was white and grey with thick puffy clouds, but no threat of rain. X tried to concentrate on everything that lay ahead. She ambled along the twisting path of compacted earth covered lightly in leaf and tree litter as it descended to the valley floor. X noticed birds flitting through the bright green leaves of the ferns and heard the gurgling river getting ever louder. She played a game of guess who and imagined all sorts of people under the homogeneous metal facades that walked the same path as her, mainly in clusters of twos, threes, and fours. Occasionally, she looked behind her to see how many others were there, enjoying the great outdoors of Xoha.

The river was wide, stony, and crystal clear. The only non-translucent part was the foamy white of bubbles as water hurried over large round boulders. X walked closer to the riverbank, drawn by the immense beauty. She marvelled at how well she could see the bottom, every stone, leaf, twig. It was in complete contrast to the muddy or sandy rivers back home where you had to guess the depth and what hazards, or creatures, might lurk beneath the surface. She sat down on a large rock, peering into the water.

"Beautiful, isn't it?" came a voice from close by.

X startled and looked up. There was a suit standing nearby, turned in her direction. "Sure is," she said.

"Are you here alone?" the person asked.

"Yes. You?" X replied.

"Yes. I just moved here last week."

"Really?" X said. "Me too."

"How are you finding it?"

"Ah, good," X said.

The person didn't reply.

"But a little overwhelming, too." X paused. She didn't know what else to say. She stared at the river again. "How are you finding it?"

"Well, mostly overwhelming, I'd say."

"It's nice to know it's not just me," X said. She smiled, relief spreading through her chest. "I might head to the waterfall now." She got up off the rock. "Do you want to walk together?"

"Sure," said the person. "That would be nice, thanks."

They crossed a beautiful wooden bridge and followed the track upriver. There was a distant crashing sound of the waterfall.

"I've never seen a waterfall in real life," the person said.

"Really? I have, but mostly small ones. Where I came from was frequently in drought. I've heard that this one is magnificent. It's sure to outrival anything I've seen before."

"I'm from the city. Suburbs really. But I never had the chance to go anywhere."

"Oh, wow. I'm sure you're in for a treat then. Living in Xoha."

"Yes. It's like nothing I could ever dare to imagine. My family hid me away because of a condition I have. These suits have changed my life. They have given me life. It's just that after all this time of not living a life, I guess I don't really know what to do with it."

"It seems like you've made a great start, coming out to the mountains by yourself. That must have taken a lot of courage."

"Thanks." There was a long pause. "Yes, I guess it did."

X looked at the person, wondering what kind of condition they had. She was thankful that they could be here, in Xoha and start living. *Perhaps this place is all it is cracked up to be*, she thought. The waterfall got louder and louder, so much so that it was hard to be heard above the roar. As they rounded the bend in the river, they glimpsed white water cascading down rocks.

"Wow," X thought the person said, but she couldn't be sure because of the thundering surge of water.

They walked out onto the wooden viewing platform and found some space between the crowd of onlookers. They stood there in silence for a long time, watching the barrage of ever-flowing water stream down over the rocky outcrops. The spray billowed around and occasionally the breeze blew droplets across the crowd, although there was no bare skin to feel it. X noticed her helmet glass getting hotter, the clear vision function swinging into action. She signalled to her companion, and they walked off the viewing platform together.

"That waterfall is enormous," she said.

"It's phenomenal," they agreed. "I'd like to stay and watch it for a while."

"Oh, okay. Sure," X said. "Enjoy, and good luck here, with everything."

"Thanks. We don't need luck anymore, though. Here, you only reap what you sow. Take care and sow well."

"Thanks," X said. She walked on, in search of the other end of the summit track.

CHAPTER TWENTY-FOUR

X sat in her seat in the waiting room, eyes closed under her helmet, repeating a mantra that everything would be okay.

"X ... X ... X. It is your turn now."

It took a moment to compute.

"Oh, that's me," X said. She jumped out of her seat.

"This way, please." The person led her into a small room with a desk in the middle and a chair on either side. "How are you going today?"

"Good, thanks."

"Are you nervous or excited about your results?"

"Nervous. I don't think I did my best the other day. The group task really threw me, not being allocated to a group, that is."

"Yes, I saw that in the comments. Very peculiar indeed. I have never seen that happen before."

X looked at the helmet in front of her. She had a sudden urge to pull it off and see who was underneath—to talk face-to-face with another human.

"It's just that, um, I'm not sure I'm cut out for this, for Xoha. I feel like I've made a huge mistake coming here. I miss my friends back home, my boyfriend. You know, I miss people. I miss seeing people and the human touch." She rose from her seat. "These suits, they're stifling, I—"

"X, before you do something rash, I must tell you that your results are remarkable. You are an extraordinarily talented person. They have placed you on the strategy team at city office. It is a much higher role than we usually give to our new recruits."

X sank back down into the chair. "Really?"

"Yes, X, really. This is the reason you came to Xoha. A discriminating boss who wanted to keep you from reaching your potential stifled you back home in your job. It is not like that here."

"I, I'm at a loss for words. This is, well, I'm so ... relieved. I thought maybe it was all in my head, my potential. No one else has ever seemed to see any in me."

"Here are the details of your job." The interviewer placed a small chip on the table in front of X. "Everything you need to know before you start there on Wednesday. Plug that into your screen when you get home. Read everything carefully. They will reprogram the chip in your suit at city office with your job details." The person paused.

The room was silent.

"I will contact your buddy and get them to come visit your house." They looked at the screen. "Sand is your buddy."

X nodded.

"I will tell Sand that they can have a proper home visit, unsuited. We rarely recommend that in the first few months. We see better results when people remain suited. They acclimatise to Xoha faster. I understand you are struggling a bit with settling in, though. The last thing we want is to lose you from this program X, or from our city. You are too special."

X blushed. "I, well, thank you," she said. "Can I give you a hug?"

"Oh, well, as long as you keep your suit on; sure."

X rushed around the table and hugged the interviewer. It was a bit of a hollow sensation in the suit. But it still made X feel a little more human. "Thank you, thank you so much," she gushed.

"Take care X maybe I will see you again after another assessment sometime. Perhaps for promotion."

"Thanks, I will. Yeah, maybe." She turned and walked to the door, buzzing.

"It seems you are forgetting something," the interviewer said.

X turned around.

The interviewer pointed to the chip sitting on the table.

"Oh, yes, right." She walked back and picked it up. "I'll put it somewhere safe," she said. She placed it in the front right pocket of her suit and patted the pocket with her right hand. "There, all safe." X smiled broadly and walked out the door.

***

The sudden ring of the doorbell jolted X from her daydream.

She wasn't sure how this whole thing was meant to happen.

Should she answer the door in her suit or not?

Now that she faced seeing Sand in the flesh, she worried about her appearance more than ever. It was like seeing someone naked for the first time, only they'd both be fully dressed, she assumed.

"Of course we will!" X screeched to herself. She hesitated in the kitchen.

The door buzzed again.

"Argh," X said. "The intercom!" X rushed to it and woke it from its slumber. "Hi Sand."

"Hi X. Can I come in?"

"Um, yes. I'm just not sure how to do this. Am I meant to answer the door with my suit on, then ... well?"

"It is okay, just unlock the door and I will come in. You know that front entry space? There is a de-suiting spot. I will show you. Just unlock the door, okay?"

"Oh, okay, sure." X jogged over to the door and unlocked it. She stood back. The door opened and in came a grey suit. They stopped and waited for the door to click shut.

"Here," they said. "See this panel? If you press on it like this, a curtain comes down from the ceiling." Sand disappeared behind the curtain.

"Wow, I never noticed that before. Must have skipped that in the house information, sorry."

Sand's voice changed to a deep baritone. "That is okay X." He stepped out from behind the curtain.

X couldn't help but gasp. He was gorgeous.

Sand smiled at her. "Good to see you X."

"Good to see you too," X stammered. She blushed. The two stood in the hallway. "Oh, come in, please. Welcome to my humble abode. Can I get you a drink?" X swept through the lounge to the kitchen. She turned to see Sand watching her.

"Yes please," he said. "I will have whatever is on offer."

X giggled.

"What's so funny?" Sand asked.

"I, um, well. It's just. I can't get over how deep your voice is and how, well, good looking you are," X blurted. Her cheeks went an even deeper red. She busied herself in the kitchen and tried to avoid Sand's gaze. She mixed up the drinks, humming a merry tune.

"X, I should tell you something. Come into the lounge room and sit down." Sand walked back into the lounge room.

X carried in two glasses of gin and tonic with a wedge of lime in each. She placed one in front of Sand and sat down next to him, taking a sip of her drink.

"Thanks." Sand took a large swig. "Wow, this is superb."

"It's a local gin, of course. I just bought it on the weekend. It's amazing."

Sand studied X's face. "This may sound harsh or premature, but I just wanted to let you know we are not permitted to get physically involved. You seem like a great person, X, but as your buddy, the Council bans relationships between us. This is a very unusual situation," he gestured to X and around the room. "They would not generally let a buddy and new recruit be unsuited together. It is a diversion from the orientation process, you know, the way things should be done. They have done a lot of research in the past and put strict rules in place to protect equality."

"Oh, sure," X said, wishing her cheeks would stop burning and return to their natural colour. "Of course. Well, uh, it's great to have you over. Do you like vegetable lasagne? Have you had it before? I made a recipe my friend Stella back home used to make. Stella's a splendid cook."

"It sounds lovely, X. I hope I did not offend you."

"Not at all. I'm not in the right headspace for a relationship right now, anyway. This is all so new and I, well, I'm just not sure I'm doing it right."

"You must have done something right in your assessment, X. They told me you got one of the highest results across the most indicators they have ever seen. It is very impressive."

"Really? Oh, wow, I thought they were just being over complimentary to make me feel better."

"Not at all. You really impressed them. They want to make sure you settle in quickly. They think you might have what it takes to be on the Council. Elections are coming up at the end of this year and they are constantly looking for the best and brightest to be nominated."

"Wow. Really?" She looked at Sand to see that his face was as serious as his words. "Right. Council. So, how do the nominations work?"

"Your employer must nominate you. At least three senior staff need to sign off on it." Sand took a drink. "Well, let us not get ahead of ourselves, hey? Something to aim for, though. It is very prestigious. Now, where is that lasagne? I am starving."

X smiled and jumped up. "It's definitely ready," she said. "Coming right up!"

Sand followed X to the dining room.

X brought the plates of steaming lasagne to the table. She returned to the kitchen for the garlic bread and salad she had made earlier, fresh from the vegetable garden she found in a hot house down the back of her yard. She gazed at the table and smiled. *Stella would be proud*, she thought.

"Oh Stelle, you see I'm not crazy," she whispered. She studied the table again. "Cutlery," she mumbled. She went back to the kitchen drawers to fetch it.

Sand stood hesitantly at the table.

"Sit. Please, sit here," she said, gesturing to the seat he stood closest to. She placed a knife and fork on either side of his plate and then put hers beside the other plate. "Can I get you another drink?"

"Yes, please. X this looks and smells incredible. I have not had a home cooked Italian meal for years. This really takes me back." He sat down, sniffing in the aroma.

X took the two glasses, emptying the last of her drink down her throat as she walked. She set the glasses down on the bench and poured another two shots of gin, topping up with the tonic she'd mistakenly left on the bench earlier.

She looked at Sand, sitting there at her dining table, and suddenly longed to kiss him. In her imagination, she grabbed his hand and pulled him into her bedroom, and they made wild, passionate love. She blinked away the sizzling vision. She hardly knew this man. What was wrong with her? His aura was magnetic. *It's because this is the first human you've seen, properly seen, for a week*, she thought. Her face dropped. How could it have only been a week?

She sighed.

X returned to the table with the drinks. "Thanks for waiting for me. Here you go, let's eat!"

X passed Sand his drink. Their fingers touched, and it was like a lightning bolt up her arm. X drew her arm back to her side and quickly sat. Her cutlery clanged against her plate.

Sand raised an eyebrow. Then he raised his glass.

X followed suit.

"To new, full, potential," Sand said.

X smiled shyly and clinked her glass with his. They both took a large sip.

"Would you like some bread?" X offered the plate to Sand.

He took a piece. "Thanks."

X crunched on her bread and chewed slowly. She was so attracted to this man. She needed to get a hold of herself. Perhaps it was the added temptation of forbidden love.

"Are you hot? Is it hot in here, or is it just me?" X cringed at the way her question came out and half wished she could hide in her suit.

Sand smiled. "No, it is just you." His eyes danced.

X looked down at her plate. She cut into her lasagne and took a small piece on her fork. She savoured the flavours as they swirled across her tongue. When she looked up, Sand was staring at her. Their eyes met, and she was stripped bare. It was as though Sand was looking into her soul. She looked at the table. "Salad?" she asked. "It's all from the garden. I was so surprised when I found the hothouse out the back there." X gestured towards the backyard.

"Yes, thanks," Sand said.

X passed the bowl to him, and their hands touched again. X withdrew her hand and picked up her water glass. She drank hurriedly until the glass was empty. She jumped up from the table. "More water?"

"No, I am okay, thanks. But after you get some more for yourself, will you please sit down and relax?"

"Oh, yes. I will. Sorry." X filled her glass at the tap and paused there, taking some long sips of water. She looked out of her window into the dark garden beyond, then steeled herself and returned to the table.

"So, what are the biggest lessons you've learned since coming to Xoha?" X asked, as casually as she could.

Sand looked at her. "Hmmm, well, let me see." Sand finished chewing a mouthful of food and looked straight into X's eyes. "Appearances are not as important as I thought they were. Discrimination and racism *were* my biggest problems back home. And hmmm. You can, uh, leave the past in the past."

"Wow, that's heavy," X said. She averted her eyes. "I did ask though."

"You did."

The couple sat unspeaking and continued eating their food.

"Have you ever told someone your real ... I mean your old name?"

Sand looked up, brow furrowed, the train of thought broken.

"No." He chewed a piece of lettuce. He took a sip of gin. "Actually, I lie. I did. But it was by accident. I told the first person I saw unsuited. I blurted it out one night, after we, um, had sex."

The word *sex* hung in the air.

"You had sex with the first person you saw in the flesh?"

"It is quite common X, to be attracted to the first person you see without a suit on. There is an animal magnetism that grows stronger the longer you go without open human contact. Can you not feel it?"

X nearly spat her mouthful of water across the table. She swallowed it awkwardly and looked down at her plate, moving a piece of tomato around with her fork.

"I will take that as a yes. It is okay. There is nothing to be ashamed of. I feel it too, but probably not as strongly as you. That may be because I am, well, in a steady relationship now."

X's eyes met his as she ventured a peek at him. "How did you meet them, the person you're in a relationship with? Was it difficult, getting to the point where you could see each other unsuited?"

"We met through work. Although we work for different organisations, we collaborated on a high-profile project with city office. Through that, we found we had a lot in common, like a natural connection, I guess you would say," Sand spoke slowly.

X tried to place his accent but couldn't. Was he European? African? She shook her head slightly and tried to refocus on what he was saying.

"One night, he asked me out for a drink after work. Then we met the required four more times. Because we were not working together anymore, we did not need authorisation from our employer to meet at home, without suits. So, he came to my house. I did not know who he was behind the suit, but I knew who he was on the inside. He is the kindest, most generous human I have ever known. He lights up my life. If I had not come to Xoha, I never would have met him. He is my soulmate, X."

"Wow," X said. "That's, well, that's just lovely. I hope I find someone else like that."

"What do you mean, someone else?"

"Well, I was dating this *guy* back home, and he was mostly ... well, he was a good guy." X sighed, looking into her glass of alcohol. "Then he asked me to marry him, right when my application came through for Xoha. And I left. I don't know that he was my soulmate. But I do worry that he was the one for me and I won't find another like him. We dated before then and, well, there's never really been anyone else. No one serious. I just, you know, wonder what will happen if I don't find anyone here. Because it seems like it's hard to meet people under these circumstances, and all that."

Sand ate the last mouthful of food on his plate. He chewed slowly, methodically. "You obviously valued the potential of Xoha over that of your relationship X otherwise you would not be here." He placed his hand gently on hers. "You will find your way here X it just takes time. Make sure you give it time, okay?"

X pulled back her hand self-consciously. She took hold of her glass and emptied it with one last swig. "I hope you're right, Sand. I really do."

"Trust me, I am," he said. He placed his knife and fork neatly together in the middle of his plate. He sat up straight, his broad shoulders stretching beyond what now looked like the narrow back of the chair. "Thank you so much for this lovely dinner, X. It has been a real treat. I am sorry I will need to get going, though."

"Oh, you don't want dessert?"

"No, thank you," Sand gently patted his stomach. "I'm stuffed." He pushed back his chair and rose from the table.

X stood up, her heart beating in her throat.

They walked to the front hall.

"You know I am here for you if you ever want to chat. Just call me or send me a message," Sand said. "You can find me easily on your contact list."

He turned to face her and embraced her in a warm hug.

It was such a pleasurable experience. X didn't want him to let go. She held tight and breathed in his sandalwood scent. The memory of Guy crashed into her consciousness and she dropped her arms, breaking the embrace.

"Thanks Sand." She stepped back from him. "I really appreciate it. See you again, maybe, sometime."

Sand smiled kindly. "Yes, maybe, X." He stepped behind the curtain and returned moments later in his suit.

X couldn't believe how quickly he got suited.

"See you X," Sand said.

The monotone voice was surprising and disappointing.

"Go out there and do the amazing things you are capable of."

"I will," she said. X released the door latch, and it swung open.

Sand walked out into the night. The cicada tunes drowned out the sound of his retreating footsteps.

The door closed softly, and X leaned against it, letting out an enormous sigh. "What a night," she breathed. X trudged back to the kitchen.

CHAPTER TWENTY-FIVE

X rushed through the doors of city office at 9:02 a.m. She was furious at herself for being late. She had no time to take in the foyer's beauty with its wooden floors and walls, high central ceiling with large, gnarled wisdom tree growing all the way up to the sky roof. Instead, she found the security desk and queued behind three other suits. She bit her lip and tapped her foot, staring into the backs of those ahead, wishing them to be faster.

The queue moved slowly, and her mind flashed back to her experience at the pop-up application centre, which, while only months before, seemed like years ago now. When she finally reached the front, the person behind the desk said, "Can I–"

"New starter X, reporting for duty," X interrupted.

"Well, hello there X, you seem very keen to be here. Let me see where you are starting today." They scanned a small screen inset into the glass-topped desk. "Ah, here we are. You'll be with Maple, on level two. Just give me the chip out of your suit and I'll program it for you."

X slid her chip from the front pocket of her suit and passed it over the desk.

The person slid it into a slot in the desk and a moment later passed it back to X.

When she slid it back into her suit, she noticed the light on her shoulder turn blue again. She looked at her arm and noticed the complete suit had turned pink again. This time, it seemed even brighter. *This will make it hard to blend in*, she thought.

"You can head on over to the lifts now and just wave your arm in front of the panel inside, and it will take you to level two."

Inside the lift X was alone with her thoughts. She glimpsed herself in the shiny lift doors and saw a robot looking back at her, facial expression masked by the slick helmet. The lift stopped at level two and the door opened out to an office like nothing X had ever seen. It was what she imagined a rabbit warren looked like underground, with stone tunnels and small rooms branching off in all directions. She saw a desk across from the lift and approached it.

"X," a familiar voice called, and she spun around. Then she remembered all the voices sounded the same.

"Maple?"

"Yes, I'm Maple. Welcome to city office. Did you have any trouble getting in this morning?"

"I'm so sorry I'm late, it's all so new and—"

"Oh, no worries at all. Come on through."

"What is this place? It's like a rabbit warren or something."

"Yes, it is a bit. This layout has proven to be the most productive for strategists. There are private spaces for everyone and the cool of the stone seems to bring a calm and direction to the team."

"How interesting," X said.

She followed Maple down a tunnel to the left, past three or four branches of other tunnels and out into an open central sort of cave.

There were screens strung around the walls of the nearly circular room, with groups of people talking and moving between.

"This is command central. Its real name is the den, but I like command central. It sounds fancier."

X laughed. "I like command central too," she said.

"So, these teams over here are working on the suburb matters, everything from housing to shops and natural infrastructure." Maple walked in between the team of light green suits. "Team suburbs, please say hi to X. She's our new starter I've been telling you about."

"Hi X, welcome aboard," someone said, raising their hand to their shoulder.

"Welcome X, great to have you here," said another, doing the same.

"Hi," said a third.

"Hello," said the fourth.

"Hi, nice to meet you all," X said, mimicking the hand gesture. She vaguely remembered it from the welcome information. It was like Xoha's version of a handshake.

"You can find team suburbs in section one of the office. I'll make sure they load the map on your chip. And by the green hue of their suits, of course. And over here," Maple said, walking over to another group of people around a screen, "these are our jobs strategists, with the pale-yellow suits. Say hi to new recruit X, jobs team."

"Hi," they said, almost in unison.

"Hi," X replied, waving her hand.

One team member returned the wave. The remainder of the team raised their hand in the Xohan salute.

X blushed, then returned the gesture.

The team turned their attention back to their screen.

"Okay, and here is the data team, with the light-brown-coloured suits. You'll notice how big this team is. They are spread out around the place. The data analysts support all the other teams at city office as well. I will see if Ocean is here. Ocean is the head of the data team. You will notice their suit is a darker brown than the others." Maple led X down a tunnel and into a small room off to the right side. "Hmmm, this is where you usually find Ocean if they are not in the den. Oh well, I am sure you will meet them later. Come back into the den and I will introduce you to the team that you will be a part of, the systems strategists. It is an exciting team to be in. They look at all the systems in place to make Xoha work, from the suits to the way we recruit people internationally."

"Oh, wow," X said. "That sounds really important."

"Sure is. Without smooth running systems, this place would be nothing." Maple led X back to the den. It was like coming out of the shadows into the sun. Another reason to call it command central. *Den* had a dingy ring to it. The light shone down from high in the ceiling, but X couldn't make out the source.

"Here they are, the systems team, in orange." Maple squeezed in alongside one of the team members and their screen. "Hello, good morning systems team. Let me introduce your newest team member. This is X." Maple pulled X forward into the semi-circle of suits.

"Hi," one of the orange suits said.

"Hello X," said another.

"Welcome to the team," said a third.

X found it hard to distinguish who was talking. They all looked and sounded the same. "Hello," she said shyly. X was glad that no one could tell she was nervous.

They all gave the Xohan salute, and she did the same.

"We are just finishing up our morning briefing," said one of her new colleagues. "Please listen in to the rest, then I will introduce you properly to the team," said the person across from X. Their suit was a darker orange than the others, the telltale sign of the team leader.

"I'll leave you here then, X," Maple said. "If you have any trouble at all or if you need anything, please contact me through your screen, call or message, and I will be happy to assist. Whatever you need to settle in here, please just ask. Have a great day."

"Thanks," X said.

Maple walked away.

X looked at the large screen the team was huddled around. It was set into a high table.

"As I was saying, the key issue this week for me is the breakdown between the security system and the citizen's reports. In order to uphold our current nine hundred-day run streak of no incidents, we need to keep one step ahead of people. We need to understand how they will react before they react. So, I am working with the behaviour team on this one, and the security team, of course."

"Sounds like you have your hands full, Seed. Do you need any extra help?"

"Seed, Seed, Seed," X repeated to herself to remember the name. Not that it would help, she could only tell it was Seed by where they were standing right now. As soon as they moved, she would have no idea who anyone was.

"No, I have everything I need. You can gift the new recruit to someone else," replied Seed.

Maybe it was a waste of time learning that name, X thought.

"Okay," said the team lead, "How about you, Field, any update on the intercity strategy?"

"Oh, yes. We had our big meeting last week, as you know, with all four cities represented to discuss our joint strategy, which is due to go before Council in two weeks' time. Actually, we could really use X's help if that would be alright? We're down one staff here since Dew got transferred."

"Great," said the lead. "Yes, that will be fine. X can start with you Field and you can help better orient X to the office as well. It shouldn't be difficult; we have a bright spark here."

X blushed. She smiled when she realised none of her new colleagues could see her red cheeks. It was liberating. "See, you've got this, X," she mumbled to herself.

* * *

Field was high energy. They talked fast and moved faster, dragging X around city hall, explaining who all the people were, what teams they belonged to and how it all fitted together. X had the impression of being swept up in a whirlwind.

"How do you remember all this?" she interrupted at one point. Her monotone helmet voice belied the exasperation she felt.

"Oh, well, it just takes time, I guess. Don't worry X, you'll get it. City office is a great place to work."

"Have you worked anywhere else here?"

"No. But I have friends that work in other places. Some stories they tell make me think this place is a dream." Field led X back to the den at a half run. "Enough chat. Time to get to work. There's so much to be done."

X stood next to Field at a smaller screen placed against the stone wall. She touched the wall's smooth surface. It wasn't as cold as she had expected it to. She sighed.

"Is everything okay?" Field asked.

"Oh, yeah, sure," X lied. "What are you doing now?"

"I am reviewing the data from City North. I think they are missing something." Field flicked through screen after screen. "Yep, as I thought, they are missing the report on wildlife numbers and habitat health. I will contact them and get them to share it with the group. While I do that, can you please ask Seed if they can provide the incident report analysis? We just need the key findings, then we will have our, City East's that is, full record."

"Incident report analysis, key findings," X repeated.

"That is correct."

"And how do I tell who Seed is? Any tips?"

"Oh, I forgot what it is like when you are new. Everyone looks the same. No worry, you will work out a system to tell people apart. But for now, you may just have to ask, I guess."

"Right," X said. She turned from the screen and looked across the room, scanning for orange suits. She suddenly realised how much her pink suit must stick out amongst these more subdued colours. *I guess I'm no equal just yet. I'm a new recruit,* she thought. She saw two orange suits across at another screen and walked over. They were deep in discussion.

"Excuse me, hi," X said.

They turned towards X.

"Um, are you Seed?"

They shook their heads.

"Sorry to bother you."

X walked around the den. There were no more orange suits. She chose a hallway to walk down. No luck there either. She wandered around past the small rooms, looking in at the ones that had open doors, which were mostly vacant. The ones that had closed doors were a mystery. You couldn't see what was going on inside. At first X was calm and curious. After a while of searching, she realised she didn't know where she was and didn't remember what she was supposed to ask Seed. X panicked. She rushed down the corridors, trying to find her way back to the den. The office was such a strange place. After a while, she found herself at a dead end. There was a room at the end with a closed door. X paused, her heart beat hard in her chest, and she felt the cool flush through her suit to counteract her increasing body temperature.

X heard the inaudible murmur of voices behind the door. She moved closer and pressed her ear to the door. She could distinguish the odd word, 'council', 'statistics', 'conceal', 'lie'. X's eyes went wide. The hair on the back of her neck prickled. She couldn't tell who was in there or when they would come out. When they did, she wouldn't be able to distinguish them from anyone else in the building, except for the team they worked in by the colour of their suit.

"X."

She spun around.

"What are you doing down here?" The person was wearing an orange-tinged suit. It could be anyone from the team.

"Um, I'm ... well ... I'm lost."

"Seems like it. Where are you meant to be?"

"I was trying to find someone. Then I was trying to find the den. Then I just stopped for a rest."

"Right. Well, I can show you the way back to the den. Who are you trying to find?"

"Seed. I need to ask them something."

"Well, that is probably Seed in there. They like that room. All the way down here. You should not be listening in at doors, though, X. It is not the done thing around here."

"I wasn't listening in ... how did you know it was me?"

"Your pink suit, remember?"

X looked down at her arm. "Oh, right. I forgot for a minute that I'm the only one who stands out around here. And who am I speaking with?"

The person paused. Suddenly, the door sprang open.

"What is the meaning of this? There are plenty of rooms available. Why are you loitering around this one?"

"Seed, is that you?" the person asked.

"Who is asking?"

"I am," X said. "It's X. But you know that by this pink beacon. Anyway, I need to ask you something Seed." X scrambled to remember the question. "It's about City East, a report. Um. Oh, the incident report, that's it. Just the key findings. Can you please share them?"

The orange suit stood still. X wondered if they'd heard the question. There was another orange suit in the room. They squeezed past, excusing themselves, and walked back down the hall.

"Well, you can tell Field that I can't share that information right now. I am due across the city for an important meeting. Send me a message and I will get back to you." They disappeared down the corridor.

X watched them go, imagining they were storming off. "Is Seed always like that?" she asked.

"What do you mean?"

"Well, they seem abrupt and not very helpful. It's like they don't like new recruits or something."

"Do not worry about that. Do you want me to show you back to the den now?"

"Sure, thanks."

* * *

"Um, hi. Field, is that you?"

"Yes, well done, X. Did Seed give us what we need?"

"I couldn't get the answer from Seed. They told me they had to rush off to a meeting across the city. They asked me to send a message. How's the best way to do that?"

"I should have known Seed would be less than helpful. They are always too busy, it seems. It is okay X I will take care of it. To answer your question, though, the best way is a direct message. You can do it from the big screens here in the den or from your personal screen. Once you log into the network, you can find any member of staff in the directory. Here, like this."

X watched Field's swift hands on the screen and marvelled at the directory. "Wow, there's a lot of staff that work here."

"Yes, there is. City office controls most of the public-facing infrastructure and services. It is an extremely interesting place to work. Now let us see how you go with your first assignment. Here it is." Field brought up a new screen, controlling it by touch. "Now I will send this to your personal screen, and you can find a space to work where you are comfortable. I will come and find you at lunchtime and we can go for a walk outside and get some food. It is okay if you do not finish the assignment today. I will follow up with you to see where you are at. Just do your best X."

"Okay sure, I will." X scanned the den looking for somewhere to work. She felt odd in the large space and walked instead down one of the long corridors. She stopped at the third door on the left. The room was empty and dark, the door open. She walked in and the light switched on automatically. The illuminated room was less enticing. She walked out again. She wandered along the corridor, trying to get her bearings in the strange building. Once she'd walked the entire floor, she found herself back at the front desk. She sighed. She contemplated going outside and sitting in the park, but she wasn't sure if that was allowed.

"It'll just take some time getting used to this place," X muttered, trying to calm the uneasiness in her stomach.

She noticed a group of orange suits walking out of the same corridor she had come down. She headed for the toilets to avoid awkward conversation. The toilets were individual rooms off a corridor near the front desk. X found the first available one and locked herself inside. The suits had a way of undoing the bottom half so you could use the facilities without getting completely unsuited. The sanitisation station was made for suited hands, not bare skin. She cleaned her suited hands and removed her helmet, peering into the small mirror. "Come on X, realise your full potential!" Her voice bounced around the small, tiled room. The timbre of it caught her by surprise. She didn't have anyone to talk to at home and the times when she spoke without her helmet on were getting fewer.

X resisted the peculiar urge to walk out the door without replacing her helmet. She'd been having these urges more and more, to walk unsuited down the road from her house without a care for who saw her. "Pull it together," she mouthed to the mirror. *I've really got to meet someone*, she thought. *Guy, Stella, how I wish you were here. I miss you.*

X shoved her helmet back on and clipped it, grateful for the cooler air. It was stuffy in the toilet. She walked back to the den and found a little nook with a seat. She sat down, pulled out her screen, and opened the work message. The assignment was a complex one with lots of background reading and statistics. X began reading through the different files. She was less than halfway through when an orange suit came over to her.

"Ready for lunch?" they asked.

X looked up and mumbled, "Um, oh, I guess so. Gee, that went quickly."

* * *

X returned from lunch frazzled. It was time to get some work done. She went to the spot she had found in the den, but a person in a green-tinged suit was there. X looked around the den for somewhere else to sit but it was abuzz with people, rejuvenated after their lunch breaks. She walked back down a corridor and tried the first open door. X sat at the table in the small room and pulled out her screen. She started reading, but soon examined the walls instead. *This place is creepy*, she thought. X used the read aloud function so she could close her eyes and listen. The voice was the familiar monotone of the suits, the same voice she heard all day. X listened to the background information on the green spaces in the city. She was drowsy. She leaned forward in her chair. A few minutes later, she rested her forehead gently on the table.

* * *

The knocking woke her, and she sat upright. A wooziness hit hard, and she put her hand to her head for comfort. The sensation of suited hand on helmet was not what she expected. X was disoriented. She had been dreaming. Of what? The images in her unconscious had shattered and fallen away as soon as her sleep was broken, but the homesickness unsettled her stomach.

"Hello, X," someone said as they walked into the room.

"Oh, hi," X replied.

"How is the assignment going?"

"Good, Field," X lied.

"Great. What have you got to show me?"

"Well, I haven't put it down yet. It's all in my head. Tomorrow, I will have it all plotted out. The strategy response, that is."

"Have you got anything at all to show me today?"

X blushed, her red cheeks hidden behind her pink tinged helmet. She felt cool air circulate faster around her suit.

"Well, uh, no." X tapped the fingers of her right hand on the table before her. "But I can tell you it's all about connections. We need to link the people of Xoha's great cities both through the green-scapes and socially through programs that focus on our need for real human interaction. And touch. Otherwise, it will become like a land of robots. The suits are fabulous for showing us we're all basically the same. As humans, there's little that really differentiates us at our core. But diversity is a strength, differences in tastes and perspectives. It seems like that might be, well, a little lost here. Perhaps that's a big opportunity for Xoha's development."

Field said nothing.

"But it's still a work in progress," X added.

"X, that is interesting. We have not been looking at it that way at all. I have been thinking we need fresh eyes on this. It did not come to me at that point that a new recruit would be perfect for the job. Someone with a fresh sense of Xoha. Someone who still knows what it is like beyond these borders. Where it is not just a distant memory. Thank you. I am excited to see that tomorrow. Can you make a presentation to the team? We have a meeting at eleven. See you then."

Field swept out of the room before X could respond.

X rushed to get what she'd said onto her screen before she forgot all those words she'd made up on the spot.

CHAPTER TWENTY-SIX

The next day X stood in the den waiting for her colleagues. It was 10:50 a.m. She shuffled her feet a little, whispering the opening line of her presentation under her breath. It was a strange sensation to hear your whispered words through the helmet. X appreciated the even tone at times like this. The suit acted as a shield and calmed her nerves. She certainly felt a lot more confident than she would have back home making a presentation on her second day at a new job.

"Hello X," someone said as they approached. X stared at the suit, wondering who it was. Their suit was the orange hue of her systems strategy team.

"Hi," X said.

"Are you ready for your presentation?" they asked.

"Sure. I've prepared something short to say with only a couple of visuals. I put them together quickly this morning. Hopefully, they come across alright."

Another team member joined them.

"I am sure you will do great," the person X had been talking to responded.

X decided it must be Field. Two more orange suits arrived. X recognised the team leader by their darker orange suit but did not know who the other people were, except the one to her left, which she thought was Field.

"What is this about a presentation?" the person directly in front asked. "From you—you have only been here five minutes, what could you possibly have to–"

"That is enough, Seed," Field said. "Give X a shot."

X cringed and focused on trying to slow down her breath.

"Okay, everyone," the team leader said. "It looks like we are all here. Perhaps we should start with the topic of the moment, X's presentation. Go on, X. Field said you had a new idea that the team should hear." The lead signalled to the team to stand around the screen in the den's corner near where they had gathered.

"Oh, well, yes. Thank you. Let me just bring up the visuals on this screen here." X fiddled with her personal screen, trying to share the content with the large screen.

"Today would be good," someone said.

X hazarded a guess that it was Seed.

"Perhaps I should start with an update from my end. It should only take a minute," the person continued.

"Give her a chance Seed, you are so impatient."

X felt her heart thump in her chest and temples. She remembered the authorisation check box in the corner and quickly ticked it. Up came a map of City East.

"Xoha's four cities are all the same," she started. "The general layout, services, opportunities are equal."

"This is not new information," Seed said.

X looked towards the team leader. They gestured for her to continue.

"You're right," X continued. "This is not new information. It is the foundation of Xoha. Equality. But each of the four cities with their three suburbs that fan out beyond, is missing out." She flicked to a photograph of the local park. "We have all these green spaces. Each city has a similar large parkland that wraps around it and bridges the suburbs but is not connected to that of the other cities. I know the distance between our cities is large. But this lack of connection is a missed opportunity. There are ways we can use these green spaces to bring the people of Xoha together." X flicked to a sketch she'd mocked up of a well-connected Xoha. "Here is just one idea of how we could do that. It's not fully worked through, as I only had a bit over an hour to pull it together." She paused. "In addition, we need to connect the people socially through programs that focus on our innate need for human interaction." She flicked to her last picture. She'd quickly taken it the night before on her way home. It was of the park, dotted with the odd suit. "We risk becoming a land of robots. These are all individuals living and working here, moving through the park. Yes, they all have the same opportunities, but how do they meet people and form relationships? I think Xoha could really benefit from a greater focus on social connections." X looked at her team. They were all facing towards her and the screen, but their steely exteriors gave nothing away. "Thank you." X stopped herself from filling the silence that followed with useless chatter or after thoughts.

"Thank you, X for that interesting presentation," the team leader said. "You have some novel ideas. It is fabulous to see you contributing to the team already. Well done."

X smiled. Then blushed. Then sighed quietly.

"I have been thinking for some time about the need for more representatives on the intercity strategy team. It sounds like that would help with the development of a strategy to increase connections across Xoha, as our new recruit has suggested is of need. Field, as you have been City East's lead on this, I think you should continue to lead, bring in X as part of our core representation and encourage the other cities to expand their representation as well."

"I like it. It sounds great," Field said.

"Of course, you will include Seed in the team too," the team leader said. "They have valuable experience we need to utilise. Oh, and before I forget, make sure you take your chip back to security before you leave today, X and they will remove your starter status so your suit will no longer be pink, but orange like ours. Congratulations, I think you are going to be a real asset to this team."

CHAPTER TWENTY-SEVEN

The train came to a stop just outside the city. X looked out the windows and then around the carriage. The other grey suits turned their heads as well.

"Not today," X said. "I can't be late today." She stood and paced up and down the carriage.

"This is the train control room. Apologies for the interruption to your service. The train has broken down. The tow service will be here in approximately five minutes."

* * *

"X, I'm so glad you're here, I was beginning to worry," Field said.

X knew it was Field because they had arranged to meet in the foyer, and there were no other orange suits around.

"Sorry I'm late. The train broke down just before the city stop. Once I finally got to the station, I was frantic and basically ran all the way here."

"Oh, no. Well, hopefully the infrastructure team is all over that. I am glad you made it because we have a problem. You know how Tide was supposed to do the presentation today. Well, they have fallen ill and will not make it."

"Oh, no. That's terrible. I hope they're okay."

"I am sure they will be. But it means you are up."

"What, me? Give the presentation? No, I ... isn't there someone else?"

"X, the group discussed it earlier and agreed you are the best person for the job. We have seen you present many times and once you get over the nerves, you are excellent. There is no time to argue. We need to get in there now."

"But I've ... well ... luckily, I came prepared. Thanks for your belief in me. Uh, I'll do my best."

"Now remember what we discussed in the last meeting, about addressing the heads of Council—speak loudly and clearly and wait until they ask you questions."

"Yes, I remember," X said.

"And be prepared for their distinctive voice. The Councillors do not sound the same as us. If you're not expecting it, it can be a little offputting."

"They don't sound like us. Right."

"You will be fine, X. It is time to go in."

X and Field walked into the large circular room on the top floor of the city office of City North. The room was silent, and their footsteps made soft clicking noises on the polished wood floor.

They joined the rest of the intercity strategy team at a raised part of the circular wooden table that took up most of the room, with seats all around. They had set up the room so all seats could clearly see presentations. The three large screens were evenly placed for ultimate viewing. X took in a long breath and let it out slowly and noiselessly. She felt her pulse regulate and her suit's cooling slow down.

"Good morning, Councillors," she said. Her throat felt scratchy, but her voice sounded the same as it always did in her suit. She waited for the pictures on the screens to sync with her voice. The video showing the first city scape began. "The cities of Xoha are exceptional places to work and live. However, they are disconnected and there is duplication of effort across the city offices." X tried to speak loudly and clearly.

She wished she'd had time to practice properly. She had read the presentation over in her head several times to make sure she was across what they were presenting. The team had let her know the Councillors would likely ask questions of everyone. But she hadn't conceived that they would ask her to present.

"Our proposal that we put forward to you today is to better connect the suburbs through upgrading the green spaces, so they lead seamlessly from one to another, encouraging people movement. We also propose to develop a network of teams working on the same issues so that we work across cities and share resources and information for a more united and efficient Xoha." X took a breath and looked around the room. It was extremely difficult to judge the crowd of identical suits. The lack of facial cues and masked expressions made her tense. She remembered Field's words about waiting for the Council to ask questions.

"If I can interject, this sounds all too much like what we had in place in the beginning."

The voice came from behind her. X's head nearly spun off her shoulders. A person in an orange suit, a few seats down, had stood to address the Council. Her mouth fell open. *Who is crashing my presentation?* X thought.

Field stood up next to X. "I am very sorry about this," they said. "We brought a united front, but someone seems to have gone off script."

"You mean you do not even know what member of your team that is?" the Councillor directly across from them asked. The booming nature of the Councillor's voice caught X off guard. She blushed a deep crimson.

Field began to respond, "I have a fair–"

"It is Seed here. I am not scared to speak up. I never agreed to this proposal, and they would not hear it." Seed swept their hands at the presentation team. "I could not sit back and have them make this mistake off the back of a new recruit's fanciful idea."

X blushed again and was tremendously grateful for the cover of her helmet.

"It seems presumptuous of you. Do you not think that we, the Council, should be the judge of this proposal? What right do you have to come in here and interrupt proceedings?" a Councillor to the right of the one who spoke first asked.

"I mean no disrespect, Councillors, I simply intended to give you a much better, counter proposal. I did not think it was fair that they present this as the only unanimous option. Please do me the good service of hearing me out." Seed strode up and back behind the team's chairs.

Field muttered something under their breath.

"Should I do something?" X whispered to Field.

They shook their head. "No, you will just have to wait and see what Council decides."

The Councillors turned their heads towards one another. They seemed to bob around a little, unable to catch one another's gaze through their impenetrable helmets. It reminded X of boats at a marina, tethered to the jetty and moved by an unseen current.

"We will need a moment to consult on this," a Councillor said.

"Please leave the room," said another.

"We will call you back when we have a decision," said a third.

X and her colleagues, and Seed, left the room in silence. As soon as the door to the room was firmly shut, there was an eruption of noise. Everyone spoke at once.

Field, who was still next to X, raised their hand. "Everyone, please, this is useless. One at a time. Let me start. Seed, how could you do this to us?"

"Calm down. There is nothing wrong with a bit of healthy debate. If you were confident in your idea, my interjection would not have made you so worried."

Another of the strategists spoke up. "You have gone behind our backs and made us look like fools. A key part of this project is to show that the cities can unite and can work together. You have jeopardised that."

Someone else spoke. "Our history has shown us that working in silos has been effective for each city individually. However, the divide between cities has become substantial. Do you know the success rate of a person if they are moved from one city to another due to a failed relationship or some other complication?"

"Less than ten percent," X chimed in.

"That is right, is that you X?"

"Yes."

"You were doing such a great job with the presentation, considering the short notice you had," the person said.

"Thank you," X said. She felt slightly better. "Don't you see, Seed," X said. "We have considered all these factors already. If you had not stormed off that day, you would have seen all the research and modelling we've completed to ensure this strategy is the best one."

"I don't need a rookie to give me a lecture."

"What is your problem with me? Why hide behind this new recruit bullshit? You've discriminated against me since I joined this team and I've had enough. If I wanted to be treated like this, I'd have stayed in Melbourne!" As soon as the words left her mouth, X regretted them. You were never meant to share personal details with your work colleagues. It was forbidden, and for good reason. You never knew who you were talking to, and that was the point. If you shared your past, people might recognise you and the risk was so much higher in a conflict situation. If they forced X to leave this city office because of an identity breach, she already knew there was only a ten percent chance of success elsewhere. Although surely they would not transfer her in this situation, they'd simply reassign her to a new job.

"Now you've done it, silly girl. Just when you were finally fitting in." The voice that rang in her ears was her father's.

Suddenly, the door to the meeting room flew open.

"You may come back in."

X looked at Field but couldn't tell what was going on inside their suit. She followed the others inside and sat at the end of the group, closest to the door next to a Councillor. The Councillor's gold-tinged suits could not be mistaken. They were luminous even in the dimly lit room.

"We have made our decision," boomed the Councillor.

X felt like she was being lectured.

"We will interrogate both proposals," the Councillor continued. "But we are all in agreement that it would not be fair to do that today. We have other business to discuss, and not enough time left on the agenda to do it justice. We will adjourn this matter until the next

Council meeting on the fifth of next month. Thank you for your time, intercity strategy team."

The group stood. X was first out of the room. She desperately wanted to run off to the toilet to process what had happened in silence. Instead, she stood in the foyer, shifting her weight between her feet. The others came out, and they formed a group at the centre of the foyer, waiting for someone to say something.

"It is time for a debrief. Seed you too. We can discuss a way forward for the proposals, as a team, so they are both the best they can be."

Field's words, delivered in the same helmet voice as always, somehow sounded desperate to X.

"This is Field, by the way. I take the lead due to Tide's absence. It makes sense as I am the lead for City East and Seed is in my team."

X checked herself. *Am I finally picking up nuance?* she thought with excitement. Everyone had told her the day would come when she would know who was speaking and find intonation, even though they looked and sounded the same as everyone else. It seemed impossible. How could anyone look or sound different when they were all the same? Perhaps the shock of being challenged at this most critical time had brought out something good in her.

"Well alright. I will come. But only so I can show you why my proposal is the only one we should present to Council."

X scowled. Seed was a real piece of work.

They all walked towards the lift. Field went to the reception desk. The remainder of the group milled around, waiting.

"Why didn't you believe you could come to us and raise your concerns before the meeting, Seed?" someone asked.

X was fairly sure it was Desert from the City South team. They were always polite with the words they used.

"I was sick of getting shut down by my team. It was the only option left to me."

Field returned to the group. "I have clearance from security for us to go downstairs with the strategy team to their den."

"We should go to the large meeting room on level four. It will be more private." The City North colleague went over to the desk and returned quickly. "All set. We only have half an hour, though."

Even though the elevator only went down one floor, X's stomach rose to her throat. She was amazed as they stepped into a room with glass walls affording views of the city on three sides. It reminded her of offices she'd been in back home. It was the first one that had felt familiar since arriving in Xoha.

Someone joined X by the window. "It's a stunning view, isn't it? I remember thinking these kinds of offices only existed back home in cities like Melbourne," they said.

X flinched. She knew blurting out her home city would come back to haunt her.

"I'm from Sydney, by the way. It's Park here."

"Oh, hi Park. Thanks for telling me that. I felt so awful after blurting out where I was from before. Knowing where you come from makes me it a bit better. Aren't you worried about what might happen to you though by sharing that?"

"Nah, it's just between me and you, right? Plus, Melbourne and Sydney are big places. Hey, if you're interested, I can look you up and send you my details. We should catch up sometime socially. I have no idea the last time I met a fellow Aussie. I've been here two years next month and I still get a little homesick. It's normal, don't worry."

"That would be fantastic, thanks," X said.

"Please sit down everyone, we have a lot to sort out and only a few minutes to do it in," Field said.

Unsuited

X sat at the table next to Park. She felt happy for the first time in weeks.

* * *

X and Field stood in front of a screen in the den. They had been researching Seed's proposal for days, looking at every angle Council might consider. Seed was absent from work for the third day in a row since the Council presentation.

"Have we heard from the City West team yet?" Field asked.

"No, we've heard from the other two, but not City West. I'll send them another message now." X got out her screen and started writing a message.

"You should just send voice messages X you know it is quicker."

"I know," X said. "But I have the chance to edit what I write. It's harder with voice. You have to get it right the first time."

"You should work on that, otherwise it will end up holding you back."

"Okay, I will. Starting tomorrow." X grinned. She liked the dynamic she had with Field. They seemed to really believe in her and try to bring out her best, even though X was sometimes resistant. She'd never had a supportive boss before. It was strange but refreshing. As she sent the message to the City West team, another popped up on her screen.

Hi X. Park here. Would you like to meet after work? I'm in City East for an appointment.

X's heart pounded in her chest. She quickly wrote back.

Sure, I'm free. Meet you at Judicious Juices, 5:30 p.m.?

"X."

"Sorry?"

"Put that screen away, would you? I asked you if you had read about the railway system failure last year?"

"Right. Railway failure. Uh yes, I did." X replaced her screen in the pocket of her suit. As she did, she saw the reply from Park flash on her screen.

Lovely. Can't wait.

X smiled. Her hand rested on her left hip.

"And?" Field said.

"Oh, right. The trains shut down after a track safety incident and no one could travel from City North suburbs into the city for two days."

"Not City North, City South. And what happened as a result?"

"Oops, yes I meant City South. The people of City South all went to buy bicycles and other wheeled individual transport to get around and there were huge pedestrian jams all over the paths in the parks and connecting green spaces."

"Yes, at first. And then?"

"Then the people figured it out and came up with their own staggered schedule of getting to work and some who rarely worked from home did. The city office learnt from the experience and mandated each business in the city maintain a more staggered and flexible approach to scheduling their staff and City South's efficiency and productivity statistics outperformed the three other cities."

"Correct. And who was leading the intercity team that rolled out the City South model across the other cities?"

"Was it you?"

"No, not me. It was Seed."

"Oh."

"So, you can see why they felt entitled to have their perspective chosen and their proposal put forward this time, right?"

"Yeah, I guess so. I don't understand why they had to be such a jerk about it, though."

"Well, Seed's approach may just have got them reassessed."

"Really? Is that why they haven't been at work since the Council meeting?"

"Seems likely, though management are yet to confirm it."

"Does management usually notify you of things like that?"

"Well, it depends. They usually notify you if it is something that could have a negative impact on your work. But probably more likely once they have a result."

"Do you think they will reassign Seed?"

"Maybe. Anyway, better not waste our time pondering over things that are beyond our control. Best get back to our research and make sure we have two solid proposals for Council in three weeks' time."

X looked at Field, wondering for about the hundredth time what they looked like, who they were underneath the orange suit. Field looked up, as if sensing X's gaze. X smiled automatically and invisibly, then turned her attention back to the screen.

CHAPTER TWENTY-EIGHT

X stood at Park's front door. She went to straighten her hair subconsciously, but dropped her hands when she heard the dull clink of metal on metal. "Will you ever get used to this?" she grumbled to herself.

She picked up the bag she'd set down at her feet.

The thick metal door was an exact copy of her own. She pressed the buzzer and waited. After a minute, a voice came through the intercom. It sounded ever so slightly different from the suit voice.

"Is that you, X?"

"Yes, it's me," X said into the panel.

"Be there in a tick."

"Sure thing."

X felt the knot in her stomach twist as she imagined the way the night might unfold. "I shouldn't be this nervous," she said just as the door swung open.

"Nervous," Park repeated. "No need to be nervous." Park stood in the doorway, suited. "We've followed the rules. All those meetings after work and the walk in the park. You are allowed to be here."

"Ha. I didn't. Um ..."

"I'm just teasing X, come inside. You'll feel better in here. I promise I'm not scary, really."

X stepped inside. Her cheeks were burning. *Think of a way to stall the unsuiting so you can get it together,* X thought. Her mind was suddenly blank.

"Here you go, you can unsuit behind the curtain." Park pressed a button, and a curtain fell softly from the ceiling.

It was just like the one at X's house.

"I'll meet you in the lounge. It's just through there." Park gestured the way.

"Thanks," X stepped behind the curtain. "I'll just be a few minutes." She slowly unfastened her helmet and took it off, placing it on the hook on the wall. Then she unzipped her suit, taking her time to step out of it like it was made of precious silk instead of the hardy colerium. She hung her suit next to her helmet. Looking at the suit hanging like some kind of toughened snakeskin, she realised it had become part of her. It was the outer layer that protected her from so much of the outside world, but also from herself, her facial expressions, blushing. She stood for a few minutes, breathing deeply. She smoothed her hair, then took a hair tie out of her pant pocket and tied her hair back into a low ponytail. When she was certain her cheeks had cooled, she picked up her bag and stepped out from behind the curtain.

The house seemed familiar, and X realised the floor plan was just like hers. A large foyer swept into a generous hall that led to the lounge, kitchen, dining and bedroom wing beyond. The colours were different, though. Warm yellow greeted her in the foyer. As she glanced around, she wondered what Park looked like, who they were.

Memories of her encounter with Sand came rushing back, and she blushed again. This time there was no helmet to hide it.

X walked slowly down the hall, padding on bare feet. There were photos of landscapes dotting the walls. The room that opened out before her was bright; lights twinkled in the vaulted ceilings and X felt like she was at home. She walked over to the brown couch and sat down. X scanned the room for pictures of people, for a glimpse of her host. There was a small image on a dresser on one wall, but she was too far away to see the detail. Just as she thought about getting up to have a look, Park, now unsuited, breezed into the lounge from the bedroom wing.

"Hola. Que tal, X?"

"Hola. Uh, muy bien," X stammered. "My Spanish is a bit rubbish, sorry," she added with remorse.

"Oh, no matter. We will speak in English then. I might be rusty from not much practice. I keep hoping to meet someone who speaks Spanish but no luck! When I heard you come from Melbourne, I thought, what a multicultural city, perhaps this time ..."

"I'm sorry," X said. "I stupidly assumed that you spoke only English, being from Sydney."

"How our assumptions remain, despite all the lessons these suits have taught us," Park said slowly.

"Oh. You're right. I hope I haven't offended you," X said.

"It's okay!" Park said with a flourish of her arm.

Park was a beautiful woman with long, flowing dark brown curls that covered her shoulders.

"Would you like a drink?"

"Oh, yes, please. I brought some wine." X reached into her bag and pulled out two bottles. "I wasn't sure if you liked red or white, so I brought both."

"That's very thoughtful. Muchas gracias, X."

"No problem." X smiled at Park and when their eyes met, she felt a shock go through her like she hadn't felt since the incident with Sand. She quickly diverted her eyes. When she glanced back, Park was studying her. X touched her hair self-consciously.

"I like red best. Are you happy for me to open this?" Park asked.

"Yes, go ahead, red sounds great."

Park swept into the kitchen, and her flowing floral top rippled out behind her. She returned a few moments later with two glasses, full nearly to the brim, with red wine. She passed one to X.

"Thanks," X said. Their hands touched briefly, and X's heart raced. She took a gulp of wine. *Seriously X, get a hold of yourself*, she thought.

"This is new for you. Isn't it? To be spending time with someone, without suits on. Here, in Xoha." Park stood looking at X and took big sips of her wine.

"It's that obvious, isn't it? I'm just a bit nervous. It's my second time. I know it's silly." X looked down at her feet. She drank some more wine from her glass.

"It's not silly," Park sat next to X on the couch.

She sat awfully close, with her knee almost touching X's.

The two sat quietly for a few minutes. Sipping their wine. After Park had drunk nearly all of hers, she put the glass on the coffee table. She waited until X put her glass down on the table too.

Park took X's hand. "You are safe here with me. I like you X, you're very fresh still, like a cool breeze on a hot summer's day. Most people aren't like that here anymore."

X sat there looking at Park, their hands interwoven. She slowly drew her hand back. "Thanks. I didn't think it would be so hard fitting in here. With everyone looking the same, I thought it would be easy."

"You've found your way with work though, haven't you? You seem to be a good fit in the team, and you have shown everyone that you're smart." Park picked up her glass and took a small sip.

"Thanks," X said, blushing. "I just …," X picked up her glass and drained the last of the ruby liquid "feel alone." The wine was delicious and silky smooth to the finish. She put the empty glass on the table.

Park finished the last sip of her wine and returned her glass to the table. Then she leaned across and kissed X.

X's eyes bulged. She put her arms up defensively, ready to push Park off. But then she felt Park's soft lips on her own. And they felt delightful. She leaned forward and kissed Park back. Park smelt like jasmine and tasted like wine, with a hint of mint. They kissed softly and slowly at first, then faster and more passionately. X felt Park's hair in her hands. She felt butterflies rise from her stomach and settle in her chest. Her heartbeat pulsed in her ears. *What on earth is going on?* she thought briefly.

X tried to stop kissing Park, but it felt so nice to be touching someone again. And to be touched. She let herself get swept away in Park's embrace and passion. There was such passion in her every move. The kissing led quickly to undressing. They made love on the couch and after the initial awkwardness X soon felt comfortable in Park's arms.

After they were spent, they lay there naked, legs and arms entangled.

"So, how do you feel now?" Park asked. "Not so lonely, huh?"

"No, not so lonely," X said. "Happy. For the first time since I arrived. And, well, not so frustrated."

Park threw her head back and laughed a deep, hearty, generous laugh. "Good," she said. She stroked the side of X's cheek with the back of her fingers. "You hungry?"

"Sure am," X said.

"Let us eat then."

Park untangled herself from X, rose from the seat and kissed X softly on the forehead. Her large breasts brushed against X's collar bone and sent a shiver down X's front that landed in her crotch. X dug her nails into the edge of the couch.

Park moved calmly through the kitchen, putting together the meal as if it were any old day, and she wasn't stark naked.

X sat and put on her underwear, then padded across the room towards the bedroom wing. "Are the facilities through here?"

"Yes, the loo is just down the hall to the left," Park called from the kitchen.

X laughed. She couldn't remember the last time someone had called it that.

When X returned, refreshed from spraying water on her face and re-tying her ponytail, she saw the table laden with bread, salads and a meat dish. X's stomach dropped. She had forgotten to tell Park she was a vegetarian.

"Come sit down lovely, time to eat." Park had put on a plum coloured, satin, short-sleeved dressing gown.

"Thanks, I might just get dressed first."

"Come, come, don't worry about that. You're beautiful. Sit, eat. Are you cold? I can turn up the heat."

"No, I'm not cold," X said. "I'm perfect." She smiled broadly and sat down at the table. "I am vegetarian, though. Sorry. The bread and salads look fabulous."

Park looked at X. "Vegetarian, huh? Well, no matter. Nobody's really perfect." Park laughed her hearty laugh again, a twinkle in her eye.

X grinned. "I guess not."

CHAPTER TWENTY-NINE

X woke to her insistent alarm. "All right, all right!" she said as she silenced it as quickly as possible. She saw the date flash on the screen and jumped up. "It's the fifth. Council presentation today can't be late!"

She heard the toilet flush and startled. Looking around her bedroom, she saw Park's clothes strewn on the floor. *That's right, Park stayed over again last night*, she thought. This was one of those times where she felt as though she was having an out-of-body experience. It was as though she was looking down on herself, judging her every move. X thumbed through her underwear drawer.

Park walked back into the bedroom. "Good morning, sunshine," Park said. She gave X a small tap on the bottom as she walked past.

"Morning," X replied. She grabbed her clean underwear and padded off to the toilet.

As she went about her morning routine, X kept repeating the opening statement of her presentation to herself. After finishing in the sanitising cubicle, she put on her underwear and wished she'd brought her clothes with her as well. She brushed her hair, marveling at how long it had gotten. She hadn't had the guts to go to the hairdresser in Xoha yet. All appointments had to be verified through city office for compliance. It had all seemed too much. X tied her hair at the base of her neck so she could easily cajole it into her helmet.

There was a tap on the door. "Can I come in?"

"Yes, I'm done now."

Park entered the room and smiled at X. "You look so beautiful, fresh from the sanitiser," Park said.

X blushed. She looked down at the floor and walked to the door.

"Is everything okay?" Park asked.

"Yes, sorry. I'm just nervous about the presentation today."

"You will be majestic, my darling."

X smiled. "I'm not sure about majestic, but I'll do my best."

X slipped out of the room and quickly got dressed. She went into the kitchen to make breakfast. Park was still using the sanitiser. She hoped Park would be organised today. She didn't like the idea of having to leave her there on her own if Park wasn't ready to go when she was. *But today we are going to the same place*, she thought. *I won't be able to leave without her.*

"You shouldn't have invited her over last night," X scolded herself. *But I didn't. She came knocking on the door at nine thirty, remember, looking for sex.* The thought made X's stomach churn.

X arranged the fruit she'd cut on a plate. She added the warm croissants and placed them on the table. She retrieved the jam she and Park had made on the weekend from the fridge.

"Smells delicious," Park said as she walked into the room. She glanced at the jam jar in X's hand. "What a brilliant weekend we had." She sat down at the table in her underwear.

"Aren't you going to get dressed?" X asked. It seemed to her Park was always eating at the table without clothes on.

"After. No hurry," Park said. She waved her arms dismissively.

X sighed. She put the jam on the table and went back for the butter and cutlery. X returned to the table and loaded her plate with fruit and croissant. She ate hurriedly, watching Park take a spoonful of home-grown blueberries. The purple juice ran down her chin and dropped into her decolletage.

"See," Park said, mouth full. "This is why I wait until after breakfast to get dressed!"

"You know no one will see your clothes anyway, so it wouldn't really matter if you spilt a little juice on them."

"You're making me think you don't like me sitting here in my underwear. What, do you find it too distracting?" Park traced her right toes up X's pant leg and rested her foot in her crotch.

X pushed her chair back from the table and stood. "Fun as this is, it's time to hustle. We can't be late today. Field would never forgive me."

X walked into the kitchen with her unfinished plate. She raised her right hand to her chest and felt her frantic heartbeat under her breast. "You've got this, X," she whispered. She put her plate into the dishwasher and walked back into the dining room.

Park was picking at her food with her fork. "Is there something wrong, X? Something more than you're telling me?"

"No," X said. "Really. It's just this presentation, that's all. I'm overthinking it and I just can't seem to get control of my nerves. It might help if we leave for the city office now and have time to walk past the lake. I think that will calm me down."

"Okay," Park said slowly. She looked X right in the eyes. "But only if we hold hands while we walk."

X snorted.

She saw Park's lips tighten.

"Oh, you're serious. Sorry. Yes, sure. We can hold hands. It's not like anyone will know who we are."

"I knew it," Park retorted. "You're ashamed of me, you're ashamed to be with me."

"That's ridiculous, it's not that at all," X said. She walked over to the table and took Park by the hand. X pulled her out of her chair. She stood close and looked Park in the eyes. "I could never be ashamed of you. It's just, this is all so new and I'm overwhelmed, that's all. You're the only person I see outside of work, and I guess I just, I don't know what this is. What we are. And I really didn't want to talk about this now because I want to go to work, so we're not late. Please don't be mad at me." X opened her arms, and the pair hugged.

"Okay, okay. I'll go get dressed. Be ready in a tick."

X sighed. "Thank you."

* * *

Walking down the street to the train, they looked like twins in their grey suits. X breathed in the lavender perfume of her suit. It was soothing, as she'd hoped it would be. After the short train ride, they alighted at the edge of the park. As they walked along the path, Park took X's hand. It felt peculiar to X, holding suited hands. Although she knew that nobody could tell who she was or who she was with, she felt self-conscious. *Stop being silly*, she thought.

They walked down past the lake. A dozen different water birds were looking for food in and around the calm water. Thoughts crowded X's head.

What is this, though?

Am I a lesbian now?

Or bisexual?

Does it even matter?

Would I still be attracted to Park if we'd met in Melbourne?

Or Paris?

Or London?

Anywhere other than Xoha?

Maybe you should ask Park about this. She might have some answers. She's been here for over two years.

"What are you thinking?" Park asked in her monotone, helmeted voice.

"Hmmm. Oh, nothing. Just what a pretty morning it is with all these birds."

"It is lovely. You were right about walking down here. It's very calming."

They walked past the sign to the fountain.

"Should we sit for a moment on that bench?" X asked.

"Well, well, you really have calmed down. Sure, if you think we have the time."

X looked at her forearm and pressed the side button to activate the digital time display. "Shit, is that the time? No, we can't stop. Come on, we need to be there in ten minutes."

X pulled at Park's arm and the pair half-jogged, half-ran up the slight hill into the centre of the city. X was glad that they'd dropped hands in order to increase their speed. She felt less like a beacon, demanding people's attention. Although they were the only ones not walking. Surely that was attention grabbing. How could you tell if anyone was staring, anyway? They were both out of breath by the time they made it to the door of City East's city office.

They were a few minutes late. X pressed the button manically for the lift. Her heart thumped in her throat.

"Come on, come on, come on." Her anger came across as monotonous repetition.

"It's going to be okay, X," Park said.

"No, it's not. I think I need some space. A break from whatever this is. From you." She gestured at Park with her hand.

Another person joined them waiting by the lift. The lift doors opened, and the three stepped inside. X swiped her arm across the scanner and the other person looked at the screen.

"You're going to the same place I am," they said.

X tried to smile at them. *What are you doing? They can't see your face*, she thought. X lifted her right hand to her head. She felt woozy from the speed of the lift.

When it stopped at the top floor, X sprang out. There was a group of suits milling in the foyer outside of the Council meeting room. Seeing her orange suit, someone rushed up to her.

"X, is that you?"

"Yes, it's me. Is that you, Field?"

"No, it is Seed of course. I have some news. Field has been in an accident, and they are in the hospital. Where have you been? I have been messaging you all morning. Well, I do not actually care where you have been. It does not matter. I am taking over the presentation. You were meant to be here like twenty minutes ago. You are too late."

X collapsed onto the floor. Someone pulled at her arm and got her to stand. "X, it's Park. Take it easy. Come on, you're going to be okay."

"Didn't you hear that?"

The door opened to the Council room, and an announcement rang around the foyer.

"The Council will see the intercity strategy team now. Please enter."

Park helped X forward towards the door to the stunning Council room on the top floor of her building.

"I've blown it," X said. "What is Seed doing? I can't believe I've blown it. This was my chance to impress them. And all for some,"– they all entered the room, and it fell silent–"mediocre sex."

Park stepped back from X, and she was standing alone. The room spun before her eyes.

"Right, well. Who is leading this presentation today? It is time to get started." The booming voice rang around the slick, wooden-floored room.

X looked at the round of Counsellors, disoriented. She was not sure who had spoken.

"I am," said Seed, raising their hand.

X found a seat at the end of the group and slumped into it.

"At your last meeting, I interjected and caused you all to reconsider the proposal put before you by the team. Since then, we have thoroughly researched both options and written detailed proposals, which we distributed to you in advance of the meeting."

We, thought X. "You weren't even there for half of it. Field and I did most of the work," X hissed under her breath.

"Therefore, I will be brief and only run through the best of the two," Seed said.

X's stomach dropped. She clutched at the table to give herself strength. "I can't let you do that," she bellowed. X rose from her seat. "Field cannot be here because of an accident that landed them in hospital, but they would never have agreed to this pitch. Seed is one-eyed when it comes to this issue. They're only going to present the proposal they championed last time. I didn't contribute to all of those weeks of research for nothing."

"Stay out of this rookie," Seed gestured towards her. "You have no right–"

"I have no right? What about you?"

"Enough. This is highly irregular. This Council meeting will not become a thrash down," a Councillor said, standing. Their voice bounced around the room. "Take a hold of yourselves. Seed, we are dismissing you from this meeting. Rookie, I'm sorry I don't know your name. We are dismissing you, too."

"X. The rookie is X," cried Seed as a security guard pushed them towards the door. The security guard had appeared out of nowhere.

"Shit. Damn. Shit," X said under her breath. Another guard pushed X through the now open door. As the door swung silently shut behind them, X heard a voice.

"Apologies for this Councillors. My name is Park. I volunteer to present both proposals to the Council on behalf of the team, if that would be acceptable to my remaining team members."

Indistinguishable murmurs were all that followed.

X turned and saw Seed waiting over at the lift. She went after them. The lift arrived before she could get across the foyer, and X found herself pounding on the closed elevator door with her fist.

"Seed, wait," she cried. "Come back here, you're ruining my life." For once, she wanted the anger in her voice and not the dull, unemotional sound emitted by her helmet. She looked around furiously for a stairwell but couldn't find one. X sank to the floor near the lift.

"What have you done, you stupid girl?" Her father's voice reverberated in her ears with such venom she looked around to be sure he hadn't suddenly appeared next to her.

X hit her forehead repeatedly with the palm of her right hand. It didn't quite have the intended effect in the suit. She rested her head in her hands. After a while, she looked around. She was alone. She got up and pressed the lift button. It still weirded X out that there was only one button for the lift. There was no up or down, just the call button. The scanner in the lift took you wherever you were supposed to go. As she got in the lift and waved her arm in front of the scanner, X had a flash of despair that the lift would take her somewhere bad. She breathed a sigh of relief when she arrived on the ground floor and quickly exited the building.

CHAPTER THIRTY

X walked through the park to the lake. It was a lovely sunny morning. She longed for the sun on her skin instead of her suit. X knew she should go back to the office to be there when the intercity team got out of the Council meeting. She sighed loudly. After a few minutes, she stopped walking and watched the water birds land on the lake, creating splashes and ripples that stretched all the way to the water's edge. It was calming.

X summoned her courage and walked back to the office. It had been nearly forty minutes since Council had thrown her out of the meeting, and she was probably pushing it to get back before the team got out. While patiently waiting for the lift to take her back to level two with its maze of offices and the den, she glanced at her reflection in the metal doors. The orange tinge of her suit had not returned when she'd entered the building. She held up an arm and saw it was a dull grey. The blood drained from X's face. "This cannot be good," she said.

The lift doors opened, and she got in. She scanned her forearm, and the lift started. X paced back and forth in the tiny space until she felt giddy. The lift stopped and the door behind her opened. X had never realised the lifts in her building had more than one set of doors. She got out. This was definitely not level two. She went over to the abandoned reception desk. This one was a dark timber, almost black. There was a button in the middle of the desk. X read the sign behind the button.

Push for reassignment

X felt like she couldn't breathe. She paced around the foyer. There was not a single person in sight. There were no visible doors out of this place, only the lift. She went over to the lift and pressed the button. A buzzer noise sounded.

"Reassignment incomplete," an automated voice said.

X dropped her head. "What the hell have you done?" she muttered.

She plodded back to the desk. She stood staring at the button, heartbeat thundering in her temples. X took out the screen from her suit and opened a new message. She wrote hastily to Sand, asking him to meet her as soon as possible. X read over the message and felt a little better. She pressed send. An error message popped up immediately.

Contact not found.

X stared at the screen in disbelief. She blinked twice. Her mind scrambled for a new solution. She suddenly remembered Maple's introduction to the team on her first day at work and their offer of help. X would send a simple message, under the guise of checking in. She searched for Maple's contact details. There was no Maple in the system. She put her screen away and felt a numbness creeping into her feet. X reached across and pressed the reassignment button. A door opened in the wall behind. She stumbled into the small dark room, and the door began closing softly behind her. The lights flicked on before the door clicked shut.

"Please remove your suit and place it in the cleanser. It will be cleaned, and your chip will be reprogrammed. Your new work instructions will be ready when you put your suit back on. This process takes approximately five minutes." The voice was the same as that of the house intercom. As soon as the instructions finished they began again.

X removed her helmet and put it on the shelf of the sanitiser machine. As she unzipped her suit, she had a sudden urge to run out of the building just as she was, shorts and a T-shirt. She imagined the wind in her hair, the breeze dancing across her skin. X closed her eyes and saw Guy, arms open, a big smile lighting up his face. She desired nothing but to run to him. To be wrapped in his embrace. Shut out the universe and just be with him. The two of them, together. Like the way it was when they went to the zoo that day. The day after they found each other again.

"I love you Guy."

Tears rolled down her cheeks and dropped from her chin onto her chest, making a dark wet patch on her T-shirt. X looked around for tissues, a towel, anything to dry her eyes and face with. She had become accustomed to the inbuilt tear absorbers in her helmet. There was nothing. She wiped her face with her hands.

"Get a hold of yourself, X. There's no running away from this," she reprimanded.

The harshness of her tone surprised her. It was always strange to hear her wild voice, stripped of its familiar robotic monotone.

"Seriously, X, what would happen if you left here without a suit on? The lift would not come. Security would, though. And they would be on you in under a minute."

X stumbled over to the solitary chair situated at the centre of the room and sat. She waited for the machine to finish. After what felt like an hour, the machine's humming stopped.

"Your suit is ready. We have reassigned you to a new team. Report to level one for your induction."

X glared at the machine.

The machine repeated its monotone message.

She wished she could find something to throw at it to stop that incessant voice. She walked over to the machine. *Level one, what team will this be?* she thought. *Will I ever get to see Field again? What about Park?*

X opened the sanitiser and looked at her suit. It looked clean, brand new, like it had when she'd first got it at the airport that day, months before. It felt so much longer ago. She put it on carefully. When she zipped it up, she realised she felt comfortable again somehow. She felt protected. X gathered her hair and tied it in a low bun, then placed the helmet on her head and fastened it to the suit. She checked her right shoulder. The light was blue.

"That's that then. Time to go meet the new team." The voice that rang around the small room sounded nonchalant instead of resigned.

X walked out of the strange little room and back towards the lift. As she walked across the foyer, she heard the suit reprogram message, muffled from behind a hidden panel. There was someone else on the floor, in this secret part of the building. Someone else getting reprogrammed. X wondered if it was Seed. She hoped she wasn't the only one that had to pay for the mistake. It was, after all, Seed's fault. She felt the scowl on her face, but when she caught her reflection in the metal door of the lift, she could see only the shiny reflection of her dark red helmet. She pressed the button. After a few moments, the lift arrived, and she got in.

CHAPTER THIRTY-ONE

X got in the lift and took the brief journey to compose herself. When she stepped out of the opposite doors at level one, she was unprepared for the bustling foyer. Suits all but filled the space. They were all pink, jostling for space. X took a sharp breath and made her way through the crowd to the reception desk on the far side of the room. She had to wait in the disorderly queue.

When she hustled to the front, she said quietly, "I've been reassigned. I'm not sure which team I was just instructed to come to level one."

"Oh," said the person behind the desk. "Please pass me your screen. I'll have a look."

X removed the screen from her front pocket and passed it over the desk. The person peered at the screen. X imagined them raising their eyebrows under their helmet.

"Hmmm. That is peculiar. I will just have to ask Meadow what this means. I have never seen this before."

The person turned and walked through a hidden door panel. X wondered about all the hidden doors she'd been past and never noticed. She speculated if there were any in her house. She felt her mouth go dry. X looked around and saw the person behind her move their head, as if to look away. She waited and waited. Just when it seemed they had forgotten her, a person returned to the desk, holding her screen.

"X, is it?"

X nodded. "Yes, that's right."

"So, they have reassigned you to our team."

X nodded. She wished this person would keep their voice down. "Right, okay," she said.

"As our team manager."

"Excuse me?"

"You are the new manager. I think you should come around this side of the desk."

"Oh, okay," X said. She walked around the desk. "Sorry, where am I? What team is this?"

"This is City East customer service. We are here to ensure that the people of Xoha have everything they need. If something goes wrong with a service or, well, anything, they come here. You are now leading the complaints team. Welcome to city office complaints."

X's jaw dropped. She stared at the sea of visitors on the other side of the desk. "I. Well. Thank you. What's your name?"

"I'm Meadow. Manager of the complaints team. Until a minute ago, that is. Former manager, I guess it is now."

"Well, this is awkward. I'm sorry. Do you think there's been a mistake?"

"No. City office does not make mistakes. They carefully consider all staffing decisions."

"Right, well. Do you think we could go talk in the office behind here? And leave our colleague to attend to these people's complaints?"

248

"Sure, you are the boss."

The words echoed in her head. X couldn't tell if Meadow was being facetious. It was moments like this that she really missed tone and facial cues. She walked up to the back wall panel and tried to push it open. Nothing happened.

"Scan your hand over the panel," Meadow said.

X blushed and waved her hand. There was a click, and the door swung slowly inward. X and Meadow walked through it into a small room with two large screens in each of the far corners.

"So, I appreciate this is not an ideal situation. But it would be great if you could give me a quick rundown of the team."

"Not ideal. I have only been managing the team for a month. It is not a great job. I think I deserve better anyway. I am going to ask for reassessment straight after this."

"Oh, right. Fair enough, I suppose," X said.

There was a knock at the door and then it opened and a person in a red suit walked in.

"Can I help you?" Meadow asked.

X had opened her mouth to speak but hadn't been quick enough.

"I have just been reassigned here. The person at the desk suggested I come in for an overview briefing."

"I'm the new manager of this team. What's your name?" X asked. She felt emboldened by her anonymity.

"My name is Seed."

"Excuse me?" X said.

"They said Seed," Meadow repeated. "Seed, meet X, the new manager who has just taken my job. I mean, they just assigned X here too. As manager."

"I cannot believe it. I thought this day could not get any worse," Seed said.

"There must be some mistake. We were already working together. Seed's the reason I just got reassigned," X yelled. The even monotone of her helmet made her words sound calm. It eliminated all the sounds of frustration, but the intense feeling remained.

"They do not make mistakes," Meadow replied. "There will be a good reason for this. Now listen carefully and I will tell you what you need to know. This is a small team of three, now five, I guess. We operate the city office complaints function."

X tried to listen, but the thumping in her ears made it exceedingly difficult. *How could they have reassigned me and Seed to the same place?* she thought. *Surely this is wrong? How am I supposed to manage this person? This is my worst nightmare. What am I going to do?*

"And that is the most important part," Meadow said.

X blinked twice quickly. The heat of anger drained rapidly from her face. "And why is it the most important part?" she asked.

"Because it is central to the complaints process," Meadow said.

"You are kidding, right? You are meant to be my new boss. This is ridiculous. I am done here. I am going to request reassessment." Seed turned to leave.

"Wait, Seed," Meadow said. "You cannot ask for reassessment when they have just reassigned you. There is a required waiting period of two weeks. Due process, remember?"

"Oh, great. Well, I am not taking orders from X. How about you stay manager, for the time being anyway? Until this mess gets sorted out. I am sure we can get the other staff to agree."

"That seems highly irregular. But then again, all of this does, really. Well, I suppose if it is alright with X?"

X looked from Meadow to Seed. She didn't know what to say. "Uh, well, I guess it would be helpful if I could mirror you, if you stay the manager for now. Then once I've got a handle on things, we could swap over." Even with the helmet mediating her tone, X knew her choice of words sounded pathetic.

"Okay, it is unanimous, then. I will stay the manager for now. We will go help Air sort out all these complaints. It is hectic out there with Leaf away today." Meadow turned and exited the door.

The noise from the foyer spilled into the enclosed office. X breathed in deeply and followed. As she walked past Seed, they grabbed her arm.

"You will never be my boss," they said. "Just so we are clear."

X shrugged off Seed's grip and kept walking, too stunned to respond.

CHAPTER THIRTY-TWO

The foyer was hectic, with pink suits moving in all directions.

"Air, it is Meadow. We are going to keep running as we were for now. We just received two more team members. Headquarters must have finally realised how understaffed we are."

"Good. I am just helping this person with a housing complaint. The next in line is here for a public space issue." Air turned their attention back to the individual across the counter.

"Right, X, come here."

X stepped forward next to Meadow.

"We will help the next in line. You are up."

"Oh, um. Next please."

The person stepped over in front of them.

"So, you have a complaint relating to public space?"

"Yes, that's right," the person said.

"Can you please detail the nature of your complaint?"

"I have already done so in writing as required. I am following it up in person, as per the stated protocol."

"Please excuse my colleague," Meadow said. "They are new to the team and obviously not good at listening, as I only explained a moment ago about the protocol. Do you have your issue number handy?"

X felt annoyed at herself for not listening earlier.

"Yes, it is UTPS, five, four, nine, three, seven."

"Okay, great. Just enter that issue number into the system and give the person the verification code," Meadow directed.

X fumbled with the screen on the desk but worked out how to enter the issue number. The verification code flashed on the screen.

"Okay, here we are. The code is XUTPS, two, four, four, five, four, nine," X said.

The person entered it into their screen and X saw a green tick flash on the screen in front of her. *Maybe this won't be so bad after all,* she thought.

"What happens next?" X asked Meadow.

"You process the complaint and respond within forty-eight hours," the person said.

"That is correct," said Meadow.

"They are new here, aren't they? Very green," the person said, leaning in towards Meadow. "Are you sure they don't need to be reassessed?"

"No, they ca–they will be all right. They have only been here for five minutes. It is nice to meet someone unfamiliar with the complaints system for a change. You do not see that very often."

"Ha. I guess you are right. Thanks for helping me with this. It is a serious safety issue I am reporting, so I hope it gets addressed right away."

"Thank you for doing your bit to make Xoha live up to its name," Meadow said.

The person raised their hand in the Xohan greeting, turned and left, making their way back through the enlarged crowd.

"One down, a hundred to go. Do you think you can handle the next one on your own? I have got to get back to managing the processing and analysis work."

"Sure," X said. *So much for allowing me to shadow you,* she thought.

"If you have any trouble, just ask Air," Meadow said.

X nodded her head. "Next please," she said.

The next person stepped forward.

"Hi, do you have your issue number ready?" X asked.

The person shook their head. "No, I don't."

"Oh. Right. Well, did you access our online complaint submission? That's the first step in making a complaint."

"I'm sorry, I didn't realise. I'm new around here."

"Oh, that's okay. I'm new too." X smiled. She drew her lips into a straight line when she realised the invisible smile would be of no comfort to this person. "Hold on a minute," she said.

X stepped sideways a few paces. "Air? Can people fill in the online complaint anywhere here?"

Air looked up from the client in front of them. X wondered what look was on Air's face. One of annoyance or indifference.

"Pardon me?" Air said.

"I have a client who hasn't completed an online submission yet. Can they do it here?"

"Yes. That is what the screens at the side there are for." Air gestured to the screens that lay on either side of the foyer.

They were like the ones in the den, set into tall tables and angled for ease of use. X felt a pang of regret at the thought of the den.

"Right, thanks," X replied. She stepped back across to face her customer. "Did you hear that? Good news, you can use the screens over there." X gestured across the room with her hand. "Looks like a bit of a queue, though. You might be better off using your own."

"See, that's the thing. I kind of dropped my screen yesterday and it won't work. So, I took it to the suit repair place, but they told me to go to–"

"I'm sorry to have to cut you off. It's so busy here, and unfortunately, I can't help until you've filled in the online complaint and come back to me. I need the reference number."

"Oh, of course. Must follow procedure. Got it. I'll be back."

X watched the person turn and jostle through the crowd to the screens on the side. For such an organised country, this complaints section was completely disorganised and inefficient.

Maybe I should go talk to Meadow about it, she thought. Then she looked at all the waiting customers and thought better of it. "Next please," X called.

CHAPTER THIRTY-THREE

X sighed as she opened her front door. The rain was bucketing down, the heaviest she had seen since moving to Xoha four months earlier. X opened the umbrella she'd found in the hall closet and braced against the wind. It wasn't until she got halfway to the train station; she realised the umbrella was pointless as the suit completely protected her from the rain. X could not believe her stupidity. She saw heads turned towards her and was glad she could not see the expressions under the helmets.

Why the heck would there be an umbrella in my house? she thought.

As she walked along, holding the useless, folded umbrella, she supposed people must use umbrellas in their own private backyards. Weird. She contemplated running it back home, but didn't really have time for that. As she considered how she could hide it at work, she realised she could not carry the umbrella any further. She stopped walking and looked at the front garden of the house she had stopped in front of. X hastily bent down. Just as she was trying to conceal the unwanted umbrella underneath a bush, she heard a noise beside her.

"What are you doing?" a voice said.

X turned around in fright and shame. "Um, I ... well ... I was just looking for a discreet place to hide my umbrella. I guess it's not so discreet now."

To X's surprise, the person burst out laughing. Although X could not tell by the lack of tone, she imagined a full, hearty laugh from the way they threw back their head.

X gave them a minute to regain composure. "I don't suppose I could store it near your front door. My house is just down the street. Number twenty-six. I can pick it up on the way home after work. I'd run it back now, but I think I'll be late."

"Sure, neighbour. Here, let me take it for you and put it by the door. Are you catching the train?"

"Oh, thanks. You're very kind. Yes, I'm trying to catch the eight fifteen," X said.

"Me too. Just a sec and we can go together. If you don't mind."

"Oh, sure," X said. She waited in front of the hedge.

The person returned; hands empty. "Right, let's be off," they said. "I'm Raven, by the way."

"Hi Raven, I'm X. You're the first bird I've met."

"Excuse me? Oh, my name." Raven laughed again. "You're the second letter I've met, but the first funny one. Come to think of it, this may be the first time I've laughed since I got here."

"I hope you arrived recently."

"Yes, a week ago."

"Oh, well, welcome to Xoha. Are you going to work? Have they assigned you a job yet?"

"Yes, this is my first day. I'm nervous, to be honest."

"That's normal. You'll be fine, though, I'm sure," X said.

"How was your first day?"

"Well, ah. It was strange really, but it was a good job, my first job here."

X and Raven arrived at the station. X checked the sign and was relieved that the train was on time. Although she had never experienced a late train in Xoha.

"So, you've had more than one job, then?"

"Yes, they, um, reassigned me a little while ago. It was a bit of a mess, really. My new job is fine, well, I'm sure it will be. It's just change can be hard, especially after the big transition coming here. How are you finding it?"

"Well, it's been good so far. As expected, I'd say."

X felt her stomach turn. *This person must think I'm an idiot*, she thought. *They seem better adjusted after just one week, while I'm still struggling after months.*

The train pulled up, and the pair alighted. They sat next to one another on a window seat on the right-hand side of the carriage. X marvelled at the sparkling clean carriage.

As if reading her mind, Raven said, "I still can't get over how clean these trains are."

"Yeah," X mused, "me neither."

The pair sat, not speaking.

"I hope I didn't offend you before, X, when I said I'd settled in easily. The truth is, I'd been planning to come here for some time and so I was extremely prepared. But it hasn't been all that easy. I guess I just say that, so hopefully one day I will believe it."

"Oh, no, it's okay. I think in a lot of ways I've made it much harder than it needed to be. I haven't made the best decisions since I arrived and, well, this was supposed to be my one real chance at a new start. And I'm dirty with myself because I think I've mucked it up."

X couldn't stop the honesty from spilling out to this person she had randomly met. This stranger. Although grey suits were both strange and familiar, in this place she now called home. But the relief she felt was blissful. Suddenly, she was grateful for the umbrella experience. It had led her to Raven, who lived in her street. Perhaps this was someone she could make friends with. She could sure use a friend in Xoha. Not a friend like Park; just a friend.

"X, that's the great thing about this place, the ability to keep getting genuine fresh starts, even if you have a few false starts. Haven't you found that with the reassignment?"

"It was supposed to be, I guess. But they reassigned me with this very troublesome person I'd worked with in the previous job. They were the reason for the reassignment in the first place, because they refused to be a team player. Alarmingly, they reassigned me as this person's manager, of all things. And the worst part about it is that the person immediately undermined my authority with the existing manager."

"Wow, that sounds rough," Raven said. They traced their left finger down the right arm of their suit. "But perhaps you need to take a step back and consider your problem from another angle. I'd be happy to talk it over some time."

X looked out the window and saw they were nearly at the city station. "Really? That would be great. Are you free on Friday night?" X blushed at her desperate-sounding words.

"I can do Saturday morning, or afternoon. We could take a walk through the park, and you could run through me through all the issues. I find being outside makes it easier to think."

"Okay, sure," X said. "Saturday afternoon works for me. I'll swing by your house around two?"

"Great."

The train pulled into the station and they got off.

"I better go. It was so nice to meet you, Raven. Have a great first day."

"It was nice meeting you too, X. Have a great day, as well."

X walked through the station. The rain was still bucketing down, but she didn't care. She was dry and warm in her suit. X felt lighter after her conversation with Raven. She looked back, but could no longer see the platform. She wouldn't have been able to distinguish Raven's grey suit from everyone else's anyway.

CHAPTER THIRTY-FOUR

X was glad the sun was shining when she left her house on Saturday afternoon. She walked along the street, noticing how the few deciduous trees were nearly completely bare of autumn leaves. It was as if they had changed colour and dropped overnight. She *had* been in her own head a lot lately. It was nice to be outside and present in this lovely scenery. X hummed a tune as she made the short stroll to Raven's house. That song, again. From back in Melbourne. She never had figured out what it was.

X tried to ignore the homesickness rising in her chest. She walked up the path to the front door at eighty-eight and paused. As she pressed the intercom, the door opened.

"Hi, X."

"Oh, hi Raven. Shall we go?"

"Yes. I've been looking forward to this all week."

"Me too."

As the pair walked the rest of the way down the street, the conversation came easily. There was a familiarity about Raven that X hadn't felt with anyone else in Xoha.

"How was your first week at your new job?" X asked.

"It was good. It took me a while to work out who was who. You really have to look for mannerisms, don't you?"

"Yes. It's difficult, isn't it? And just when you think you've got it, you talk to someone about a project you're working on and they say, 'X, this is so and so, who did you think I was?' It's so frustrating because they know exactly who you are, and you mistake them for someone else."

"It looks like I have a lot to look forward to," Raven speculated.

X and Raven walked past the station and into the park. The path was busy with walkers. The sky overhead was a piercing blue with only half a dozen wispy clouds strewn across it like scuff marks on a newly polished gym floor.

"I'm glad the rain cleared away," X said. "It's such a beautiful day."

"I'm glad you don't need your umbrella," Raven joked.

X gave Raven a playful shove. "Okay smarty, tell me you've never done something here automatically like you would have back home. I mean, your previous home."

"Hmm. Well, I nearly forgot my helmet the other day after I was using the facilities at work. I'd taken my suit off completely just to have a break for a few minutes. I find it stifling sometimes, you know. Anyway, a noise from another cubicle distracted me and I wanted to check it out."

"What was the noise?"

"It sounded like someone crying, but I couldn't be sure. Anyway, I put my suit back on and had a problem with the fastener. Then I heard the noise again and so I unlatched the door. For some unknown reason, I paused in the doorway to run a hand through my hair. I guess it's an old habit of mine and realised I was missing my helmet. I quickly shut the door and put it on."

"Was there anyone in the corridor? Would they have seen you?"

"I don't think so. It was a close call, though."

"Gee, that's lucky. What happened to the person crying?"

"By the time I got out into the corridor, the other cubicles were empty and it was all quiet. I guess they were okay."

"Huh. They must have been."

X looked sideways at Raven. She wondered what they looked like, where they'd come from, why they'd left. It seemed like her head was constantly full of questions about the surrounding suits. It was painful not being able to know people, to only have such a shallow view of almost everyone around you. The thin malleable armour blocking out so much humanity. X wondered if anyone else felt like that or if it was just her.

"So, tell me about this reassignment of yours. How did you know the person you ended up being reassigned with?" Raven asked.

"Well, we were working on an extensive project in my last job, and the manager asked me to consult with them, but they wouldn't engage. We had a presentation coming up, to Council no less, and they were obstructive to the process. At the original Council meeting, the person objected to our proposal. So Council made us return to the next meeting and present the two core proposals, under a united approach. Then, on the day of the presentation, my supervisor had some kind of accident and could not attend, which I didn't find out until we were in the foyer waiting to be called into the room." X took a breath.

"Oh, that sounds super stressful," Raven said.

"It was. Especially since the team manager asked me to present the project to Council and then this deadbeat person interjected once again."

"Oh, no."

"Yes. It made me furious and, well, I guess I lost my cool and ... well, I blew it. Next thing I knew I was on a different floor of city ... of the place I was working. It was so strange, somewhere I didn't know existed. Then I couldn't leave until I had completed the suit reprogramming process, and they had reassigned me." X cringed at nearly giving away her previous employer to Raven, which she knew was against the rules.

"Wow," Raven said. They lifted a hand to their head and then lowered it back down. "What happened then?"

"So, I show up to my new job and they tell me I'm the manager. My suit is a darker tinge than the others, except for the original manager. I guess theirs didn't have a chance to change back. It was all very sudden. I was so confused." X noticed a bird close by her foot. She wondered what the birds and animals thought of these suits. She kicked her leg out at it and the bird flapped its wings. It flew a short distance and pecked at the grass.

"You sure know how to keep a person in suspense," Raven commented.

"Oh, sorry. What was I saying? That's right. So I'm the new manager and just when I was trying to sort that out with the current, or previous manager, awkwardly I might say, this person comes into the back office. They have also just been reassigned."

"No, it couldn't be them."

"That's right. It's the very person who stuffed up the presentation to Council. I was incredulous. How could they reassign us to the same workplace and the same team? It seems like this person is trying to ruin my career."

The couple stopped on top of the bridge and looked into the still waters of the lake. The birds were out in their hundreds, maybe thousands, even.

"That sounds intense," Raven said. "Did you have time to speak to them? Did you lay down some ground rules now that you're the boss?"

"Not exactly. They convinced the manager to stay manager and therefore I'm their peer."

"Oh, that doesn't seem right. I didn't think you could alter assigned roles."

"You're not meant to. I can't get my head around it. This person seems to have an issue with people who are new to Xoha. They use the term 'rookie' like it's a dirty word. And seeing that these suits nullify most intonation that seems like a real skill."

Raven chuckled. "Shall we sit on the bench over there?"

"Sure."

They walked over to the wooden bench criss-crossed with shade from the thick branches of a large, nearly leafless tree, and sat down.

"Have you been able to learn how the place runs and what the manager's role is?" Raven asked.

"Yes. I've been watching and learning. Originally, I asked to shadow the manager, you know, as a compromise when I first came in and there was pushback from Se—from my, ah, nemesis." X put a hand to her head self-consciously. "But the manager just made me work out the front at the desk like the remainder of the team. It was busy, and they didn't have a very good system in place. I've been mapping out a better one that I think will work, and I'm just biding my time until I can try it out."

"And your nemesis, they are doing the same job as you? Is there anyone else working in that role?"

"Yeah, the rest of us all do the same role. There used to be only two people and the manager. But when we got reassigned to the team, one of the three also got reassigned. So, there's four of us in total now. It's a small team."

"So, here's what I would do X, if you don't mind me saying," Raven offered.

"Sure, happy to hear any suggestions."

"Go in there on Monday morning and tell the manager 'Hey thanks for giving me time to learn but I'll take over from here'. You obviously know what you're doing, and you have ideas on how to improve things. Take back the authority that they undermined."

Raven looked in X's direction. At least, that was how it appeared.

X nodded slowly.

"Get in early. Before that joker who's trying to bring you down. Act like the manager and you will be the manager. Your suit shows you are. The others will fall into line. If they don't, report them to the next level up, or whatever the process is."

"Do you really think that will work?" X asked.

"Sure, if you don't back down, it will. Perhaps this is a test from Council, to give you another chance to prove yourself. Think about it. What better way to see what you're really made of than to reassign you with the very individual that made you fail?"

"Huh, I hadn't really considered that. Maybe you're right. Thanks Raven, this has been really helpful. All I need now is some courage and it might actually work. Hopefully, I'll find some before the weekend is through."

Raven laughed. "I'm sure you already have some left over. Coming here to Xoha took courage. Don't we know it? Think about how far you've come. It's not a small thing."

"You're quite the motivational speaker," X replied.

"Ha, thanks."

X studied Raven's helmet, but all she could see was the reflection of blue sky and tree branches.

"Hey X, can I ask, did you have trouble climbing the ladder before you came to Xoha? I know they don't like people talking about the past, but—"

"Yes. That's why I came, really. I kept missing out on promotion after promotion, and, well, I'd had enough."

"Don't let it happen again, then. You do not know what this other person has done in their life, do you? What their qualifications are, who they're friends with. They started at the same base as you did when they arrived here. Remember that and believe in yourself and what you're capable of. That's obviously why you came here."

"Yes, it is." X looked at the lake. She watched a bird dive. It was under the water for what seemed like a full minute, then it popped back up and shook itself free of any evidence of its trip below the surface. "I won't forget that again."

CHAPTER THIRTY-FIVE

X walked into the complaints office early Monday morning with her head held high. She was the first one there and felt bolstered by her chat with Raven.

"You've got this X," she said with conviction but heard only a flat, unconvincing drone.

X began out the back of the office. She turned on a screen in the corner and reviewed the statistics from the previous week, then month, then year. X went into the storeroom that was connected to the office through the typical hidden door in the wall panel. She searched the shelves. At the back of a bottom shelf, she found what she was looking for. Rope dividers. X presumed they were there from the old days when Xoha was first set up. She dragged the heavy metal poles out into the foyer and began setting up some queues. She was halfway through setting up the third line when a colleague arrived.

"What's all this?" they asked.

"This is the new complaints queue. Left for public space issues, including safety concerns and public transport. Middle is for work and system complaints. Right is for home and other personal complaints."

"That's not you Meadow, is it?"

"No. This is X. Your new manager. If you have a problem with the new setup, I suggest you join the middle queue. Otherwise, get over here and help me finish this before the others get in."

The person paused for a moment and then joined X in setting up the last barrier. "Well done, X. I've been waiting for you to step up and take control. I think it's rubbish what Meadow and Seed did when you first started. I've been here for two years, overlooked three times for the manager position, but you don't hear me complaining. You've got to do what they assign you to do. That's how it works here. Sometimes you can't see the reasoning, but it's all part of the mechanics that make this place special, that make it work. The complaints process is integral to that. It's an honour to work here."

X realised she'd missed the opportunity to talk one-on-one with Air until now. "Thanks, Air. You've really put things into perspective. Now, I was thinking we need some digital signs, and we need better people flow once they enter the foyer. The screens on the side aren't quite in the right place. Any ideas?"

"Well, um, let's see. We could create a small waiting area at the very front and section off the screen there. I'll also reprogram it so that people get the information onto their personal screens once they enter. We can have the floor plan pop up and colour-code the queues."

"Fabulous. That sounds great, thanks. I'll go out back and get some chairs while you reprogram." X smiled. It was all coming together. At least Air believed in her. They would have her back when the others arrived. She thought she had a better chance if it became two against two.

X pushed the panel and strode into the office. She almost leaped out of her suit.

"What are you playing at X?" The person, who X quickly assumed was Meadow, was standing before the left-hand corner screen.

"How did you get in here?" X asked.

"There's a back entrance to the office. Anyway, that's not the point. What have you done with my foyer?"

"How did you … know?" X looked at the screen and saw the foyer. "Oh, right. Well, it doesn't matter." She took a deep breath. "Meadow, I'm the manager here now. Things are going to change. I've been–"

"Oh, I can see what you've been doing. You're very game to–"

"No," X said. "You're very game. They assigned me as manager here. I didn't ask for it. It was a directive. That's how this place works. That's what we're here to protect. We take complaints to ensure we've got it right. To analyse the data and make changes if we need to. With the power of control over how people live and work comes great responsibility to always ensure we are upholding the values of no discrimination, of equality. And they have asked me to oversee this important function, to manage this team. And, well, I'm going to do it to the best of my ability."

"Nice little speech," a voice said from behind.

X spun around. She glanced sideways at the screen to see Air still reprogramming in the foyer. "I'm glad you're here, Seed. You need to know the new setup here. I'm the manager and we're changing things around to provide more streamlined processing of complaints. I've got Air reprogramming the foyer screen and then they'll organise the digital signs to place above each queue. If you have any good ideas, I'm happy to hear them. Otherwise, join the middle queue to make a job complaint when we open in five minutes. Or you could just get to work." X stormed through the back door into the storage room. She placed her hand on her chest but couldn't feel her racing heart through the metal suit. *Maybe this is the coat of armour I've always needed,* she thought.

X grabbed a stack of three chairs and carried them through the now empty office and into the foyer. There was a red suit behind each section of the desk. After she'd set out the chairs, she examined the new setup. "This is great," she said. "A big thanks to Air for helping make this happen. It's going to be a great day."

Someone (she supposed Seed) grunted.

CHAPTER THIRTY-SIX

X spent the next few months making improvements to the system she'd implemented at the complaints office. Seed had surprisingly fallen into line and seemed to enjoy the newfound calm at the office. Meadow seemed relieved that X had taken over and although they told X they were planning on getting a reassessment, the weeks went by, and they were still there. X tried to remember what they'd said when she arrived, something like it not being a great job. *I guess it's what you make of it,* she thought.

* * *

The morning of the last day of winter, everything changed. X turned up to work early as usual and went straight out the back to analyse the complaints from the day before. There had been a worrying increase in complaints of indecent exposure. Two people in the suburb of Eastleft had submitted complaints the day before. This took the weekly tally to twelve.

In the latest reports, both individuals were on their way to work and walking through the park towards the city. One said the incident happened at eight fifteen, while the other said they happened upon it at 8:23 a.m. The first had used their emergency alarm to call law enforcement. Two units had arrived at the park at 8:25 a.m. and 8:29 a.m. respectively, both from different directions, but by the time they got to the individual that had raised the alarm, the offender had fled. Air had received the reports as they were looking after the system complaints queue that day. X looked up the reports from earlier in the week. They were from different times of day, but always when people were on their way to or from work or at lunchtime.

What intrigued X most about these reports was the lack of information. The description of the offender was vague, a person without their suit holding a sign. The report had photos taken from security cameras attached, but they were locked, along with all other details. Even X, as manager, couldn't access the restricted content. Usually, all complaints, even those where law enforcement was involved, had open access to information so the manager could assess them in the context of other complaints. Often the ones that came directly from law enforcement had the most information, as they just provided access to the file in the law enforcement system. These were usually the easiest to manage as they came to a natural outcome through the justice system, which was very efficient and streamlined across Xoha.

"Of course!" X said.

Someone knocked and entered the office. "Good morning, X. Of course, what?"

"Oh, I was just reviewing the stats and came across some recent repeat activity that's very interesting. I just realised I should see if there are similar cases in the other cities."

"Alright," her colleague said. "I'm on systems complaints today."

"Oh, so it's Meadow then," X said.

"Yes. You're still having trouble recognising me then?"

"Yeah, well, I have had my head buried in this—"

"I'm just teasing, X. I'm so glad it's Friday, aren't you?"

"Sure," X said. "Hey, can you look out for any indecent exposure complaints—an unsuited individual carrying a sign—and let me know, so I can handle it?"

"That sounds pretty minor. Is that what your repeat cases are?"

"Yes."

"What's the sign say?"

"It's classified."

"Oh, so you can't tell me, but I might hear it if someone tells me, anyway. Come on X, you can trust me."

"Not even I can access it."

"Oh, that's strange. Yeah, sure, I'll let you know."

"Thanks. Can you also let me know when Air gets in? I mean, ask them to come see me. They lodged the reports from yesterday."

"Sure, but you know you can just look at the foyer cameras on the screen."

"Yes, but I'm using it for my analysis right now."

"Can't do two things at once."

"Sorry?" X looked up at Meadow.

"Sure, will do. Happy Friday."

"Yeah, you too."

Meadow left the office, and X logged into the intercity portal to search for similar reports across Xoha.

***

"Boss, you wanted to see me?"

X looked over her shoulder. "Air. Yes, I did." She walked over to them. "You took two reports yesterday about an indecent exposure in the Eastside Park. Do you remember?"

"Um, yes. One was a person who'd called law enforcement and once I found the report in the system, I let them know it was all taken care of. The other, yeah, that's right, it was kind of weird. The person came in on their lunch break. They'd scheduled the time after submitting the complaint online when they got to work. I looked up the reference number. Most of the detail was inaccessible. You know, locked. I asked the complainant some questions. Like, what did the sign say, but they said they couldn't say. I ticked off the attendance box on the file and the report disappeared from the screen, so I told them it was complete, and they left. The whole thing took less than a few minutes."

"Hmmm. Odd. Thanks Air."

"Do you know why there's all this secrecy?"

"No. They must have a reason. I'm sure it's no big deal."

"Yeah, might just be a glitch in the system. It seemed like a fairly minor thing, the indecent exposure, I mean. Probably some newbie not coping with the change and went for a walk unsuited in the park. We've all dreamt of doing that at some point, aren't I right?"

"Huh. Yeah, I guess so," X said, blushing.

* * *

When the late alert came through for the weekly report, X jumped. She'd been poring over the files from all four cities the entire morning and had completely forgotten the deadline. She scrambled to pull it together during what should have been her lunch break.

X was determined to work out the pattern that was emerging from indecent exposure reports across Xoha. The first complaints came a month ago. By the end of the day, she had an outline of activity that spanned nearly the entire country, except City West. X had been there once after a trip to blue lake. It was very similar to City East. In fact, it was tough to tell each city of Xoha apart. The key geographical features were the only actual difference. It was hard to see them from many parts of the suburbs. Mostly, each suburb was indistinguishable from the next. All trains from the suburbs went to the city. Trains from the city connected to two other cities and the airport, which lay in the centre of the country, an equal distance from each of the four cities. That meant it was extremely difficult to get lost.

"Bye, X, have a great weekend."

X looked up from her seat. She shifted position and felt the tension in her neck and shoulders from being hunched over the portable screen for the last few hours. "Bye, Air. Have a great weekend too. That is Air, isn't it?"

"Yes, it is. How can you tell?"

"Just a lucky guess. Hey, I've been meaning to say thanks for all your hard work lately. I think we've really got things running smoothly here now. You've played a big part in making that happen."

"Oh, well thanks, X. Nice of you to say. By the way, everyone else has already left. You going soon too?"

"Yeah, in a minute."

"Good. Don't stay too long, go out and enjoy yourself. It's the weekend. Work can wait until Monday."

"Sure. Yes, you're right. It can wait."

X watched Air leave the office and walk into the foyer as the door swung gently shut. She couldn't help but feel uneasy about this string of complaints. Something didn't sit right.

"Get a grip on yourself, X," she said.

She quickly packed away the screens and switched on the backup. X turned off the lights and walked out into the foyer. As she stood there waiting for the lift, X knew they could access anything she did, both personally and at work. But she felt a little more comfortable using her personal screen. It was less obviously linked to her work.

X walked back across the room. She suddenly wondered about the secret doors. Meadow had given her a huge fright the day she imparted her authority over the team by appearing out of nowhere. X walked along the panelled wall, pressing the wall and waving her forearm in front of it every few steps. It seemed strange for a secret door to be somewhere here, only metres from the main door panel behind the complaints desk. X couldn't find anything. She vowed to remember to ask Meadow next week, then returned to the office via the usual door. She turned the light on, found her screen, replaced it into her suit pocket, then left.

CHAPTER THIRTY-SEVEN

X awoke in a pool of sweat. The nightmare fell away as she opened her eyes and saw her bedroom, just as it was the day before. The dream had been full of dark corridors and conspiracy and although she couldn't grasp its detail; she knew it involved Meadow, Seed, and Field. Park had been there too, completely cold, indifferent towards her. She wondered how Park was, remembering with regret those awful words she'd said that had ended things so abruptly between them. X had tried calling and messaging, but there had been no reply. *It was probably for the best,* she thought. *We were way too different. It would never have lasted, anyway.* Her chest heaved, and she breathed deeply. The calmness slowly returned.

X looked around the room. She really loved her house. It was comfortable, homely and spacious—the polar opposite of the tired old apartment she'd left back in Melbourne.

"At least you had someone to love and care about you in Melbourne." Stella's voice was in her ear.

She turned her head, but there was no one there. Just her, in the comfortable but lonely room. X rose from the bed, shaking off the sheet and the memories of home. She didn't need them weighing her down. Right or wrong, she'd made her decision and now she was stuck with it, the good and the bad.

X considered going for a run but remembered how uncomfortable it was in her suit. She'd been meaning to get one of the new sports suits that were being issued. The high number of complaints her office, and the other city complaints offices, had received about the standard issue suit being completely impractical for high-intensity activity had spurred innovation. They issued the sports suits at no cost; you just had to place an order and go down and pick it up. It didn't seem that challenging, but X hadn't found the time. Instead, she used the sanitising cubicle and ate some breakfast absentmindedly.

Saturday. What to do on Saturday? she thought.

She considered going to the yoga group she had found that met at the park, but the thought of doing yoga in a suit was very unappealing. It just didn't seem right. X decided to go to the local farmer's market to buy some more fruit and vegetables. The market always had a good vibe and perhaps being around people would stave off the loneliness. After putting on her suit, she left the house and strolled down the street. She paused in front of Raven's house and looked at the time.

8:23 a.m.

Not that early. But it was Saturday. She followed her impulse and pressed the door buzzer.

The panel made a small zapping sound. "Hello?"

"Hi, Raven, it's X. I was just passing on my way to the farmer's market and thought you might want to join me. Would you like to come … to the farmer's market?" X held her hand to her head, embarrassed by her awkwardness. The sensation of metal glove on helmet was so uncomfortable it only added to her embarrassment.

"Um, no, not today. I've got someone here. Thanks for the invitation, though. If you're around tomorrow, we could take a walk in the afternoon."

"Oh, right, sure. Yeah, tomorrow afternoon sounds good. I'll drop by then."

"See you X, have fun at the farmer's market."

X sighed. She couldn't tell if this was genuine or teasing. She hurried back down Raven's path and along the street. X felt a stabbing pain in her heart. Raven had someone with them. She'd been trying to get invited over to Raven's house for weeks and every time she'd invited them to her house, there had been a clash. From their first chance meeting, X had been attracted to Raven. She longed to see them unsuited.

They're making up excuses, she thought.

Raven's not interested in you. They can tell you're desperate.

Raven is probably in a relationship with that someone who is there, at 8.23 a.m. on a Saturday.

They haven't told you because they don't care about you.

They don't need you. Nobody needs you.

You shared too much with Raven.

No wonder they're not interested.

You're pathetic.

A new pang of hurt stung her gut.

* * *

X wandered aimlessly around the farmer's market. She'd picked out the food she wanted within a few minutes. The brief chats she'd had with the vendors hadn't been at all satisfying, and she scowled inside her helmet at the couples and trios that seemed to surround her.

X left. She ambled towards home. She had no reason to rush. There was nothing waiting for her. As X walked through the park that wrapped around the city, her mind wandered back to work and the indecent exposure in the parks across the four cities of Xoha. X wished she saw that person now, unsuited in the park. What would their sign say? At least it would add a little excitement to her day, her weekend. She could certainly use some of that.

X thought about arranging a stakeout to find the person herself. She knew the remaining suburbs that hadn't been 'hit' by the offender yet. She felt a rush of excitement.

"Why shouldn't I do it?" she asked herself.

X decided to wait until mid-week, to see what moves they made on Monday and Tuesday. She pondered how she would get out of work. Perhaps fake an illness or make up an intercity meeting that she needed to attend. Better yet, arrange a real intercity meeting and go to the park at lunchtime on the way back. *Yes, that's it,* she thought. *Create a legitimate reason to be there.*

X came to the playground on one side of the park and stood watching the families play. The way the kids interacted in suits fascinated her. They looked so cute in their mini-sized suits. X hoped she would get a glimpse of a baby. Most times, the shields of prams concealed the baby so you couldn't see them unless you were right up close. It wasn't really the done thing in Xoha, to walk up to a family with a pram and peer down through the shield. Even though that's what X felt like doing right at that moment. She thought about how the authorities in Xoha didn't assign a gender to babies. Adults could choose one if they wished, but it wasn't mandatory.

X marvelled at how, even in suits, the children liked to do the kinds of things kids did back home. Her childhood memories were a blur. But the fun of running, jumping, and skipping seemed to be universal. She thought how wonderful it would be to have a baby in Xoha. But X was old school. Traditional. She would like to have a baby with a partner. She was certain that partner would be a man. X wanted to have a family. And she would really like to do it in the not-too-distant future. At least find someone. She'd been feeling her body clock ticking faster this past year, which was weird. She was still young. But time had a habit of running away.

"Which one's yours?"

X jumped, startled from her daydream by the stranger. "Oh. None actually. I was just passing by and … well … um–"

"I'm glad I'm not the only one who likes to watch the kids. But not at all in a creepy way. I'm sorry, that sounded creepy. Do you know what I mean?"

"Yeah, totally. I just like to see them play and interact in their suits. It's fascinating."

"Me too. There is something about them, a freedom they seem to enjoy that we adults can't sustain."

"When you put it like that, it sounds depressing."

"Well, it kind of is sometimes."

There was an uneasy silence.

"I'm Aqua, by the way. I live up that street there." The person gestured up a street X could just make out beyond the park.

"Hi Aqua. I'm X. I live further out." She flicked her wrist and looked at the digital display. "Oh, is that the time? I actually need to get going. Have a nice day."

X walked away, heart thumping in her throat. *What did you do that for? You could have made a new friend, or more, with someone who likes kids,* she thought. X strode home, her frustration mounting the closer she got to Raven's house. She rushed past it, as if worried that someone might come out the door. Even though she was unrecognisable in her dull grey suit, she felt somewhat conspicuous.

After completing the unsuiting ritual, she flopped on her bed and felt like she was back home in Melbourne, in her old life. She suddenly missed Guy terribly. Maybe that's why she fled from meeting someone new at the playground earlier. Even though it was early afternoon, and she hadn't eaten since breakfast, her eyelids seemed too heavy to stay open. She rolled over onto her side and pulled her knees up. She thought about Guy and Stella and drifted off to sleep.

*

Walking along St Kilda beach, she saw Stella off in the distance in her pink yoga top and leopard print tights. She jogged over to her.

"There you are," Stella said. "I've been looking for you. Shall we start the class now?"

X nodded. She found her mat already laid out on the sand and started stretching. The sun felt glorious on her skin, and she smiled. She looked around her yoga class and saw the familiar faces. Then she turned, and she was in Guy's apartment, sitting on the couch.

Guy entered the room and handed her a glass of wine. "You look so lovely today," he said. His voice was husky. His sandalwood scent filled her nostrils.

They gulped down the wine, and then they were between the sheets. Guy's light kisses caressed her neck. Then he was on top of her. They rolled over, and she was on top of him. She felt like a light was shining, then bursting out of her chest until she was in ecstasy.

*

X awoke panting, in a ball of sweat. As she rose from her bed to get a glass of water, a cloud of regret shrouded her. *Why did I leave?* she thought. Her stomach grumbled. Resolving only to focus on the hunger, she headed for the kitchen.

After stuffing her face, X sat down on the couch with a glass of wine. The food distraction had been short-lived. X longed to get a message to Guy. She knew there was no way to get anything digital out of the closed and perfectly secure Xoha network. X thought about all the texts they'd sent to one another at bedtime. If she'd received a 'goodnight' message from Guy right then, she would have replied with her usual 'sweet dreams' with an additional 'I love you'. She got up off the couch and scrounged around for some paper. She looked in half-a-dozen places before locating a slim notebook at the rear of the sideboard drawer. Thankfully, there was a wooden pencil with it. She scrawled out a love note and then folded it meticulously and put it in her pillowcase. That night in bed, she tried to send Guy the message telepathically.

CHAPTER THIRTY-EIGHT

X headed out early for her meeting with Glade in City West. She had arranged it on the pretense that she was testing a new process and wanted to run it past another complaints manager to see if it might work in their context. Perhaps she could help them roll it out, too. X wanted an opportunity to return to City West later on. In case there was action from the repeat offender. She had an unsettling imperative to investigate. X knew she should probably try to work with law enforcement on this plan, but was compelled not to engage with them. She wanted to check it out herself. Perhaps it was just the prospect of seeing someone unsuited out in public. It made X feel extremely excited.

Glade had only been available after lunch, at such short notice, but X went mid-morning so she could be in the park at lunchtime. She'd checked the system before leaving. There had been no reports of indecent exposure that morning. When she arrived at the edge of the park, she looked left and right and didn't know where to wait.

Westside Park was large, like the other city parks. After she entered through its gates, she headed left and meandered along, looking for higher ground or some other vantage point. There was a slight rise but no bench to sit on or bridge to stand on, like at her local park. After standing for a while, she sat on the grass. Nothing happened. A few people in suits walked by. Twenty minutes passed. Her stomach rumbled. X was sure there had to be a drinks kiosk in the park and so went back the way she had come. She ventured into the other side of the park.

X found the kiosk and a lot of commotion. While she waited in line, she watched as a person give a report to a law enforcement officer in a khaki green suit. Their partner walked around, talking to the small groups of people milling nearby. When X got to the front, she ordered a purple smoothie.

"What's all this fuss about?" X asked, heart palpitating in her chest.

"Oh, it's quite shocking. There was a person here, without their suit on. They were standing over there." The person behind the counter gestured to the grass on the left of the path. "They seemed to appear out of nowhere. The security cameras picked them up, of course, but they fled before law enforcement arrived."

"Gee, that's full on." X fidgeted with the front pocket of her suit. "Did they have a sign?"

"As a matter of fact, they did. That's a strange thing to ask, though."

X blushed. "Oh, well," she stammered. "You know, I just guessed they might have been trying to get people's attention, or something." She swallowed. "Did you happen to see what it said?"

"No, I couldn't see it from here. They held it up, but it was facing the other direction. Law enforcement may have been able to see it through the eyes around the kiosk."

"Hmm. How weird. Has this, um, happened here before?"

"Not in the six years I've been working this kiosk." The person passed the cold drink to X. "Anyway, here's your smoothie."

"Thanks." X took the drink and walked across to a group of onlookers. She steeled herself. "Hi, did any of you see what happened?"

The three people turned towards her. "No, we didn't," one said.

"Really? It's very disconcerting having law enforcement here." No one spoke. X waited. "Very disconcerting," she repeated. X got the impression they'd been told not to say anything. She looked around and decided there was only one option.

X waited until law enforcement left and followed the person they had interviewed along the path. She desperately wanted to run up to them and question them about the sign, but was a bit put off by the onlookers' reaction to her questions. The person was walking fast, really striding out. At least they were heading towards the city, which was where X needed to be. She sipped her smoothie through the helmet straw hole and tried to keep up.

"I can't believe I was so close," X muttered between sips. She knew if the person got out of sight, she'd lose them in a crowd and have no chance of finding out what was on that sign. After ten minutes she could still see them, but the gap between the two had increased to where X would have to jog to see where they were going or risk losing them around a corner. X pitched her half-drunk smoothie into the reuse receptacle alongside the path and tried to pick up the pace.

She saw the person turn down a path that led to the city centre and jogged a few paces to get a view down the shady arcade. A few minutes later she realised the person had entered city hall. She followed through the doors not far behind them and saw them wait at the security desk.

"They obviously don't work here," X said.

By the time she joined the queue, she was a couple of people behind them. *Please, please, please be going to the complaints department*, she thought. *That way, I have a legitimate reason to follow you.* She couldn't hear what was being said between the person and the security personnel. X watched them take back their chip from security and click it into their suit. The suit turned the familiar visitor pink.

X checked the time. She had five minutes until her meeting with Glade. X waited in line, tapping her foot on the floor like a petulant toddler. She strained her neck to see the person walk through the security gates to the lift. She couldn't see the lifts very well from where she was standing. X was sure she had lost the target—unless they were going to the complaints office, and even then, it would be nearly impossible to get any information from them.

Finally, after what seemed like ages, X advanced to the front of the line.

"Hi. I'm here to see Glade, the complaints manager. I'm from City East's city office." X handed over her chip to the security personnel.

The person took it and scanned it. They typed something into their screen, scanned it again, and handed her back the chip. "Thanks X. Just scan in on any of the lifts and they will take you to level one. Head straight to the desk and someone will show you through to the back. Have a nice day."

"Thanks." X took the chip and inserted it back into her suit. She hurried through the barriers and looked around. There were people moving in all directions and only one pink visitor suit. It disappeared into a lift. X sighed. She was too far behind. She pushed her way into the next available lift. X arrived swiftly to the foyer of a familiar-looking level one.

The complaints office was buzzing with people and disorder. X walked to the desk and stood to the side. Perhaps her target had come up and she could hear their interaction. It seemed like a long shot in this madness. It was time for her meeting. *Maybe I can get something useful out of Glade*, she thought. X stepped forward and raised her hand. "I'm here to see Glade. I'm from the intercity office," she shouted.

A dark red suit moved forwards. "Hi, you must be X."

"Yes, that's right."

"It's nice to meet you. This way, please."

X followed Glade to a panel in the back wall that opened into another familiar room. The back office.

"Welcome to our office."

"Thanks for having me, Glade. I appreciate you meeting with me at short notice."

"No problem. So, tell me about these exciting changes you've made to the City East complaints office. Do you want to sit?" Glade gestured to the small booth in one corner of the room.

"Sure, thanks." X detailed the changes she'd made, outlining the positive impact they had made to the functioning of the office. Glade listened intently. When X had finished, Glade asked about a dozen questions. They seemed eager to learn and X was sure they'd have the office running as smoothly as hers in no time. X waited for a gap in the conversation. Her heart fluttered, and she smoothed down her suit as she would have done to her clothes in the old days. There was a pause.

"Glade, I was wondering if you've had any complaints about indecent exposure lately. I know it might seem like an odd question." X restlessly fiddled with the front pocket of her suit. "We've seen a huge spike and I'm convinced it's all from the same person. I've been looking at the data for patterns and anyway, I just wondered if you'd noticed anything similar."

"Indecent exposure," Glade said. "Hmm. Not that I know of. I have seen no complaints like that for years. We used to have a stack within a couple of weeks after new arrivals."

"Oh, really?" X's heart skipped a beat.

"Yeah, but they changed the integration process and fixed the problem, or so I thought."

X chewed on the side of her lip awkwardly in her helmet. "Would you mind checking in the system in case something's come in today? From the data, it looked like the offender may be headed in your direction. As long as it's not too much trouble, I would appreciate if you could have a look."

"Oh. Well, sure. Let's have a look here." Glade touched the screen on the wall beside them. They entered the inquiry into the system. Up came a report entry from twenty minutes earlier. Bingo.

"Well, what do you know," said Glade. "There was a report from lunchtime in Westside Park, from the middle section." Glade tried to open the report, but it was locked. "That's strange. I can't get any detail on it. It's been locked. Did you have this trouble with yours?"

"Yes," X said. "It is strange, but probably just a public safety thing."

"Perhaps." Glade looked up from the screen and turned their head in X's direction. "I have only come across one locked report in my time," they said.

"Oh. And do you know why it was locked?"

"Well. I am only telling you this because you are a manager. Manager to manager, you know."

"Sure, okay."

"They locked the report because it involved city office personnel and they could not risk them getting involved. Or, you know, messing with the files or something. They quickly reassigned the person involved, though."

"Oh." X felt her stomach drop.

"If this has been going on for some time, as you say, and they can't catch the offender, well, that seems bad. Have you had any reassignments?"

"Not from my office, no."

"Mine either. This is most peculiar X."

X felt the hairs on the back of her neck prickle. What if the report involved someone from the complaints office? Perhaps she could check in the system for reassignments from the other city complaints offices. Although that information would probably be secret. It wasn't someone from her office.

"When I first joined the office, they had just lost someone to a reassignment," X said.

"When was that?" asked Glade.

"A few months ago."

"It seems unlikely to be related if it was before all this started happening." Glade shook their head.

X remembered Meadow had said they might ask to be reassigned. But that was months ago too. X felt like her head might explode. There was silence. X looked at Glade's dark red helmet and wondered what lay underneath.

Glade stood.

X hesitated, then stood. "Well, I'd best be off, I suppose. Thanks for meeting with me. I hope you got something out of it, and you can get some wonderful outcomes."

"Thank you, X, it's been great. You should come back in a few months. I'm sure we will impress you with the changes we will have made by then."

"Sure, that would be great. And if you're ever visiting City East, come say hi at the complaints office."

"Okay, will do. I will see you out."

"Thanks, but there's no need. I'll make my way back out. Bye for now." X left the complaints office. She was eager to get back to work so she could do some further investigation. She began planning an excuse to come back to City West the following day.

* * *

"How did you go, X?"

"Really well thanks, is that you, Air?"

"Yes, it's me. You're getting quite good at that now, knowing who's who."

X smiled. "I suppose I am. The office set up there is so similar, they had the same chaos as we used to."

"Do you think they will make any changes?"

"Yeah, I think so. The manager seemed keen on it. Anyway, I best be getting back to it."

X disappeared through the back panel door. "Hi Meadow," she said confidently when she saw the familiar suit out back.

"It's Seed," they replied.

"Oh, sorry. I was on such a roll. Hi Seed." X rolled her eyes. "Have you been taking care of the reporting for me?"

"Yeah," said Seed. "I've been looking through today's reports. There's something I can't figure out."

X walked over to look at the screen Seed was standing in front of. "Let me see."

"This, here. See how these reports from last week are linked to a new report in City West? But I cannot clear it from the system. It seems like it has been tagged."

"Oh, don't worry, I'll fix that. I think it must have been something I did the other day. I was working on an intercity report." X's cheeks flared hot inside her helmet. She was relieved that the suit's cooling kicked up a level.

"It's not just that," Seed said. "There is also a … um. I am not sure if I should tell you this. There is also a red flag in the system."

"What do you mean? What red flag? You should definitely tell me about red flags. I'm the manager. It seems like something I should know about. I know we've had our differences in the past, Seed, but you've proven to be a valuable colleague here in the complaints office." X paused. There was no response. "What red flag?" X's dull voice belied her exasperation.

"Well, I guess I am obliged to tell the manager."

X couldn't hear it but assumed there was sarcasm in Seed's voice.

"But not here. Come into the storeroom." Seed walked through the back door.

X followed. Her stomach dropped.

Seed locked the door behind them. "You need to take," they said, pausing, "it off."

"Huh?" she replied, then watched astounded, as Seed removed their suit in a smooth motion and before her stood a handsome man of around forty, in a T-shirt and faded shorts.

He put the suit in the metal trunk that sat next to a shelving unit full of cables. He gestured to X to do the same.

She quickly obliged and removed her helmet. "I must warn you I didn't put on more than underwear today," she whispered.

Seed raised his eyebrows.

X blushed, this time without a helmet to conceal it.

Once they had safely stowed their suits, Seed said, in a much higher voice than X expected, "They have put a tag on someone in this office. Which means they likely track that person's every move, every connection, conversation."

X's eyes bulged. "This is to do with the indecent exposure cases, isn't it?"

Seed nodded.

"Who are they tracing? It's Meadow, isn't it? I've been working this through in my head and I think they're connected somehow."

"No, X, it is you."

"What? I don't understand."

"When did you start looking into these cases?"

"Not long ago, maybe a week or two."

"Well, it looks like they flagged you in the system since the first incident over a month ago."

"How did you find the flag? I couldn't see it. This doesn't make any sense. I've only come to know about it recently and–"

"Don't you see, X? The person must be linked to you. Maybe someone you knew before you came here, someone from your past."

X's eyes were like saucers. Her head felt like it might burst with the grenades of questions rolling around her mind. The most urgent one that hung in her throat, threatening to escape her mouth, was: *How do I know I can trust you?*

It was the last thing she should say to him. She knew it would not get the desired result. X looked from the door to Seed, to the trunk where her suit lay. She didn't know what to do.

Seed followed her eyes, awaiting her response.

"Oh, right. Of course. So, by locking the details in the system, they're trying to protect me from someone that has tracked me down and come all the way here to find me. To hurt me, maybe?" X said. *Get the hell out of here, X,* she thought. Sweat trickled from her brow down the bridge of her nose. She swiped at it furiously, longing for the protection of her suit.

"Do you think someone is trying to hurt you?"

"Well, no. I don't think so, really." X chewed the end of her thumbnail. "But I suppose Council is trying to protect me, protect us all from some potential threat."

Seed looked at X with questioning eyes.

X felt her throat constrict. It was an effort to swallow. "Well, thanks for bringing this to my attention, I–"

"What do you plan to do?"

"Well, I'm not sure yet. At least I know I have a confidante to come to once I've thought through all this. It's a lot to process."

"Of course, this is just between you and me. But be careful X, if there is one thing I know, it's that the past can bring us down." Seed smiled kindly at X.

She wondered if she'd been wrong about him all along. "Thanks, I will," she said.

CHAPTER THIRTY-NINE

X paced up and down her living room. The suit refresher hummed in the background. She turned over the facts in her head. There was a person she knew who had come to Xoha and was out in the streets without a suit, holding a sign. She couldn't find out the description of the person or what the sign said. This information was classified. X wished she had a contact in law enforcement. She sat on the edge of the couch and studied the map she had made of the locations the person had been seen. She had scribbled down most of the dates of the sightings. Her handwriting was messy from lack of practice, and she squinted at it, trying to decipher the rushed strokes.

By her calculations, the unsuited individual would be at the Westside Park, left section today or tomorrow. Sometimes the reports came one day after the other. Other times, they were a few days apart. X wondered if that was to keep ahead of law enforcement.

"Why haven't they just blocked the park entrances?" she asked the empty room. Her question hung in the air, and she looked around the living room, suddenly suspicious. *What if they've bugged my house?* she thought. *Best not say anything out loud.* She longed to talk to someone about it, to run it over with someone external to this whole thing. *Raven,* she thought. *But can I trust them?*

X went to the refresher and paced back and forth until it finally signalled the finished beeps. She hurriedly put her suit on. She took out her screen and opened a new message. X paused, staring at the 'To' box, trying to decide who to send it to. X didn't have Raven's details. There was nothing appealing about rushing up to their house and pressing the intercom. Been there, done that. She decided on Field. X hadn't spoken to Field since before the Council meeting. Perhaps if she could just talk things over, she could get this whole business straight in her head. Field was sensible, and experienced, and she felt like they had a good connection. X typed out a brief message, not wanting to give much away or sound as desperate as she felt. She re-read it one last time and nodded to herself, then pressed 'Send'. The reply popped up instantaneously:

Contact not found.

X looked at her screen in disbelief. She returned it to her suit. Then she paced up and down the living room once more. And again. After the third time, she took a deep breath, bit the side of her lip and left the house. X power-walked down the street, then hesitated at Raven's door. She knocked vigorously, then shook her head. *Use the intercom, you silly girl,* she thought. X pressed hard on the door buzzer.

"Hello," the familiar monotone voice said through the intercom.

"Raven, it's me, X. Can we talk? It's, um, kind of urgent."

"Ah, well."

"Please. I don't know who else to turn to."

"Sure, X. It's just, I'm not alone."

"Oh. Right. Sorry."

"It's okay. Do you want to come in?" Raven asked.

X fought her desperate urge to shout yes. Here was the invitation she had been waiting for. After months of wanting to see Raven in the flesh, an opportunity. But they weren't alone.

"Come in, X. You sound frantic. And that's hard to do in a suit."

The door clicked open, and X entered the house, debating her next move. She both wanted and didn't want to take off her suit at the same time. She kept it on. X walked reluctantly out of the entrance hall. She felt uneasy in her suit inside a house.

"Thanks, I just needed to talk something over with you. It's a work thing," she called out as she entered the lounge room.

Raven's floor plan was the exact opposite of X's. The bedroom wing was to the left and the kitchen and dining room beyond the lounge to the right. Raven was in the kitchen pouring a jug of liquid, with ice cubes, into two glasses. His back was to X. He was slim built with sandy blonde hair. As X walked in, he turned around.

"No need to be shy, X. You can take off your suit."

"Oh, no, it's not that. I can't stay long, I need to ... ah," X faltered as a familiar face entered from the bedroom wing.

Park's long hair was shiny clean, and she was wearing only a robe.

X couldn't believe her eyes. "Park. My goodness. I, um, how are you?" she stammered. She leaned on the back of a chair to steady herself.

"You two know each other?" Raven said, astonished.

Park looked at X, bewildered by this person in a grey suit.

"I shouldn't have, uh. I've made ... well ... I should, uh ... I'm going to go. Sorry." X turned and strode out.

She heard them call after her. She couldn't get out of the house fast enough. As the front door swung gently closed behind her, she jogged down the path and ran into the street. X ran all the way to the park, through the gates, and flopped down onto the park bench. Tears streamed down her face. She felt the soft cloths at her cheeks, catching the deluge. Her suit's climate control went into overdrive.

The park was empty. X undid her helmet and threw it on the seat beside her. She looked around, wild-eyed. She breathed in deeply and smelt the fresh grass scent and a subtle, sweet floral overtone from a nearby bush. There was no one else in sight. It was as if an artist had painted thick white stripes across the cobalt blue sky. X unzipped her suit. She felt her pulse go thump, thump, thump, in the side of her neck. The sudden need for freedom was all-encompassing.

X sat next to her suit with her legs hugged to her chest and her head resting on her knees. She glanced along the path in both directions. No one. The sound of a bird nearby startled her, and she sprang from the bench. X laughed at herself when she saw the bird digging in the garden bed. She looked around again. She did a full 360. X looked at her suit, then the bushes that stretched away in a curve, following the path. She grabbed the suit.

Once she was happy that the suit was fully concealed underneath the bush, she walked across the grass behind. For the first time in an extremely long time, there were no thoughts in her head. She walked slowly in her skimpy yellow singlet top and short cotton shorts. The grass felt like magic under her feet. Goose bumps raised on her arms, and she looked down wondrously as though it was the first time she had ever seen such a thing.

Run, she thought. *Just run!*

X sprang forward. She sprinted across the gently sloped grass until the stinging pain of a stitch made her stop. She collapsed forward, squatting, panting, completely out of breath. A huge smile crossed her face, and she stood. After a few deep breaths, she was off again. This time she leapt and cartwheeled in crooked lines back in the direction she had first run. She felt amazing. Exhilarated. Liberated. Unshackled. Happy. Deliriously happy.

X lay down on the grass, arms and legs spread wide in a star shape. She gazed at the mixture of blue and white above. Slowly the purples, pinks and peach of sunset appeared. They were mesmerising. She remembered gazing for endless hours at the sky above the school oval as a kid, back in the outer suburbs of Melbourne, wondering if her mum's spirit was out there somewhere, in the enormous expanse. X rose, brushing off the grass from her backside and shaking the thoughts of her old home, her old life, her old self, from her head.

She stood up straight and looked towards the path. That's when she saw them. They were close to the grass, standing on the path near the bushes where X had left her suit. They stood, suited, frozen mid-stride, a robot malfunctioning. She felt the colour drain from her face. Her thoughts raced, bombarding her brain like swooping magpies in the springtime. X stood still, looking straight at the person, eyes blazing into their grey helmet. They seemed to look straight back at her. But the helmet masked all expression.

X swore, took a sharp breath, and diverted her eyes. She felt the grass in between her toes and looked at the beautifully manicured parkland around her. Then she smiled, jogged over to the person, and gave them a big hug. Or at least that's what she tried to do. The person retreated slowly backwards as she approached. X persisted, wrapping her arms awkwardly around the metal upper body of the stranger. Then she ran for the bushes and her hidden suit. She crawled in amongst the foliage and tried to pull her suit on whilst concealing herself as much as possible. After flailing for a few seconds, she crawled out and stood. She brushed off her feet and stepped into her suit. She zipped it up, grabbed the helmet, and shoved it on her head.

Her blood pulsed frantically, and she felt the internal cooling kick in as soon as she fastened the helmet. Then she jogged off, away from where the person had been. X turned around in a circle and couldn't see anyone. She walked briskly but stifled the desire to run in case she came across someone. She would look inconspicuous if walking and wished, now more than ever before in her life, to blend in. To be unseen. Unnoticed.

X stayed off the paths, preferring to weave a course out of the side gate of the park. She knew the side gate led to Eastleft. She could walk along the streets there, unknown and unlinked to any reported incident at the park. X saw the lights along the paths switch on suddenly, illuminating two law enforcement units entering from the very gate X was heading for. Their red and blue lights flashed a warning to escape. She used the cover of darkness to sneak into a grove of trees that stretched down the park's perimeter towards the lake.

CHAPTER FORTY

When X got to work on Monday, everyone else was in the back room already. X clicked the button and looked at the time on her forearm. She wasn't late. X walked towards one of the big screens. They hadn't switched it on yet. She turned to see her three colleagues crowding around her.

"We got your memo, X," the middle person said.

X stifled her impulse to scream 'what memo?!'. "My memo," she said, glad of the monotone voice emitted by her helmet. "Good."

"I can't believe there was an indecent exposure incident in our neighbourhood last night," the person added.

X's eyes bulged. She decided the person speaking was Meadow or Air. "How did you know—"

"The memo said to come in early so we would avoid peak time and any further incidents," the person to X's left interjected.

X thought the interjector must be Seed. Her head spun. *What the hell is going on?* she thought. "What should I do?" she mumbled.

"What's that?" the one to her right, who hadn't spoken yet, asked.

"Okay," X said loudly. "I called you all here early for a team meeting." X contemplated her next move. "First, let's get this screen loaded." She flicked the switch on the wall near the screen. The office screens flashed blue, then loaded the home screen. "So, let's go over what we know," X said. "Seed, can you please start?"

The person to her left answered. "Just that it was an indecent exposure in Eastside Park middle section. Law enforcement didn't catch the person. They questioned a person who encountered the unsuited individual and made a full report."

"Thank you," X said. She felt victorious that she guessed who Seed was earlier. "Meadow, how many cases of indecent exposure have we had in City East in the past month?"

"I'm not sure. I think half a dozen," the person standing directly in front of X replied.

"Eleven," the person to X's right said. That had to be Air.

X turned and looked at Air. It was hard to stare someone down while wearing a helmet. "Eleven. Right." *Ten by an unknown perpetrator and one by me*, she thought. "So, what I would like is to be notified immediately of any further reports, as I should manage the complaints personally."

"Do you think that's wise?" Air asked.

"Yes, I do. I am the manager, after all. Meadow and Seed, please set up for the day. Air, I'd like to speak with you further in private."

There was an uncomfortable silence. Meadow and Seed moved off to do their work.

X's heart beat thunderously in her chest, so much so, she was sure Air could hear it. X considered her options.

Air stood in their spot, steadfast, perhaps defiant.

"Why did you send a memo from me to the team?" X asked.

"I didn't."

"Alright," X said. "Assuming that's the truth, you know who sent it and that it was going to be sent." She took a step towards Air. "You also know I am linked to these cases of indecent exposure."

"I can't tell you anything," Air retorted. "I can't tell you what you want to know."

"And what do you imagine it is I want to know?"

"What the sign says."

X gasped, despite herself. She had been right; it was Air that had been feeding information back to Council about this. *Air is the insider Seed warned me about*, she thought.

"What I can tell you," Air stepped forward, so they were right in X's face, "is that Council knows everything. Where you have been, who you have talked to. Who you have slept with." Air paused.

X's mouth gaped beneath her helmet.

"What you have eaten," Air continued. "This conversation."

X looked in horror at Air. She felt queasy.

Surely law enforcement is close to catching them, aren't they?

It's only a matter of time, isn't it?

Is this my only chance to find them?

Who is it?

Why me?

What on earth does the sign say?

The questions swirled in circles around X's head, bumping into one another, jostling for space, like sheep in front of a freshly laid hay bale. Her knees felt as though they might give way. She had to get away from Air. She felt obliged to find this person before law enforcement did, but she wasn't sure why.

X gritted her teeth. "You've been most helpful, thank you." Her stomach flipped. "You can go now. Back to work, please." The even tone of her helmet diluted the impact of her words. Air remained in their position. If it weren't for the suits, Air would have literally been breathing down her neck. X braced herself for the response. Without a word, Air turned and walked out of the office. The door swung silently closed.

X shivered despite the even temperature inside her suit. She toggled the control for the nearby screen so she could see the foyer. She studied her colleagues. They looked busy enough. The first customers had trickled in.

Why hasn't law enforcement ever got there in time? she wondered.

X tried to concentrate back on the screen. There was really nothing to see, though. There were three red suits behind the counters, facing a growing group of pink suits.

Why didn't they catch me yesterday?
Why didn't they suspect I would be in the park?
Weren't they tracking my location?
What the hell am I going to do?

X wished there was a power-down button on her suit. Or at least a thought blocker.

She paced back and forth, glancing at the screen every minute. At a break in the flow of visitors, she typed a brief message and sent it to Seed. She saw him check his screen and come to the door. She couldn't tell if he had said anything to the other two. X walked to the storeroom. She heard the click-clack of Seed walking across the floor. Once in the storeroom, Seed locked the door behind him. Without saying a word, they removed their suits and put them in the metal locker.

"Thanks for meeting me," X said as soon as the lid was down.

"We can't talk long," Seed replied in a hushed voice.

"I know. Do you know why law enforcement would sit off these cases, turning up only after the offender has left?"

"There could be two likely reasons. Either the offender never wears a suit, and the Council has lost track of them. Or they are waiting for the inevitable. It's a setup."

"What, you mean they want me to meet this person, so they can catch me too?

"Something like that. X, you know you're playing with fire if you keep chasing this down, don't you?"

"Yes, I know. It's just I can't let it go. It's all too strange. I have to know what the sign says."

"All I can say is, be careful, X."

"What's the worst that can happen if I get caught by law enforcement? I would get deported, right? And banished?"

"It's not that simple. They don't let people leave as easily as they'd have you believe. There's a dark side to Xoha, X. And believe me, you don't want to get caught up in it."

X looked into Seed's eyes. She saw a deep pain. It was sickening. "Right. Thanks. Well, we best get back to work then."

Seed pulled X close and whispered in her ear. "If they're living unsuited, I might know where you can find them, or some information about them. Meet me at the fountain at six tonight and I'll give you a map. Do not say a word about this to anyone."

X nodded her head slowly, eyes wide. Seed smelt like cedar and bergamot. X fought an impulse to kiss him. He let go of her shoulders. Then he opened the locker. Without another word, the two swiftly put on their suits. Seed unlocked the storage room door and left.

X stayed a while in the storeroom looking unseeingly at the shelves of cables and metal components. The words 'living unsuited' replayed over and over in her head.

CHAPTER FORTY-ONE

X walked along the footpath on her way to the park. She heard a rustle and immediately turned to look over her shoulder. There was nothing there. Nothing she could see, anyway. She had a funny sensation, like she was being watched. *They probably are watching me*, she thought. X walked a little faster. She felt the panic rise in her chest. "Come on, be reasonable. It's probably just a bird," she chided.

Before yesterday, she had done nothing wrong, broken no rules. Sure, she'd got into trouble at work and been reassigned. But that wasn't against the law. It was just a misunderstanding that had put her in an awkward position in front of Council. The most powerful people in Xoha may know about her, but surely reassignment was insignificant in the scheme of things.

X walked along the deserted path. She had seen a couple walk down the path of the last house in the street, but that had been a while ago now. The park was deserted. Her fingertips rose to her left armpit. She didn't feel for the impression where the panic alarm was, but her hand lingered there. X felt trepidation, not relief, when she rounded the bend in the path and saw the brightly lit fountain. She lowered her right arm back to her side and honed her focus on the fountain.

Her eyes searched the darkness for signs of another human being. There was no sign of Seed. There was no sign of anyone. She walked around the large digital fountain, marvelling at the hologram of carved stonework. It really looked like the famous Trevi Fountain. X had visited Rome after finishing university, a popular stop in the European backpacking-right-of-passage for many Australians. A pang of nostalgia stung her belly. She wished she were on holiday in Europe right now. Instead, she was here, in Xoha, in a deserted park and potentially walking into a trap.

Before she had even finished a lap of the large fountain, she was engrossed in its beauty and entranced by the sound effects. She stood on the spot, looking, watching, now oblivious to her surroundings. There was a zap and a flicker, and the display changed to the Peterhof Fountains, or so the sign said. X marvelled at this lovely, unfamiliar sight. Within seconds, she was transfixed again.

The subtle sound of footsteps brought X back to the park, the night, and her mission. X turned and watched a person in a grey suit approach. She noticed the subtleties of their gait and relaxed a little. The suit walked like Seed. She allowed herself a small victory smile.

Seed put out his hand and X took it. He led her to the back of the fountain and pressed in close to her.

"Hi X. We are safe to talk here briefly."

"Hi, oh, okay."

"The fountain jumbles the suit's system, and you go off radar here. But we can't talk for long. If they are tracking either of us, they will get suspicious."

"Do you think they are?"

Seed nodded his head. "Here's the map. Put it in your pocket, quickly now."

X took the folded paper and put it carefully in the front pocket of her suit.

"Make sure you only read it when you're at home, unsuited. Best to put it in a book, just in case there are eyes in your house. Pretend you're reading something while you study it. You won't be able to refer to it after you leave the house. You have to memorise it. Got it?"

"Really?"

Seed didn't move.

"Okay, yes. Sure. Got it," X said. "Thanks," she added.

"When you go out, make sure you leave it at home, somewhere safe. In case you're intercepted. Now off you go. Don't leave it too long. They change locations every week, sometimes less. You should be alright until Thursday."

"Oh, okay. Right."

Seed stepped backwards. He turned and dashed away.

X wanted to yell after Seed, reiterate her thanks. Or ask him how he knew all this. Instead, she stepped away from the back of the fountain and walked in the opposite direction. She bit her lower lip. *I have three days*, she thought. *Best go tomorrow and get it over and done with.*

CHAPTER FORTY-TWO

Work was excruciating. X watched the clock inch forward. She tried to bury her head in the numbers, but they only swirled around with elaborate imaginings of home, Xoha, Seed, the map, the unknown person holding an unknown sign. It was all too much. She hoped these helmets didn't record people's thoughts or transport them to a database. She envisaged an office like this, with someone like her sitting there, getting paid to work with the computers, analysing all that rich data. It was a sobering image. A shiver ran down her spine.

X kept her head down and conversations with colleagues short. The day dragged onwards.

Finally, her shift ended. She raced home to study the map, which she had left safely enclosed in one of the few hard copy books she owned.

* * *

X woke with a start. The book was next to her pillow where her hands must have dropped it when she fell asleep. The map was covering her face. Once corner stuck to the side of her mouth that had obviously been drooling onto her pillow. Yuck. She carefully peeled it off, making sure to not rip it.

How did I fall asleep so quickly?

X had meant to study the map just one more time, before heading out in the dark to find the location, and hopefully solve this strange mystery that had been stalking her every waking minute. She closed the map into the cover of her book and walked drowsily to the toilet.

When she came out, X saw the early morning light filtering through her door from the lounge room. She must have left the blinds open. She shuffled to the kitchen. It was 5:03 a.m.

If she hastened, there was enough time to go to the location Seed had given her before work. X gulped down a glass of water and ate a breakfast bar. She put on a pair of leggings and a top just in case the morning's activities included unsuiting. It was a fair assumption they would. She threw on her suit and left the house, trying to be quiet so that the neighbours and anyone else around wouldn't hear her. She knew it was completely out of character for her to be walking out of the house so early. If anyone saw her, they would likely get suspicious, or at the very least, interested in what she was doing. Neither would be helpful.

X made her way swiftly down the street. It surprised her to see a few people out walking so early, but she casually returned their monotone hellos. The map was very particular about the route she must take to the underground meeting point, so she followed it to the letter. She didn't have time to stop and appreciate the beauty of Xoha at dawn. The purple-grey light cast a peaceful glow on the houses and trees of the streetscape. X weaved up and down paths, making her way to the park and then around the edge to a bush area she didn't even know existed. It was between Eastmiddle, where X lived, and the next suburb over, called Eastright.

After a little way in, the bush got so dense; she had to walk sideways to fit down the path, or risk scratching her suit on the branches that closed in from both sides. She wanted nothing to draw unnecessary attention to her and wasn't sure how she would explain the damage if questioned. A vision of how ridiculous she must look made her laugh. She turned around hastily, instantly regretting making the sudden noise. There was nothing in sight but the greens and browns of the plant life.

The tree trunk was enormous. Nestled in a small clearing a few hundred metres off the track, there was no mistaking it. Its thick bark was brown black and lined with deep rivers and cracks. X wondered how old the tree was. She approached it slowly, craning her neck to see its green canopy, high above. The hollow was dark and faced west, with no dull morning light to hint at what was inside. X looked quickly around her. When she was confident that she was alone, she stepped forward and disappeared into the tree.

It was dark inside, but her helmet auto-adjusted, and she could see a space big enough for two or three people. It looked like an ordinary inside of a tree, but she scanned the walls for the concealed button she knew was there, which would reveal the spiral staircase that led down into the underground shelter. The unsuited must have several hideouts and X wondered if they were all like this. She also wondered how Seed had found out about this secret location. She hadn't found an opportunity to ask. Maybe she was better off not knowing.

What if this is all a big joke? X suddenly thought. She visualised Seed waiting outside the tree trunk with a bunch of onlookers, all laughing at her gullibility. She half smiled. *That would be a little funny,* she thought.

Then she saw it. It looked like a bump in the tree, something that others could undoubtedly overlook. She reached out and touched it. Nothing happened. Then she remembered she was in the world of the unsuited. She ripped off her helmet and unzipped her suit enough to free her arms. The scent of decaying wood, damp and pungent, encircled her. She realised how much she had missed the smells of nature. Her nose was nearly always shielded from the outside world by her helmet. The smell inside the suit, whilst pleasant and changeable, was under her control. Nature offered a bouquet of scents that ebbed and flowed, depending on the season and the weather.

When she touched the raised part of the tree with her bare hand, it felt cool. The smooth wood had a notch underneath with a small, round button. She pressed it and a panel to her right slid silently open, revealing the small staircase. X removed the rest of her suit and draped it over her left arm. She clutched her helmet tight. The earth was spongy under her feet. She stepped forward to the stairs, nearly bending in two to fit through the tiny door. Her feet made a slight dinging sound as they passed over the cold, hard metal steps. X descended to the bottom, right hand lightly tracing the railing.

At the bottom was a heavy metal door with an intercom to the side. She let her suit fold over itself on the floor beside her and placed her helmet on top. X pressed the buzzer, not knowing what to say. The panel lit up and a camera lens focused on her, no doubt sharing her image with those behind the door. X felt self-conscious. She smiled feebly at the camera.

"State your name, why you're here or who you're here to see."

The voice made X jump. She wasn't used to hearing a human voice through an intercom. The year and a bit she had been in Xoha, had conditioned her to the monotone robotic voice of everyone and everything. It sounded like a woman, but she couldn't be sure.

"Um, hi. I'm X and I'm here to find out something. I think you can help." She nibbled the corner of her lip.

There was silence.

X shifted her weight from side to side, then swallowed loudly. "It's, um, the identity of the person involved in the indecent exposure cases of late. A person holding a sign. I think something may somehow link us, but I don't know what it is."

"Please state your name."

"It's X."

"Your real name."

The colour drained from X's face. It had been so long since she'd used her own name, the one given to her at birth by her mum. The only thing she had left in this world that had come from that fabulous woman. She thought about how she had lost her mum's earrings back in Melbourne before coming to Xoha and her stomach twisted into a knot. The time she had spent in this so-called land of equality flashed before her eyes.

Her name.

The very thing which had been hardest to deny. Which she'd almost had to erase from her memory because it hurt so much to think about. She squeezed her eyes shut. "My name is Evalie."

There was an audible gasp as the buzzer sounded and the door swung open.

X, that is Evalie, walked into a bright room. It looked like a dormitory with bunks around the walls. Squeezed into the corner was a small, round wooden table with three chairs. There were also shelves of clothing and accessories, some of which Evalie hadn't seen since Melbourne. Hair accessories and wigs. Ties. Sunglasses and hats. All things that were useless while wearing a suit with a helmet.

Standing before Evalie was a woman with long brown hair and green eyes. "He's not here. But he'll be back soon. It was his turn. To do the first morning lookout. To check the cameras and everything."

The woman spoke in short, quick bursts.

"Oh, I'm Ivy, by the way," she said breathlessly. "That's my real name. It can be confusing as it sounds like a Xohan name. Words can't relay how excited I am to meet you, Evalie! We've been waiting for you." Ivy stepped forward and caught Evalie in a big hug.

Evalie hugged her awkwardly back. Hugs were the thing she'd missed most, and yet she was floundering. It felt so strange. "Sorry, who? Who will be back soon? Who is *he*?"

At that moment, the door swung open behind her. "Evalie!"

Evalie whirled around to see Guy standing there in ripped jeans and a faded T-shirt. She gasped, hand across her mouth. Tears welled in Evalie's eyes as Guy ran to her and enclosed her in a big hug. She was crying and laughing at the same time. She couldn't believe it was him. It was Guy. Her Guy. In Xoha. She hugged him fiercely.

Guy leaned back and looked at Evalie, brushing tears from her cheek with his left thumb.

"Guy, I ... what are you doing here?"

"I'm here because of you, Evalie. Nothing matters but you. I want to be with you. I love you. You're the only one for me. I'd follow you anywhere, everywhere. Even here."

"But I ... I left."

"Yes. You did. But not because of me."

"Well, no. Not because of you, exactly. But I–"

"I want you to know that I believe in you. You are, well, like no other. I didn't hear you back home, and I'm sorry for that. My listening has improved, I swear. I didn't understand what you were experiencing and I ... well, I was dismissive. I didn't see it until later. Until I found out about Xoha."

"Oh, Guy."

"I hope you can understand that I didn't get what an easy run I'd had in life and, well ... I thought everyone had the same experience. It has become painfully clear that I was wrong. I'm sorry you felt like you had to come here to ... you know, succeed."

Evalie tried to find words, but they eluded her. She looked down at the ground.

"I know your experience here hasn't been what you expected," Guy continued. "This Xoha, this equality, it's an illusion. You know that, right?"

"Well, ... um, yes. I guess. I'm just ugh. It was such a big decision, and I couldn't involve you in it. And being here, trying to settle in. Well, lately, I've been miserable. Then I didn't understand what was happening with work. The indecent exposure cases. That was you?"

"Sometimes, yes. It's been a team effort." Guy winked at Ivy.

Ivy smiled back at him.

"We wanted to mix it up to make it more difficult for law enforcement to find us." Guy turned to Ivy. "It's all clear out there."

"Great, thanks," Ivy said. She left through a door Evalie hadn't noticed before.

This place is intriguing, Evalie thought. *A real secret hideout. I feel like I'm in a movie.*

Guy took Evalie's hand and led her over to the table. They sat facing one another.

"So, tell me," Evalie said. "I've been dying to know what was on the sign."

Guy laughed. "The sign simply said *Evalie.*"

Evalie looked into Guy's eyes and felt at home in a way she hadn't felt since leaving Melbourne. "Oh Guy, what have I done? How are we going to get out of this?"

"It's okay Evalie, we will find a way. To leave. To go home, together."

"What am I meant to do now? After I leave this hideout, I mean. Is it even safe for me to go?"

"Yes. You must leave. You must keep living like you have been. Like today didn't happen. But without the incessant searching for us, though." He grinned.

Evalie blushed.

"We will find you. When the time is right. When we can find a way out. Together. For now, you need to trust me, though."

"Right, okay. But I want to help. Can I come back and visit here and help with arrangements?" Evalie looked at Guy.

He shook his head softly.

"Can … can I see you again?"

"We need to be extremely cautious. We can't meet *here* again, that's for sure. You were lucky you found Seed, and he was able to give you the map. Your suit is being cleaned, so the history of where you've been since you left the house this morning will remain secret. Do you have the map?"

Evalie's face fell. "Oh, I left it at home. Wasn't that what I was meant to do? In case I got stopped and searched out there?"

Guy reached out and took Evalie's hand, which was resting on the table. As he did so, he brushed aside some kind of gadget. "Good. Yes, that was the safest thing to do." Guy squeezed Evalie's hand gently. "Just in case."

"So how did you get here anyway and become a part of all this?" Evalie gestured around the room with her free hand. "It's pretty intense." Her eyes fixed on the torch-like gadget on the table. "And what's that?"

"Well, um, that's a suit disabler. But there's really no time to explain it all now. It just ticked over six thirty. You'd better be getting back to your day." Guy dropped Evalie's hand and picked up the suit disabler.

"Oh, yeah. Okay." Evalie looked into Guy's dark brown eyes. "I don't know how I'm going to pretend like this morning hasn't happened."

Guy stood up. Evalie pushed her chair back and stood also, keeping her eyes locked on his. Guy pulled Evalie in close and they kissed. It was sweet and hungry all at once. Evalie felt her heart flutter, and a tingle danced down her body, coming to rest in her pelvis.

"I'll see you out," Guy said.

"Oh. Okay. I still can't believe you're here, that you're not some figment of my imagination. Or this isn't all just a dream or a movie or something."

Guy chuckled. "You haven't changed a bit. And here I was worried that this place might have got under your skin."

"You're the only thing that has ever really got under my skin," Evalie said. She raised her eyebrows. Then blushed.

They both laughed. They walked back to the door and as it swung open, Evalie saw her suit hanging on a hook that she hadn't noticed in the gloom at the foot of the stairwell.

"Emmi must have sorted that out for you. She's on close lookout today, hiding around the main entrances to alert the team below of any activity. She's stealth. You never actually know where she is. I think she must have been a ninja in her former life."

Evalie gave Guy a funny look. She brushed her feet with her hand and stepped into her suit. She pulled on her suit. Evalie's moves were fluid, graceful, like a dancer. She zipped it up, then paused. Before she put on her helmet, she kissed Guy one last time.

"Don't be a stranger," she said.

Guy smiled. "I'll be in touch soon. And don't go talking about this to anyone, okay? Especially not Raven. You can't trust them."

Evalie bristled at the mention of Raven. Her eyes dropped to the floor. *Does Guy know all about what's gone on here, about my relationships?* she thought. When Evalie looked back up, Guy was staring at her.

"It's not so much, Raven," he said gently, "as the company he keeps."

"Right. Okay." *Park*, she thought. *I've been such a fool.* "Sure, I won't tell a soul. I love you." Evalie put on her helmet.

"I love you too," Guy said. He looked at her with a sparkle in his eye. "This suit, wow! You look *so* sexy." Guy made both eyebrows bounce up and down.

Evalie laughed and gave him a little shove. "Now I get why you came all the way here," she said. "You've got a suit fetish."

Guy flung his head back and laughed his hearty belly laugh.

Evalie realised how much she had missed that. How much she had missed everything about Guy.

"See you … later. Not too much later, though." Evalie turned.

"Bye, Evalie. Remember who you are out there," Guy said.

"I don't know who you are talking to," she said. "I'm X." Then she climbed the narrow spiral staircase back up to ground level.

CHAPTER FORTY-THREE

Evalie flopped onto her couch. She'd done it. Somehow, she'd made it through the week and could relax. It had been a grind since the early morning rendezvous with Guy. He was all she could think about. Not being able to talk about him with anyone was excruciating. She missed having a best friend, someone she could trust. She wondered if Stella would ever forgive her. If she and Guy got back home. It felt like a massive *if*.

Evalie had received one message from Guy during the week. It was a folded piece of paper she found in her veggie garden, tucked under an ambling pumpkin vine. She wondered if there were more messages hidden in places she hadn't yet discovered. It was a small piece of paper with scrawled handwriting she didn't recognise as Guy's.

Love you. Meet you soon.

Instructions to follow.

Yours truly xx.

Evalie had gone on a note hunt, searching all around the garden and even in her house. She had found nothing. She distracted herself on Saturday, visiting the market in the morning. Again, she had been happy to blend in with the crowd. This time, she didn't have any pangs of regret when she saw two suits together, even when they were holding hands.

In the afternoon, she booked in for a swim at the private pool. It was bizarre being the only person in the water, but she was happy doing slow laps up and back in the warm water. She watched the rippled water emanate from her body out towards the sides of the pool. It was only the second time she had been for a swim. She wondered why she hadn't come more often. The water felt glorious on her skin and although she found it hard to get into a rhythm with her breathing; she persisted. When she came out from the sanitising cubicle, she felt lighter. That was until she put her suit on.

Evalie walked home from the station, meandering along in the fading light. Her stomach churned with nerves. *What if I can't find the meeting place?* she thought. The thought of meeting up with Guy made her both excited and anxious. Since the visit to the strange tree hideout, she had felt more uneasy about her situation with each passing day.

As Evalie turned up the path to her house, she scanned the bushes and trees for hidden notes. There was nothing. She reluctantly went inside. After combing through her garden, she went back inside and cooked dinner. Evalie sat down at her table alone, with a glass of wine full nearly to overflowing. She sighed. She couldn't decide if it was the loneliness, regret, or fear for the future that was behind the sigh. Perhaps it was all three. After cleaning up, she flopped back on her couch again. *How will I ever get through this?* she thought.

* * *

Unsuited

The days dragged and there was no word from the unsuited. Evalie felt like it had all been a dream: studying and following the map, the trip to the underground hideout. She became more and more distracted and uneasy. Then one Sunday afternoon, while she was trying to take her mind off things in her garden, a note floated down beside her, like a leaf from the enormous tree above. At first she thought it *was* a leaf and didn't look up from weeding the garden bed. But as she went to gather the pile of weeds she'd made; she saw the folded paper. She jolted when she saw it. It was thin and green, folded into its own little envelope. Evalie bent down cautiously and picked it up. After a brief hesitation, she gently unfolded it. Her pulse quickened as she read the note.

I have found a safe suit. Meet me at the station.

Third bench, platform 3, 5:45 p.m.

Just bring yourself.

Evalie turned the note over in her hands. It had the same scrawly handwriting as the previous note. She looked up at the tree and the sky above. Then she scanned the garden. She couldn't tell where the letter had come from.

How could they have known I was outside?

An apprehensiveness settled in her gut. Evalie re-folded the note and put it in the pocket of her gardening pants. She went inside. It was 3:50 p.m.

Evalie grabbed a glass from the cupboard and poured some cold water from the fridge. As she stood drinking in her kitchen, conspiracy theories ran rife in her head. Her heart pounded in her temples. She felt like her head might explode.

Evalie headed for the sanitising cubicle. It was not as satisfying as a shower. It never was. There was a slight relief in feeling clean, though. She padded into the lounge room and flopped onto the couch. After she had run every scenario over in her head, she decided she had to go. Hopefully, the note was legitimate, and it would be Guy she was meeting. She chewed on the side of her lip. If not, she would have to face this new reality.

I don't have any other choice. I must go, she thought.

Necessity resulted in Xoha being highly controlled. To eliminate inequality, they had taken bold decisions and removed personal freedoms. They had inbuilt control into the suits in the name of freedom. She had believed in the system. She had put her trust in the Xoha of her dreams and hopes.

I've given it my best shot, haven't I? she pondered.

Now it seemed she should return to her proper home, in the real world, with the love of her life.

What if it's a trick? What if law enforcement is onto me?

Evalie didn't know what the penalty was for going against the system, for fraternising with the unsuited. The dark side of Xoha could not be good.

How bad it could be?

A shudder coursed through her body. She rolled over and buried her head in the couch cushions.

CHAPTER FORTY-FOUR

As the time clicked closer to 5:45 p.m., Evalie sat in her suit at her kitchen bench. She drummed the fingers of her right hand subconsciously on the countertop. She stood up, but then sat back down. The fingers of her left hand tapped a new beat. She was too scared to say anything out loud in case they had bugged her house. If only she could have someone go with her to the station as a backup. Or even better, if she could send someone there in her place, just in case it wasn't Guy she would sit down next to.

Evalie remembered Guy's warning about Raven.

What about Seed?

She checked the time. It was too short notice now. If only she had thought of this sooner. She summoned her courage and left the house. She walked with head held high, down her path to the street.

When Evalie reached platform three, she stood at the end, surveying the scene. The platform and benches were empty. It was eerily quiet. Evalie guessed that this hour on a Sunday wasn't a popular time for travel. *No need to panic*, she thought. *You are five minutes early, after all.*

Evalie studied the board. The next train was due in seven minutes. If it was Guy that Evalie was meeting, she had no idea if they would get on the train or where they would go. She wandered down the platform and back to kill some time.

Evalie had to grit her teeth so as not to pace back and forth like a mad person and draw unwanted attention to herself. Not that there was anyone to draw attention from. No one she could see, anyway. As she walked along, the hairs on the back of her neck prickled. Evalie turned slowly and looked around. There was a person standing further down the platform. They were facing her direction, but she had no idea if they were looking at her or not.

Evalie walked to a bench and sat down. She scanned the platform continuously for any signs of threat, ready to walk away at any moment and return home.

But what is there to return to? she thought.

I must see Guy; I have to be with him again.

This is too much.

I can't take it anymore.

Evalie stood with all the confidence she could muster and walked directly to the third bench. It appeared to her the suit she had seen earlier was now sitting on the fourth bench. Although she couldn't be sure it was the same person.

The note said third bench. I'm sure it did, Evalie thought. Cool air circulated through her suit. Evalie floundered. *Yes, third bench. That's what it said.* Just as she was about to sit down, two law enforcement officers appeared beside the fourth bench. Evalie stepped forward, past the bench. She quickened her pace and headed towards the end of the platform and the stairs. She heard low monotone voices but couldn't make out any words. Evalie's heart rose into her throat and her fingers curled into fists.

At the sound of a scuffle, Evalie turned around. She saw the khaki green law enforcement suits apprehend the grey suit. They dragged the person towards the other end of the platform. Evalie stood rooted to the spot. She felt the air in her suit kick up a notch and realised she was panting. She tried to force herself to breathe slowly and deeply. With eyes wide and hands still in fists, Evalie turned back towards the exit and made a quick retreat. She looked for somewhere to hide, where she could still see the platform and the third bench. There wasn't anywhere in this stark, brightly lit space.

Was that Guy? What if they thought that was me?

The thoughts made her sick to her stomach. She leaned against the end wall and waited, willing the nausea away. The train came and went. Two people in grey suits got off and headed straight past her to the exit.

Nobody got on.

No one else came onto platform three.

No one sat on the third bench.

She waited, not knowing what else to do. The time lurched slowly forward. She waited as long as she could. Then the empty platform became overwhelming, and she left.

As Evalie walked along the quiet street to her house, she tried hard to stop the tears from overwhelming her. She felt so desperately hopeless. The anxiety that churned her stomach at the station turned to a dull ache. Halfway home, she thought she heard footsteps behind her. Evalie turned her head slowly, but kept walking. She couldn't see anyone. She picked up the pace. By the time she got to number twenty-four, she was practically running.

The sight that met her eyes at her neighbour's house made Evalie's blood run cold. There was a law enforcement vehicle parked across the path, lights flashing. The red and blue lights pierced the gathering darkness, creating an eerie dance of colours. Two officers in khaki green suits dragged a grey suited person down the path towards the vehicle. Evalie ducked around the rear of the vehicle, trying to blend into the night. She hoped the lights wouldn't illuminate her dull grey suit. It suddenly dawned on her that anonymity could easily result in mistaken identity. A sobering thought. She snuck down her path, out of sight. Her hands shook as she removed her key from the forearm of her suit and unlocked her door. As soon as she was inside, she collapsed onto the floor. After she heard the click of the door closing, she ripped her helmet off. Tears came flooding down. She felt like she was going to hyperventilate. There was no increase in airflow to regulate her breathing. The sobs racked her throat and convulsed her body.

When the deluge abated, she peeled herself off the floor and undid her suit. After pulling it off, she padded to the laundry and put it in the cleansing machine. Evalie slid down to the floor next to the machine and put her head in her hands. Her mind raced with all the catastrophes that were bound to be coming her way.

At nine o'clock, she peeled herself off the floor once more and got ready for bed. She felt exhausted. When she looked into the mirror in the cleansing room, her face was red and splotchy. She sprayed it with cool water. As she brushed her teeth, she realised she hadn't had any dinner. She couldn't stomach the thought of food. Evalie curled up in bed and fell into an uncomfortable sleep.

*

She walked along the cobblestone alley. It was familiar. It looked like the place where she bumped into Guy, when she was with Stella. The buildings looked different, though. They were black stone, with gargoyles hanging off the roofs. She heard a noise and turned her head. There was a person in a grey suit. She turned the other way. Another suit. She spun around. Grey suits surrounded her. They pressed in on her. She felt like she couldn't breathe. She tried to call out to let them know they were crushing her, suffocating her, but no sound came. Her lungs were being squeezed. She slipped down, clutching at the suits, but her hands slipped off the shiny metal. All she could see was grey. She gasped for air. There was none.

*

Evalie awoke to her alarm, disoriented. She poked at the flashing screen to make it stop. The memory of Sunday's mishaps came flooding back and Evalie screwed her face up in pain. She jumped out of bed and began pacing across her bedroom floor.

I have to go to work, she thought.

No call in sick.

No, go in.

Stupid girl, can't even decide what to do.

Evalie left her bedroom and distracted herself with breakfast. She felt extraordinarily hungry. After finishing a bowl of cereal, a serving of fruit and yoghurt, and a piece of heavily buttered bread, she stood staring out the window into her green garden. The urge to run was strong.

But where would I run to?

How could I escape by myself?

She didn't know where to start. If she hadn't just eaten a ridiculous amount of food, she would have contemplated going for an actual run in her suit to clear her head. But her stomach was so full. She decided the safest option at this point was to go to work.

Evalie arrived at work to find everything, as it should be. Although she had been willing it to be okay the whole journey in, she could scarcely believe it was. She busied herself in the back office as usual. As she sat checking through her Monday morning list, she noticed two colleagues enter the complaints foyer on the main screen at the same time. She watched as they walked across the floor towards the office. Evalie wondered which two they were.

"Good morning," Evalie said as they walked through the door. She was relieved that her suit helped moderate her excessive enthusiasm.

"Good morning, X."

"Morning."

They walked over and stood near her.

Evalie considered what to say. "How was your weekend, Seed?"

There was no response.

"Oh, Meadow, then. How was your weekend?" Evalie tapped her foot absentmindedly on the floor.

"It was good thanks, X. How about yours?" Meadow was standing slightly to Evalie's left.

"Oh, fine thanks. It was a fine weekend. How about you, Air?" Evalie turned to the right and looked at the suit facing her. She longed for a sign of the person beneath the benign exterior.

"Uneventful. Just how I like it," Air replied.

"Okay, good. How about you both go set up for the day?"

"That's it. Are there no extra directions today? Are you still trying to find out about indecent exposure activity, or have you resolved all of that? You seem to have gone quiet on that recently."

Evalie blushed. "Nothing has changed. Of course, if you hear anything about an indecent exposure incident, I would appreciate it if you came and got me immediately."

"Yes, boss," Air said, then turned and left the office.

"What was that about?" Meadow asked.

"I'm not sure," Evalie said.

The office door opened.

Evalie looked up. "Oh, there you are Seed, good morning."

"It's not Seed. About those indecent exposure reports. You might want to check a message that just came in."

Evalie flicked out of her list to the main screen. The message flashed before her eyes.

Indecent exposure offender apprehended.

Evalie stifled a gasp. She stared at the screen. The words danced around in her head before they sank in. *Guy, no!* she thought in desperation. She forced the words out through gritted teeth, "That's that settled, then. On with our day."

The scene from the train station the night before played over in her head. The grey suit dragged down the platform by two law enforcement officers. Guy, dragged down the platform. Out of the station. Captive. In a foreign land. A criminal working against the system. She squeezed her eyes shut tight and fought back the tears. She heard Air and Meadow leave the office.

As Evalie pretended to work, she looked up at the screen often in anticipation of Seed's arrival. At ten o'clock, she sent him a message. She got a brief response saying he was unwell. Evalie tried to stem the dread that was seeping in. She avoided her colleagues as much as possible. It wasn't difficult, as they were busier than usual without the third person behind the desk. Evalie was relieved when the clock ticked over five and it was closing time. She opened the office door and called out.

"Thanks Air and Meadow. I'll finish up here. You can go home now."

"Okay, bye X."

Evalie guessed that was Meadow.

"See you." The person Evalie thought was Air put their hand up in the Xohan salute and departed for the lift.

Evalie watched the two of them go and then wandered around the foyer. She straightened up the queue ropes. A wave of anxiety washed over her.

What on earth am I going to do now? she thought.

Evalie rushed back into the office and searched for the indecent exposure reports. She hadn't dared do it while Air had been there. They all had 'file closed' as their status.

It's over, Evalie thought. *I'm on my own now.*

She drew in a deep breath and slowly exhaled. Evalie stood up straight, turned off the screens and the lights, and left the building.

CHAPTER FORTY-FIVE

E valie paced up and down her living room. The thoughts came in fast, bombarding her like balls of ice in a hailstorm.

Why didn't law enforcement come for me?
They know where I am. Surely.
Why didn't they take me from the platform?
Is it only the unsuited they are after?
They must know where I've been.
Haven't they been watching me?
Maybe they haven't.
But they flagged me in the system.
Maybe they don't care about me.
Perhaps one case of indecent exposure is not that big of a deal.
What am I going to do?
Maybe they've got what they really wanted, Guy and the rest of the unsuited.
It's just me now.
It's just me.
I have to think of a plan. Think, Evalie, think!

Evalie sat down on her couch and laid back, feet resting on one armrest. She surprised herself by not crying. She didn't even feel like it. A strange calmness descended over her. Evalie looked around at her comfortable surroundings. It really was a pleasant home, and she felt contented here. She shut her eyes and pictured her old apartment. There was nothing she missed about it. She opened her eyes. It was suddenly clear to her. The only plan she needed was her original one. All she needed to do was to reach her potential. Do what she came to Xoha to do. She could do it. Go back to managing the complaints team, day in–day out, week in–week out. Not that bad. She was proving herself. She had proved herself already. Perhaps this was all there was.

Perhaps over time she could forget the past few months had ever happened. Forget about Guy.

Oh, Guy, where have they taken you? she thought. Evalie burst into tears.

***

Evalie awoke with a stiff neck. She sat up on the couch, stretched, and checked the time.

9:30 p.m.

She looked at her screen on the coffee table. It was showing three new messages. She grabbed the screen, hoping deep down they were from Seed.

They were from Park. She tentatively opened the first message.

X, hope everything is okay. If you need to talk, I'm here for you.

Evalie saw the message was from a few hours before while she was napping on the couch. The next message had come a few minutes later.

I forgive you, by the way. Water under the bridge.

Evalie stared at the words. Her cheeks burned with fury. She read the first message again. Then the second. A strange sense of relief swiftly replaced the anger. She opened the last message; it was time stamped at nine fifteen.

Raven and I are just friends.

Evalie stared at the last message. She mouthed the words. Her lips curled into a smile despite herself.

You can't trust her. Remember what Guy said, she thought.

Don't trust her.

But they took Guy away.

I may never see him again.

Park may be all I have left.

CHAPTER FORTY-SIX

Evalie sat on a stool at the kitchen bench, looking out the window at the faded light and growing shadows in her garden. She would have waited outside but was worried she wouldn't hear the intercom. She felt a slight apprehension. Or was it excitement? At the sound of the doorbell, she jumped up and flew to the intercom button.

"Hello," she said.

"I'm here," came the reply.

"Come on in," Evalie said and pressed the door release.

She saw the grey suit enter and go straight to the de-suiting area. The curtain fell softly from the ceiling. Evalie walked back into the kitchen and poured two gin and tonics. She was just putting a slice of freshly cut lime into the second glass when Park walked into the room. She looked beautiful as ever, and Evalie felt a pang of betrayal in her chest.

"X, it's so good to see you." Park walked over to her and gave her a hug.

It was all Evalie could do not to bury her face in Park's hair and let loose. She could just tell it all, let everything out, and then see what happened. The embrace was so satisfying, Park's arms were warm, and her jasmine scent intoxicating. Evalie gritted her teeth and broke the hug. She handed Park a glass.

"Thanks," Park said.

Evalie gestured to the lounge room and followed Park to the couch. She sat apart from her, watching Park curl her legs up beside her and toss her hair to one side, while resting her glass on the arm of the couch. Evalie leaned forward and put her glass on the coffee table.

"So—"

"What—"

"You go," Evalie said.

"What happened at work that you were so upset about the other day?" Park asked, concern in her voice.

"Um, well, I have just been having some trouble with a co-worker, that's all. They seem to undermine my authority. I don't know, really. It was something I've talked over with Raven before and I thought, ah, he might help."

"He is a good listener," Park commented.

"Yeah, he is. Look, ah, I don't know why I asked you around here, really."

"For the company."

"Right. Yes, I guess so. It's just, well, I'm not really looking for a relationship or anything."

"I don't have any expectations, X. I'm just glad that we can be friends."

"Okay, good. Friends," Evalie said, looking down at her hands in her lap. She lifted her glass and took a long sip.

Park watched her curiously. "So, what happened to you after that day at the Council meeting? They reassigned you, no?"

"Yes. Let's just say it was not a fun experience. Although, things have gotten better since then. Well, they had, until recently." Evalie peered at the melting ice cubes in her drink, swirling the glass slowly and watching the tiny bubbles fizz slightly at the edge of the glass. She looked across at Park, who was finishing the last of her drink. "What about you? How are things in the strategy team?"

"Ah, things are good with me, X. The team is fine, a few unfamiliar faces ... a few new suits, I should say." Park laughed a hearty laugh.

Evalie smiled feebly.

"There were big changes from that day." Park put her empty glass on the table. "Well, thanks for the drink. We should do this again soon."

"Oh, are you going to go? I mean, you just got here."

"It's just it's getting kind of late. And I—"

"No, of course," X said.

"What are you doing on Friday night?"

"Um. I've got nothing on Friday."

"Good, good. Come to my place then."

"Sure, I can come over after work. Do you want me to bring some food? I mean, if that works for you."

"After work sounds great. No, I will do some cooking. Perhaps you can help me. It will be like old times."

Evalie glanced sideways at Park, trying not to look alarmed. She saw the coy grin on Park's face and laughed. "Right. Like old times."

Park rose from her seat and walked across to Evalie. She leaned down and kissed her on the forehead. "You take care until then, my friend. I'll see you Friday."

Evalie felt her pulse quicken. She went to get up.

"No, don't get up. I'll see myself out."

Park left the room and Evalie gulped down the remnants of her drink. She waited until she heard the front door click shut before returning to the kitchen for another drink. And then a third. And fourth.

* * *

Evalie pressed the buzzer on Park's door. She remembered back to the first time she'd visited Park's house and marvelled at how much had happened since then. This time, she didn't have an urge to straighten her hair, and she had brought just one bottle of red wine.

"Come in," the voice said, and the door lock released.

Evalie waited until the heavy metal door had swung open and walked into the entrance hall. She de-suited and carried her bottle of wine down the hall into the living area. Park was sitting on the couch with two empty glasses on the coffee table.

"Hello, my darling, there you are. I knew you would bring wine. I even have the glasses ready."

"Hi," Evalie said. "Well, I couldn't come empty-handed now, could I?"

"Sit, sit," Park said, patting the cushion beside her. "How was your week?"

Evalie sat. "It was okay. How about yours?"

"Mine was excellent. We have a Council presentation coming up and I got all my sections finished, which was good."

"Right. That is good."

Park opened the bottle and poured a generous serve into each glass. "Here you go." She handed a glass to Evalie, lightly brushing her hand along Evalie's forearm as she did so.

"Thanks." Evalie gulped her wine, relishing the silkiness on her tongue and the deep cherry flavour.

"How were your colleagues this week? Still having problems like before?"

Evalie thought for a moment. "No. That seems to have sorted itself out. Ever since, how can I put it, something outside of the office got resolved. It doesn't seem to be a problem anymore. My colleague isn't making waves anymore. I don't think." Evalie's cheeks flushed. It was an effort not to say anything that would elicit further questions from Park.

Park edged closer to Evalie. "That's good to hear. So, everything is going well for the both of us then."

"Yes, I guess it is." Evalie felt the back of Park's hand run along her thigh. She willed herself not to give into the temptation of being close to someone again.

Park took Evalie's half empty glass and rested it gently on the coffee table. She turned to Evalie. "I've missed you, X," she said, "More than you could know. We really have something good together. Like fireworks. I know you feel it." Park leaned in and kissed Evalie.

At first, she resisted. But it felt good to be wanted, and she kissed Park back. She blocked out all the confusion, the swirling thoughts and emotions. She blocked out any thoughts of the past or her future and let her body give in to the lust.

CHAPTER FORTY-SEVEN

Park and Evalie wandered hand in hand past the market stalls. The riot of colours of produce on display contrasted with the grey suits that crowded the stalls and filled the rows in between. It was busier than usual today. The air hummed with robotic chatter. Evalie breathed in deeply, but the internal scent of the suit was unsatisfying. She longed to smell the vibrant aromas of the market stalls. Evalie dropped Park's hand at the cheese stall and wandered up to the counter.

"Hi there, what can I get for you?" the green-suited stallholder asked.

"Can I have a wheel of the double brie, please? Oh, and a slither of the blue. Thanks."

"Certainly, great choice." The stallholder picked the cheeses from the fridge and wrapped them in paper. They placed them in a small paper bag. "Here you are. That will be seventeen fifty."

Evalie made the payment using her suit and took the bag. "Thanks. Have a great day."

"You too."

When Evalie turned around, she couldn't see Park. She couldn't distinguish which one of the grey suits she was wearing. There were several people milling around the stall and many walking past. She waited beside the stall, looking out for the telltale signs of her friend.

Is that what Park is to me, a friend?

She saw someone turn from a stall further on and breeze back towards her. She laughed to herself and shook her head slightly. Park was one of a kind. Unmistakable. She was carrying a small bag like Evalie's with the words 'Xoha Chocolate' printed in looped brown lettering on the front.

"Park," she called out as the suit got closer. She waved her right hand.

"X. I got the chocolate, you have the cheese, now we can go, right?"

"Sure. Let's go."

The couple walked back past the stalls to the exit and then on through the park towards Evalie's home. Evalie felt a sense of ease, of comfort. She hadn't felt that way since before she had noticed the reports of indecent exposure. It still hurt her to think of Guy and the unsuited, but the sense of inevitability and the consequences of the choices she had made had overwhelmed her. Fulfilling her purpose was the only option left that she could control.

***

As they neared her house, Evalie noticed two regular-sized suits holding the hands of two smaller-sized suits. They turned down the path to number twenty-four. Kids in suits always made her smile. They looked so cute—a replica of the adult they were walking with, indeed, of any adult. She pushed away the memory of the law enforcement incident at that house weeks before.

"Nice to see families out and about on this fine day," Park said.

"Yeah, it is," Evalie replied. She opened the door to her house and let Park go in ahead of her. "Shall I make a cheeseboard?" Evalie asked.

"Yes, of course," Park said. She removed her helmet and suit in the entrance, not bothering to use the de-suiting area.

Evalie did the same. She took the bag of cheese and put it on the bench before taking her suit to the cleansing unit. "You can pour some wine and take it outside, if you like," she called. "It will be beautiful in the garden."

Evalie used the facilities and sprayed her face with water, checking her reflection in the mirror. The face that looked back at her was happy, relaxed. She smiled.

Park was outside when Evalie walked back through to the kitchen. Evalie busied herself preparing the platter. The cheeses she had bought took centre stage on the large wooden paddle, surrounded by some crackers and dried fruit. She fished around in the drawer for a cheese knife. Evalie heard Park come inside.

"Oh, they are so beautiful, thank you!" Park exclaimed.

Evalie looked up in surprise. Park was turning her head from side to side, chin raised. Evalie looked at Park's ears. The blood drained from her face. She dropped the cheese knife, and it clanged as it struck the bench. Evalie glowered at the diamond teardrop earrings in Park's ears.

"Where the hell did you get those?" Evalie's voice was so harsh it shocked her.

"Sorry? Are they not a gift? They were in a little jewellery box on the table outside with a bow on top." Park gestured outside. "I thought that's why you sent me out there."

Evalie ran to the door and pulled it open in a flurry. She picked up the crystal earring box off the outdoor table, the box she had not seen since Melbourne.

Park came through the door, holding the earrings out to Evalie. "I'm sorry. I didn't know they were yours, that they weren't for me."

Evalie turned her left hand over in a cup and Park placed the earrings softly in her hand. Evalie immediately clasped her hand shut. She rushed back inside. Tears sprang to her eyes and there was nothing she could do to stop them. She ran to her bedroom and slammed the door behind her. Evalie placed the box on her bedside table and buried her face in her pillow. She battled for air against the thoughts that were piling in on her.

What on earth is going on?

Who put the earrings there?

How did they get into my backyard?

How did they find them in the hotel?

What does this mean?

How am I going to explain this to Park?

Evalie sat up on her bed. She unclenched her left hand and carefully put the earrings on. She felt her earlobes with her left thumb and forefinger. Evalie shuddered and drew in a long breath. Her body relaxed a little. She reached over to the side table and grabbed the little box. She opened the hinged lid slowly and peered inside. Evalie noticed something black on the base. She glanced up at the bedroom door. Evalie gently pulled out a square of black paper and unfolded it. The silver handwriting was unmistakably Guy's.

Plan B. Meet at the fountain. Sunday 7:00 a.m.

Evalie gasped. Her hand covered her mouth and heart thundered in her chest. Tears streamed down her face anew. She tried hard to compose herself. Evalie wiped her hands on her leggings and carefully refolded the note, replacing it into the bottom of the earring box. She opened her wardrobe and found her favourite jacket, which she hadn't much use for in Xoha. Evalie hid the box deep inside a fleece-lined pocket. Then she went into the cleansing room and sprayed her face with water again. She didn't dare look in the mirror. She walked back through to her bedroom. Evalie paced up and down twice before she opened the door and walked out to the lounge.

Evalie looked around for Park. She was outside. Evalie padded softly across the floor and took in a deep breath. She opened the door and joined Park at the outdoor table. The cheeses had been half devoured.

"So, the present was not for me, but for you. Who is coming into your garden and leaving things for you? How is this even … what is going on, X?"

"I can't tell you because I don't know."

"You must report this to the authorities. You know that, right?" Park looked at Evalie. "What are you doing wearing them, X? You can't, you shouldn't—"

"They are my earrings. I don't know how they came back to me. I lost them at the hotel the morning before I came to Xoha. The person at the hotel said that if they found them, they would send them back to me. I guess it just took them a long time to find them."

"Okay. If the authorities returned them, why would they put them in your back garden, with a bow on the box?"

"I don't know."

"And why did you get so upset?"

"I was just shocked, I guess. Sorry."

"This is too strange." Park drank the last drops of wine and plonked her glass on the table. "I think I should go. I have some things I need to do."

"Oh, okay. But you're fine, right? We're fine?"

"Yes, I'm fine X."

"Please don't go reporting me, reporting this." Evalie waved her arms in an arc. "I'll make some enquiries on Monday and see if I can find out about the box, the earrings."

"That's a strange thing to say. Why would you think I would report you?"

Evalie shrugged.

"I wouldn't report you. It's your puzzle to solve." Park rose from her seat.

Evalie stood, too. They hugged briefly. Evalie followed Park through the house to the front door.

Park put her suit on and clipped her helmet. "See you tomorrow then?"

"Um, yeah. Sure. See you tomorrow." Evalie opened the door and watched Park walk across the porch. She disappeared down the path. Evalie closed the door. She leaned against the cold metal and sighed.

CHAPTER FORTY-EIGHT

Evalie sat on the park bench overlooking the fountain. The morning light softened the vibrancy of its digital image. It looked less realistic but was still impressive. She checked the time.

6:55 a.m.

Despite her best efforts to sit still, Evalie's right knee bounced up and down a little. The park was quiet at this early hour on a Sunday. She stared blankly ahead. Thoughts crowded her mind, and there was no space to appreciate the beauty of the Latona Fountain. With one minute to go, Evalie nibbled on her lower lip. She wanted to stand. And run. She wanted to tear off her suit and get the hell out of there.

Suddenly, she saw him. He walked towards the fountain from the east path. Despite being suited, he stood out. That walk. It was Guy. She had to stop herself from jumping up and running to him, hugging him. Never letting go. Instead, she waited, and he sat down next to her. His hand brushed the side of her leg and even through the metal, Evalie felt a spark that set her heart a flutter.

The two of them rose instinctually and went to the back of the fountain. They huddled in close to one another.

"I thought they arrested you, I-"

"Yes, I know; I'm sorry. But there's no time for that. We need to go now. To the train. We're heading for the coast. That's all I can say."

"Okay."

Guy turned and walked, then noticed Evalie's hesitation. "Come on, E, we have to go."

"It's just. I am ... well, I'm scared." Evalie braced herself for the flippant comment or the hurry up. She held her breath.

Guy turned back. He leaned in close, so their helmets were touching. "Me too."

Evalie exhaled.

Guy continued in a low voice. "I can't ... I can't say everything is going to be okay. But whatever happens, we're in this together. I've got your back, Evalie, and I know you've got mine. So, let's go."

They walked away from the fountain. Evalie felt relieved. But there was a looming trepidation. She couldn't allow herself to think about what she was leaving behind. How Park would react when she didn't show up and wasn't contactable. She pushed it all away and focused on placing one foot in front of the other.

* * *

They stood on the platform of City East station waiting for the train. They were standing a little way apart, turned slightly away from one another so they could monitor each end of the platform. Evalie bit her lip and tapped a beat on the side of her leg with the fingers of her right hand. She tried to find topics of casual conversation, but all she had in her head were the hard questions bumping against each other and twisting her gut ever tighter. Even though it appeared they were alone, for now at least, it wasn't a good time for a heavy talk. Evalie stayed silent. Guy did too.

Slowly, a dozen people joined them on the platform. Evalie was a little surprised at the influx of passengers. She tried not to think the worst of every grey suit. Surely they were just keen to beat the crowds to the natural beauty of Xoha. When the train arrived, the two alighted and sat next to each other in the middle of the second carriage. Four others joined them in the carriage.

Evalie looked out the window at the familiar scenery. She still marvelled at the beauty of City East and its surrounds. It didn't take long to get into the dark green forest. The electric train passed quietly through the landscape. The browns and greens blurred as the train sped past. Further on, the trees thinned out to low scrub. Then the mountains came into view. Their deep blue mass stretched upwards to the sky. The tops hid in thick cottony curls of cloud. Patches of gold blotted the scene from the first rays of the morning sun.

"Magnificent," Evalie said.

Guy put his hand on Evalie's leg. "It really is."

The train stopped for five minutes at the transit station for the mountains. The four other grey suits in their carriage got off. No one got on. As the train continued to City South station, Evalie shifted in her seat and snuggled into Guy. It didn't feel that comfortable in the suit, but the closeness soothed her. She closed her eyes.

* * *

As the train slowed, Guy moved and Evalie opened her eyes, blinking herself back into the train and their journey. The train stopped. They got off and crossed the platform to board the awaiting train towards City West. As they got near to the waiting train, Guy suddenly put his hand in front of Evalie. Then he stepped ahead of her and changed direction to walk down the platform. Evalie followed him, heart rate rising.

What did he see? she thought.

The train left the platform. They left through the exit. Once they were alone on a path that wandered through City South, Evalie swallowed hard. "What happened back there? What was wrong with the train?"

Guy turned his head to look beside and behind them. "Law enforcement was on the train. I saw two khaki green suits standing in the carriage. It could be nothing, but I didn't think we should take any chances."

"Oh. Right."

"I saw two others get on at the other end of the train."

"I'm embarrassed to say I didn't see them. What are we going to do? There's no other way to get to the coast, is there?"

"No." Guy raised a hand to his head. "I don't know."

"Shall we go get a drink? I'm thirsty."

"I'd prefer not to make any transactions here. They can easily trace them."

"Oh. What about with my suit, would that be less obvious?"

"Maybe. I still don't think it's a good idea, though. Sorry."

"No, that's okay. I get it. Let's go sit down on that bench over there for a minute."

Guy followed Evalie to the bench. He paused before sitting down next to her.

"We can't wander around here all day, especially with nothing to drink. I think we should go back to the station and get on the next train."

"I guess."

"We've got to keep going. It's our only option." Evalie stood and put her hand out to Guy. "I've got your back. Come on, we can do this."

Unsuited

Guy took Evalie's hand. They walked hand-in-hand back to the station. The two grey suits stood waiting for the train. Again, they stood slightly apart, faced towards either end of the platform so they could monitor for khaki green suits, or anything remotely suspicious. Evalie was thirstier with each passing minute. She tried to repress the feeling and focus on the platform. She was relieved when the westerly bound train arrived moments later.

* * *

Evalie nearly jumped for joy when she saw the seaside station in the distance. She and Guy stood ready for the train to stop, then burst through the doors onto the platform. There were only three others that got off the train. They exited the station and walked down an adjoining path. The sky was completely overcast. The clouds hung low, and the seabirds screeched as they passed overhead. Evalie tried not to take it as an ominous sign.

She noticed the air in her suit increase as they picked up their pace. She walked beside Guy, matching his steps. Her mind flashed back to the many nights they'd walked together in Melbourne. It seemed like a lifetime ago. Mostly they'd strolled back then. This stride was serious, with a clear destination, although Evalie knew nothing about it. Observing the closed shops, she realised she could have been anywhere in Xoha. It all looked the same. Every town and suburb, every station and path.

The dull monotony was suddenly clear. This was the price of the version of equality she'd signed up for so naively all that time ago. She felt like screaming, like ripping off her suit, running to the sand and dancing on the beach. Splashing in the water and diving under the waves. She'd been mesmerised by this place, but it was an illusion. Just like the fountain. The disappointment sank heavy in her stomach like an overdose of carbohydrates. The ugly truth of Xoha disillusioned her. But most of all, she was upset with herself for being sold such a fanciful dream.

As they came to the end of the path, they turned left and headed towards the boats. The marina was quiet. There was not another suit in sight. Evalie and Guy walked out onto the jetty, past a variety of boats, their white berths bobbing up and down, boards groaning and straining with movement. Evalie smiled as they came up to a boat with curly lettering. She mouthed the name, "X Stream."

Guy climbed aboard and held out his hand for Evalie. She took it and allowed herself to be pulled on board. Evalie immediately felt uneasy, even though the rocking was negligible. They walked across the deck, headed for the cabin. Guy closed the door at the top of the stairs and locked it. They climbed down the steep steps, one at a time.

Guy led Evalie through the kitchen and into a small bedroom. He removed his helmet and suit and signalled for Evalie to do the same. Guy took the suits and disappeared out of the bedroom door. He came back a few moments later, holding a glass of water.

"Don't worry, I've got the best motion sickness medicine money can buy." He went over to a set of drawers and pulled out a packet. "Here, take two of these." He handed Evalie the tablets and the water.

"Thanks," she said. She swallowed the tablets and guzzled the water. "I must admit, I was worried when I saw the boats."

Guy smiled feebly. "We definitely don't want a repeat of our last time on a boat together."

Evalie flopped down on the bed.

Guy disappeared back through the door.

Evalie looked up when she heard him return.

He was carrying a plate of bread, cheese, and dried fruit. "I thought you might be hungry."

"Thanks. Oh Guy, this isn't just a hideout, is it? I'm not sure I can go back there, you know, to my house. I can't continue living this lie any longer. When I thought they had taken you, I tried really hard to fool myself I could manage here. I was completely clueless about what else to do. I had no option. But I can't—"

"Evalie, it's alright," he whispered. He cleared his throat. "I know. I feel it too. We sail for Melbourne tomorrow. The crew is meeting us here at four thirty in the morning. We will be out of the harbour for our 'fishing trip'"—Guy motioned quotation marks in the air with his fingers—"before five. All we have to do is get past the border control boats and we will be sailing across the Tasman Sea and on our way home to freedom. I have a new chip for your suit with the permit for offshore fishing. First, we need to clean it to remove today's journey from your current chip. Then we'll crush it and throw it overboard, just to be safe. The new one will replace it, with no record of your time here. Hopefully, law enforcement doesn't have real-time tracking on your chip."

Evalie's head swam. "So, our escape is this boat. We leave tomorrow morning. We are going to sail all the way back to Australia. Guy, I don't know if—"

"We don't have any other options, E."

The desperation in his voice frightened Evalie. "Right. Well. Okay. It's just a lot to take in."

"I know it is. Here, have some food. I'll be right back."

Evalie picked at the plate of food whilst listening to Guy's footsteps climb back up onto the deck. She lost them somewhere up above. She chewed on a piece of sourdough bread. While she perched on the edge of the bed trying to absorb the details of the plan, she realised she was hungrier than she had thought. By the time Guy returned a few minutes later, she had finished three quarters of the plate.

"I'm sure it's a good plan. Thanks for all this."

"Sure. Well, the food must be good." Guy smiled at Evalie. "Here, give me some."

Evalie passed the plate to him.

He took a couple of pieces of cheese and placed the plate on the side table. Then he put the cheese back down and licked his fingers. "Hey, before I forget, or get distracted." Guy looked at Evalie and raised his eyebrows.

Evalie smiled and gave Guy a gentle shove.

"I need to show you the suit disabler. Seriously though, in case we need it, which I hope won't happen." Guy reached across to a drawer under the side of the bed. He took out a small, flat, torch-like object.

Evalie recognised it from the tree hideout.

Guy held up the disabler in front of Evalie. "All you have to do is press it onto any part of a suit and flick this switch. I can't actually demonstrate as it's pretty powerful."

"Oh, okay. Don't then."

"It makes a kind of zapping sound, and it completely disables the suit. The person will crumble to the floor and the suit will turn dark green."

"Right. That seems fierce. Can I hold it?"

Guy passed the disabler to Evalie. "Only use it in an emergency, okay?"

"Yeah, I get it. How long does the effect last for? I assume it wears off." Evalie turned it over in her hand.

"Yes, it's only temporary. It lasts about twenty minutes."

"Okay. Best put it away now. It's a bit creepy." She passed it back to Guy.

"Sure. Remember, it is *here* if you need it." Guy returned the disabler to the drawer. He closed the drawer and sat up straight on the bed. "And it takes a minute or two to recharge once you use it. So, if you're trying to disable more than one suit, remember that it won't work straight away."

"Yep, got it. I'll remember. Any other neat weapons I should know about?"

"No, I think that's it."

"Good."

"Oh, there is something else you should know about."

"What's that?"

"The chip reader. In case you need to find out someone's background. It's located at the opposite end of the disabler. You need to remove the chip from the suit and stick it in the slot in the end. I'm sure you won't need to know any of this, though."

"Hopefully."

"The plan will work, Evalie. It's a good plan."

"I trust you."

Guy smiled at Evalie. Then put a large piece of cheese in his mouth and chewed, loudly.

I forgot he was a loud eater, Evalie thought. She chuckled to herself.

"What's so funny?" Guy asked.

"Nothing, I was just thinking about how much I've missed watching you eat."

CHAPTER FORTY-NINE

Evalie and Guy lay next to one another on the small cosy bed. The plate beside the bed held only a few crumbs. Evalie looked at Guy and felt that he'd aged substantially in the time that had passed while they were apart. Guy brushed her fringe from her face. His fingers trailed down her face to her shoulder.

"How are you? Any motion sickness?"

"I feel fine, thanks. That food really settled my stomach, and well, the medicine seems to work too."

Guy's hand traced the rest of Evalie's body. Evalie moved closer and kissed him with the force of desire caused by separation, loneliness, and regret. They made quiet, passionate love. The boat rocked gently in the breeze. The creaks of wood grinding against wood and the lapping of the water all but drowned out their heavy breathing and occasional primordial groan. Their naked bodies intertwined; they lay together on the bed. Evalie's whole body tingled, and her left leg twitched.

"Wow," Guy said. He peered sideways at Evalie.

"Yeah. I've really missed that," Evalie replied.

They lay without speaking for ten minutes. Guy kissed Evalie's nose.

"I was wondering how we were going to keep ourselves amused on this little boat until bedtime."

Guy snorted a laugh. "We never had trouble finding things to do between the sheets."

"True. That was always the easiest part of our relationship." Evalie traced a finger down Guy's chest. She studied the black hair and the way it just stopped, giving way to a smooth stomach and then further down more hair, thicker and curlier.

Guy clasped her hand in his. "That tickles." After a few minutes, he released Evalie's hand. "Have you, uh, been with anyone else here?" He tried to look casual, but Evalie could see the anxiety in his eyes.

"Well, it has been more than a year." She studied Guy's face. Disappointment and hurt flashed through his eyes.

They moved subconsciously apart, so there was a little space of sheets between.

Evalie lay on her back, looking at the ceiling. "Full disclosure," she said. "I need to be honest with you. Not telling you the truth has led us to, well, here." Evalie paused, absentmindedly flicking her right thumb against her pointer finger. "I've had a couple of romances, kind of. Well, a relationship, I guess, with a woman." Evalie didn't stop to look at Guy's reaction. "I don't know if she's familiar to you. You said something about being careful about the company Raven kept." Evalie glanced at Guy.

He had his eyes closed.

Evalie sighed. "Anyway, her Xohan name is Park. It became complicated and turned ugly. Of course, you don't know who people are until you see them unsuited and—"

"Evalie, it's alright. You don't have to tell me all the details. I'm glad you're being honest with me. That's what I want for our relationship too. But you don't need to be, well, *that* honest." He opened his eyes and looked at her.

She turned her head to face him. "Oh. Right. Sorry."

"You don't need to apologise. You've already apologised enough. I don't want you to feel guilty about this part of your life. Hopefully, it will soon be far behind us. A distant memory."

"Okay. Well, thanks. It's just really hard to, you know, forgive myself for this." A tear rolled down Evalie's cheek, and she brushed it quickly with the back of her right hand. "Have you been in any relationships?"

Guy laid back and stared at the ceiling. Then he took her hand. "I have. Just one. Full disclosure." He studied Evalie's face.

Evalie tried her hardest not to let the hurt show in her eyes. "I was gone. I get it." The words came out strained, and Evalie wished she had her helmet to mediate them.

"Yes. You were. But that doesn't make this easy. This is so difficult to say to you. And you have to promise to keep it a secret. It's over for good. It was really more of a backlash against losing you. A way to deal with the pain. Not a very good one, granted." He rolled over and looked into Evalie's eyes. "I'm truly sorry."

"Who was it, Guy? This sounds—"

"Stella."

Evalie jerked away from Guy and covered her open mouth with her right hand. Tears sprang to her eyes. "No, oh no." She sat bolt upright on the edge of the bed. "I can't believe this. My Stella? Does Tejas know?"

"No. And he can't ever know; it would kill him. It's over and it was nothing. Just comfort between two people who had lost someone and didn't know how to deal with the pain." Guy paused. "I made a promise to Stella that we would never see her again. Or Tejas. Both of us. Well, I promised I wouldn't see them. You were gone. But I'm sure it applies to you too. It was before I came to look for you."

Evalie sprang off the bed. "I can't believe ... I ... you, and Stella? Guy! How could you? I need some fresh air."

"Ev, you can't go outside without a suit on. You can't risk it here. Someone might see you."

Evalie stormed into the kitchen. Her face flushed magenta. Blood pounded in her ears. She knew she had no right to be this furious after all she had done. But Stella and Guy? It was inconceivable. She swiped at the cups on the bench. They flew off and crashed onto the floor, making a loud clatter but not breaking. She wished they had smashed into a million pieces. She dropped to the floor, knees in hands and buried her head. Tears flowed freely.

Guy didn't try to soothe her. He stood in the doorway for a few minutes, then disappeared back into the bedroom.

When Evalie unravelled herself and got off the floor, she saw the cups were back on the bench. She hadn't even noticed Guy in the kitchen. She felt awful. Exhausted. She padded softly through to the bedroom. Guy lay on the bed, eyes closed. She searched for the time and found a small clock on the side table. It was early evening. She looked at Guy lying peacefully and wondered if he'd fallen asleep. She used the tiny bathroom and hopped into bed beside him, naked. He rolled over to face her, but she rolled the other way.

He reached out an arm and lay it across her side. Her nipples prickled. She shuffled closer to him. She felt his manhood awaken. He gently caressed her breasts and his fingers wandered down across her stomach and down further into the hair and further still. Then he was inside her. She moaned and flipped over. This time they had loud wild sex and as Evalie climaxed for the first time in such a long time, she realised she wasn't mad at him anymore. She nearly wasn't mad at herself either.

CHAPTER FIFTY

The alarm entered Evalie's consciousness as if from another realm. She rolled onto her back and stretched out her legs. Then an arm. The bed was empty beside her. She opened her eyes. Guy was standing beside the bed, dressed in black, long-sleeved underwear. He walked over and switched off the alarm, then leaned across and kissed Evalie's forehead.

"Time for action. The crew will be here in ten minutes. It's best if we're suited when they get here."

"Right," Evalie said. She yawned. "Do you have any clothes for me? I didn't bring a thing with me."

"Yes, it's all organised. Everything you need is in this drawer. There's breakfast in the kitchen. Don't forget to take some more of the motion sickness medication once you've eaten something. I'm going to get my suit on and go up on deck."

"Mm, hmm," Evalie said sleepily.

"Come on sleepy head," Guy chided. "You've really got to get up now."

"Okay, okay." Evalie got out of bed and walked seductively past Guy to the bathroom. "If that's what you'd prefer."

"I tell you what I'd prefer," he said. He tried to catch Evalie, but she slipped past him and shut the door swiftly behind her.

Her laugh bounced around the walls. As she splashed her face with water, she peered at herself in the tiny mirror and saw a happy person beaming back. She dressed quickly and gulped down the juice and bread, along with two tablets. Evalie left the medicine in the kitchen cabinet for later. She was just getting her suit on when she heard voices outside. Most likely the crew. The voices were monotone, as usual, but there was something about them that made Evalie stop what she was doing and try to listen. There was an urgency about them. They were in a precarious situation, and she had to keep her wits about her. No more delighting in the experience of sexual satisfaction. Evalie clicked her helmet in place and patted the blue light on her shoulder; she was ready. As she climbed slowly up the steps, she listened. There was only the hum of the engine and the sound of water lapping against the boat and its mooring.

The deck was empty. Evalie's stomach sank, and she regretted eating her breakfast so quickly.

Where has Guy gone? It's four thirty-five; we're supposed to be setting off in a few minutes with a crew of five, she thought. *It was five, wasn't it?*

Guy had given no instruction about how to contact him if he wasn't there. There was no 'Plan B' this time, well, none that she was aware of. Evalie reached for her screen but thought better of it. Any digital communications would surely be too dangerous. She wandered about on deck, studying the ropes and trying to get her head around it all. *What if that was law enforcement I heard on the boat earlier?* Evalie shuddered at the thought. "Come on Guy, where are you?" Evalie muttered as she looked out across the marina.

Unsuited

The sky was cloudy with no stars visible. The frosty morning air made Evalie's suit switch up the heat. Evalie wished she could feel the morning air on her face. She looked around. There was no one in sight. For a split second, she considered taking off her helmet. Then she remembered her predicament. She went to the cockpit and looked for any clues as to where Guy had gone.

There was nothing that stuck out. The two chairs were empty. Evalie went back down into the kitchen and walked through to the bedroom and bathroom. She was panicking.

What should I do?

How long has it been since I heard voices outside?

She looked at the time.

4:46 a.m.

How long should I wait?

Evalie sat down on the bed and took some deep breaths. She needed to figure out how to work the boat and get out of here. She wished Guy had let her in on the plan earlier so she could have been much more across the details.

Would I leave without him if I knew how to? she thought.

Her father's voice echoed in her mind. "You're not good enough. You're a disappointment and you don't deserve Guy. He will figure it out soon enough and leave. That's probably why he's not here now."

Evalie raced up the steps onto deck and started untying one rope that secured the boat to the jetty. She was going to get this boat out somehow. She was not staying in Xoha another minute.

I'm done with this place, she thought, desperately. *If I have to live a life at sea, I ...*

Evalie fell to her knees on the deck, helmeted head in hands, and cried. Big sobs wracked her body. The soft tear absorbers sprang into action. Her insides felt like a twisted tree.

When the worst had passed, she sat, solemn, holding her knees to her chest. Then she heard something. Footsteps. Someone was coming along the jetty. She rose to her feet and grabbed hold of the rope she had partly untied. The three suits strode to the boat and got onboard.

"X, thank goodness you're ready. We have to leave now. Right now."

"Ah, well okay." Evalie looked nervously at the three people. The two that hadn't spoken got to work untying the other ropes. Why had Guy called her X? She wanted to ask if it was him. Instead, she dropped the rope and followed the person into the cockpit. "Where's the third?" she asked.

"They didn't make it. There was a mixup this morning when they were trying to get to the boat. Turns out they weren't on our side E," the suit said, lowering their voice at the end. "It's not safe for us to use our real names," they whispered into her ear. "Once we're out of the harbour, we'll know who we can really trust."

Evalie nodded in reply.

"Now you took your medication, didn't you?"

Evalie breathed a sigh of relief. It was Guy. She knew it now. "Yes, I did. What do I call you?" she whispered.

"Just call me Y," Guy said. "We can be X and Y."

X snorted.

"Okay, maybe not. What about Skipper, then?" Guy said.

"What are the others calling you? And how did you learn to sail a boat, anyway?" Evalie asked.

"They've been calling me Captain. And I learnt to sail when I was a teenager, I guess. My parents had a boat moored out at Mallacoota. Anyway, we could really use your help on deck. Introduce yourself. They'll tell you what to do." Guy gestured to the suits on deck.

"Oh, okay. Sure," Evalie said. She joined the two strangers on deck. "Hi, I'm X," she bellowed. "How can I help?"

One of the crew turned to her. "Well, grab that rope over there, would you?"

Evalie walked across and grabbed the rope.

"That's it, and wind it back around there, like the other one."

Evalie did her best to follow the instructions. She felt awkward.

The suit to her left untied the final rope from the jetty and called out, "Right, we're off."

The boat's engine revved, and the person jumped back aboard as the boat moved away from the mooring and began the slow punt out of the marina. Evalie felt relief wash over her. They were free! The feeling was quick lived as apprehension about the trip ahead seeped through her.

The person who had jumped back onboard came over. "You'll find it easier if you do it this way." The rope coiled neatly with ease.

"Oh, right. Thanks. I have a lot to learn about boats."

"Well, I hope you're a quick learner, in case we're stopped out here." They gestured towards the ocean.

"Right. I don't suppose you could give me a crash course, then?"

"Hmmm. Just follow me around and watch what I'm doing. If you have questions, just ask."

"Alright, sure." Evalie followed the suit around the deck, watching their actions. Occasionally, they explained what they were doing.

Some words were foreign, others familiar from the many nautical-related metaphors she'd heard. But knowing the metaphors wasn't really going to help her now.

I'm all at sea, Evalie thought. She cringed at her attempt at humour.

The person went to the cockpit. Evalie sighed and followed them in. The other two crew members were already in there. Evalie couldn't tell who anyone was. It was unsettling.

"So, that nonsense back there delayed us by about forty minutes," one suit said. "The border control boat should cross our path in about an hour, as we head south and out into the open sea."

Another suit studied an old map, yellowed and faded.

Evalie took out her screen. "Is this thing of any use now, or is it too dangerous?"

"Nah, it's useless," the suit with the map replied. "We're too far from land already. This boat doesn't have a connection to the Xohan network."

Evalie nodded. "Right. Okay."

"Now we need to be prepared for border control to intercept us within the hour," the suit without the map said. "We really need to be prepared for all scenarios. And remember, this far from land, all the suits will be grey. So, we won't be able to tell who anyone is if border control does intercept us."

"There are four people on our boat, with four fishing permits. We should be okay," Guy said from behind the wheel. "If we get stopped, we just need our stories to align. We are fishing for the Xoha Seafood Alliance. Everyone remember that, okay?"

"Yep," said the map holder.

"Sure," said the other one.

"Xoha Seafood Alliance," Evalie repeated.

"The primary concern is that our missing ship mate has likely got a message to law enforcement," the person without the map said. They leaned against the side wall. "That could cause some major problems for us."

"I don't mean to speak out of turn," Evalie said. "But why don't we just cross the border to New Zealand? We could easily get on a plane to Australia from there."

"It's too risky, X. New Zealand signed a no questions asked extradition agreement with Xoha last year, in exchange for some exclusive manufacturing and intellectual property rights for the suits. It turns out they're very useful to protect the population against communicable diseases. Even though it has been twenty years since the COVID-19 pandemic, China, Russia and North Korea have become big buyers of these suits. New Zealand is one of the chief beneficiaries."

"I never heard about that." Evalie shifted from one foot to the other. "I guess it's not the sort of information they like to share in Xoha."

"No. They have every reason to keep the outside world a secret," the person with the map said.

Evalie pressed her teeth into the corner of her lip. The question burned in her throat. She breathed in sharply. "What's the worst that could happen if border control sees through our fishing story?"

"A life of misery as Xohan slaves," someone said.

"Right, that sounds like something worth avoiding," Evalie responded with a nervous laugh. She wondered if they were joking, or if it was possible they could become Xohan slaves. She considered a followup question, but she wasn't sure she truly wanted to know the answer.

The boat pitched and Evalie grabbed for something to hold on to. Her stomach dropped and then rose into her throat. *It seems awfully rough for a day that started without wind,* Evalie thought. She supposed the protection of the marina may have distorted her weather expectations. They must be in open water now, away from the protection of the land. The wind whistled through the boat as if whispering a dismissive taunt about their futile attempt to leave Xoha. The impressive technology of the suits filtered the likely pungent smell of salt and seaweed out. Evalie smelt only the hint of delicate jasmine and vanilla fragrance within her suit.

* * *

Evalie checked the time. It had been half an hour since they left the safety of the marina. She paced back and forward. She could barely hear over her suit's temperature control system, and the wind and water thrashing the sides and deck of the boat. Evalie was worried about how long it would be until the motion sickness medication wore off.

But that's probably the least of my worries, she thought.

She wished she could talk openly about all her fears but didn't know who these strangers were on the boat with them, and Guy had said something about finding out who they could trust. It was all very unnerving. She bit her lip. "Focus Ev–, X. Focus," she muttered softly. The only trouble was, she had forgotten what it was she should focus on.

* * *

Evalie tried to help, but felt completely useless. She watched as the sailors untied and tied ropes to adjust the sails to the prevailing wind. The boat responded, changing course, and taking them closer to their fate. It felt tiny out here, this little amalgamation of wood and metal, in the vastness of the waves, with the sea rolling and pitching in a continuous roller coaster of blue-black and the occasional outburst of white foam. She was glad to have her suit on, to protect her from what were likely icy winds. It was strange being out on the water, exposed to the elements and yet completely protected. Evalie suddenly wondered if she would miss her suit if they made it back to Australia. It had become a cosy cocoon, and although sometimes stifling, it was also comforting.

The predawn light hinted at an overcast morning. Evalie didn't quite know what to do with herself. She hung around on deck, trying to follow the moves of the strangers whilst keeping out of their way. She eventually got sick of being in the wrong place all the time and snuck back below deck. Whilst sitting at the small table, she saw a map stuck to the wall. That's when she realised how she could help. Navigation. It was something she had been good at since she was a child. Finding her way with a map had got her out of a variety of awkward situations. Of course, it was a skill that many of her generation didn't have, always relying on tracking and map technologies to show them the quickest route to their destination. Perhaps that was the one thing she could thank her dad for, teaching her to read maps.

She went back upstairs to the cockpit. "Guy," she blurted, "I've got it! I'll be your navigator."

"Shh, it's Captain to you. That's what we agreed, wasn't it?"

Evalie clapped a gloved hand over her helmet. The sensation felt ridiculous.

"So, navigator. Right. I guess I could use some help. Have you ever seen a sea crossing map before though? It's a lot different from a road map."

"Let me see. I'm sure I can work it out. I've always had a knack for directions. The knots are too tricky. I'm really struggling out there. I feel like I'm just getting in the way. Your friends seem to have it covered."

"Okay, well, sure. Here is the main map we're working from." Guy passed the map to Evalie.

She studied it for a good time before nodding her head. "Yes, I see. It is complex, but we're following this line here, aren't we?" Evalie traced her finger across the Tasman Sea. "Which will take us to the Victorian coast. We should dock in somewhere near Port Welshpool, is that correct?"

"Yes, that's right."

"So, we're almost heading due west, then."

"The currents run down the east coast of Australia, so we need to head a few degrees north to account for that. But if you head west, you can't miss Australia from here. It's just a matter of finding a port to dock at when we hit landfall. A smaller port is preferable. We are more likely to get clearance to dock and we can apply to the government to cancel your death ... I mean, to get your citizenship rights reinstated. Hopefully, we will buy ourselves some time, anyway."

"What did you say?"

"A lot. Weren't you listening?"

"Don't play the fool with me, G—Captain. You said something about cancelling my death—"

"When you agreed to come here, what did they tell you would happen to your citizenship? What did they say they would tell your family and friends?"

"I agreed to renounce my Australian citizenship. They told me they would take care of packing up my apartment, my things. They would send people trained in counselling or something, to tell my family and friends and my boy—and you. Isn't that what happened?"

"Not exactly. They told me you were dead."

"What? But why? Why would they do that?"

"That's how I got your earrings. They brought them over to my place, posing as police officers, and told me you were dead."

"I ... they told you I was dead! I had no idea. My mum's earrings. That's so sick. I've been wanting to ask about the earrings but I haven't had a chance. So much has been–"

"That's not all of it–"

"Does dad think I'm dead too? And Stella? Is that why you–"

"Just let me finish. I really need to tell you this. Your dad was the one who worked out you weren't dead, that you'd come here."

"My dad, but–"

The boat jolted sideways. Evalie gasped. There was yelling on deck, but she couldn't make out any of the words.

CHAPTER FIFTY-ONE

Four grey suits stormed the cockpit. Two apprehended Guy. *Border control,* Evalie thought. She edged her way out and flew down the steps to the kitchen. The other two guards pursued her. She took two steps towards the bedroom, then they grabbed her arms and thrust them behind her back.

"What is the meaning of this?" she asked.

The guards shoved her backwards into the kitchen cabinet. They held her arms tight.

"I demand to know what's going on," Evalie continued. "My boss at city office will surely have something to say about this. They authorised me to come here and witness the testing of the systems offshore. I'm due back by midday. They will be waiting for me."

"We are just doing our job. We must stop all boats attempting to travel beyond Xohan borders and take any persons we find back to shore," one suit said.

"What? Attempting to travel beyond the borders, don't be ridiculous," Evalie scoffed. "I am just doing my job, too. They asked us to sail out as far as we can to see that the systems only work until the perimeter of Xohan waters. This is for an important city office project. Council approved it."

"What are you talking about? We haven't heard about any such project. They would have notified us."

"It's classified. That's why you haven't heard. I've already told you more than I should have. Now unhand my crew this instant or the Councillors will hear about this, and you'll all be reassigned."

"Council has approved this?"

"That's right. Council gave me strict instructions that we've been following to the letter. If you're familiar with the way they like to work, you'll know they don't suffer fools and are very keen that we implement plans as directed."

"Yes, we're familiar with the way of Council."

The hands holding Evalie released their grip on her, and she pulled away.

"Bring my crew back and leave our vessel," Evalie said, bolstered by the reaction of her efforts. "You can consider that an order from the Councillor's themselves."

The guards climbed back up the steps. Evalie heard orders given in short bursts. When she reached the top of the steps, she saw Guy being pushed back into the cockpit. It was hard to see if he was okay.

"Welcome back Captain. We shouldn't have any further trouble from them."

"What did you say to them?" Guy asked.

"I just told them the truth. That we are on a mission as directed by Council."

Guy's head spun around. He paused, then walked over to Evalie. "Right, of course. The truth."

Evalie suddenly had a horrible thought. *What if this isn't Guy? What if it is one of the border control guards pretending to be Guy?* Evalie waved her hand dismissively.

"Now, let's get back to our mission. I'm just going to check that things are okay on deck." Evalie considered crossing her fingers, but it felt weird in a suit. She wondered if there was a way to validate the suits on the boat to ensure they were the same people as before and not imposters from border control. This was no time to risk being trapped by the border guards in the very lie that had potentially set them free. As she walked through the door, she had an idea. She could ask Guy a question that only he would know the answer to. After she was sure it was him, she could get him to help her come up with a plan for verifying the identity of the other two, whom she barely knew.

Evalie stood on deck, holding onto the rail. There were two suits checking the sails. She let go of the rail and walked around, looking for any sign of another boat. *It couldn't be that far away from us already, surely*, she thought. She spotted a boat off in the distance. Its dark grey shape loomed off the starboard deck.

"That was intense," she called out to the suit closest to her.

"Yeah," they replied.

The boat turned abruptly to the left, and Evalie fell onto the rail. She grabbed desperately at the metal to steady herself. They appeared to be turning around. Evalie felt the dread rise in her stomach.

We're turning around, she thought. *Someone is taking us back to Xoha.* She felt like screaming. She examined the suits on deck and realised they could be anyone. How could she know if they had been plotting against her and Guy from the beginning? She raced back down the steps and into the bedroom.

No time for questions. She would have to use the suit disabler. *I will start with the suits on deck*, she thought. *And then Guy, or whoever it is, in the cockpit.*

Evalie struggled to come to terms with the fact that it might not be Guy in the cockpit. But she knew for sure that he would not have turned the boat around.

"You're so naïve. It must be a border control guard. They all must be border guards." The sound of her pessimistic father's voice stunned her.

She shook her head vigorously. "Leave me alone!" she shouted. The helmet suppressed the intended authority of her voice. "I'm done with you and your negativity. It's over. I am capable. I am enough."

Evalie retrieved the small weapon from the drawer under the side of the bed. She wished she had tested it the night before, or at least seen it in action.

What did he say? she thought. *Hold it against the suit and flick the switch.*

She smirked at the recollection of Guy and the memory of them in bed together that danced through her head. Her cheeks burned invisibly under the veil of her helmet.

"Concentrate," she warned. "Time to disable the robots," she added in a whisper.

Evalie heard a noise. There was someone in the kitchen. She flattened herself against the wall, slightly behind the door, which was fixed open with a powerful magnet at the bottom.

"X," a voice called.

Evalie stifled her reflex to respond. She stayed silent and waited. If the three people on her boat were border guards, she would have to disable all of them.

But then what? she thought. She stifled the panic rising in her throat. *Where is Guy?*

She realised that if he wasn't on this boat, he must be on the other. Border control must have turned this boat towards the other one, which meant they were getting closer to it.

How will I get Guy back? I can't sail this boat alone, she thought.

Evalie knew she couldn't leave him here after all he'd done for her. Being apprehended was also not an option. It was absolutely clear. The only option was to disable the suits and then work out what to do next.

Evalie heard footsteps across the floor, nearing the door to the bedroom. She listened closely, fairly certain she could only hear two feet. She waited until the suit had just entered the bedroom, then leapt forward and zapped the middle of the suit with the disabler. The suit shone a sick-looking green and collapsed into a pile on the floor next to the bed. The buzzing sound and zap of the disabler rang through the small room. Evalie's heart pounded in her ears. A metallic taste hung in her mouth. She knew she didn't have long before someone else came. Evalie swiftly returned the disabler to her front pocket and un-clicked the helmet in front of her. She pulled it off the limp body.

It was a woman with long brown hair. She looked familiar. "Ivy," Evalie said. "I think you are our friend." Evalie felt stomach acid rise in her throat. She swallowed hard. Her throat burned. As she was trying to replace the helmet, she heard footsteps descending from the deck. Two sets. Evalie didn't have time to move the limp person out of sight. She hung just behind the door. She would need to push the first person into the second, then zap them, so the disabler had time to recharge.

Evalie steadied herself. There were no voices this time. She retrieved the disabler from her suit pocket. When she heard them close by the door, she leapt out and pushed hard. Without hesitation, she zapped the first suit, and the person crumbled before her. The suit turned the same ill-green as the first disarmed one. This time, the person fell in the doorway, partially blocking it. The suit behind was off balance, but didn't fall. The person scrambled in the kitchen. Evalie counted to fifteen. She heard the person climb the steps. Evalie clambered over the suit in the doorway. Her foot got caught in a part of the suit. Evalie kicked wildly, until it was free, trying to ignore the fact it could be Guy underneath that suit. She held tight to the disabler in her right hand and pulled herself up the stairs with her left.

When she got to the top step, she saw a flash of the suit out on deck. Evalie propelled herself forward with all that she had. She flew onto the deck metres away from her target. She could see the other boat, no longer a shadow on the horizon. It was less than fifty metres away. The person started waving their hands and jumping up and down. They were yelling something she couldn't understand. For the first time, her helmet wasn't translating for her. The words were foreign and urgent.

Evalie wasted no time. She came in close behind and pressed the disabler to the back of their suit. They turned just as it zapped and fell to the deck, green and limp, like the others. Evalie saw the crew on the other boat and gasped. There were at least ten suits on deck. *Where had all these guards come from?*

She hoped like hell Guy was the unidentified crumpled mess below deck.

Evalie rushed into the cockpit. She needed to buy a little time. Evalie looked at all the controls. She saw the autopilot switch glowing.

The guard had locked the steering wheel in place. Evalie grasped at the wheel and unlocked it. She slowly turned the wheel to her left.

"No sudden moves. Easy now," she mumbled.

She felt the boat shift course, away from the border control ship. Evalie fled back down to the bedroom. She stared at the crumpled green suit in the doorway. She pushed it as gently as she could, trying to get it fully into the bedroom. It nearly worked. Only one foot poked through the doorway. There wasn't much room with Ivy lying beside the bed. Evalie cautiously unhooked the helmet. She slipped it off and gasped. The familiar features were duller than usual, but there was no mistaking who he was.

"Seed," she mouthed. She didn't dare say the name aloud.

Evalie raised her hand to her mouth, but only felt the hard exterior of her helmet. Her mind raced at pace with her elevated pulse.

Friend or foe?

Accomplice or captor?

He led me to the unsuited.

Was he already on the boat before?

A ship horn sounded.

Evalie jumped.

Is there another boat out there?

Did the border guards call for backup?

Evalie wanted to curl up in a ball on the bed and wait for it all to be over. She played the scene over in her mind.

"They will capture you. Then what?" she asked herself impatiently.

The dread that descended into the depths of her stomach propelled Evalie into action. She pushed Seed's remaining foot inside and pulled at the bedroom door, squeezing it shut.

"Sorry," she murmured.

Evalie hoped the sound of the door opening would be enough to alert her once they awakened from their daze. She glanced at the time. There were probably only a few minutes left. She scrambled up the stairs onto the deck to the third body. She removed the helmet more easily now that she'd had practice. It was not Guy.

Her heart skipped a beat. The woman had shiny black hair tied in a tight bun. Her features were unfamiliar. A stranger.

"Who are you?" she asked.

Seed, Ivy, and an unknown, Evalie thought. *But no Guy. What should I do?*

"What the hell can I do?" she asked herself.

Evalie thought about trying to drag the unknown person below deck. She paced back and forward and looked out at the sea. There was nothing but water ahead. She dared not look behind. Evalie felt the blood drain from her face. Her mouth was dry, and she started yawning. Thoughts invaded her now thumping head.

The tablets. In the kitchen.

It's too risky right now.

You should focus on the suits. And getting Guy back.

He must be on the other boat. But there are so many of them.

How will I find Guy?

Could I disable them all?

Could I leave him here and come back for him later, with back up?

I could get the Australian government involved.

Would they help him?

Above all the mind chatter rose her mother's sweet voice. "He risked everything for you, Evalie. You can't just leave him."

Evalie was relieved to hear her mother's voice after all this time. She knew she was right. "Plus, mum, who else can sail this damn ship!"

CHAPTER FIFTY-TWO

Evalie paced up and down in the cockpit. She looked straight ahead and left the wheel locked, keeping the boat steady on its current trajectory. All she could see was the ocean in front and all around her. When she had dared to look around the back of the boat, she hadn't seen the grey ship from earlier, as expected.

It was an eerie feeling now, being alone at sea. There was a foreboding air about, even though she couldn't feel any air on her face; she wished she could. Evalie couldn't get her mind around why there were still four people on her boat, including herself, but Guy was gone. Did they swap him for one border guard? It made little sense. Evalie felt her queasiness intensify.

She unlocked the wheel and turned it carefully, feeling the ship respond. The sails flapped nosily in the breeze. She would need to fix them at some point, tighten them or re-tie them or something. But for now, the boat had changed direction. She locked the wheel once more. The boat travelled due west. If she was reading the instruments correctly, that is. If only she could get a message to Guy, so she could identify him from the other suits on deck. She hoped he was conscious, unlike her current companions.

If only there was a way to tell who the third person on her ship was and what the intention was of the three. The questions bombarded her brain.

How will I know whose side Seed is on?

What about Ivy?

Were they hoping to escape like me?

Surely, I can trust Ivy, the unsuited.

But what about Seed?

Evalie retrieved the map from the kitchen, where she had dropped it when the guards apprehended her. She tried to flatten out its creases, then poured over it. She traced the route from the west coast of New Zealand to the east coast of Australia. It looked easy enough to get from A to B on a flat render, but the pitching sea was a constant reminder that the journey would never be easy. She traced a finger back and forwards across the great expanse of the Tasman Sea. Evalie attempted to replace any of the varied tragic scenarios her imagination offered in quick succession with a vision of her and Guy on deck, spotting the great brown land for the first time. In her imagination, they were euphoric. They were safe. Free. They were in love.

A ship horn sounded. It shattered her daydream and brought Evalie back to the moment. In the urgent clarity that followed, she remembered the chip reader.

Why didn't I think of this before?

I will find out who these people are. Maybe they can help.

The boat went over an enormous wave, pitching higher and then lower than it ever had before. Evalie grabbed for something to hang on to. Her stomach lurched more sharply than the boat, and she began salivating profusely. She would be no good to anyone if she started vomiting. Evalie went to the kitchen and grabbed the tablets from the overhead cupboard. She tipped two out of the small cannister into her hand and let them fall onto the bench. Then she crushed them with a suited fist. She used the map she was still carrying to maneuver the tablet dust into a glass and filled it with water. Grabbing a straw from the utensil drawer, she stirred the glass feverishly and pushed the straw through the hole in her helmet. She sucked the liquid tonic down in an instant.

Evalie retrieved the disabler and examined the end, where she could insert the chip. She thought about trying her chip in it to see who she was now, if anyone was to read her chip. Evalie shook the frivolity from her head and instead made her way to the bedroom door and nudged it inwards. She opened it wide enough to get in and stepped past Seed to Ivy. The green had nearly faded from her suit completely. There was no time to waste. The suits would be awake soon, probably, hopefully, woozy from the aftereffects of the disabler.

Evalie opened the front pocket of Ivy's suit and took out the small chip. She plugged it into the reader. Nothing happened. The boat pitched suddenly, and she felt the nausea rise in her throat. Evalie wished the motion sickness tablets would start working. She grabbed at the edge of the bed and steadied herself. Annoyed, she went over to Seed, who was lying half on his side. It was a little more difficult getting to Seed's front pocket. After being delicate, she sighed and wrenched the chip free. Evalie clasped it in her hand. She rushed out of the room. As she went to climb the stairs, she paused.

Should I go back and try to restrain them? she thought.

But with what?

Rope.

Obviously.

You're on a boat, genius.

Evalie closed her eyes.

No, find out who they really are first.

She blinked her eyes open and moved to the small nook that made up the dining room and sat at the tiny table. The boat pitched again. It seemed like the boat had changed direction. Although, it was hard to tell. Her head swam.

"Focus, Evalie," she chided.

Evalie studied the chip reader. She swapped the chips over. Still nothing. She pressed a button on the back that looked like the volume control.

"I am Seed," the machine said. "I am assigned to City East complaints office."

Evalie smiled. "Phew." She breathed deeply and swapped the chips over once more.

"I am Forrest," the machine said. "I am assigned to Xoha border control."

Evalie flinched. "Ivy was unsuited before she came here," Evalie whispered. "Surely this is just a cover. Yes, she would have needed a cover. But why border control?"

The uneasy gurgle of Evalie's stomach was a less than comforting response. She raced up the stairs to the deck and retrieved the chip from the remaining unknown suit. She put it in the reader.

"I am a Councillor of Xoha," the machine said.

"Oh, crap," Evalie said. "I've disabled a Councillor." Her mind went blank.

There were no racing thoughts or internal voices to lead her in any direction. She knelt down on the deck.

"Think, Evalie," she yelled. "For goodness' sake, think."

She returned the disabler to her pocket and began painstakingly replacing the helmet onto the head of the limp woman. As she studied the woman's features, she could not believe how young she looked. Surely, she was not much over twenty. How could she hold such a prominent position? When the helmet clicked into the suit, the woman stirred. Evalie panicked, reaching for the disabler. As she brought the disabler out of her suit pocket, it slipped from her fingers and fell onto the deck. The disabler clinked, bouncing end on end, leaving her grasping the chip. Evalie gasped and chased after it. Before she could grab it, it fell over the side. With a small splash, the blue-black waters claimed it.

The woman tried to stand. Evalie inspected the chip in her trembling fingers. Without blinking, she grabbed the chip out of her suit and replaced it with the Councillor's chip. She watched as the gold colour flowed down the arms of her suit to her fingertips. She put her chip alongside the other two in a neat row in her pocket. Seed's, Ivy's, hers. Without a chip, the suit before her would have only generic settings. Evalie mustered a renewed strength. Her suit felt amazing. Whilst the Councillor's suit had been grey before Evalie disabled it, her suit now shone gold with this new chip. Evalie felt lighter and stronger at the same time. It was bizarre.

"Get up," she said. Her voice boomed with a new authority. Evalie stood over the confused woman.

A ship horn sounded.

Evalie looked out and saw an approaching grey vessel. She knew the others must be awake now below deck.

"What, who are you, where am I?" the grey suit asked. The voice was meagre compared to Evalie's.

"This is the Councillor speaking. Get up."

"But I'm the Councillor."

"Nonsense. You are an insubordinate who has tried to take down all Xoha stands for." Evalie pinned her arms behind her back. The captive flinched but didn't struggle. Evalie stood behind her, looking out to sea at the boat that was not far away.

"You will never get away with this charade," the captive said. "Border control knows who I am, that I am the Councillor. They know all about you, too. You are Ivy from Manchester who went off grid after that failed relationship with a Councillor. The unsuited. What a thing to start. Did you think you could erase all the progress made by those who worked hard to establish this equality from the beginning?"

So, it is Ivy downstairs, Evalie thought. *Wow, the leader of the underground. Perhaps we are just collateral damage, me and Guy.* It was a sobering thought.

"What are you talking about? You're Ivy," Evalie boomed.

"Nobody will believe that."

The other boat came up alongside, ready to tether to them. "You are under the control of the border guards. We are going to board your ship," the monotone voice that came from the ship was surprisingly loud.

Evalie observed the loudspeaker in the hand of the grey suit on board and wished she'd had time to get the loudspeaker from the cockpit of their boat.

"This is the Councillor." Evalie walked to starboard so they could clearly see her from the other boat. "I turned on my suit's colour since our job here is done. I have captured Ivy. Bring me the ship's captain, the one you took from this boat earlier. We will exchange the captives so I can get this ship safely back to the harbour."

"We will steer it back, Councillor."

"No. I need to question the captain. I trust you have realigned the captain already, and there's no need to worry about further acts of disobedience."

"Well, yes, of course, Councillor."

"Do not listen to this infiltrator. It is a trick," the Councillor said. "I am the real Councillor. This here is Ivy in the suit, she is—"

"What utter rubbish. Only the true Councillor can activate a gold suit," Evalie thundered. "There's no way an unsuited scoundrel could do that."

Evalie hoped that none of the people on board would question this fabrication.

"Where are the others on your boat? Can't those border guards steer your ship?"

"We want the captain for questioning, not to steer the boat. Do not make me give my order a second time."

Guards threw the ropes over the side. Three guards boarded the boat. Two apprehended the sullen Councillor. Perhaps they had decided it was futile to prove their identity until they were back on dry land. Evalie was intent on never getting back on Xohan soil. She was certain it would be the end for her.

The third guard approached her.

"The captain is um—"

"Bring the captain to me this instant. Whatever their condition," Evalie barked. Her suit barely altered the tone of the voice coming out. Evalie felt satisfied that, for once, her intention and the words coming out of her helmet matched.

The guard bowed their head slightly and walked back to the edge of the boat. They called across to the boat. "Bring them out."

Evalie composed herself.

Three guards came, carrying a limp suit. The suit was a lacklustre grey.

"What have you done to h—the captain?"

"They were lively on board, Councillor, so we did what needed to be done to, um, calm them down."

"Right," Evalie said. She held back tears. "Now I'm going to delay the journey back until I can get all the information I need from this person."

"Can't you wait until we're back at port?" one guard asked.

"Are you questioning the Councillor's methods? We all know how it will be when we get back. I need the critical information now. Before the process they will put in place as soon as we step off these boats, interrupts us."

The guard bowed their head in submission.

A newfound confidence bolstered Evalie. "Now return to the ship and be on your way. Get that Ivy back to port so she can go through the process. I've already had my chance to interrogate her. I have a few critical gaps that the captain should fill, and then we will have the full story."

"Yes, Councillor," the guards replied.

Evalie gazed at the forlorn mess of a suit in front of her. She longed to rush to Guy, pull off his helmet and check that he was alright, but she knew she couldn't. Instead, she stood watching the guards untie the other boat from hers. It slowly retreated backwards, turned, then faded into the middle distance of the watery horizon.

Evalie moved slowly. She heard a low whistle. She saw the shadows dart on the side of the deck and felt her doom.

"It's X. Seed, for God's sake. I stole the Councillor's chip, then pretended I was her, and she was Ivy. Don't hurt me." The words flew out of her mouth.

The suits came into view, one behind to her left and the other to her right. She raised her hands up in the universal sign of surrender.

"That's Guy there, I think. I hope. We need to check he's okay."

"Take your helmet off," one suit said. "Show you are who you say you are, Evalie."

Evalie looked into the distance and saw a blip on the horizon. Nothing else but water. She unclipped her helmet and held it in her hand in one smooth motion. She hurried to Guy and took his helmet off. Evalie's heart threatened to rocket out of her mouth and onto the ship deck. Tears ran freely from the corners of her eyes, tracking wildly across her cheeks in the wind.

"Guy," she croaked. "Come back to me. What have they done to you?"

Wisps of hair swirled around Evalie's head where they'd broken free of her hair tie. Seed and Ivy came to her side. They removed their helmets and placed them on the deck.

"Let's lift him gently and take him below deck, out of this weather," Ivy said.

"He'll be okay," Seed added.

They picked Guy up and carried him cautiously and awkwardly down the stairs. Then propped him up against a wall in the kitchen. Evalie sat next to him. She stroked his cheek with her gloved hand. Then she unzipped her suit, shrugged it down and pulled her arms out so she could stroke his cheek again with bare fingers. Guy didn't stir.

"What do you think they did to him?" Evalie's voice was meek.

"Probably something similar to what you did to us," Ivy answered. "I'm sure he will come around soon."

Evalie's eyes flashed. "Yeah, sorry about that. But he's not green like you were. The suit, I mean."

"There are different ways to disable a suit," Seed offered. "Anyway, we need to get out of here. It's not safe."

"Do either of you know how to sail?" Evalie asked. She bit her lower lip.

"I'll handle it," Ivy replied.

"Oh, thanks. Thank goodness you're here with us, Ivy. I have your suit chip in my pocket, by the way. And yours too, Seed. I took them to find out who was onboard with me. Sorry again for disabling your suits." Evalie took the chips out of the pocket and held them out to Ivy and Seed.

Ivy grabbed hers and replaced it into her suit, then skipped up the stairs.

Evalie looked sideways at Seed as he took his suit chip back from her. "Well, this is pretty wild. How did you, um, why did you decide to escape?"

"It was after that night when I gave you the map. I went and had a conversation with the unsuited and they convinced me to help with their plan. It was, it *is* a massive risk, you know, X. We are not out of the woods yet. Can I still call you X? I'd prefer to."

Evalie nodded.

Seed sat down at the little table. "We might not make it yet. I'd prefer to be Seed and you be X until we make it to Australia."

"Okay. Well, thanks, you know, for helping us."

CHAPTER FIFTY-THREE

Guy grunted. He blinked his watery eyes open and stared at Evalie.

"Where are we?" he whispered.

"Safe; for now." She smiled at him. "Seed and Ivy are here."

"Good." Guy's voice was raspy. He grabbed Evalie's hand. "I feel a little faint."

"Do you want some water?"

"Sure, thanks."

"I'll get it," Seed offered. He rose from his spot at the little table.

"How did you get me back? The border control ship. It was much worse than I'd imagined."

"Yeah, well, they sent a Councillor. Seemed like they were most interested in Ivy. They said she started all this, the unsuited?"

Guy nodded slowly.

Seed brought the cup of water to Guy.

"Thanks mate." He took the cup, hand shaking. He raised it cautiously to his mouth, then took a few long sips.

"They didn't seem interested in me. Anyway, I used the disabler, like you told me to. Then I remembered the chip reader. I checked the chips. I convinced them that the Councillor was Ivy. And traded her for you."

"Smart going. Although it can't be long before they get back to the port and then the lies will unravel. They will be on our tail with the fastest ships they have. So Ivy's up there driving the boat?"

"Yes."

Guy finished the water. "That's much better. I'll go help Ivy in the cockpit. Where's my helmet, and yours?"

"Oh, we left them up on deck," Evalie said.

"I'll go get them." Seed sprang to the stairs.

Guy stood up slowly. "Can you two manage on deck?"

"I'm sure we'll manage," Seed called from halfway up the stairs, then disappeared.

"We need to speed up and push this boat to the limit if we're to make it safely into Australian waters," Guy said. "They will try to chase us to the end."

"Are you sure you're okay?" Evalie asked. She looked at Guy with concern.

"Yeah, I'm fine. I feel much better now. Come on, let's get this boat moving."

Evalie smiled gravely. She tried to push the dread from the pit of her stomach. Evalie returned her arms into her suit and zipped it up.

As Guy and Evalie emerged onto the deck, Seed handed them their helmets. "Can you take Ivy's too?" he asked. He held out the remaining helmet to Guy.

Guy nodded. "Sure thing."

Evalie followed Guy to the cockpit so she could put her helmet on out of the wind. She hummed a tune as she fixed her hair. It was *that* song again. The one she never learnt the name of.

"I love that song," Ivy commented.

"Do you know what it's called?" Evalie asked. "It's been stuck in my head for ages."

"I think it's called 'going home'."

"Well, that's apt, isn't it?" Evalie remarked. The apprehension drained away and hope trickled back into her heart. She grinned.

Ivy chuckled. "Yeah, I guess it is."

* * *

Evalie yawned as she entered the cockpit. "Seed said he would take first watch."

"I'll be alright for a few hours yet too," Ivy said.

"Are you sure?" Guy asked.

"Positive."

"Thanks. We've been going at a good pace; I think we should be right if we keep it up through the night." Guy rose from his seat and followed Evalie downstairs into the bedroom.

"It's been a massive day, I'm wrecked," Evalie said. She peeled off her suit and jumped under the covers.

"I suppose I'm putting this in the cleanser for you, then?"

"Thanks, hun," Evalie said. She rolled over onto her side.

When Guy returned, Evalie looked like she was asleep already. He joined her in the small bed. She stirred a little.

"Do you really think we can make it?" she asked sleepily.

"Yes, I do." Guy shifted uncomfortably in bed. "Evalie, there's something I must tell you. Are you still awake?"

"Hmm?"

"It's about your dad, well, your mum, actually."

"Hmm? Tomorrow. Tell me tomorrow, I'm too tired."

"But I don't think I can wait until tomorrow. I've tried to tell you so many times already."

There was no reply. Guy leaned in close to Evalie and heard her deep breathing. "Your mum isn't dead," he whispered.

* * *

Seed and Ivy stood on deck, searching the horizon with tired but keen eyes, passing the binoculars between them. Evalie looked out from the cockpit, eyes flicking between the two on deck and Guy.

"Any minute now," Seed shouted. "We will see it on the horizon."

Evalie crossed the fingers on both ungloved hands and squeezed tight.

Ivy jumped into the air. "Land ahoy!" she exclaimed.

The End

THANK YOU FOR READING

Thanks for joining Evalie (X) on her quest for equality!
If you enjoyed the book, I would really appreciate a brief review (on your chosen review site) as it will help new readers find my book. It might seem insignificant, but it can really help, especially independently published authors like me.

Thanks, you're awesome!

ACKNOWLEDGEMENTS

Without the support and unwavering belief from my husband, this book would never have got here. Thank you, I love you.

A big thanks to Maria Rodgers O'Rourke of MRO Communications (https://mrocommunications.com) for your skillful review and editing of my manuscript using the Story Grid method. Your generosity of spirit and respect for the writing craft enriched and transformed this book. Thanks also to Vanessa Wright, who I found on Reedsy for her copyedit/proofread of my book for the second edition.

My heartfelt gratitude to all the friends and family who have believed in me, encouraged me and cheered me on along this journey. Also to my small number (so far) of super fans. You know who you are. I love your work.

AUTHOR'S NOTE

I had the idea for Unsuited many years ago. At the time, my focus was on writing short stories. I came back to the idea of a world where people wore suits a few times, but knew it was a much bigger story. It percolated in the background while I developed other stories. The first novel I tried to write was about an ordinary police officer, named Mike, who had extraordinary experiences on the job and the effects these had on his family and social life. Using real life inspiration, I wrote 21 chapters, but they didn't hang together. I couldn't find the story arc. So I switched to my idea of people living their external lives in suits, anonymous to the world, and built from there. When I met with my structural editor, she asked me what I wanted the story to be and I decided I wanted the backbone to be a love story. I weaved a few missing elements into the story and was pleased with the result.

Writing the novel was a huge thing for me.

Then came the publishing. I started my own business and came up with the name Temja Publishing, by adding my surname, Tippett, and then the initials of each of the four members of my family. Searching the internet, I found a meaning for Temja from Old Norse, to tame. As an author, this seems fitting, as we are always trying to tame words into sentences, paragraphs, chapters and stories.

Independently publishing my novel came with many challenges. There are many skills to learn and decisions you must make to end up with a finished product. Some I had help with, from professionals (such as editors and graphic designers). Others, such as formatting or which spelling to use, were a combination of copyeditor advice, gut feel and internet advice, such as:

https://www.writerscentre.com.au/blog/qa-lent-vs-leant-vs-leaned/

https://www.grammar-monster.com/easily_confused/lasagna_lasagne.htm

I hope that none of my choices put you off the story. Know that I tried my best and am proud of this novel. If you find an error or something not to your liking, I hope you will forgive me.

This second edition comes with improvements from the original (no longer available). There were many fixes to cheeky typos that were missed in my original process, helped phenomenally by the use of ProWritingAid software. There were also some new descriptions and scene-setting additions that were augmented by ChatGPT through using Microsoft Bing's Copilot and ChatGPT (3.5) directly. The print version also comes with book club questions at the end of the book. I used Claude AI (paid version) to assist with developing these.

ABOUT THE AUTHOR

My love of books and writing has been longstanding but complex. It's something I have kept coming back to, studying a short course here and there amongst a busy life of work, study and raising a family. It wasn't until my dad, a technical writer, left this world prematurely that I made a commitment to write a novel. Publishing short fiction with the Monash Writer's Group and getting a 3rd place prize and high commendation for two stories (at WordFest) helped with the momentum for the full-length work.

I'm working on multiple projects, including a middle-grade children's fiction series (Teleporting Twins) and an anthology of my own short fiction. I value kindness, creativity and diversity. My interests outside of writing, reading, watching and listening to stories include cooking, spending time with family, travel, experiencing new cultures, flavours and ways of thinking, as well as running, yoga, mindfulness, fitness and learning new things. I live in Melbourne with my husband, kids and Foxy the cat.

Connect with me online
Website: www.ericatippett.com
Email: admin@ericatippett.com
Instagram: #ericatippettauthor

BOOK CLUB QUESTIONS

Here are some suggested questions to spark discussion about *Unsuited* (Warning: spoiler alert).

1. How would you feel if you had to wear an anonymity suit in public at all times? Would the promise of equality be worth losing your identity and individuality?

2. What emotions did you feel as Evalie had to decide on whether to go to Xoha; and then tried to fit in to Xohan society? Would Xoha have lured you in as it did Evalie?

3. Were you surprised by the secrets Evalie discovered about Xoha and its leadership? In the end, do you think Xoha achieved its egalitarian ideals?

4. Discuss the multiple meanings of "unsuitability" explored in this book. Who is truly "suited" or "unsuited" for Xohan society by the story's end? Are Evalie and Guy "suited" for each other?

5. How would you describe Evalie's personal transformation from the beginning to the climax of the novel? Do you relate to her journey of self-discovery?

6. Does the Xohan culture's enforced anonymity prevent meaningful human connections? Is anonymity compatible with intimacy?

7. What did you think about Evalie and Guy's escape plan? Would you have risked everything to get out of Xoha?

8. Were you surprised by the twist revealing that Evalie's mother might still be alive? How might this impact Evalie's view of herself?

9. Discuss the role of Evalie's father in her life. How does he influence her decisions regarding Xoha and Guy?

10. How did reading about the Xohan culture make you reflect differently on norms in our modern society regarding privacy, surveillance, and technology?

11. Discuss some symbols and motifs that stood out to you, like Evalie's mother's earrings. What might they represent about identity and memory? What about the triquetra?

12. What did you think about Evalie and Guy's relationship? Why do you think it took something so extreme, like moving to Xoha, for it to mature and develop?

13. Discuss some of the moral dilemmas faced by characters like Evalie, Guy, and Seed. Do you agree with their choices?

14. Why do stories about totalitarian futures remain popular? What core human fears or questions do they bring to the surface?

15. Would you recommend this book to a friend? Compared to other dystopian stories, what makes this one unique?

www.ingramcontent.com/pod-product-compliance
Lightning Source LLC
Chambersburg PA
CBHW010437100726
47904CB00008B/2378